To Bathe in Eden's Glory

Christopher Cass

This Edition:
Copyhouse Press

First published in the United Kingdom 2013 by Vanguard Press

Second Edition published in the United States 2015 by Baker's Boy Books/Amazon

This edition published in the United Kingdom 2015 by Copyhouse Press Ltd

Copyhouse Press Ltd

International House, 24 Holborn Viaduct

London

United Kingdom, EC1A 2BN

ISBN 9780993321023

To Pauline Maud
1928-2012

Acknowledgements

Sincere thanks to my friends and family who suffered
the early drafts while I got a grip.

Also, to those at The Essex Regiment Museum,
Madame Tussauds, The National Gallery,
The London Transport Museum, Talbot House,
Dr. Martin Mather
and everyone who aided my research.

Finally, thanks to the generation that inspired this novel,
both those who lived to record their experiences
and those who fell.

God the Holy Ghost

He stands, hands clasped in solemn prayer
For those who are no longer there,
Commending them to Him above,
Our all embracing God of Love,
But, tell me Padre, please explain,
Where was God when the gas cloud came?

To Bathe in Eden's Glory

The only quotes are on page 47/48 attributed to Bloch,
which date from the late 1800s and the song lyrics
which originate from the period 1914-1918.
Versions included are based on versions found in the
EMI publication 'Oh! It's a lovely War'.

All poetry by Christopher Cass.

To Bathe in Eden's Glory

PART ONE

CHAPTER ONE

The scent of sizzling bacon teased the boy from his dreams. He stretched luxuriously, letting the sunlight into his eyes, blink by blink, until he could look out at August's rich horizon. How he loved the summer; a painting in a hallway had unlocked nature's kaleidoscope, now he saw the harvest in all its hues.

He'd seen the painting only once, when he'd been hauled before the Squire for scrumping Manor apples. It had been hanging over the mantel of the biggest fireplace he'd ever seen. His father had been called. He'd thrashed him, there and then, so hard the welts had lasted for weeks.

His mother had never belted him. She'd smacked him once or twice, hardest one Christmas for sharing the mincemeat with the dog, but that had been ages ago. Now, summer fruit filled the piecrust and cricket practice the long evening hours, until his twilight tramp home to dreams of Lords, England and the Ashes, twenty to get and him the last man in.

He drifted back to the batting crease, padding away a googly from his swollen bladder. Most lavatories were sentry boxes at the bottom of the garden; the Bowden's was brick built and semi-detached to the coalbunker beneath his bedroom window. It was also occupied. To use his chamber pot was beyond the pale. Instead he squirmed under the covers, counting the rooks in their lazy circuit of the woods, until the rustle of roughly quartered newspaper sprang him into his britches and down the stairs.

His father emerged from the lavatory, braces at half-mast. Scuttling past, the boy nipped his nose, ripped open his fly and peed into the abyss in blissful relief.

Across the fields, the Church bells tolled into oblivion. The family didn't go to service, his father wasn't overly religious, but still the boy loved the plaintive call to worship as dearly as his mother's summons to breakfast - bacon and egg, his Sunday treat from weekday dripping.

At the table he portioned bread, egg white and bacon into equal, yoke dipped mouthfuls. A swig of hot, sweet tea disintegrated his final bread crust. The family heirloom ticked off the seconds of his father's silent appraisal. The plate was satisfactorily spotless; the boy was excused.

Beyond the outhouse, a glut of white roses tumbled over the ramshackle garden shed. He breathed their perfection in passing, following the cinder path up through his father's vegetable garden to the far reaches of the back fence and his own tiny plot. He'd been given some seeds late in the spring and now a multitude of bright red poppies bobbed gently in the breeze. They laughed at his 'weeds', but he didn't care. Here, hidden by the bean canes, he could be Gordon at Khartoum, Cardigan at Balaclava, Kitchener at Omdurman or even Nelson at Trafalgar, when the wind blew waves in the wheat.

A whiff of grass fire carried on the breeze. It was a pity his new neighbours had moved in; their back garden had become his Waterloo, where, armed with his willow sword, he'd driven back the Napoleonic nettles single-handed.

Across the divide, Harold Scott straightened his aching back. His shirt was sweat soaked, his brow matted, his hands blistered. They'd done well, he swinging the sickle, his daughter feeding the sheaves to the bonfire's flames.

"Move round," he called to her. "No, the other way."

The smoke enveloped her, until a gust of wind carried it up and away over the fields.

Scott dried her cheeks, happy to see some colour in them. She'd been a sickly city child; now, God willing, her health would improve. Losing one daughter to diphtheria was lesson enough.

"Come on. Let's see if your mother's made some lemonade."

Glass rim and straw brim tilted in endearing tandem at the kitchen table.

"She's full of bonfire," Marian Scott, complained, sniffing the girl's tresses disgustedly. "It's not right, working on the Sabbath."

"I'm sorry, dearest, but there's so much to do. I'm sure God will forgive us, just this once."

"Heathen is as heathen does," Marian muttered, returning to the sink.

Sullen shoulders, a silent back, the irritable scraping of potatoes: Scott stifled a sigh; God and Caruso; through the move Marian had missed both. If he really put his back into it, he could appease her piety with Evening Prayer, but the mighty tenor was now halfway to the West Country. Not that he imagined for one second that even Caruso's magical voice could offer his wife any lasting solace. For Marian, bereavement was only the tip of the iceberg.

Scott took his daughter's hand. Sackcloth and ashes were no Queen's Jelly for a child. "Come on, my pet, back to work. If we keep at it, we should have it cleared in time for evensong. How's that, Marian? Lunch at one?"

As father and daughter waded back into the wilderness, Marian cast potato and knife into the peel choked sink.

"Why, in heaven's name, did we have to come to this God forsaken place?" She sobbed.

The newcomers' return brought an abrupt cease-fire at Rorke's Drift. The boy crouched behind his palisade; the Zulu faded through the wheat field, conceding the river's reeds and rushes to the sentinel alders that buttressed its banks. Along the shallow valley to the Southwest, the water mill's weather vane was just visible above the trees, while to the Northeast lay the dell, rising to Clayman's farm and Sparrowhawks wood, carpeted with bluebells in springtime and now verdant with August fern. No feathered war bonnets broke the plane, no assegai clacked on hide shield; the Zulu had gone.

Riding the astral plain, the boy led a scouting party along the rutted back lane and down into the native Kraal. All was deserted, reverted to shops, inns and High Street houses, as gnarled and knotted as the crossroads' oak, whose forebears enframed their wattle and daub.

Venturing on over the Georgian stone bridge, he checked his father's yard, then the doctor's Queen Anne house and the early Victorian vicarage, before emerging on the far side of the river, on the time trodden path to town. The Manor's gatehouse stood unbreached. Natal was saved. Tranquillity stretched over the parish; 'We thank thee all our God' drifted back, sliced into bars by the newcomer's sickle.

The boy sat, cross-legged, furrowing the earth with a dried twig. The meaning of life was a question, not of reality, but of philosophy, and, as yet, reality was all he knew. When he took his education from man, then his mind would be drawn into the ever-expanding surrealism of intellectual thought. For now, conclusions reached themselves unquestioned. The turning of the soil would always bear more truth, embedded in his subconscious, than academia.

The smell of roasting beef drifted down the path. Sunday, for all its confinement to house and garden, had its compensations. He re-sighted the Boer commando through a knothole in the paling. From Zululand to the Transvaal was no time trek at all.

* * * * *

The days shortened, the haystacks dampened, the village schoolmistress counted heads and the class trooped in. After a short prayer and an even more discordant than usual 'Oh God, our help in ages past', partly due to the warping of the upright piano in the corrugated summer heat, the teacher announced the new arrival. Her name was Laura. The boy had seen her in her garden and walking in the village with her mother, but she hadn't gone fruit picking with the other children, they hadn't spoken. Her father worked in town, cycling there and back in his Sunday best. According to Violet Coombes, whose mother knew everything, he changed his collar three times a week, not counting Sundays. He was civil, his wife snooty.

The girl smiled shyly, when she was introduced. It gave the boy a funny feeling. Her desk was on the far side and slightly in front of his, allowing him a covert glance when the opportunity arose. She was the prettiest girl he had ever seen, and clever, raising her hand to answer with a modesty that provoked no animosity, at least among the boys. She read well, hardly stumbling over the longest words. She didn't speak like them, she spoke more like the teacher; not like gentry exactly, not like the Vicar, but not like them.

At playtime, he kicked a football about with the other boys, but found his normal immersion compromised. He looked for her. At first she stood alone by the steps, then Miss Cooper led her to a group playing hopscotch. He heard his name called; the ball skidded towards him. Trapping it skilfully, he dribbled past two players and squeezed his shot inside the pile of jackets and jerseys that served as a post, but when he turned in triumph, she wasn't watching, and he felt oddly deflated.

Her mother met her from school. He and the Crutchleys followed them home as far as the farm cottages; from there he trailed them alone, unsure of overtaking them or of what he would say if he did. Lingering by his mother's azaleas, he watched them walk the final hundred yards to their own gate, suffering the perplexity only a girl can imbue in a boy.

After tea he took a stroll past her house. His heart pumped harder as he drew near, as if he were going in to bat, then sank to the depths of a golden-duck, when he found her garden bare.

Crossing the stubble fields, he followed the weir's thunder to fathom the day's events in its vortex. The tremor in her voice, her loneliness on the school step, his goal, her nervous smile, all came vividly to mind; he remembered nothing of the other girls, apart from Edith Taylor wetting herself in arithmetic.

Moving along the footbridge, he freed his confusion on the vermilion sunset. It was a pity school had to start and cricket stop, while there were still evenings like this. He sighed deeply at summer's passing and headed back along the riverbank, flailing his way through a swarm of midges. Near home, he cast a final glance towards Laura's back garden, but she wasn't there.

His father's boots awaited, his last chore of the day. As he applied brush to leather, his mind wandered back to the classroom and Laura's first, shy smile.

"Watch what you're doing!"

He looked at his boot-blackened sleeve; in the autumn of his infancy he was experiencing the first manifestations of unrequited love.

* * * * *

Laura went straight to bed after supper. Her first day at the village school had tired her, but she was happy; she'd heard Miss Cooper tell her mother what a bright child she was.

Pulling on her nightgown with all the modesty browbeaten into her, she took one last look at her new world. She recognised the boy trailing along the riverbank, but nothing more. Her mother's footsteps propelled her into prayer. After a goodnight kiss, her eyelids closed on the sunset to reopen on Never-Never Land. Peter Pan swooped from an azure sky.

Downstairs, her father settled into his armchair, pipe clenched between his teeth, the Times held before him like a safety curtain.

"Laura looked tired," he said.

Marian's crochet hook clicked angrily against a knuckle. "What do you expect, having to hobnob with that filth? They're no better than gypsies. Plough hands' and labourers' brats the lot of them. They probably don't bath but once a year. I wouldn't allow any of them within a mile of her, let alone sitting at the next desk, but oh no, her father knows best. It's not enough that we have to live amongst scum; our own daughter has to become one of them. It's a wonder she didn't come home with the nits."

"She won't catch anything," Scott assured her.

"Oh won't she? But of course it's all right for you, you're not the one who'll have to suffer the indignity of a shaved head. She's to keep her distance and I've told her so."

Scott lowered his broadsheet. "For heaven's sake, Marian."

"Well it's not right. I told you before, you should talk to the Vicar, get her up to the Manor with children of her own kind, not that vermin."

"I've talked to the Vicar. He's seeing what he can do."

"Seeing what he can do isn't doing. A pack of them even had the gall to follow us home, filthy little heathens."

"Marian, they're children."

"You didn't see them. Little Satans, every last one, with nothing but the devil's work on their minds, especially that dirty little brat from down the road. He came past later, staring in the window. You'd think butter wouldn't melt in his mouth, but I know what he's after, young as he is. I warned you. We should never have come. From a decent city living to this, scraping by in a pigsty with not even a proper lavatory. It makes my blood boil. What kind of future is she going to have, stuck out here among this riffraff, tell me that?"

"At least she'll have a future," Scott snapped. "Unlike her sister."

His remorse was instant. It was on Marian's insistence that the family had stayed in London despite the diphtheria epidemic. The crochet hook fell; Marian's face crumpled. She shrank from his touch.

"I'm sorry, Marian. It wasn't your fault. It was no-one's fault. You're right; of course she should go to the big house. I'll speak to the Vicar again on Sunday."

* * * * *

By the end of September Marian Scott's wish had been granted and Laura was attending the Manor school. The Vicar himself taught the children there, ten in all, the doctor's small sons, the head gamekeeper's brood, the estate undermanager's twins and now Laura.

The boy saw little of her after that; they were neighbours, but lived a world apart; the Manor's converted nursery and the lessons taught there had little in common with the village classroom, with its tin-roof and elementary curriculum. Now and again he would catch a glimpse of her in her garden at weekends, but she seldom ventured out and, when she did, it was always with her mother. She seemed such an unhappy woman, her mother.

- CHAPTER TWO –

The winds of October whistled down the valley, clogging the lanes and footpaths with autumn leaf. Some children were kept from school to scare the starlings and gather acorns, but, as 'Bonfire Night' approached, the classroom filled. The previous year the Vicar had arrived early with the Church's traditional 'Penny for the Guy'. This year the truants were taking no chances.

'Guy Fawkes' was a village affair, held, as all national celebrations were, in the Manor's Paddock. The children stuffed the guy, their fathers lopped the firewood and his Lordship, with grander estates more suited to a pillar of the establishment, supplied the fireworks in absentia.

As with many such men, his Lordship's closet had its skeleton, its backbone being a disastrous episode in the same Zulu Wars the boy was so fond of re-enacting, when nepotism and title had ridden roughshod over acumen to procure him a command. Nevertheless, after a suitable sabbatical, he'd proceeded to build a solid Tory reputation on the foundations of his patriotic plebiscite. The blunders forgotten, he'd been hailed 'a Hector of Empire' by the editor of the local Chronicle.

He'd played no active part in the more recent South African Wars, preferring to fight the Boer with rhetoric from the palace of Westminster, while his son boxed their ears on the Veldt. Unfortunately for his son, the Boers had fought back. An impressive requiem had been held in Ashleigh's parish Church, a scaled down version of the grander St. Giles in the Field 'In Memoriam'. Now a portrait in the nave and a brass plaque in the chancel reminded the parish's peasantry that true heroism was the preserve of the aristocracy.

The night of November the fifth was clear and cold, threatening frost by morning, but that was of no immediate concern to the multitude gathered round the blazing bonfire.

"You'd better get a move on or you'll miss the fireworks," the three musketeers were warned, as they fenced the flames for their roasted chestnuts.

The boy remounted the tree stump he'd defended against all-comers, his chewy treats scorching his jacket pocket. He was just prising apart a charred shell, when the first rocket embroidered the heavens.

"Oooohhhh!" Exclaimed the crowd. "Aaaahhhh!" They all replied.

"Give over," the boy protested, barged from his perch by Athos and Porthos. However, his anger was short-lived, for Laura was there, just feet away. More salvoes soared and detonated, more constellations formed and fell, but he only had eyes for her.

The last Roman Candle fizzled to extinction. The crowd applauded, gave three irreverent cheers for his Lordship, and began to disperse. As Laura took her father's hand, her sparkling eyes met the boy's, prompting a tidal wave of shyness that all but drowned him. By the time he resurfaced, she'd gone.

He knew it was love, but it wasn't the love he knew. He loved his parents, but he wasn't struck dumb by his mother, he didn't get the collywobbles when his father walked in, unless he had good cause, and then it was a different kind of collywobble. This was the kind people teased you about, the kind you kept to yourself, the kind people married for.

He knew the difference between dogs and bitches; he knew the embarrassment of a willy rising of its own accord in class, particularly when he had to stand to read or answer, but he couldn't equate that with his yearning to see her smile again, to be the reason for her smile. Most of all, as he headed back to the bonfire, he wanted to kiss her.

Next morning, he was up with the larks. His parents would still be in bed when the Scotts went to worship, winter Sundays were days of rest where his father was concerned, one of his few adherences to the Christian faith. Laura would walk right past the parlour window.

Relying on his bed-generated body heat to keep the cold at bay, he emptied the ash bucket over the garden path and went to the lavatory. The lamp on the sill gave just enough heat to keep the seat from frosting. He loved the smell of paraffin. Loading the coalscuttle from the bunker, he heaved it into the house and set the fire.

The paper flared, the kindling spat, the coals hissed and finally caught. By the time he returned from the sink, hands clean, face and neck icily invigorated, the family cat had ensconced itself on the hearthrug.

Leaning over it, he drew the heat through his outstretched fingers, until his chattering teeth quieted enough to eat a wedge of bread and the dregs of last week's dripping. He missed the crust-devouring dog. Sam had gone to heaven to be with the boy's brothers, both killed by the same Boers that had killed young Squire, his mother had told him. Not like the rabbits, they'd gone in the stew; 'needs must,' his father had said.

A watery sun filigreed the trees, stirring the birds to song. The cat opened a sly eye, tuned an attentive ear.

The boy set to work on his boots, wondering whether his third brother would visit. Too young to fight the Boer, George had joined the family business and married Elizabeth, an orphaned cousin of the Whites. The couple had moved into an old cottage at the far end of the village. Now they had a baby and another on the way. The boy hoped they didn't come, a refuge from his screeching nephew wasn't easy to find on cold winter Sundays.

He and his parents might go to his grandparents for tea; they did that sometimes, his grandparents on his mother's side. His father had left home at twelve-years-old and never mentioned his kin. He'd walked all the way from Suffolk. The village smithy had taken him in, but there'd been no call for another blacksmith, only a plumber. By his fourteenth birthday the boy's father had set himself up in business.

The clock in the hall chimed out the half-hour. Risking his father's wrath, the boy tied his bootlaces. The parlour window was not close enough to the lane, the garden gate too open to inquisition. If he got caught sneaking back in, he could always say he'd been feeding Crutchley's old nag, he'd done that before on a Sunday. Donning cap and scarf, he stole from the house.

Patches of frozen mud crunched underfoot as he hurried along, anxious to make Clayman's bend before the Scotts came into sight. From there he could pretend he was coming from the village.

He reached the farm gate and waited. The cold seeped through his woollen gloves; his ears began to ache, his toes to burn. He kicked his heels and swung his arms. Maybe they weren't going to church today; maybe he'd missed them; premise played upon premise until his maybes became 'can't be' and 'must have', and Crutchley's old nag no excuse at all. Despondently he started back.

Ten yards on, his dejection was turned on its head. The Scotts were coming. He slackened his stride, but the lesser the gap, the more his pulse raced. His gait became awkward, so awkward he stumbled. Perspiration chilled the back of his neck.

Twenty yards became ten, ten five. He reached for his cap. "Morning," he gurgled.

Through blurred eyes he saw Laura's smile dissolve into distress. He followed her fear to find himself impaled on the venomed lance of her mother's abhorrence.

"How dare you, you filthy little wretch," the woman screamed at him.

He was completely stunned. No one had ever hated him before. He could only stare blankly after her, as she dragged Laura away.

Running home, he took the stairs two at a time to bury his head in his pillow. Hell hath no fury like a woman scorned, and no pain greater than that of a child scorned in its innocence.

- CHAPTER THREE -

The boy saw little of Laura through an icy winter of recurring colds and confusion. What had he done wrong? Had she turned to her mother for protection? For the first time in his life he missed school.

The Scotts kept to themselves and became the 'Hermits', their house 'The Hermitage'. The father was seen paying the household bills and voting in the two General Elections that year, as the Commons battled the Lords over Lloyd George's 'People's Budget', but sightings of mother and child were restricted to school on weekdays and Church on Sundays.

It would have quickened the boy's heart to have known that Laura, from her bedroom window, saw considerably more of him. Every girl needs a hero and he was hers, the only man to have stood his ground in front of her mother, albeit he'd been pinned to it. The butcher's boy, having suffered a similar fate for genially addressing her mother as 'missus', was now halfway down the lane before he'd even knocked, while the grocer's lad hid behind the rhododendrons.

The atmosphere in the house had worsened; her parents no longer slept in the same room. Her father spent longer at work, leaving early and returning late. At weekends, despite the cold, he worked in the garden, although there seemed little to do.

Upstairs, her mother's room had become a penitent's cell, austere but for a crucifix and two agony-illuminating altar candles. At this Spartan shrine to suffering mother and daughter knelt in daily devotion.

Laura knew her mother was different from other women, she never laughed, she seldom smiled, and, when she did, it was such a bitter smile; but, then, she reasoned, other women hadn't lost a daughter.

It would have taken a more Freudian mind than a ten-year-old's to root out the cancerous corpse of Marian's childhood from beneath that simple shroud. Crucified on the cross of illegitimacy and her own mother's prostitution, Marian had learnt well Christ's torment. Immersed in the cleansing pool of faith, the nails had rusted in her soul, as the antichrist himself had assailed her with lust for her deliverer, a man of God, who, after her mother's horrific death in unaided childbirth, had suffered the bleating of his bucolic flock, until he'd procured Marian's salvation in city anonymity.

It was this secret legacy, this manic fear and hatred of anything rural, that had fuelled Marian's refusal to leave London despite the epidemic, committed her first born to the grave and her own soul to Gehenna.

Now Laura had been cast into that same Gomorra. She must stay away from 'that' boy, from all Satan's children, she was told. But a hero scorned is a hero enhanced and temptation was never explained.

16

The Edwardian era passed with Haley's comet in a blaze of funereal pageantry. After a year of national lament, political crises, suffragist anarchy and the murderous Dr. Crippen, mourning gave way to bunting for the Coronation of George V. His philandering father had proved more popular than expected; the monarchy was on a high and the villagers celebrated loyally and royally. Even the Hermits obeyed the bugle calls of empire to flag-wave and cheer the mace-tossing Drum Major, as he wheeled his band about the enclosure with as much pomp and precision as divots and dung would allow, following the first rounds of the gymkhana and the awesome excretions of an exhibitionist elephant. The tug of war teams looked apprehensively on while the groundsman searched for a shovel.

There were agricultural competitions for the men, hedging and ditching, log splitting and ploughing a furrow; baking, embroidery and flower arranging for the women, races for children and parents alike and a boxing tent, from which local heroes would be borne throughout the afternoon. However, if the day's crowning glory was to be a firework display, its main attraction was a travelling fair.

The surrounding communities flocked in, packing the fairground, marquees and beer tents, and it was some time before the boy caught sight of Laura, standing by a coconut shy with her mother. Her father was trying his luck. There was something odd about it, but his view was obscured. By the time the path cleared, they had gone.

Plugging his last pellet into the airgun, the boy sited left of centre, pulled the trigger, hit the bullseye, collected his prize and ambled off to the refreshment tent. Much as his mother loved dogs, he dreamed of giving the plaster-cast spaniel to Laura. After so many recuperative months, one glimpse had left him a pining puppy. He picked the petals in lovesick envy, as he passed the coyly flirtatious on the merry-go-round.

"Hey, young un, you been to the big tent yet?" His brother ended the daydream, broken lipped from the boxing ring but beaming proudly, his wife beside him, baby in one arm, toddler clutching the other. "Reckon you should; you never know what you might find."

The village council had donated materials for a children's painting competition, with prizes for village and Manor schools alike. After his first uncertain brushstrokes, the boy had taken to it like Stubbs to a horse.

The sun shone, the boy hurried on, working his way through the bustles and britches to the marquee's far gallery. His parents were waiting, his father's yellow waistcoat puffed out like a Wagtail's. A paternal thump on the back sent him tottering forward.

"Well done boy, well done!"

In pride of place in the village school section was his portrayal of 'The King Reviewing his Troops'. Looking at it now, the king looked more like the old king than the new one, and there was something fishy about the horse, but the soldiers were good, from Grenadiers and Coldstreams, to kilted Scots and turbaned Sikhs.

The picture bore two rosettes, both embossed with '1st Prize', one crimson for 'best in school', the other purple for 'best in show'. His handwriting effort also sported a genuinely unexpected '3rd'.

"Oh, I'm so proud!" His mother hugged him.

Instinctively he looked round. Daniel Dicks, the only eyewitness, gave him a wink and a thumbs-up; his embarrassment evaporated.

Looking right, he scanned the Manor entries. He'd thought Laura's 'Coronation Coach' wonderful on earlier viewing, although, in hindsight, the horses did look a bit like gangly sheep and the people inside a bit short of leg room, in fact, of legs altogether, which was why, he supposed, the judges had only given it a commendation. However, her immaculate longhand had also swept the board.

How he longed to lead her to her triumph. The Vicar's sister beat him to it. He gazed over, lost in whimsy, until he realised that Laura was smiling back. It was a smile that answered every question, a smile he returned in besotted abundance across the prize begonias.

Suddenly his friends were there, pulling him away to the duck-hooking stall.

"Look what we won! It's easier than pissing," Joe Crutchley aired his way with words, a flair he invariably backed up with a practical demonstration.

"He did it against the beer tent, Bowdie, with people inside," Frank Cudlip confirmed.

The spell was broken. Laura was back under her mother's wing. With a regretful sigh, the boy scampered off to hook his own commemorative mug emblazoned with the royal likeness.

The races were held mid-afternoon. The boy won the junior sprint ahead of Ernie Thompson, the gamekeeper's son, breasting the tape rather too impressively for someone about to be shackled to the cack-footed Joe Crutchley in the three-legged. They ended up in a heap, finishing an ignominious last but one.

His brother did no better in the men's sack race, leaving his sister-in-law to restore family pride by coming third in the women's egg and spoon, behind Cissy Brewer, the village belle, and Winnie Truelove, the village bike, soon to be tandemed to an unsuspecting Elmsfordian.

Laura came fifth in the girls' dash and fourth in the three-legged with Amy Holland, although her mother seemed far from happy about it.

At five o'clock, prize winners and supporters gathered in the marquee. One by one, the Manor school children were called to the table.

"Laura Scott."

The boy mooned over every step, aiming an ingratiating smile at her mother, only to have it gorgonically frozen.

"Rodney De'Ath." It was an unfortunate name for both doctor and son.

At last the village schoolchildren's turn came, "Daniel Dicks," and then, to raucous cheers from Joe Crutchley and company, "Richard Bowden."

As the boy turned back, book token in hand, he saw Miss Cooper with the Scotts. She was waving him over. He swallowed hard; she couldn't be, but she was and more urgently, people were beginning to titter, with one scowling exception. Keeping his eyes riveted on the teacher, he braved the lightening bolts of Mrs. Scott's malevolence.

"And now for the two main awards."

As if in a dream, he was being ushered forward with Laura, hand in hand.

But infatuation's dream for one was revulsion's nightmare for another, for Marian Scott, the worst nightmare of all. Each day she'd delivered her daughter into the Vicar's safekeeping, then home again, while, from behind every curtain, every sly smile, the coven had seethed. But, today, from the first, they'd made themselves known, lying in wait under the gatehouse arch to tag the sacrificial lamb.

She'd torn the heather from Laura's bonnet. She'd wanted to turn back, but Harold had told her that she had to go on, that all would be well. But then she hadn't realised that he was one of them, not even at the coconut shy, when he'd let the warlock cast his spell. 'A ghost from the past,' the gypsy had claimed. She'd stared the man to hell, but his eyes had been Laura's and her shield as glass and her soul as innards on Beelzebub's altar, as her mother's had been that same lifetime ago.

She'd dragged Laura away, but the witches had stalked them, closing in packs, until they'd hobbled Laura to one of their own, and Harold had stood by, and she'd screamed in his face and seen its true colour, Lucifer's crimson.

She'd run to the tape and ripped off the bonds, the day had been over, she'd thought she had won; then the collar of God had become the yoke of Satan and the trap had been sprung and she'd reeled in horror, as Laura's hand had been delivered into that of the anti-christ's own.

How the coven now gloated, how it gleefully bleated. She reached out to strike them, to strike them all down, beseeching her Saviour to give her the strength, but their grip was like iron, dragging her down and out through hell's window to her mother's grave, open and corrupt, where Satan was waiting, bestial phallus in hand.

Wells was there, her childhood mentor, Emily, her first born, dead in his arms. He held out a bible, but the pages were blank, so she screamed out the scriptures, long learned by heart. But the Devil's eyes were the cauldrons of hell, consuming her prayers like moth wings in flame, while his serpent swelled with omnipotent pulse, burning her blind with its red molten venom. She was held, she was naked, he rent her asunder, impaling her soul, and she gave it ecstatically.

The Doctor was on hand. They carried Marian to the Manor. She'd suffered a stroke; one side of her face was hideously contorted, the other perfect and peaceful. Her heartbeat was erratic but there.

The onlookers pressed; few had ever been inside the Big House.

"Would everyone please clear the room," De'Ath ordered. "You may stay, of course, Mr. Scott. Mr. Holland, would you ask Mrs. Stafford to oblige us with a blanket or two and a pillow, if she would be so kind."

19

Scott looked apprehensively round for Laura. The boy had stayed with her. The boy's mother was with them.

"It's alright, Mr. Scott," she said. "We'll look after her."

Scott baulked at Marian's repulsion at such a thing, but the very social leprosy she had afforded the community, it now afforded him. The Bowdens were his nearest neighbours; it was nonsense to refuse.

The unabated gaiety of the fairground only emphasised the anguish the gypsy read in the young girl's eyes, as the group walked solemnly by. Closing his shy, he followed his intuition to the big house and its breeze blown curtains.

Even now, in all its distortion, the likeness was unmistakable. He'd been barely sixteen, her mother the same. They'd made love in a barn, then the fair had moved on.

He'd planned to go back when they'd laid up for the winter, but they'd been too far away and his father had been gaoled, his duty had been with his family.

He'd counted the months, then the weeks, then the days, until the time had come and he'd pulled their caravan onto the green. His lover had been sent away, a local had told him; 'a right little tart she turned out to be.'

The fortune-teller had consulted her cards; whoever the father was, it wasn't him, she'd assured him. He'd had no reason to doubt her.

He lowered his head in bitter weeping.

The hurdy-gurdy trailed the Bowdens across the valley and over the footbridge, the river below only inches deep at this time of year. The boy looked wistfully at Laura's hand clasped in his mother's, wishing it was still in his.

"Try not to worry dear, the doctor's with her," his mother consoled her.

"He's a good man, he'll look after her alright," his father confirmed, while he remained tongue-tied.

Nearer home, his father told him to go on with his mother, that he would be home shortly. Despite the circumstances, his heart quickened, then beat a tattoo, when his mother told him to show Laura the garden, while she made some tea.

He led her along the cinder path to his own special corner.

"Have you been down the old mill?" He found his voice at last, desperately trying to contain his Essex burr. "It's good down there."

"Mother doesn't like me leaving the house," she told him.

"It's quite something when the wheel's going round. Perhaps I could show you one day?"

"I'm afraid mother would never allow it."

Her face sank further.

"This is my part of the garden. Them's my poppies," he boasted, trying to lift her spirits.

"They're very nice," she said absently.

He sauntered to her side.

"She'll be alright, you'll see."

His reward was a smile, inspiring even in its sorrow.

"You'll be stopping the night with us, my dear. You'd best go along with Mrs. Bowden and fetch your things," Mr. Bowden told Laura on his return.

"Will my mother be all right?"

"She's staying at the Big House," he answered evasively. "They'll see if she's well enough to come home in the morning. Your dad'll pop by in a bit."

"What a damned shame," he said to the boy, after mother and girl had gone. "Pretty little thing, too. What do you reckon to her?"

"Ah, she's alright as girls go," the boy said dismissively.

"Oh, I see," Bowden chuckled. "Well, just you be nice to her. She may be needing a friend." He settled contemplatively back into his age-ravaged armchair. "Perhaps you and me'll be having a little talk before you're much older. Best fill that big pan in case she wants a wash."

It was the nearest Bowden would ever get to explaining the facts of life to his son. "Dah, what he don't know now'll come natural enough," he would excuse himself. "After all, no one told me and I didn't do so bad."

After supper the family watched the firework facsimile of King and Queen flicker across the valley, bringing the festivities to a close. As the image faded, young hands united. The Bowdens shared the union with a nudge and a wink.

* * * * *

The following morning Doctor De'Ath summoned one of Elmsford's new motor ambulances on the Manor's telephone. He'd kept vigil with Scott through Marian's delirium and it was her mental rather than her physical state that now compelled him to risk the potholed trip to hospital.

His fears proved well founded. When Marian regained consciousness, her eyes were wild, her speech incoherent and volatile. Whenever a man came near, she would fly into a rage, threatening physical violence, then she would rock back and forth, hugging her knees and chanting a hotchpotch of repentant psalms. Nothing medically could be done, Scott was assured, the damage was irreparable, there was no alternative but an asylum.

Faced with the stigma of madness and its likely backlash on Laura, Scott agonised over what to do. Finally, he sought out a private sanatorium and fabricated Marian's death. He set the funeral in Hertfordshire, Marian's birthplace, distant enough to deter mourners, and, three days after her committal, acted out the charade by taking Laura there for the day. By chance, there had been a recent burial. The grave was unmarked, its flowers still fresh, its adoption easy.

Marian's only close acquaintance had been Reverend Wells, her childhood mentor. As far as Scott was aware, communications had broken down with their move to the country, but what if the man wrote? He could hardly tell him she was buried in his own parish, and even if he invented another location, what if Wells insisted on visiting the grave? Scott left it to providence. As for his own family, his parents lived nearest, and they were thirty miles away in London. They might think it odd not to be invited to the funeral, but he had every excuse, they'd disapproved of Marian from the start. Besides which, they hated travelling.

Once a month he cycled into Elmsford to catch the train the twenty miles to Leaford and the asylum, where, under a false name and often in a straightjacket, Marian remained in an unfathomable underworld of her own. Other than to settle the account, the journeys were always pointless.

To keep house, Scott hired a charwoman for two mornings a week, until Laura was old enough to do the cleaning herself. The loss of her mother had its effect on the girl, but the Bowden's neighbourliness greatly reduced its impact. She spent most of that summer holiday with her grandparents in London, and the remainder with the boy, under Mrs. Bowden's supervision. There was nothing to fear, they were both still children.

- CHAPTER FOUR -

In early August, Bowden and son were summoned to the Manor. Arthur had stood in that hallway twice before, once to get paid for some plumbing work, and once to fetch the boy home after the squire's son had caught him scrumping Manor apples.

"This'd better not be something similar," he warned the boy for the umpteenth time, dragging him away from the big painting over the hearth. "Worth a king's ransom, that. Now stand up straight."

At last they were ushered into the library, musty with cigar smoke and crammed with the wisdom of ages, bound in leather of russet and ochre. Bowden felt as if he were walking into autumn. Squire Stafford was standing by a massive oak desk, the Vicar beside him.

'How the other half live,' Arthur mused, contrasting Stafford's pristine, cherry red chesterfields with his own scuffed and tufted relic of an armchair.

"Bowden, thank you for sparing the time," Stafford said. "It's precious to us all, so we won't beat about the bush. Reverend…"

"Oh, I…" Plainly the Parson had expected the Squire to do the talking. "Yes, well, what we have to say concerns your.. er.. son, Mr. Bowden."

The boy flushed. Immediately Arthur was on the defensive.

"He's not in trouble again, is he?"

"Again, Mr. Bowden?"

"He was caught scrumping apples a year back."

"Oh, no, no, nothing like that. I'm sure we've all scrumped a few apples in our time."

"Not from my orchards, I hope," Stafford frowned.

"Quite, Mr. Stafford. No, actually, Mr…er… Bowden, it's quite the contrary."

"Well, go on Vicar," Stafford prompted.

"Yes, well.. er.. it has been the.. er.. custom of his Lordship on certain auspicious occasion, such as the recent Coronation of our beloved sovereign, to mark the er.. occasion by means of a benevolence, such as a tenancy, or the inauguration of a monument and such like. You may remember the stained glass window in the transepts…"

"If you please, Reverend," Stafford reminded him of the clock.

"Ah, yes, well, on this.. er.. particular occasion er.. his Lordship has honoured us with a scholarship."

Perspiration soaked Arthur's collar; his shirt stuck to his back.

"Well that's all very well, Vicar, but I don't see what that's got to do with us. The boy's got his own life to lead. With all due respect, I ain't sending him off as no manservant, if that's what you're thinking."

"No, no, Mr. Bowden, I don't think you quite understand. Your boy is to receive the award."

Arthur was dumbfounded.

"Mr. Bowden?"

"What? You mean go to a proper school, like?"

"Exactly, Mr. Bowden."

"My word." Arthur scratched his head. "Well, I don't know what to say, Vicar. I know Miss Cooper wants him to stay on 'til Christmas, but, well, this'd be for years; a proper education. Surely one of the doctor's lads or Mr. Holland's boy would be better suited?"

"It is his Lordship's expressed wish that the recipient should be a boy from the village school," Stafford confirmed.

'And I bet I know why,' Arthur silently surmised. A long running feud between his Lordship and a local farmer had ended in tragedy. His Lordship's standing had never been lower. "Are you sure the boy's bright enough, Reverend?"

"Miss Cooper seems to think so. She speaks very highly of him. I must say.. er.. Mr.. Bowden... it is a great opportunity for him."

"Well, yes, I can see that. Will he have to leave home, like?"

"No, the scholarship is to Elmsford Grammar School; he will be a day student."

A 'phew' escaped the boy's lips.

"Quiet, boy. Well, I don't know what to say, gentlemen, really I don't," Arthur knitted his brow. "I was expecting him to start earning his own keep, not go spending more of mine. I mean, a place like that; he'll be needing a uniform and books and Lord knows what; a bike, too, if he's to go into Elmsford every day."

"The scholarship takes care of all that," Stafford said impatiently. "At least, initially. Surely, after that, the means can be found?"

'Alright for you to say, money falling out of your arse,' Arthur thought resentfully. "Look, Vicar, can I give you an answer tomorrow? This needs thinking about."

"Surely Mr. Bowden, but no longer or another boy will have to be chosen."

* * * * *

The boy began his first term in the red braided black blazer and grey flannels that would clothe him through his adolescence. On his first day he saw the copper beech, resplendent in its cardinal glory. It was rumoured to be as old as the school itself, founded in 1549 by Edward VI, but this was unlikely. The school had moved location in the 1880s; the tree had existed long before then, but its exact age was unknown.

An old Georgian rectory sheltered behind its foliage, an annex to the modern main building across the playing fields. Throughout his school days, the boy would cherish the desk in the rectory's bay-window, basking in the tree's ancient aura. For him it was, truly, a tree of knowledge. Once he was caught in complete contemplation, returned by the ear to the present tense of Latin grammar. He had his knuckles rapped with a ruler and was told he would never learn his Cicero by staring at a tree. To him the tree was Cicero, but he kept his peace, evading the crucifixion normally metered out to vacuous Vandals and Visigoths.

His social superiors gave him less leeway. It took a string of victories in the boxing ring to give his innate amiability the time and space to complete the acceptance process. Within eighteen months, he was as much a fixture of the school as it was of him.

He cycled there and back with Laura, who, thanks to her father's promotion, began attending Elmsford's St. Saviour's Priory. On his mother's insistence, "after all the Vicar's done for you," he even joined Laura at Church and Sunday school. However, his most precious moments were those fate allowed them alone. Inevitably, as the relationship endured and matured, nature teased them, but, however strong, they resisted its temptations, a self-denial that became both the agony and ecstasy of their passion, as binding as the act of consummation itself.

There was talk of 'Kaiser Bill and his blooming dreadnoughts.' A few young blades impressed themselves with vows of 'putting the ruddy fool in his place', but no one took the arms race seriously. England was unchallengeable; not even the Kaiser was daft enough to try his luck against the might of the Empire.

The Titanic sailed and sank, the dockers, miners and rail-workers went on strike, Isadora Duncan shocked society, Scott's namesake perished in the Antarctic, Emily Davison martyred herself for Women's suffrage and Ulster rebelled against Irish Home Rule, but, for the boy, life, in those celestial years before the world was plunged into a holocaust to end all wars, could hardly have been more adolescently idyllic.

- CHAPTER FIVE -

The white roses flowered early in 1914, predicting the long, hot summer to come. Every other day, the boy would cut two fresh stems, one for Laura and one for himself. Laura had turned fifteen in April, he sixteen in May. They were as romantically in love as only youth can be and, in both gift and acceptance, each bloom was a plight of the purity and passion that sustained them through the frustrations of spring.

The boy had become a competent artist, sketching a portrait that was essentially Laura. He'd given it to her for her birthday. Time seemed not only on their side, but eternal, marriage, if a dream away, one certain of fulfilment, one that governed, supported and in many ways diminished all other aspirations. Rich or poor, they would be together always; nothing else mattered.

* * * * *

The assassination of Archduke Franz Ferdinand, heir apparent to the Hapsburg Empire, passed unnoticed in the village, barring Squire Stafford's grunt when he read the insignificant report in the Times. Irish Home Rule was by far the prevalent political issue, the third ranked topic of Tap Bar debate after the impending drought and expected bumper harvest.

It was more keenly noted by Chapman, the boy's History Master, a student of European politics and a great admirer of Bismark, who had predicted that the next war would result from 'some damned foolish thing in the Balkans'. Chapman regretted the German Chancellor's demise. He had no time for the Kaiser, whose megalomania he greatly feared would prove Norman Angell's 'The Great Illusion', with its assertion that economic interdependence made armed conflict between the European superpowers impossible, to be, itself, delusional. In Chapman's view, General Von Bernhardie's 'war is a biological necessity' was far more likely to impress an Imperial mind unbalanced at birth and as belligerently retarded as the arm that rattled the sabre.

With examinations over, the schoolmaster dedicated the last two weeks of term to a crash course in Current Affairs, charting each move on the political chessboard into a chilling hypothesis. The spark from the assassin's revolver could ignite the European powder keg.

A Serbian pawn had killed an Austrian Prince, providing the perfect pretext for the annexation of Serbia that Austria had long been contemplating. If attacked, Serbia would turn to Russia for protection and so set in motion the complex cogs and counter cogs of Europe's political time bomb. Germany would support Austria; Russia would call on France, her military ally and Germany's traditional enemy. Even if, as far as Chapman was aware, the Anglo-French 'Entente Cordiale' stopped short of military obligation, should Belgium neutrality be violated,

England, as its principal guarantor, would be duty bound to take on the violator, theoretically either party, but, in essence, the Kaiser's Germany, long considered England's enemy.

However, the schoolmaster could find little evidence to support his fears. The Kaiser left for his customary summer cruise; Austria's aged Emperor, Franz Joseph, declined even to attend his detested nephew's funeral; it seemed the episode was forgotten.

Term ended and Chapman headed off for his holidays, happy to have been wrong, until Austria's ten-point ultimatum to Serbia stunned the world on July the 23rd. On the 25th, the Government announced a 'precautionary period', then, on the 28th, exactly a month after the fateful assassination, Austria declared war on Serbia.

The British fleet, already assembled for the Spithead review, was sent to its war stations. The Stock Exchange closed; the bank rate soared by 6 percent overnight. 'Not a single British life shall be sacrificed for the sake of Russian Hegemony of the Slav world', the Daily News declared, while the Times urged immediate countermeasures against a possible German advance through Belgium to take the Channel Ports. 'Hegemony' was very much the word of the moment.

Declarations and ultimatums followed one upon another over the bank holiday weekend. Then, in the early hours of August 4th, German troops entered Belgium. By day's end, England was at war.

Chapman stood at his guest house window, looking down at the cheering crowd gathered on the promenade. Before long they were swaying in the lamplight, singing Rule Britannia and God Save the King.

"What is it, daddy? Are we at war?" His twelve-year-old daughter asked, running into the room.

"Yes, my darling, it seems we are."

"Now, Constance, go back to bed," the girl's mother said, turning her by the shoulder. "It's the middle of the night."

"But they're singing."

"They'll go home, soon, I promise."

In truth it had been a war waiting to happen. Now, thanks to a Serbian extremist in a small town called Sarajevo, the excuse had been duly provided.

* * * * *

In Ashleigh, one or two daredevils marched off to Elmsford's recruiting office; as for the rest, they'd plant their seeds, tend their crops and celebrate victory when the time came. 'Business as usual' was to become, not just a catchphrase but a national philosophy. The Empire hadn't been involved in a European war since the Crimea, which, as Amos Crutchley told Arthur Bowden over a pint of Mild and Bitter, "weren't in Europe anyway. Don't know why we want to get involved. Leave it to them French, that's what I say. Got the best army in the world, they have, barring ours, of course."

If Barley Mow memories reached back to the harvest of 1870, they didn't stretch

27

to foreign fields and the blood-soaked soil around Sedan.

"And, if that bloody fool Kaiser tries coming over here, well, just let him try, that's all; our navy'll soon make an 'and of him; blow him out of the water they will, him and his blooming Dreadnoughts."

If Arthur shared Amos's confidence in the navy, he had little in the army. He'd lost two sons in the Boer debacle, one to a bullet in the brain, the other to typhoid at Bloemfontein. Now, thanks to a pint too many at the previous year's Elmsford Carnival, his third son, George, was about to shoulder arms, having joined the territorials for the price of a best Sunday suit.

"What the hell was you thinking?" Arthur had berated him at the time.

"It weren't just me, dad, Charlie and the others've joined up and all. Anyway it's not like it used to be; just two weeks a year, that's all, more of a holiday than anything. Even if there's a war, we won't have to go nowhere, home defence only," George had assured him.

Now the whole battalion had volunteered for overseas service.

"Couldn't say no," George had confessed sheepishly. "Couldn't be the only one."

Beatrice, Arthur's wife, was distraught. "You won't let them take the boy, Arthur, not our Richard; promise me you won't," she pleaded.

And so Arthur promised; it was the only comfort he could offer her. Besides, Richard was far too young and it would be over by Christmas.

The following week Beatrice joined Richard and the Scotts at Church. Stubbornly, Arthur stayed at home. He'd lost all faith ten years before, when the old Vicar had raised a plaque to his Lordship's dead Viscount with never a mention of the Bowden's lost boys. He'd decided, then and there, that, if God existed at all, He'd been dispossessed by the Aristocracy. However, he found solitude no substitute for Beatrice's periodic reports on the progress of Sunday lunch. Broodily, he went to meet her.

A list of all those serving their country had been posted in the Church porch, regulars at the top, 'Stafford, S. P. Lt., Essex Regiment. Cudlip, J. R. Pr., ditto,' then the volunteers and territorials, beginning with 'Bowden, G. A.' Arthur's eyes blanked in anger.

"He's gone, then?" Old Joe, the blacksmith, took him by surprise.

"Oh, hello, Joe. Yes, the bloody young fool. I told him no good would come of it. It's a wonder they took him, state of his teeth. They sent one of the White boys back, and his were no worse than our George's."

"Ah, but George was already in."

"Worse luck. His mother's worried sick. She's in there now, praying her heart out, for all the good it'll do her. After what happened to his brothers, you'd've thought he'd have had more sense."

"He'll be alright," Old Joe said reassuringly. "From what I hear it'll all be over before he's boarded the boat. There's a notice up by the post office, same as that one up there if I'm not mistaken. Old Ma Beasley read it to me."

"What, this one here?"

"That's the fellow."

"'Official War News. German plan of invading France seriously delayed by resistance at Liège and intervention of French cavalry,'" Arthur read stiltedly. "'Consequently French have carried out mobilisation and concentration without hindrance. Various minor Belgian and French successes reported. German crews to quit the German vessels 'Goeben' and 'Breslau' at Constantinople. No British casualties.' Well, that's something, I suppose."

"What's that other one there beside it?"

"This here?" Arthur scanned it, saving himself the obstacle course of another recitation. "It's a note from the Vicar saying they're going to ring the church bell every noonday, so that them within hearing can spare a thought for the boys with the colours."

"Better spare a thought for the horses, and all; Army took the best of 'em yesterday, shires, carriage, even Clayman's old bay, and they'll be taking a lot more once the harvest's in."

"Thought you said it was all but over?"

"Well, if it isn't I reckon I'll be down to mending bicycle tyres; won't be no horses left to shoe. Here we go."

The Church doors opened. Beatrice emerged with Richard and the Scotts.

"I've just got to see the Vicar. They're forming a knitting circle for the troops," she told Arthur, as though his appearance had been prearranged.

"What about my dinner?"

"Won't hurt to keep. You wouldn't want our George going without, would you? It might be cold out there."

"Dah, they'll all be home before you've put needle to wool. It's all but over from what it says up there."

"Well, not according to the Vicar it's not, and what he says comes from the Lord Lieutenant himself."

"Ah, but that comes from the government."

"Well, I know who I'd rather believe."

Beatrice's defiance gave Arthur two options, a public scene or a face saving compromise. He chose the latter. "Well, don't be long, I've got things to do. Women, I don't know. Can't do with 'em, can't do without 'em. Morning, Mr. Scott. Mr. Petty, here, was just saying they've taken all the horses."

* * * * *

In late August, an entire Territorial Brigade passed through the village. It was a sight never before witnessed, as if the whole British Army was on the march, the officers smart and well-horsed, sword hilts glinting in the sun, the footsloggers, crippled by their new army boots, falling out in droves.

"Office workers and factory hands, most of them," a sergeant called to Arthur, watching from his yard. "Just can't hack it. But they will; they will."

By lunchtime the villagers had handed out their entire crop of early apples and plums, and still the columns came on. It was late in the afternoon before the last blister cases were loaded into the hotchpotch of commandeered brakes, carts and trade vehicles that brought up the rear.

"Well, that seems to be it," Richard said cheerily, before the officer of the rearguard turned in his saddle to flash Laura the kind of smile that would induce any girl to wave back and reduce any schoolboy to gutfuls of inferiority.

"I'm glad you're not one of them; I'd die if anything happened to you," she tried to make amends on their way home.

"Actually, it would be me doing the dying," Richard moped.

"Don't say that, I mean it."

"Oh, I'm sure you'd find someone else," he compounded his own misery. "You seem to have no shortage of admirers."

"What? Oh, don't be so silly. It would have been rude not to wave back."

"Really."

They wandered on.

"So, is that what you'd do if anything happened to me, find someone else?" Laura reverted to female logic.

"Of course not. Look, I was only joking, all right? Anyway, nothing's going to happen to either of us. Mother would be straight down the depot if I so much as looked at a recruiting poster," Richard ground to the crux of the matter.

"You wouldn't go, would you?"

Laura's concern only fed the boy's truculence. He shrugged his shoulders.

"Promise me you wouldn't."

It was too much to ask of a sulker racked by his girlfriend's flirtation with a smarmy bloody subaltern on his broad bay bloody mare. He couldn't help himself.

"Well, after that little display, I'm surprised you care."

Glaring at him with all her mother's ferocity, Laura stormed off down the track, leaving his ribcage reverberating with hollow wit. He felt like a goat.

* * * * *

The following morning, a heavy knock caught Laura at the kitchen sink.

"Who is it, please?" She called down the hall.

"Sergeant Morris, ma'am. Army business," the knocker barked through the letterbox.

She dried her hands and opened the door. A stout soldier was standing on the step.

"Begging your pardon, Miss, but his your father at home?" His Cockney accent was affected with all the 'h' Oxford he could muster.

"I'm sorry, he's gone to work."

"Your mother, then?"

"I'm afraid my mother's dead," Laura lamented a little guiltily; her mother had been far from her thoughts recently. However, her sorrow was short lived; there was something comically canine about the man.

"Hoh, h'I sees," he pronounced.

She just stopped herself from blurting, 'you old seadog, you,' as 'A life on the ocean waves' shantied mischievously through her brain.

"Hwell you sees, Miss, h'I've got some billetings to do hereabouts, hwhich necessitates the happraising of hevery house hin the harea to sees how many heach can take."

Every 'h' was emphasised to infinity, the 's's, like Laura's reaction, were natural. She desperately wanted to repeat his 'h'I sees '.

"You gets paid, Miss, two shillings a day for heach man. But with you halones in the house, well, h'I'm not so sures as hit would be propah."

"Yes," she managed to squeeze through buttoned lips, only for the seams to give way to a grin made cheekier by its tightness. It was a grin he completely misconstrued and returned, the jagged teeth of his lower jaw overlocking those of the upper. His barrel chest expanded to full capacity. He looked exactly like a Bulldog.

"Hall the same, Miss, hif you don't mind, I'll just pops me heads in and have a look around."

It was all Laura could do not to corpse. "I suppose it would be all right; but I go back to... Normally there's no one here during the daytime." To say school would have spoiled the fun.

"That's all right, Miss, nor is we," he told her, ducking unnecessarily under the lintel.

She could sense his bloodshot eyes tennis-balling from one swinging hip to the other, as she led him upstairs.

"They honly takes up the one room, they hall sleeps together, see."

Laura showed him the spare bedroom.

"Very nice, very cosy, Miss, but far too good for the likes of them."

"Surely, sergeant, nothing's too good for our brave boys?" She couldn't help a saucy inflection.

His moustaches twitched, his lips quivered. "Perhaps we could takes ha look hat the parlour, Miss?" He almost croaked.

She had to turn to smother her laughter. "Please, this way."

Again she felt his eyes on her.

"Yes, hif we clears the settee hout of harms way hand rolls up the carpet, this'll do nicely." He regained his composure at the parlour door.

"But, wouldn't the bedroom be more appropriate?" The devil in her refused to die.

His cheeks chameleoned through the entire red spectrum. "No, no, Miss, this'll do fine, really it will," he blustered, blundering into the Welsh Dresser. "Oh Gawd!"

Laura clutched her sides, fighting for breath, as he juggled air in front of the rattling cups and plates. The crockery settled. He blew like a relieved whale.

"It's alright, Miss, no harm done. Well, I've seen hall I comes for. Mustn't linger. Thank you very much, Miss. H'I'll pop backs tonight hand sees yer dad."

With a final, focusless look round he lurched out, leaving Laura in complete hysterics.

A familiar knock followed hot on the sergeant's heels. The boy's face, still sullen from the previous day's stupidity, did nothing to aid Laura's composure.

"I see you've landed two of them, then," he huffed.

"Two whats?" She borrowed from the sergeant.

"Two of our country's finest. There's a chalk mark on the door."

"Where on the door?" She stifled a giggle.

"There," he showed her. "Looks like we'll be lumbered with three at our place. We didn't get an 's' though; don't know what that means."

"S for h'ssspecial, of course," she chortled.

"What on earth's wrong with you?"

"Oh, nothing, nothing at all." She fought desperately to keep a straight face. "No, the sergeant wasn't sure. He said that, has I was halones here with father hat work, hit mights not be propah!"

"Absolutely; it wouldn't be right at all," the boy puffed, ignoring her mimicry with all his might.

It was too much for her; she couldn't contain her laughter.

"What?" He complained.

"Nothing, nothing at all. Oh, I do love you, Richard Bowden."

She fell into his arms and immediately his cloud evaporated. They'd seldom had the opportunity to hold each other so closely. It became an embrace not of adolescents, but of adults.

"Where's your father?" He asked softly.

"He's gone to work."

All conviction failed them. Their lips met with unprecedented voracity and they were lost to passion.

Laura couldn't say for how long his mother had been calling. It was like being dragged from the deepest sleep by a subliminal voice. His hands were in her clothing; his manhood was pressing hard against her hip. She panicked.

"It's all right, it's all right," he reassured her. "She won't leave her baking. I'm needed at the yard. Dad's short-handed with George gone."

She looked into his eyes, full of joy, almost of conquest, behind the cornea's mandatory guilt. She'd longed to give herself to his touch. Now she had, and she was glad. His mother called again.

"She must know you're here."

He frowned in the affirmative.

"Then you'd better go, before you completely ruin my reputation." She tilted her head up for one last kiss. It would have to be enough, for now.

"I see you've landed two of them, then," Mrs. Bowden echoed her son's words, as she followed Laura into the kitchen twenty minutes later. "I'm not sure it's right, what with you alone here and all, but then I suppose things is different now there's a war on. Still, it's better than us; we've got to put up with three of the blighters."

"Yes, Richard said," Laura told her, filling the kettle.

"I hope he didn't stay long; he's supposed to be helping his father. Your dad not home?"

"No, he had to go to work."

The girl seemed flustered. The Bowden suspicions were aroused.

"Bet he had a job keeping a straight face, what with that sergeant. Talk about putting it on. I had to bite my tongue to stop myself from laughing."

"Actually, he'd already left. The sergeant said he'd call back tonight."

"Oh well, all in a good cause; though I know someone who won't be too happy about it," Mrs. Bowden worked back to the prevalent issue. "One look at him heading up the lane and he was out of that gate faster than a greyhound. Bet he had something to say about it, didn't he?"

"No, not really. He only popped in for a minute, after the sergeant left."

Beatrice may not have been using a stopwatch, but the boy had been there considerably longer than that. The breakfast plates were still in the sink. Little more than children they may be, but Beatrice was neither stupid nor blind enough to imagine that, after three years of courtship, they didn't know what was what.

"Laura dear, you didn't... you know... do anything silly...."

"Mrs. Bowden, of course not. No, actually, we had words yesterday, but it's all right now. When the time is right we'll give you all the grandchildren you want, I promise, but only then."

The girl's happiness was infectious, her forthrightness convincing.

"I'm glad to hear it," Beatrice smiled. "I hope you didn't mind my asking, only, I wouldn't want anything to spoil it for you."

Laura took her hand affectionately. "There's no need to worry."

"No more to be said, then. I'm going down the shops, is there anything you want?"

Scott returned in the late afternoon. The sergeant followed soon after. He'd thought it best that, "hunder the circumstances," he and a fellow N.C.O. stayed with the Scotts. For their two shillings a day, the government required breakfast and evening meal; "nothing fancy, mind, just ha bit of something to keep the wolves haway. Hits just for the h'one night; we'll be moving hon in the morning."

Laura prepared ham and pickles, straining her ears for the cockney banter emanating from the dining room. Only when her father appeared did the 'h' affectation do likewise.

"Hwe'll beds down hin the parlour, sir, hif that's halright with you," she heard the sergeant say. "We've gots hour hown gear."

Her father repeated her offer of the spare bedroom.

"Thank you kindly, sir, but the parlour'll do us. Can'ts be bedding down amongst the down, if you gets my drift. Hif the men gots wind of it, they'd thinks we'd gone soft and that would never do."

After their meal, the sergeants went into the village, where the locals were entertaining the troops, leaving Scott and the lovers in the garden to enjoy the sunset from a rustic bower Scott had constructed for that very purpose. A cutting from the Bowden's rose tree had yet to climb the trellis-work, but, given time, it would provide the perfect canopy.

Across the valley, a column of weary recruits were marching along the main road, trailing the sunset back to their billets. From the village pubs, the faint strains of a harmonica and a cockney chorus of 'Dolly Grey' added counterpoint to nature's evensong.

"Well, what do you make of it all, young Richard? Do you wish you were going with them?" Scott asked, puffing on his pipe.

"Not really, sir. Besides, mother would have a fit. It's bad enough with George going. I had two brothers killed in South Africa, you see, fighting the Boers."

"Really? I didn't know. Poor woman," Scott sympathised.

"You never said?" Laura queried.

"Mother gets too upset. Besides, I didn't really know them. I wasn't even walking. But that's why, you see."

"Yes, quite. Anyway, they say it'll all be over by Christmas. Let's hope they're right," Scott closed the subject, knocking out his pipe.

Twilight fell. The sergeants returned, bearing their beer like a badge of honour.

"Quite a crowd you've got there; haven't been stood so many drinks since the declaration. Hwell, we'll be turnings hin now, Sir, if that's pardonable. Gots an hearly start in the morning. Breakfast'll have to be hat six sharp, I'm afraid, Miss."

"All right, sergeant," Scott acknowledged with a grin. "Goodnight to you."

"Goodnights to you, Sir, Miss...... young man," the hero added patronisingly.

Laura lay blissfully in her bed, watching the moon rise. It had been a strange day, a growing up day. Sometimes the boy seemed such a boy, and then..... She glowed in the warmth of his touch, until the sin of it seared her cheeks. Yet there was no shame in her guilt, and little even of that, if she was honest; how could she feel guilty over such a beautiful thing?

She squirmed ecstatically. There could be no going back now, but equally there must be no going further. The basics of how babies were made were no mystery, but there were so many unanswered questions. He mustn't enter her, that was the main thing.

But she didn't want to think of that now, at least not in a wrong way. If only they could be married, then none of it would matter, but it would be years, years.

Down in the parlour, the Bulldog was wagging his tale.

"She would, y' know, I'm damned sure of it, the way she was coming on to me this morning. You should've seen it. I'd've taken her up on it, and all, only I didn't have the time, see, more's the pity."

"Come on Harry, pull the other one," his companion yawned. "Pure as the virgin bleeding snow, that one. I told you before, wishful bloody thinking, mate, that's all that is. You'll get yer leg over soon enough, when we get over yonder. Eat you alive, them French girls, so they say."

"Yeh; and if the frogs don't get you the crabs will. Leave it out. Had it up 'em so many times, if they stood up straight their innards'd fall out. I'll settle for a sweet, unsullied English rose any day of the week, thank you very much."

"Well it won't be her, not this side of the pearly gates. Besides, she can't be no more than fifteen; they'd hang you from the nearest gallows, which is what I'll be doing to your bollocks, if you don't shut yer fucking cake hole and let me get some kip."

- CHAPTER SIX -

The hamlet's first 'Form B.104-82B' of the war fell to the Cudlip's threadbare carpet. Jos's mother cried out her anguish. Of three sons and three daughters, Jos had been the eldest. His sister Margaret was there in an instant. Her mother was standing in the hall, her face in her hands. Margaret picked up the single sheet.

"Regret to inform you, Joseph William Cudlip killed in Action 23rd Aug. 1914. Lord Kitchener expresses his sympathy."

There was nothing more, just nineteen words, the official conclusion of a life. Margaret was immobilised; if only the armies of Europe had remained so.

"He was a good boy, a brave boy," her mother said, before sinking convulsively to her knees.

* * * * *

The causes of the War, the egotistical power struggles of the mighty, the cancerous greed of trade and industry, the false pride engendered in nations by their profligate rulers, all sat secure behind the moral misguidance of the masses. 'An eye for an eye,' Christianity preached, while conveniently forgetting to turn the other cheek. Loyalty to King and Country could not be questioned; it was one's duty to sacrifice oneself for the status quo.

Nevertheless, when his Lordship descended on Ashleigh's packed Church Hall to exhort all men between nineteen and thirty five to join up and slay the dastardly Hun, vehemently pounding the table to reinforce his crie de couer, only one man volunteered, his own Manor Farm foreman. It was a bitter blow for the Hero of Isumbwana.

However the problem was not the call, but the caller. Little more than a month later, Field Marshall Lord Kitchener succeeded where his Lordship had failed, aided and abetted by reports of bayoneted babies, the burning of Louvain, the 'Angel Bowmen of Mons' and mounting casualty lists.

Wherever they looked, posters proclaiming 'YOUR COUNTRY WANTS YOU' bullied the nation's manhood, the steely eyed Field Marshal staring men down, pointing at them implicitly. 'We don't want to lose you, but we think you ought to go,' the seductresses sang in the music halls, while, out in the alleys, the white feather brigade waited to shame cowards into action.

And so they went, some lying about their age, others tiptoeing to reach the statutory height, which had to be increased by three inches to 5' 6" to keep the numbers manageable. From colleges and factories, offices and farms, inoculated with the serum of righteousness, the Empire's manhood followed its conscience: underage Sidney White, determined to join his soldier brothers, Albert Truelove,

Percy Cudlip out for revenge, Ronald Petty the blacksmith's boy, Ernest and Cecil Thompson, William Taylor, Henry Harold Cooper the teacher's brother, sons all, lovers many, husbands and fathers some.

One or two would slink home, rejected as unfit, ashamed to face those ignorant of their shortcomings. Others would be billeted at home, leaving for drill each morning, as they had for work, indistinguishable except for an armband; it would be a while before the army could cloth and accommodate them, but the point was they were 'in'.

What price a little contempt? What price a white feather? What price pride? Nelson would have been proud, Wellington contemptuously pleased. Lord Kitchener was highly gratified; he had asked for one hundred thousand; he would get twenty times that number.

* * * * *

At Saint Saviour's Priory the glamour of war was infectious. It was every girl's dream to walk out with a young officer, although, with so many boys of acceptable status answering Lord Kitchener's call, even a rank and filer of the right background would do. Some had already waved their menfolk off to war. Before the day was out, these had decorated their lapels with red topped pins. During the lunch break the 'Harlots' ceremonially ripped a pillow apart in the cloakroom, only to find its feathers a disappointing dapple grey.

Behind all this patriotic fervour was Joanna Hetherington, chief 'Harlot' and deputy head girl. She came from a military family. Her father was a major in the Guards, her brother a lieutenant in the same regiment. Both had already seen action, as had a subaltern to whom she was 'all but engaged'. The pins were her idea, one for each relative, including potential fiancés. Black pins would signify a death. From the outset, she was the most decorated, bathing in the respect her matrix demanded.

Laura wore no pin.

"What, no one in your family? Poor you," she was told.

At the Grammar the atmosphere was no less fervent. Following Haldane's lead six years before, the school had set up its own Officer Training Corps and those cadets who had recently completed their senior year were now, to a man, with the colours, albeit in the ranks. Younger masters had also joined up. An improvised register of all Old Boys serving their King had been posted on the common room notice board, names envied and admired.

As Kitchener had appealed to the nation's manhood, the Headmaster appealed to his pupils, making enrolment in the cadets practically compulsory. Games lessons were given over to drill, gymnastics to obstacle course training.

Richard didn't tell his parents he had joined, or even Laura. Khaki was in critically short supply, not even the army proper had enough to go round. If he kept his mouth shut, there was little chance of them finding out. Besides, as one of the most popular boys in the school, it was his duty to set an example.

* * * * *

"Heard about all them German spies, Arthur?" Amos Crutchley assailed Arthur Bowden with the latest gossip from Elmsford market. "Rounding them up by the cartload in London, guns, explosives, the lot. Apparently they was all in on it, barbers, waiters, even the bloody bakers, some of them here thirty years or more, just waiting for the word. Christ, they could've poisoned the whole lot of us. Can't even trust the bread you eat nowadays. Still, the old Cossacks'll soon put a stop to them. Shiploads, the stationmaster told me; bringing them down from Scotland, eighty thousand or more. Said they got out at Crewe for a stretch and left the platform all covered in snow."

"What, in September?"

"Well it snows early where they come from, and it don't melt like ours. Anyway, they're on their way over yonder, so it'll soon be over now."

"Well it so happens we've had a bit of excitement of our own, while you've been off gallivanting. Old Johnson caught a spy red-handed, standing by the crossroads drawing maps of the place, bold as brass. Claimed he was from the Ordnance Survey. Got right uppity, he did. Said it was the fifth time he'd been hauled in in as many days. Johnson's got him down at the police house now. Reckons he might be tied in with that house over in Eastleigh, the one them foreigners rented a while back."

"Hollanders weren't they?"

"So they said at the time. Johnson says there's a tennis court up there built on ten feet of solid concrete. Gun platform, he reckons, all conveniently lined up on that new wireless works in Elmsford. He's keeping an eye out, in case they come back."

"Well, I'll be. Mind you, old Stafford's got something similar with that flat roof of his; and his girl went off to Germany not long back."

"Nah. It looks flat, but it ain't; it's pointed like that," Arthur angled his hands, "only you can't see it for the parapet. By the way, they're casting round for Special Constables, if you're interested. There's a meeting next Wednesday. Sounds like old Johnson'll be needing all the help he can get."

Arthur went to the meeting and volunteered; Amos excused himself. "Got had up for poaching a while back; they wouldn't have me."

After some basic training, Arthur found himself guarding the parish's hayricks and telegraph poles for two nights a week.

"Now you be careful with that truncheon of yours," Crutchley warned him. "That there's a lethal weapon; could give a spy a nasty crack on the head with that, if he don't shoot you first."

* * * * *

By mid-October, two of Joanna Hetherington's red pins had been replaced by black, father and son being killed on the same day, in the same action. At the

Grammar, two names had appeared on its 'Roll of Honour', two weeks later, two more. Jaws set; eyes hardened; rhetoric exacted vengeance on the filthy Hun.

Chapman, the boy's history master, was one of the few who did not rattle the sabre. Having deduced the pattern of events leading up to the conflict, he now deliberated on its likely course, aided by a translation of an obscure thesis by a Polish banker named Bloch, who had written in 1897, 'through industrial development... the soldier... has so perfected the mechanism of slaughter that he has practically secured his own extinction,' going on to describe the course of events with astonishing foresight.

'At first there will be an increased slaughter on so terrible a scale as to render it impossible to get troops to push the battle to a decisive issue. They will try... and they will learn such a lesson they will abandon the attempt... The war... will become a kind of stalemate in which neither army... (will be)... able to deliver a final and decisive blow. Everyone will be entrenched in the next war, the spade will be as indispensable to the soldier as his rifle.'

As the war map unfolded into November and entrenchment swallowed the 'noble' slaughter of open warfare, it seemed the Pole's predictions were being borne out. If the defences being dug from the North Sea to the Alps, proved unbreachable, far from being 'Over by Christmas' or 'Home before the leaves fall', already a bygone German boast, Chapman saw, like Kitchener, a war lasting years. He had little faith in the much vaunted 'Russian Steamroller', which, on the evidence of Tannenberg, was in danger of being flattened itself.

But to voice his fears would be to sign his own dishonourable discharge, a fate already suffered by Adams, the Calvinist Classics Master, for daring to question the veracity of the 'Angels of Mons' story, the mythical bowmen reported to have come from the clouds to their countrymen's aid.

"What do you expect of a Presbyterian?" Isaiah, his High Church superior had ordained, the glass eye that spawned his nickname cast forever heavenward. "Don't know why the Head took him on in the first place."

"Touch of the Darwin about him, if you ask me," the Maths Master had added his sixpen'th. "Never did like the fellow."

No, to open one's mouth in anything but patriotic belligerence was to be labelled, at best alarmist, at least defeatist and at worst downright traitorous. It could even lead to a prison sentence for speaking 'to the dishonour of the nation'.

For the boys in his educational care Chapman saw little hope of reprieve. There had already been talk of conscription, a subject as inflammatory as the blessed 'Angels' in the daily staff room debate, though more because it singed the nerve endings of national honour than for any issues of personal freedom.

"It's a damned insult to the nation's manhood and politically perilous to boot," Blundell, the school's P.E. teacher cum Cadet Captain had argued on the basis of his own bulging battalions and those of Lord Kitchener, ironically the proponent of compulsory service. "Not only does it infer a national weakness of character that simply isn't there, but, by so doing, it threatens to undermine the very superiority on which the Empire is built. 'Now God be thanked, who has matched us with His hour.' That's the spirit! Look at Mons, look at the Marne! One hundred to one and still we beat them!"

'With the help of the odd Angel or two and, more to the point, a million conscripts Français,' Chapman had mused amid the 'here, here's.

"God help us if it ever comes, that's all I can say; and God help those called to command them," the would-be brigadier had declared. "I mean, if a man lacks the character to enlist of his own free will, what earthly use will he be? We'd end up with an army of duffers!"

On the evidence of the conscripted German Army's showing, Chapman had thought a duffer's usefulness pretty obvious, and there were also the questions of conscience and underclass recalcitrance, but again he'd held his tongue. Besides, as far as his pupils were concerned, compulsion was not the issue.

For the first time in his life he sceptically pondered the Victorian values educated into every Englishman: honour, chivalry, duty. What chance did these boys have against such a trinity, against themselves?

The schoolmaster sat sadly at his desk, his calculations strewn before him. No, it was going to be a long war. What was it Grey had said, "the lamps are going out all over Europe, we shall not see them lit again in our lifetime?" The way things were going, few would have a lifetime to look forward to. The great nations of Europe were hell bent on destruction.

He wondered when his turn would come. He was thirty-six.

* * * * *

And so the pattern evolved, the blueprint for four years of carnage and deprivation. As Christmas approached the country settled into the mantle of war. The peaceful hot summer days of June and July seemed a lifetime ago. The first harvest of the seeds sown in Sarajevo had been plentiful; the grim reaper's grin widened at its projected abundance.

- CHAPTER SEVEN -

On Christmas Eve, Arthur Bowden persuaded Scott to join him for a festive drink at the Barley Mow, where the price of a pint had increased to fourpence, sixty pints to the pound.

"Haven't put no limit on it yet, though there's talk they might. Be a sad day when you can't get a proper drink. We'll be off then, mother," he called to his wife in the kitchen, then, "and I want that tree finished before I get back," to Richard and Laura, busy with the Christmas decorations in the parlour.

It was the chance Laura had been waiting for. Even at the Priory, war had loosened the moral shackles. Intimacies, real and imaginary, had become the yardstick among the Hetherington set, for whom a reputation lost was now a reputation won, provided the laws of love, overseas service and, above all, self-sacrifice applied, dispensations the school's 'Zealots' jesuitically denounced, although there were some hiding behind the Zealotorial mask whose secret sexuality would have put many a 'Harlot' to shame.

Prudently, Laura kept her sex life to herself. Compared with some, she had little to boast about and it would be suicidal to do so given Richard's schoolboy status. Even so, the stimulus was there and she allowed Richard free licence under the mistletoe, cat-eared to any break in the culinary cadence emanating from the kitchen, where his mother was slaving over a hot stove.

"Come and taste this, one of you! Richard?"

Mrs. Bowden's call turned passion into panic.

"Just a minute!"

"I'll bring it in!"

Laura dived behind the Christmas tree, struggling with her catches, while Richard scrambled to the door to bar his mother's progress. She beat him to it with a plateful of mince pies.

"Try one of these, both of you," Laura heard her say, followed by Richard's yelp as he scorched his fingers.

"They're hot!"

"Well of course they're hot. They've just come out of the oven. Where's Laura?"

"Behind the tree," Laura called. "Hurry up, Richard, I can't hold this forever."

"What's wrong, dear? Is he leaving you to do all the work? Men! Worse than useless. Here, hold this."

Through the pine needles, Laura saw Beatrice thrust the pastries at her son, intent on lending a hand. Her cheeks turned to wax, her fingers to wood. She was still hopelessly undone.

The hissing and spitting of a boiling pot came to her rescue.

"The apples! Eat them while they're hot," Beatrice ordered, forcing the plate onto Richard and scurrying off down the hall. "And don't leave Laura standing there, give her a hand!"

41

Laura's hooks and eyes were completely skew-whiff.

"Do you think she twigged?" She asked, as Richard extricated the snared cotton.

"I don't think so."

"All the same, we'd better be careful."

A second intrusion could be their own undoing.

* * * * *

On Christmas morning Mrs. Bowden was up with the larks, putting the finishing touches to the family feast. Normally, Richard would have been snug in his bed, drooling in expectation, but this year he was full of dread. The Scotts were coming to dinner, perfect in itself, but so were Elizabeth and the children.

He managed to fill the pew with his grandparents at church, leaving his in-law across the aisle. His grandfather Gurny was eighty two, his grandmother seventy eight; they had been married for sixty two years. He could have sworn his grandfather broke wind, when, knees cracking in arthritic unison, the old couple knelt to pray, but it could have been one of the Beasleys in front, and it was more cabbage than rotten egg; anything was preferable to pairing Elizabeth with Mr. Scott.

With the death of Ray Brewer at Ypres and with Herbert White posted 'missing', the mood of the congregation was sombre and supportive rather than joyful. Service was concluded with an emotional 'Onward Christian Soldiers'.

Richard's father was waiting by the porch.

"Last one home gets no pudding," he told his grandchildren, leaving only Elizabeth for Richard to shepherd. Shackled to the pace of the elderly, the ordeal proved prolonged. By the time they reached the house, every bone was aching with cold, except it seemed, Elizabeth's jaw.

Richard stoked the fire; his father decanted the sherry.

"Ooh, Pale Cream; we are honoured. It's only 'cause you're here, Mr. Scott, otherwise it'd be the cooking variety," Elizabeth rattled on. "Now, are we all here? I've had a card from George. Not much of one, mind you, but better than nothing. Here you are, Mum; you read it first then pass it on."

It reached Richard well thumbed and wept over. It was not a Christmas card, but a Field Service Postcard, listing a number of pre-typed alternatives, to be struck out as appropriate:

'I am quite well

I have been admitted into hospital (sick

(wounded

and am going on well

and hope to be discharged soon.

I am being sent down to the base.

(letter

I have received your (telegram

(parcel

Letter follows at first opportunity.

> I have received no letter from you (lately
>   (for a long time.

George had deleted all except the first sentence and the last, defying the printed warning of destruction should the sender add anything more than his signature by post-scripting, 'Merry Christmas'.

"He never was much of a letter writer. That's why I don't send, see, so he don't have to answer," Elizabeth offered her excuses.

The presents were distributed. Richard gave Laura a locket, receiving a set of watercolours in return. Under the lid was a card, beautifully hand-embroidered with forget-me-nots. He felt unworthy, inadequate, a pauper before a princess, and then like a king, when she discovered the painstakingly painted miniature rose in the locket's inner sanctum.

Nevertheless, he was a king ever fearful of the flaws in his bloodline and the havoc they could reap. So far the children had been on their best behaviour, but it could only be a matter of time.

The tureens were brought, the goose carved, the plates filled.

"I can see you, young George," Elizabeth warned her son, about to swap his sprouts for his sister's roast potatoes.

Richard squirmed, willing them to behave, only to find mortification belching forth from his grandfather's oesophagus.

"Beg pardon."

"Really, Jeremiah," Mrs. Gurny scolded her husband.

"I can't help it," Gurny claimed.

"It's alright, granddad, you enjoy it," Elizabeth encouraged him.

And enjoy it he did. Richard didn't know where to put his face, until the old man's sphincter erupted in sympathy.

"Gweat gwanddad's let one go," young George squealed. Bowden spluttered; Mrs. Bowden turned the colour of beetroot.

"How could you, Jeremiah," Mrs. Gurny glowered.

"Weren't me, it was the dog," Gurny grinned sheepishly. "Anyway, it's no good keeping it in."

Only Scott's composure offered Richard any grain of comfort, until even that was ground under the millstone of parental pride, when his mother, in desperation, treated Scott and Laura to the kind of grin-and-bear-it biography which would have any self-respecting hero heading for the outposts: his sharing the mince pies with the dog one Christmas; his first tipple, "Oh, he did pull a face. Do you remember that, Arthur?" His insistence on clearing the grate, "so Father Christmas wouldn't dirty his trousers," a moderated version of the legendary 'burn his bum'. Out came calumny after cringing calumny, until the last morsel of pudding had cleared Gurny's gullet and Richard's father was able to raise his glass without fear of interruption.

To 'King and Country' and 'absent friends' provoked the expected tears, which Scott dried with toasts to the cook, to the Bowdens' hospitality, and, with genuine gratitude, their friendship, after which the men adjourned to the parlour to enjoy Scott's brandy and cigars and talk of the War before a blazing fire.

None had any first-hand experience; Gurny had been a farm labourer all his life, Bowden hadn't strayed ten miles from the village since his boyhood arrival, and Scott had swapped classroom for office at eighteen, retaining his old school tie. However, his trade was timber, a vital commodity to the war effort, and, thanks to the enlistment of senior managers, he now talked with 'people in the know', via the offices of Montague Mayer, the War Office's sole provider, on a daily basis. A lot of what he heard was classified, but the government's fears for the Essex coast were no secret.

"The whole county's going to be garrisoned. We've been asked to supply enough lumber to build a fair sized town and then some."

If not yet obese on Government contracts, Scott's firm was putting on considerable weight.

Gurny, despite his illiteracy, had sagacity on which to base his judgement.

"How they can sit there and say it'll all be over by Christmas is beyond me. Well, it's Christmas now, ain't it, and I don't see any sign of them Germans giving in."

"You're right there," Bowden agreed, refilling Gurny's glass.

"Thank you kindly; don't mind if I do. No, there never was such a thing as a short war. Look at the bloody Crimea, or them Zulus for that matter; them weren't done for inside a couple of years, and they was nothing but savages. And as for them old Boers what made an 'and of your own poor boys, Arthur, God bless 'em, took us ages to beat the buggers and what was they? A bunch of bloody Dutch farmers. Now we got the whole bloody German Army ag'in us. No, I reckon I'll be long gone before this one's over."

"You've got years left in you yet, Jeremiah," Bowden assured him.

"Well, maybe not years, but a sight longer than some of them poor devils over yonder, I'll be bound," Gurny muttered.

Richard began to pale. He'd felt giddy from his first puff on his first cigar, but had continued to partake as part of the ritual of acceptance, interspersed with sips from his very first glass of brandy. Excusing himself, he slipped into the hall and out of the front door.

His throat filled, his cheeks puffed. He couldn't be sick in the front garden. Sneaking through the gate, he gagged his way round the perimeter to bow to the inevitable behind the back fence.

His regurgitated dinner steamed repulsively between his feet. Sweat dripped from his brow. He closed his eyes, but that only made things worse; he opened them wide and all was confusion. His fever turned to shivering, and then shivering back to incineration as door-released laughter mocked him down the garden path.

He crouched, praying he hadn't been seen. The lavatory door opened and closed. Now he could make a dash for it, but, as soon as he stood, vertigo claimed him.

He gripped the fence, hanging on until the door creaked again and a second squall of laughter told him his secret was safe.

He threw up once more on thanksgiving's cue. This time he regained his

44

faculties quicker. His cheeks still burned, but he felt infinitely better. After another recuperative minute he headed back.

The hall was empty. He gave thanks and re-entered the parlour. If anyone noticed his pallor, they didn't say. He'd just made it in time; a minute or two later the women joined the party.

"You're cold," Laura said quizzically, slipping her hand into his.

"I slipped out for some air," he told her, directing his foul breath to the floor.

The afternoon was taken up with parlour games, Laura excelling at charades, Richard at Napoleon, while Gurny dozed by the fireside, waking for tea at five. Richard ate large helpings of cold meat and pickles, followed by trifle and his grandmother's Christmas cake.

"I don't know where he puts it all," his mother said.

"He reminds me so much of my George," Elizabeth observed approvingly, her mood lightened by a liberal consumption of Gurny's elderberry wine.

After tea, the children were put in their grandparents' bed while the cards were brought out for cribbage. Only once did the lovers snatch a few seconds alone, when Richard went to the kitchen for a mince pie and Laura followed to adoringly enlighten him on the remnant of peel lodged between his teeth. Even when they fetched the coats, a furtive kiss was all they could manage.

Elizabeth roused the children. The Gurnys were staying the night.

"Be a dear and take young Doris," Beatrice said, hoisting the infant into Richard's arms. "Betty's had a bit too much to drink."

An ominous dampness soaked into his sleeve.

"I think you'd better check your bed," he told her.

The moon was bright, the lane icy, too icy for an inebriate. Elizabeth fell, taking young George with her.

"Are you alright?" Richard asked.

"No bones broken," Elizabeth reported, picking herself up. "Oh do stop blubbing, young George. You can't be hurt, you fell on top of me."

"It's broke," the child wailed over his funnel-less steam train.

"There, there; uncle Richard'll fix it, soon as we get home, won't you uncle Richard?"

They stumbled on, Richard shifting his niece's weight from side to side. How women managed to carry children so effortlessly was beyond him. He'd seen them walk miles cradling two at a time. In future, he would stick to cats.

"Home at last."

The house was cold; the morning's slack had long since burned out.

"See what you can do with the fire, while I put the kids to bed, there's a dear," Elizabeth ordered, relieving Richard of the baby.

He'd just induced a flame, when she clumped down the stairs.

"I do believe I'm a bit tipsy," she giggled, plonking herself in a chair. "Here, get us a drink; it's over on the sideboard. You'll be needing something inside you for the walk home."

45

"Thanks all the same, but I'd better be off," he excused himself, hanging up the poker.

"Oh, go on, it's Christmas," she protested, fetching for herself and pouring two large measures.

"Really, I'd rather not."

"It's poured now."

He took the glass.

"Well sit down then. I'm not gonna bite you. That's better, make yourself comfortable. I do like your Laura, she's alright she is, and her old man's not half as stuck up as he's meant to be, once you get to know him."

The boy agreed, conscious of being studied in the firelight. He swilled the alcohol round his glass. He'd never had a conversation with his sister-in-law, nor tasted gin.

"You're just like my George, sitting there," Elizabeth told him, swinging a leg over the arm of her chair. "'Cept the way you talk, mind. Must be that school of yours."

"Perhaps it'll all be over soon and he'll come home," the boy offered.

"Bloody fool to have joined up in the first place. Didn't have to go; had the choice; could've stayed at home; but, oh no, he had to be one of the boys," she said tersely. "You and that Laura've been going for a while now."

"Three years."

"Three years. Why, George and I was married within six months. Still, I 'spect there's not much you don't know about each other, hey?"

The meaning in her vixen eyes was crystal clear. The boy blushed.

"I really should be going."

"Finish your drink first. Mustn't waste good gin."

His taste buds revolted, returning the alcohol's vileness to the tumbler. Still he'd swallowed enough for his stomach to mix a head-spinning cocktail with the evening's elderberry wine.

Elizabeth refilled her glass and immediately half drained it.

"Have you had her yet?" She asked bluntly.

"Ah... no..." He stuttered, taken aback. "We promised we'd wait."

"Poor dear, you must be desperate. Does she, you know, help you out a bit, in a manner of speaking?"

Her manner of speaking was distinctly slurred.

"We get by," he answered evasively, this time managing to empty his gruesome glassful. "I really must be going."

Elizabeth went to get up.

"You're gonna have to help me, boy."

He hauled on her arm, but she was immovable. He hauled again and the room began to kaleidoscope into a carousel of pots, pans and ceiling stains. Elizabeth spiralled up from under him, her laughter like an echo, her gin-sodden breath no repellent.

'I shouldn't be doing this,' wisped through the clouds, but he was undone, her grip firm, the pleasure overwhelming.

"You little devil..."

He looked at her through sex-focused eyes, fearfully enslaved to the surge in his loins. Then her smile faded, her eyelids drooped and her fingers fell away, leaving him on ecstasy's threshold.

Again the room span. He slid to the floor and forced his head between his knees, remembering someone saying it helped. The blood pumped round his skull. His breathing deepened. His lace holes came into focus. He looked over at Elizabeth, comatose in her chair. Should he try to wake her? What should he do?

He opted for salvation. Levering himself up, he lurched towards the door.

The icy air wrapped his head in its compress. He filled his lungs and staggered into the night.

Somehow he made it home, battling the bile that burned the back of his throat, only vaguely aware of his bursting bladder and the gin sweat that soaked into his collar.

The family were in bed. He flopped onto the stairs. His fly remained open; his frost flaccid penis was poking through his underpants like a hibernating mole.

"Is that you, boy?" His father whispered from the landing.

"Yes," he replied, frantically covering himself.

"They got home alright?"

Again he gave the shortest affirmative.

"Goodnight, then. Don't forget my boots."

"Goodnight."

His father's boots would have to wait. Vowing he would never drink again, the boy monkey-crawled the stairs to collapse, face down, on his blissfully dank eiderdown.

* * * * *

In the impenetrable darkness of Christmas Eve, George Bowden stood head and shoulders above the parapet, as laid down in Army regulations, on 'sentry go'. Bowden was reliable and, with the Germans only sixty yards away, sergeant Hollis needed men he could trust, particularly those too miserly or too stupid to catch on to a bit of bribery and corruption.

It was almost eleven o'clock and the front was strangely quiet. A few flares had gone up fifteen minutes earlier, ghosting no-man's-land with their green-white glare, but, since then, not even a rifle shot had cut through the cold. A frost was settling; there was snow in the air.

George slipped his hands further into his sleeves. His uniform was tattered, but he was better off than most. Some men's chilblains were poking through their boots.

There'd been a terrible, clothes-stiffening frost two weeks earlier. Only the old sweats who'd cannily wrapped their feet in straw-filled sandbags brought from rest billets had managed to conjure up enough warmth for a few hours shut-eye. Then the rain had come, raising the temperature but turning the trenches into a quagmire. What dugouts there were had flooded, forcing the men to sleep on the firestep, or in shallow funk holes they'd hollowed out for themselves.

Soaked to the skin, the tails of their greatcoats hacked off to lessen the weight of mud and water, they'd worked incessantly, clearing out the sumps, revetting the collapsing walls and staking out the few strands of barbed wire that had finally been issued. Front line or support, reserve or in billets, the misery had been the same; even a captain had been sent down with trench foot.

Now, freezing to death was, again, nature's order of the day. The Germans had sent over a few 'Whizz Bangs', but nothing serious; the elements posed a far greater threat to life and limb. A couple of frostbite cases had lost toes, one a foot. Some shaggy goatskin jerkins had been issued, but George hadn't been one of the lucky recipients. The rest of the consignment had been blown to smithereens, along with the carrying party.

He shuffled his feet. The Battalion had seen no real action since the fighting around Ypres had petered out. A party of Jocks to their right, had carried out a trench raid a few days earlier, simply to boost morale, so it was said. They'd got hung up on the German wire and 'suffered the consequences', as sergeant Hollis was so fond of putting it. 'Slovenly on parade and you suffer the consequences; dirty buttons and you suffer the consequences; don't oil your rifle and you suffer the consequences; go with a poxed up tart and you'll suffer the consequences.' Fritz had retaliated with a bombardment, but it hadn't stretched to George's sector.

Still he'd witnessed enough horror to last him a lifetime. He'd seen young Brewer sliced wide open, eyes aghast at his spilling entrails. He'd seen limbs blown off, bodies ripped apart, men buried alive. He'd seen the young lieutenant's brains when a lump of shrapnel had taken the top of his skull clean off. Death was ever present and, after just six weeks, George looked on its arbitrary butchery with the hardened inertia of the abattoir. Only the demise of a close companion resuscitated any sense of emotion.

"Quiet tonight, ain't they?" Hollis said, appearing beside him.

"Well, it is Christmas, Sergeant."

"Christmas be buggered. You just keep your eye on the bastards, my lad. They may have 'Gott Mit Uns' on their bloody belts, but they ain't Christians like us; well, not proper ones, anyway."

"And there was I about to hang me stocking on the wire."

"You'll be lucky. The only present you're likely to get from Fritz is a bayonet up the arse. Klaus he may be, Santa he fucking well ain't, and you're speaking to one that knows."

'So you keep tellin' us,' George silently groaned. Hollis had had his cheek carved by a shard of shrapnel minutes before they'd gone over the top. He'd scurried back to the aid post faster than a pigeon could fly. 'Cut himself shaving, more like,' the malicious rumour had gone round.

"Hey, Sarge, look at this."

A strange light had appeared in the German lines.

"What the fuck are they up to?" Hollis growled.

Another light appeared and then another.

"Give 'em a round, let 'em know we're alert."

48

George levelled his sights. He could just make out movement, then a familiar outline emerged.

"Hold up, Sarge, it's a bloody Christmas tree."

"Well, bugger me. Is that a bloke up there beside it? He must be fucking nuts."

The rich baritone reached them, soon joined by others, bridging the gulf of desolation with 'Stille Nacht, Heilige Nacht'.

"Well, would you bloody believe it. Trust old Fritz to have a bleeding choir," Hollis chortled. "Perhaps he ain't such a bad old bugger after all."

"But it ain't Christmas yet, can't be more than eleven."

"Not for them, sonny Jim. They're an hour ahead."

"How's that?"

"Never you mind. That's how I've got the stripes and you ain't. And a happy Christmas to you too, Fritzy!" Hollis hollered over.

The singing went on all night, warming George like army issue rum, then acting like a lullaby, as he dozed in his damp, cramped funk hole after morning stand-to, while Charlie Clayman, his village compatriot, fried their breakfast bacon over some meagrely rationed ammunition box splinters.

"Tea up," Charlie roused him.

"Christ, what's this?"

"Da. Ruddy stuff came out in chunks," Charlie excused the icebergs of condensed milk bobbing about in the brew. "Bread's the same, frozen solid. Clean though; better than having muck all over it. Anyway, never mind all that, look what Santa's brung you."

George put down his mug and took the brass gift box Charlie handed him. It was embossed with the likeness of the Princess Royal. Inside were a greetings card, a pack of cigarettes, tobacco and a pipe.

"We all got one; present from her majesty, no less. It says, 'With best wishes for It; Happy Christmas and a Victorious New Year,' on the front there, and 'The Princess Mary and Friends at Home' on the back."

"I can read you know," George complained, proving the point by reciting the inscription on the yellow cigarette pack. 'Her Royal Highness Princess Mary's Gift Fund, 1914. Bugger me."

"Swap you the baccy for the fags?"

"Done."

"Still no firing, then?"

"Not a fucking dickie bird. They ain't fired at us and we ain't fired at them. Don't seem right somehow, seeing as it's Christmas. They've been singing away like they was on Church Parade, and shouting across, 'Happy Christmas, Tommy.' Silly buggers. If I've told 'em once, I've told 'em a thousand times my name ain't Tommy."

Hollis hurried past, fear etched on his face.

"On your feet, damn you; they're coming over!"

George and Charlie grabbed their rifles and scrambled onto the firing step.

Across no-man's land a party of Germans were out of their trenches, picking their way over the frost-arrested decomposition of friend and foe killed during the November slaughter, some with their hands in their pockets, others with their hands in the air. One was waving a white handkerchief.

"No shoot, Tommy, no shoot! No fight today, okay? Kommen sie, Tommy, kommen."

Further down the line, an English officer was calling over in broken German. Before long he'd clambered onto the parapet. Soon the whole line was out.

Sign language reached across the divide; proffered hands were warily shaken. Tongues loosened, syllables multiplied, grips became firmer. A tall, unkempt German in a pork pie hat pulled a bottle of schnapps from his greatcoat pocket.

"Drink, Tommy," he managed.

"Cor, bloody good stuff that," George spluttered, wiping the tears from his eyes, as Charlie Clayman, likewise, felt the fire.

The Germans laughed. George shrugged in bankrupt apology until he remembered his cigarettes.

"Her royal highness's fags, George? Are you sure?" Charlie frowned.

"Dah, she won't mind. Anyway, she's half German herself, more than half from what Mr. Warren was saying the other day; probably sent her uncle Willi a Christmas card," George said, making a mental note to delve further into the ancestry he'd overheard outlined whilst standing guard outside the officers' mess. "Besides, they ain't hers no more, they're mine; she gave them to you and you gave 'em to me."

"Ach! Englisher cigaretten; ver' gud!" The German cried, matching George's pack with some British Virginias. "We have also. From my frau."

"Bloody hell! And we have to make do with ruddy Trumpeters, or, worse still, them sodding Ruby Queens," George complained. "Where'd the hell he get them from, I'd like to know?"

"One of them submarines must have captured a shipload," Charlie hazarded a guess, incapable of conceiving that an English exporter would take 'business as usual' to quite so literal extremes, via Holland.

Hans, Jurgen, George and Charlie, Fred and Freidrich, Dick and Deiter, all and sundry, Fritz and Tommy, looking on as burial parties chipped and chopped at the frozen sod to commit their comrades where they'd fallen, side by side, as the mourners stood. They'd all pulled the trigger. Prayers were said. Never much of a believer, still George bowed his head, the poor buggers deserved that much, whatever the colour of their cloth; "Amen."

Black sausage and black bread were produced, bully beef and 'Pearl' biscuits, plum and apple jam and a fat cigar. Pockets were rummaged for family photos, mementoes exchanged, George's new pipe for its 'Little Willie' counterpart, goodwill to all men. In the afternoon a patch was cleared and a good-natured football match rough and tumbled its way to the inevitable stalemate of the Western Front.

When dusk fell the men returned to their trenches, adversaries, but now brothers in adversity, the Germans to their drier earthworks on the high ground, the British to their waterlogged breastworks of the low. Charlie had scrounged a couple of Picklehaubes.

"Here, stuff one of these in your knapsack."

"Cor, thanks mate. My kids'll love that."

"Don't make no sense, does it?" Charlie pondered. "I mean, if they'd as soon be back in Kaiser-land and we'd as soon be home, what the fuck are we all doing here?"

"Does make you wonder," George admitted. "By the way, here's something I bet you didn't know; their time's different to ours."

"Do what?"

"Them Germans, they're an hour ahead. I checked that bloke's watch."

"Which bloke?"

"The tall one."

"Dah, you read it wrong. Either that or yours has stopped."

"No, straight up. Hollis told me the same last night. Apparently it's all to do with the sun rising in the East and Germany being nearer to China than we are."

"Dah, he's having you on. If they had the drop on us by an hour, they'd be in the horse lines before we was even awake."

"Well it'd explain why we keep getting stuffed to buggery every time we go over. Anyway, when its day here, it's got to be night somewhere, ain't it? Stands to reason."

"Yea, in Timbuktu, maybe, but not betwixt and between. Christ, I could walk from here to there in the time it takes to widdle."

"Well you ask Hollis, if you don't believe me."

"What, so he can make as big a monkey out of me as he has you? Time's time, me old mate, always has been, always will be, and theirs is no different. If you ask me, old Hollis has spun you a right load of cobblers and you've fallen for it hook, line and sinker!"

The Christmas truce was never to be repeated. Some of the field officers responsible were summarily sacked. The following year a barrage would be ordered to deter fraternisation. After all, if the men decided to make it permanent, what then?

It lasted up to a week in some places, in George's sector, just three days. On the fourth, his battalion was ordered back to billets and given a stern dressing down by their Divisional Commander. 'Treachery' and 'Cowardice' were the words that really stung. Punishment was an incessant regime of drills, fatigues, route marches and carrying parties, hour after hour, day after day, night after night.

From that moment on, for George the enemy were no longer the Fritz in the opposing trenches, but the sanctimonious staff bastards, who, from the comfort and security of their commandeered chateaux far behind the lines, had the gall to berate him for a simple act of Christianity, while they tucked into their Christmas dinner.

*****

As Boxing Day dawned, Richard talked himself out of a confession. All it would do is hurt Laura, and for what? Really there was nothing to tell. He'd kissed his sister-in-law, or rather she'd kissed him, and groped him a bit, well, more than bit, but that was all. Where things might have led had she not passed out, he didn't care to contemplate. Anyway, she'd got him drunk and that would never happen again. Still he felt like a louse.

The family moved to the Gurnys' for lunch. Elizabeth arrived at twelve. Richard had been dreading the encounter, but she showed no flicker of embarrassment.

'Too drunk to remember,' he concluded.

The children were on their worst behaviour. Slapped legs followed clipped ears, wail followed wail.

"They're missing their father," Mrs. Bowden excused them.

"I'd father 'em, if they was mine," Arthur Bowden promised her.

After what seemed an eternity, four o'clock mercifully came round and the Bowdens left for tea with the Scotts.

Laura's meticulously laid table and her mother's lingering aura did nothing to put them at their ease. They ate like servants, always waiting to be offered, never filling the best Worcester plates. A little forced laughter thinned the ice, but nothing would crack it. As soon as manners allowed, the Bowdens made their excuses, leaving Richard with Scott and Laura for the evening.

Between these three there were no such barriers. Richard was far more forthcoming with Scott than with his own father. Scott was the only person, outside of school, whom Richard had told of his cadetship, although why he had joined, he didn't exactly know himself.

Duty and loyalty had been factors, as had the fear of ostracism, but, fundamentally, he had volunteered because, whatever his intellect argued, his instinct couldn't condone his self-exemption. The same self-respect he'd dented just hours earlier had demanded it. If he were called, he would go, knowing only that he must. It would mean breaking his promises to his mother and Laura, but to keep them would break his soul. Whether he would kill was another question only face to face reality would resolve.

After ten rounds of whist and a light supper, Scott climbed the stairs, leaving the lovers by the front door to end Christmas as they had begun it, manacled to frustration.

- CHAPTER EIGHT -

The new year arrived uneventfully in Ashleigh. There was little to celebrate. The Bowdens raised their glasses with the Scotts and sang 'Auld Lang Syne', toasting peace and, for the sake of conscience, victory, although it had little deeper connotation than George's safe return.

School resumed, but this term Laura would cycle home alone, while Richard stayed on, ostensibly to catch up with his studies. He learned his drill and his military manual, and he learned to shoot with the one .22 rifle the army hadn't requisitioned. He was awarded a lance corporal's armband, which he kept in his locker. The tree in front of the Georgian annex bared its winter sadness.

In the middle of January, the casualties invalided home from Ypres began to appear on the streets. Outwardly cheery for the most part, glad to be out of it with their lives, even the seriously disabled carried their scars stoically. Only in solitude did their incapacity grip them in suicidal despair.

Yet they were men apart, men who had aged years in as many months, men who preferred a soldier's company and spoke in whispers, ridiculing the patriotic bunkum of journalists and armchair generals, while bitterly condemning the incompetence of High Command.

"Stay out of it, boy; don't be a bloody fool like me," they would tell their brothers, while, in the same breath, disparaging 'the shirkers' who stayed at home. But they spoke little of their experiences, even amongst themselves.

Many of the less seriously maimed would, in the aftermath of future battles, find themselves re-boarding the troopship to Golgotha. For some it would even be a welcome return to a comradeship that was now a part of them. At home they were strangers in their own land. For others to understand what they had been through was impossible. Home was not home anymore; the Hell of Flanders had claimed them and there they would be torn asunder, brothers in arms, until the ceasefire sounded for everyone.

* * * * *

While storms left Windsor Castle rampart deep in flood water to the West, and Zeppelins bombed Great Yarmouth and King's Lynn to the East, it was the trumpeting of his Lordship's overbearing twenty-one-year-old that disturbed Ashleigh's winter solace. Accompanied by her friend, the Baroness de Beauville, whose brother's ancestral birthright was now occupied by the Germans, Lady Alice, or, as the locals called her, Lady Superior, had embarked on a recruiting crusade of her own, touring his Lordship's estates to coerce all able-bodied dependants into joining up. In February her mission brought her to Ashleigh. Undaunted by a dismal turn-out on the Manor steps, she took to the fields and workshops. Forewarned, the men removed themselves. It took twenty minutes of fruitless searching before she stumbled upon her first victim, Walter Taylor, whose brother, William, had already gone to war. She checked her list.

"W. Taylor?"

The boy nodded.

"Well, Mr. Taylor, I must tell you frankly..." The tirade of shirked duty and virtuous indignation that followed would have floored Jack Johnson. "Are you not ashamed? Even as we speak, the German hordes are in this lady's house stealing her belongings and doing the most unspeakable things to her maid servants. Had she not escaped, she, too, would be the subject of their depravity. Will you not defend the people of Belgium; will you not defend this lady's honour?"

"Leave the boy alone!"

The call came from across the field. There could be no doubting her hailer, small and stocky and about her own age. Two rather more reluctant figures flanked him.

"And whom might you be, young man?" She called back haughtily.

For Cyril Tate it was the decision of a lifetime; for thine may be the Kingdom but the serfs shall be meek no more. He hunched his shoulders and strode across the furrows.

"Never mind me, you've got no right to go on at the lad so."

"How dare you use that tone with me," her Ladyship cried. "Do you know who I am? I have every right. This man ought to be in uniform, and so, I believe, should you."

"Me, that's different, but, him? You must need your bloody eyes tested, woman."

This was not only insolence beyond measure, it was naked effrontery.

"How dare you! I'll have you dismissed this instant." Superiority had not only to be asserted, but crushing. "He is W. Taylor, I presume?"

"Well he ain't doctor Livingstone, that's for sure."

"Then he has no excuse. It is the duty of every able-bodied man of nineteen years and over to serve his country."

"The lad's only fifteen and a half, as it happens, missy. He's tall for his age, I'll grant you, but that's not reason enough for him to go and get himself killed for the likes of you. Christ Almighty, she'll be after them down the bloody school next," Tate called to his cronies, still cringing by the hedgerow.

"You insolent swine," her Ladyship screamed. "How dare you contradict me? The Estate Manager himself supplied this list. I'm sure he knows this man's particulars better than you."

"What you got on that list there is his brother William. Now you'd be real proud of him; joined up at the start, silly sod. No offence, Walter."

Her Ladyship rustled through the pages. "There's no mention of another Taylor here, William or otherwise."

"Well, there wouldn't be, would there? He's long since gone; but that's what's happened; old Holland's scrubbed off the wrong one, or a relative of yours has."

The inference to Squire Stafford's bastardy by his lordship was the final straw.

"I'll report you," her Ladyship raved. "You'll never work on this nor any other estate again, I'll see to it myself. Cowards have no place here. By the time I've

54

finished with you, you will have nowhere to go but the army, none of you!" She spread her net to the bystanders.

"I'll see you in hell before you see me in uniform," Tate rejoined, farting in the path of his cap-doffing ex-supporters now turned petitioners. "Was that you?" They shrank from the challenge. "Must've been her then."

"Oooh!" Her Ladyship stalking off, fuming.

"You tell 'em up at that big house of yours, if the country needs men, all must go, and that includes your lot," Tate called after her. "I hear they need nurses, too, but I don't see you volunteering. What's the matter? Too much blood on your hands already? You wanna get yerself off to the front, missy; do you the world of good."

Within the hour Tate had been identified and dismissed, but it wasn't to be their last meeting. In the Spring of 1918, a more mature Lady Alice would drive a badly gassed Tate to safety through the inferno of the German offensive. His prophesy would, indeed, come true, he would see her in hell, and she, although she would not recognise him, would see him in uniform.

* * * * *

Tate's premise of 'all must go' was shared by the majority of Ashleigh's farm lads in the February of 1915, loathed to do their bit while their betters sat snugly at home. In late February the Parliamentary Recruiting Committee canvassed all households for those willing to enlist. Willing or not, the paperwork had to be completed. For some illiterate dissenters, like the Crutchley clan, getting an inept or malicious executor, like Mrs. Beasley, to mark their card was simply asking for trouble.

"Hello Mrs. B. Sorry to disturb you, but is Arthur in?" An agitated Amos Crutchley asked Beatrice, arriving at the Bowdens' door one evening.

"Yes, Amos, he's through there. Why? Is something wrong?"

"You could say that. It's that Beasley woman. She's landed us right in it."

"You'd best come through."

"Arthur! Thank God you're here. You know them papers they sent out about joining up? Old Ma Beasley's made a right muck of it; put the whole ruddy lot of us down as enlisting, the silly old faggot, even our Dan and he's not yet fourteen. I told her 'no'. Now I got this letter, and from what I can make out it's saying we've all got to go into Elmsford to attest or summat. I could bloody murder her, really I could. She said she could read and write proper. You gotta help us, Arthur. I mean, you being a Special, there's got to be something you can do."

"Well, I don't rightly know that there is, Amos. What, she put you down and all?" Arthur chuckled.

"Well I'm glad you can see the funny side, Arthur, 'cause I'm bug.... blowed if I can. Beg pardon, Mrs. B.," Crutchley glowered.

"Amos is right, Arthur. It's no laughing matter," Beatrice reminded her husband.

"No, suppose not," Bowden admitted. "But why ask her in the first place? Your boy can write; he went to school with our Richard."

"Joe? Yes, he can write, but he ain't no better at understanding forms than the

55

rest of us. Besides, he's raring to go, the young fool. That's why I asked her in the first place. He's nigh of an age, and from what I hear they ain't too fussy when it comes to a month or two; even a year or two in the case of young Cudlip. You wait 'til I get my hands on that woman."

"It's that Tom of theirs," Beatrice said. "The one that's gone missing. He was always her favourite. Won't talk to his mother; says she should never have let him go."

"Well, if she's done it out of spite, I'll have her up before the beak, so help me I will. I mean, there's got to be a law against it. She can't go around deciding other people's fate for 'em."

"Come on," Arthur said, pulling on his jacket. "We'll pop along and see Mr. Scott. If anyone knows what to do it's him."

* * * * *

In mid-March, George Bowden came home on a seventy two hour pass, scaring the daylights out of Elizabeth, who'd just climbed into her weekly bath, delayed since Friday. For long minutes he held her, until the kitchen steam permeated his clothing. In the heightened aurora of Elizabeth's cleanliness, George stank like a smelter.

Leave men were given a bath and a change of freshly stoved and fumigated clothes before boarding the boat. Rather than risk the queue, George had toyed with the idea of hiding his filth under his new greatcoat, inherited from a fresh faced six-footer who'd leapt onto a five foot fire step in broad daylight to take a look at the hun. However, without the appropriate chitty, George had been warned, he wouldn't be allowed on the boat. He'd shuffled forward, counting the green bands on the hospital ships and trying to decipher, 'Taisez vous. Metiez vous. Les oreilles ennemies vous écoutent,' to keep his agitation at bay. He'd made the gangplank with just five minutes to spare.

Sea breezes and an open deck had nullified the fumigant during the crossing, but in the clammy confines of his railway carriage its regenerated malodour had turned the woman next to him green. It was having the same effect on Elizabeth.

"Christ George, you smell like a giant mothball."

"Clean uniform."

"You could've fooled me. Anyone would think you were diseased."

"Watch out!"

Woken as much by sixth sense as the commotion, the children were bounding down the stairs. Elizabeth covered herself.

"Pooh, you smell all funny, Daddy," little Doris freed herself from his arms in crinkle-nosed condemnation. "You've been standing too close to the fire."

Sitting one on each knee, George fended off all the questions children ask, especially bloodthirsty boys. Had he won any battles? Had he killed any Germans? Had he chopped them all up like they did the Belgian babies? And then from little Doris, was he home for good? Did he have to go back? Did he like being a soldier?

He sought salvation in his pack and the Picklehaube Charlie had scrounged during the Christmas truce. The children were awestruck, trying it on in turn, before transmogrifying their father into a fearsome faced, child devouring Hun.

"Fe-fi-fo-fum..."

George chased them, screaming and giggling, round the room, growling, "you can't shoot me; you can't shoot me," until young George levelled his arm and did exactly that, prompting him to collapse in a series of histrionic death throes. Warily, the children approached. A gurgling started; the monster opened one eye, then the other, wide as a monocle. His nose twitched, his fingers twiddled, his feet waggled, and he leered back to life to pursue them up the stairs and back to bed.

"Get in," Elizabeth ordered on his return, topping up the zinc bath.

"But I had a bath this morning," he protested.

"Well you're having another one now. I'm not letting you in my bed smelling like that."

Fresh on or not, George's underwear was far from clean. Elizabeth slung everything into a bucket, then scrubbed him with carbolic.

"Leave off. I've already done all that!"

"Then what are all them little bite marks, then?"

"I'll bite you, if you're not careful," he grinned lecherously, reaching inside her dressing gown.

Resistance was futile. Rising like Neptune, he carried her up to bed and the fulfilment of his long suppressed passion.

The following morning, after a re-enactment of the previous night's conjugals and a breakfast fit for a hero, George wandered down to the yard. His father was rummaging through a stack of old piping. Not known for displays of emotion, he greeted his son with a nod.

"When did you get back, then?"

"Last night. They let me off for a couple of days."

"No uniform?"

"Nice to be out of the bloody thing for a while. No, Betty's got it out on the line, airing. They douse it in this stuff so you don't bring home any undesirables. Stinks to high heaven."

"Bad is it, son, over there?"

"Oh, not so bad, Dad. I'm still here ain't I?" George grinned. "What you up to, then?"

"Nothing too drastic. Burst pipe at the Vicarage. Won't take more than a couple of hours. Seen your mother?"

"No, had a lie in then came straight here. She at home?"

"Yeh, shouldn't be going nowhere. The boy's off at school."

"Best place for him. Don't want him mixed up in this little lot. How's he getting on with that Laura?"

"Fine, boy, fine. Made for each other, them two. She's right pretty, all growed up. He could do a lot worse."

"How about her father?"

"Scott? He's nice enough once you get to know him. More human, somehow, since his wife passed on."

George smiled. "I ain't been gone that long, Dad. Look, I'm holding you up. I'll get along and see mother."

"Alright, boy. Perhaps we'll have a drink later; I'm sure they'd like to see you at the Mow. I'll be done by two at the latest."

"Alright, I'll meet you there, then. Unless I can be of some help?"

"No, no, you go on to your mother, she'll be tickled pink."

"See you later, then."

"George?" His father called after him. "Nice to have you back, son."

"Nice to be back, Dad; real nice."

His mother swamped him with ham and poached eggs, heedless of his protests that he'd already had breakfast.

"Look at you, boy; don't they feed you in the army? Steak and kidney pudding tonight, just as you like it. You and Elizabeth will be coming, won't you?"

What could he say?

At the Barley Mow everyone wanted to buy him a drink, but he found their jingoism impossible to swallow.

"It's in all the papers," they gloated over the headlines that only some of them could read. Here, fact lay in the fiction written miles behind the lines. In the trenches, the crass tabloids and broadsheets were the lavatory paper, "not that they ain't got enough crap in 'em already," George avenged the scathing reports he had read of the Christmas truce.

"So what's it really like, then?"

How could he tell them? Even if they believed him, they could never understand. He changed the subject to conscription, the Tap Bar's favourite topic, splitting his sides when he heard of Cyril Tate's run-in with her Ladyship and Mrs. Beasley's enlistment of the entire Crutchley clan.

"Amos had to take the boys' birth certificates and God knows what to the recruiting office and swear it was all a mistake," Arthur Treadwell related the outcome. "Even then, the captain in charge was none too convinced."

At five o'clock, the Bowdens made their way home.

"Reckon we'll be in for a feast tonight, boy," Arthur said, licking his lips.

"Steak and kidney pudding," George told him.

"You'd best come home more often!"

The whole family was waiting, the Gurnys included. The steak and kidney pudding was followed by trifle, another of George's favourites. He was given the honour of clearing the bowl. He could hardly move, he was so full.

After dinner the Scotts joined the party. In Scott and Richard, George sensed an audience of more kindred spirits, but he didn't want to elaborate in front of the women. He simply prayed that the War would end before Richard came of age, with the cheery qualification of "with us winning, of course."

The hours flew by; no sooner had he said goodnight, than he was saying goodbye. In the early hours of Thursday morning, he shouldered his rifle and pack and tiptoed from the house. The road to Elmsford was paved with memories, the train to London packed with premonitions. His family and friends had welcomed him home with open arms; in Flanders' fields, the Germans would not be so accommodating.

- CHAPTER NINE -

At the Priory, Joanna Hetherington's pin-wear had developed into a differential and deferential spectrum denoting army, navy, men on active service, those in training, those wounded and those lost. With no pin to her name, Laura found herself increasingly ostracised. She could have unearthed a serving relative, her uncle Sidney had joined up soon after the outbreak, or even invented one, but the rebel in her did neither. Then, in late term, Grammar School cadets were included in the system.

Although it was known that she had a boyfriend at the grammar, Laura had remained tight lipped about Richard, afraid that people might delve into his background. When she still appeared pinless, her ostracism worsened. Then, opening her desk one morning, she found a clutch of white feathers under the lid. A tear escaped. The sniggering swelled into open guffaws, then hushed abruptly. A hand rested on Laura's shoulder.

"What is the meaning of this?"

"She's walking out with a coward, Sister."

"He's not even in the Cadets. He can't be, or she'd be wearing a pin."

"No wonder she's been so secretive."

"SILENCE!" Sister Constance ordered. "I've never heard such nonsense! You should be ashamed of yourselves, all of you. Laura is not responsible for the conduct of others; none of you are. A man's conscience is the concern of himself and his Maker and no one else, least of all, you. I am sick and tired of all this petty persecution. I will tolerate no more of it, do you understand? If it happens again I will personally report those responsible to Mother Abbess. Now go to assembly and, in future, try to behave like civilised human beings."

For the rest of the day Laura was a leper in a colony of Barbary apes. She found feathers in her coat pockets, 'Coward' notes in her locker. The only person who'd deign to speak to her was Hillary Jordan, daughter of a known pacifist. 'Cowards' girls together' was the chant aimed at them.

That night, wretched and racked, Laura rode home alone; Richard was staying on at school. Why was he never there when she needed him? Why did there have to be a war? He wouldn't go, he had promised her. They could say what they liked, Richard was no coward. Just because he hadn't joined the Cadets; so what? Even if he was pigeon-hearted, as they said, at least he would be a live pigeon. Why couldn't they just leave her alone?

Richard called round after tea, but, when the opportunity arose, she shied from his lips.

"Is everything all right?" Scott asked, when she moped back into the parlour after seeing Richard out.

"Yes," she forced a smile. "See you in the morning."

Pecking him on the cheek, she went to bed.

Laura suffered the hate campaign until the Easter break. Even then, Richard wasn't there to lean on. Inexplicably, he'd gone to stay with some idiot school friend. How could he? She was going through hell on his account; he'd known something was wrong, and still he'd gone. From the very beginning she'd risked her reputation just by associating with him. If the girls ever found out he was a simple plumber's son, she'd be a laughing stock. She was being scorned and humiliated, and for what; for someone who didn't even care anymore?

"Well, blow you, Richard Bowden!"

* * * * *

How a little subterfuge can breed the Siamese twins of jealousy and delusion. While, haunted by Joanna Hetherington's laughter, Laura's masochism roamed the corridors of Richard's Easter retreat, in reality he was in an army barracks.

A mix up with transport had caused the Grammar cadets to arrive too late to undergo anything but a cursory parade before lights out. Those four hours were crucial in establishing sergeant Baron's authority, the first step towards honing the best platoon. Now, through his cubicle wall, their loss and the novelty of bedding down on boards and palliases were making themselves apparent. Schoolboy jokes became jibes, a fatuously flung boot a full-scale artillery duel.

Baron swung his legs from his bunk, straightened his cap and reached for his swagger stick, his from the days when he had worn a crown on his sleeve and had men to command, not a bunch of raw, middle class cherubs, fresh from suckling on their mummy's titties. Late it may be, but today was still April the first and he would make a belated fool of more than one of them before the day was out. He slammed open the door and turned on the lights. The cadets' scramble for the safety of their blankets was futile.

"So, you think this is all a bit of a lark, do you? Come away for a bit of fun and frololicking, have we? Play at soldiers for a couple of days then back to mummy to tell her what a big brave boy you've been, while she pats you on your head and wipes your bloody arse for you?" His voice had escalated in velocity; now it rattled the rafters. "Stand to attention when I'm talking to you!"

They sprang up in their vests and pants, gratifyingly intimidated. He scowled down the line. "Look to your front you ignorant little prick!" He attacked a particularly weasely specimen.

Still someone saw the funny side.

"That man, two paces forward!"

It was a trick the boys took a week to twig and earned Baron a bum-eyed reputation. The offender stepped out. Baron locked eyeballs with him.

"And what would your name be, laddie?"

"Simms, Sir," the boy said, his snigger now nerve fixed.

"So you find all this amusing, do you, Simmmmms?" Baron unsheathed the name like a bayonet from a scabbard. "Well, let's all share the joke, then. Speak up

61

man," he bellowed, "What's so bloody funny?"

"Nothing, Sir," Simms quaked.

"Speak up so we can all hear you."

"Nothing, Sir," Simms raised his voice to a squeak.

"Nothing what?" Baron screamed in his face.

The boy froze.

"Sergeant," a whisper came to his aid.

"Shut up, that man!"

"Nothing, Sergeant," Simms croaked.

"That's right, Simmmms. No officer on parade here, is there Simms?" Baron turned to the others. "And there's nothing funny about this little lot what you've let yourselves in for neither, nothing funny at all. And the sooner you load of snivelling farts realise it the better off you'll be. I didn't give you permission to move!"

Someone had scratched a nervously itching nose.

Baron re-inspected the ranks, tapping his swagger stick malevolently against his thigh, while he let the chill enter their bones.

"Stand still!"

The minutes ticked by; still he held them. Sooner or later someone would break. Someone did.

"What the hell do you think you're playing at?" Baron descended upon the miscreant, who'd reached for his shirt.

"I was cold, Sergeant," the boy chattered.

"Cold is he?" Baron sneered. "The poor little lamb is cold. Top of the hut, at the double! I'll teach you what bloody cold is! Left right, left right, left right!"

The culprit high stepped to his punishment.

"Now fetch that latrine bucket."

The emergency pail stood in the corner, 'Cadets for the use of', a quarter full of freezing water and the urine of two boys who had foregone the queue for the urinal.

Heads turned.

"Eyes front, damn you! Now, you, pick it up and pour the contents thereof over your delicate little head."

The boy looked horrified.

"Do it, man!"

Hesitantly he lifted the pail.

"Higher, higher, I said! Your head's up there, not down by your bollocks! Now tip it, man, tip!"

The boy gasped, as the icy effluent cascaded over his shoulders.

"Right. Now get a mop and clean it up. And be quick about it! The rest of you, get this place in order."

Within a minute the assorted ammunition had been reclaimed; it took the drowned rat six to dry the floor to Baron's satisfaction, polishing the last droplets away with his vest. Baron ordered him back into line.

"Right. Now I don't want to hear another peep out of you lot until reveille. Got that?"

Marching to his cubicle door, he scanned the room one last time, shouted "dismiss," and switched out the lights.

None escaped Baron's wrath; his authority was absolute and unsparing. After every exercise, the cadets were allowed thirty minutes to get cleaned up; a trace of mud or a dirty button and the criminal was liable to fatigues, peeling potatoes, slopping out latrines, washing the barrack room floor. Yet, as vindictively motivated as these humiliations appeared, they were designed for a purpose, to instil discipline, to break the individual spirit, to compel those in Baron's charge to obey with the unquestioning precision of automatons.

'Theirs not to reason why, theirs but to do or die.' Nothing had changed since the charge of the Light Brigade, except the magnitude of the blunders and the numbers indoctrinated into doing the dying. At Balaclava, six hundred had galloped to destruction; while the Cadets swallowed the first bitter pill of Army discipline, sixty thousand littered the valley of death around Ypres, the flotsam and jetsam of April 1915's foolishness.

In attack the boys advanced in the same time honoured, text book fashion that had annihilated the Armies of 1914; in defence, they stood head and shoulders above the parapet, perfect targets. But there were no machine guns to mow them down, no artillery to pound them into oblivion, no wiser souls to teach them differently. Their betters knew best, it was written in stone, a stone so settled that not even an Armageddon would loosen it. When all was done, the Generals would be fêted, the cannon fodder forgotten. Bankruptcy would dominate Britain's post-war politics, not manhood's missing millions.

* * * * *

Laura found Richard's letter on the Easter Monday breakfast table unopened. She was lucky, in that respect, most fathers would have read their daughter's mail. Sullenly, she tore open the envelope, expecting to have her suspicions confirmed, that he didn't love her anymore, that he'd found someone else. Instead she read of how he worshipped her with every cry to the sun, with every whisper to the moon, of how their time apart was interminable torture. He would be home for her birthday.

She pressed the words to her lips in joyful acquittal.

When Scott came home that evening, he was thankful for the change in her. He'd been to the asylum; one Marian was enough. He, alone, knew of Richard's true whereabouts, a secret Laura might have shared had she studied the letter's postmark. Scott said nothing; his mind was elsewhere. Marian's doctor had offered him tea, sympathy and a discourse on 'Shell Shock', a term new to him.

The authorities didn't recognise it either, quite literally, the specialist had told him. "As far as they're concerned, the only cure is the Firing Squad. A very incensed General even had the audacity to call me a 'Quack'; said it was all poppycock; that even to suggest such a thing was tantamount to treason. 'Good God, man; you'd have every Tom, Dick and Harry in the Army claiming they were 'Shell Shocked' if they thought they could get away with it," the doctor had mimicked. "It would be comic if it weren't so criminal."

A troop train had steamed through Leaford station, while Scott was waiting on the platform, its cargo waving cheerily from the windows, 'we'll kick the Kaiser's arse' and 'next stop Berlin' etched in the grime.

"God have mercy on them," he'd sighed, "and on young Richard, if it's not over soon."

* * * * *

The accident happened during trench digging on the Cadets' penultimate day. It was Bretterton's turn to take charge, Baron's bête noir, or 'pee brain', as he was now known. His section was working on a traverse dug the previous afternoon, sumping, revetting and constructing a dugout. There were four boys inside, squaring off the walls, while the rest piled sandbags onto the corrugated iron roof. Richard warned him that one of the supports had missed the overlap, but Bretterton was too scared of Baron to admit his mistake and start again. The boys worked on; the roof began to sag.

"We've got to stop. It won't take any more," Richard reiterated his warning.

"Not likely, Baron'll have my guts for garters."

Another bag thumped down above their heads. The metal groaned, the support shifted.

"It's too late, get them out!" Richard yelled, instinctively reaching up to take the strain.

His heart pumped, his shoulders shuddered, his legs locked against the others' scramble for safety. He heard Baron's voice, saw the man's boots, then his knees buckled and he was engulfed.

He came to in a hospital bed. His right arm was in plaster and hurting like blazes.

"Edge of corrugated caught it. Snapped it clean in half. Miracle it didn't take your arm off," an orderly told him cheerily. "Ruddy good job it wasn't your back."

That afternoon his company commander came to see him, along with an embattled sergeant Baron. Whatever Bretterton's failings, militarily Baron would be held responsible. His embarrassment was Goliathian.

"It was no one's fault, Sir, the support just split," Richard forswore.

"Then it should have been checked, Sergeant," the Captain said.

"Yes, Sir," Baron snapped, his cheeks purple.

'Pee brain had better watch out,' Richard concluded, when his visitors left.

- CHAPTER TEN -

Richard arrived home with his arm in plaster, bearing muddy football boots as false witness. Laura's compulsion to rebuke him was irresistible. There was little he could do, being right handed he couldn't even compile his father's ledger. Everyone agreed that the paso doble of a drunken spider would be more legible than his left-handed scrawl. For the remainder of the holiday Laura had him very much to herself.

She revelled in her physical ascendancy, making fun of his every bungle. However, as the nightmare of the summer term crept closer, her reaction to his advances, whether fumbled or not, became retarded by her mental malaise. Ecstasy, she discovered, was a matter of the mind.

But to confess the catalyst of her gloom would be to open the can of morally contentious tapeworms that fed on her confusion in all their writhing juxtapositions. It would mean her surrender to the will of the Pin Brigade. It could force Richard's enlistment, a victory Joanna Hetherington would smugly claim. It could ultimately lead to his death, an impossible responsibility.

Yet, fundamentally, she was a child of her times. However much she reasoned to the contrary, deep within her a sense of shame took root in the undersoil of middle class morality. She had no room for manoeuvre, she was trapped in martyrdom.

Richard, for his part, lacked the insight to understand. As Laura had jumped to the wrong conclusion, he similarly reacted, and so the misconception of one deepened that of the other. A veil was drawn; the veil became a curtain, the curtain a wall, the wall a fortress. Hope's hand reached through the portcullis, but disillusion's blinding fog made contact impossible.

* * * * *

By the first day of term Richard was cycling one-handed, but their pair-riding of the past was now a tyre track on the back roads of memory. At the Grammar school gates, Laura rode on with barely a wave. Disconsolately, Richard wheeled his bicycle to the bike sheds, answering 'an accident' all the way to his form-room and a queue of plaster-signers.

"Quite the hero," someone said, before the bell sounded for assembly.

The hall's hammer-beamed roof, Victorian rather than Tudor, led the eye to the effigies of Chaucer, Shakespeare, Milton and Bunyon and the illuminated legend, 'Lives of great men all remind us, we can make our lives sublime,' stained in glass, unstained in glory, a window, not to the world, but to the soul.

On the stage beneath, the staff took their places, rising as one when the headmaster swept down the aisle, gown flowing, tasselled mortar board bobbing above the congregation. Joscelyn was a man in his late fifties, an imposing six footer with wild grey hair and side whiskers. He had been a housemaster at Rugby and was a strict disciplinarian. Being 'Jostled' had its own particular meaning at the Grammar School.

The organ pipes overflowed with the overture. The boys took up their hymn books for 'Fight the Good Fight', which was followed by a particularly genocidal lesson from the Old Testament, read by the Head Boy. All stood. The boys bowed their heads and muttered amen to the Headmaster's prayers for God's favour 'in this mortal hour', for the Country's merciful deliverance from the Germanic hordes and for the victory which was unquestionably God's will. 'Isaiah' Allsop took the blessing and Masters and Prefects resumed their seats for Joscelyn's first address of the Summer term.

"It is with great sadness, gentlemen, that I draw your attention to our Roll of Honour and the addition of four names, names those senior amongst you will know; W. N. Carling, C. D. Moss, T. W. Naylor and R. S. Younger, boys of pride, boys of courage, men who died fighting for the deliverance of their nation.

Walter Carling was a fine boy. He captained the school at soccer and would have gone on to captain his college had duty not called him to a greater destiny. In death, as in life, he is a shining example to us all.

Cedric Moss was his contemporary; a scholar of such brilliance that he would surely have gained great status among the academics of our nation, had his young life not been cut, so cruelly, short.

And Robert Younger, a boy whose headstrong behaviour occasioned our frequent meetings, yet, when duty called, made the greatest sacrifice one can make for his King and country.

Which brings me to Thomas Naylor. I remember Naylor as a shy boy. He did not share Carling's sporting prowess, nor did he shine academically like Moss, but he pursued the goals set him to the best of his ability and no headmaster can ask more. And, when it came to the field of honour, he gave of himself equally. While those around him fell back, he, alone, stood his ground in the face of impossible odds, pouring fire into the enemy until he was overwhelmed.

It is with great pride that I tell you now that in recognition of his heroic action the King has awarded Thomas Naylor, old boy of this school, the Distinguished Service Order."

Joscelyn paused to let the magnitude of the decoration sink in.

"Gentlemen, let us mourn our dead."

Heads were hung. Each tick of the clock was followed by a louder tock, each interval stretching farther into eternity, from where the lost reached back to bid their farewells.

"Thank you, gentlemen."

Feet shuffled. However, instead of leading the school off, Joscelyn motioned masters and prefects to re-take their seats. The ranks re-straightened.

"And now, gentlemen, we have an award of our own to bestow. The recipient is a boy popular in the school and deservedly so. He came to us via a scholarship, and, during his time here, has further demonstrated that same endeavour to elevate himself to the prefecture he will, today, so deservedly receive."

Richard froze. Surely Joscelyn wasn't talking about him? He broke out in a cold sweat.

"However, that is by no means all. During the recent Cadet Camp a situation arose which endangered not only the life of the boy in question, but the lives of those around him. Showing no regard for his personal safety, he single-handedly supported a collapsing trench, enabling his comrades to escape unharmed. As a result, he had to be extracted from the debris. I have it on the authority of the commanding officer himself that, but for this boy's prompt action, lives may, indeed, have been lost. I would now ask the boy in question to step forward; Richard Bowden."

Richard stumbled to the stage on a roll of cheers and adrenalin. It was like standing on a cloud, with everything crystal clear, but completely unreal. He was back in his form room before any of it began to sink in, the Headmaster's handshake, his prefect's tie, his bronze medal in its silk lined case, richly enamelled with the school badge and inscribed 'For Conspicuous Valour'.

His classmates crowded round, bumping and boring.

"Let's see, Bodders, let's see!"

'Crikey,' he thought, 'I've won a medal.'

* * * * *

At the priory Laura's term began as the previous one had ended, with a vicious snipe from one of Joanna Hetherington's cronies. But, as the day drew on, the hatred inexplicably thawed. Someone asked the dreaded question: "Is your boyfriend's name Bowden?" She had no choice but to admit it. Yet, instead of the expected sarcasm, there seemed to be embarrassment. Then someone said how proud she must be of him. Someone else actually apologised; "why didn't you say?" She was completely bemused, she thought the whole world had gone mad, until she met Rosalind Edwards during the break.

"Would you please thank - Richard, is it? - for me. If it hadn't been for him, my brother might have been killed."

"I'm sorry?"

"My brother. Your Richard saved his life."

"Where was this?"

"At cadet camp."

Laura's depression sank to the depths. It was a case of mistaken identity; her Richard wasn't even a cadet; he'd been staying with some imbecile school friend, also obviously not a cadet, and breaking his arm in the process.

The hell she would face when the girls found out consumed her; it took rationality some time to claw its way to the surface and slot the pieces into place. So why did he stay on at school so often, and where had he been at Easter, exactly? Was it possible? Could he have been a cadet all along without telling her?

His deceit stung her cheeks, but, the more she pondered it, the more the impossible became possible and the possible compelling. It had to be him.

An unshakeable posse joined her after school. At last the hero wobbled up.

"So, this is the famous Richard," Emma Stubbs purred, the same Emma Stubbs

67

who'd taken a swipe at Laura that morning. "My; no wonder you've been keeping him under your hat."

Laura flushed. How dare she! She gritted her teeth and completed the introductions.

"I'm so pleased to meet you," Emma breathed from the harem, leaving boldness at the starting gate along with the giggling also-rans.

Short of creating a scene, there was little Laura could do except surreptitiously seethe and divert Richard's attention to Rosalind, whose timid gratitude turned his cheeks perjury crimson.

It was all the confirmation Laura needed. Her soul soared into the ascendancy she knew was hers.

The ogling was intense. Emma was seduction itself. Laura dragged Richard away before her fury got the better of her.

"I'm sorry," he apologised as they pedalled down the High Street, "I should have told you, but I couldn't, not after I'd promised. I hadn't intended to join, but there was no way out."

Laura stopped in midstream, forcing the traffic to swerve around them. To be intimate in public was nothing short of scandalous. She didn't give a hoot. Throwing her arms round his neck, she kissed him full bloodedly on the lips, to a cacophony of catcalls from the loungers outside the King's Head.

A honking steam bus ended the embrace, propelling them on past the Shire Hall, the Police Station, the ball-bearing and new wireless works and onto the Ashleigh road by the Grammar School playing fields.

Laura set a strenuous pace, challenging him to keep up, until, reaching Ashleigh, she yelled, "race you," and set off hell for leather. She freewheeled through the village with Richard gaining by the yard, then, as they swung right at the Butcher's shop, she picked up the pedals and left him standing, skidding to a halt outside the Bowdens' with two lengths to spare.

"Dare you to try that when my arm's mended," he gasped.

"Whenever you choose," she panted, complacent in victory.

"You two been racing?" Mrs. Bowden appeared at the door. "Must be out of your mind, you with your arm in a sling, Richard. I don't know, and you're supposed to be the brainy one. Well, once you've got your puff back, you can pop down the bakers. I forgot your father's bread this morning."

Mrs. Bowden baked her own white, but she'd never got the hang of her husband's favourite brown. "It's always too yeasty," she explained to Laura for the umpteenth time.

"I'll come, too," Laura said, leaning her bike against the fence.

"Make sure it's the brown, dear," Mrs. Bowden called after them. "That arm's addled his brain."

They took the shortcut across the fields. The dell was deserted, a broad oak beckoned.

"I've missed you," he whispered.

"I've missed you, too." The very thought of his lips made Laura tingle. "I'm sorry, I've been such a fool."

68

"I'm the fool, trying to hide it from you. After all, it's only the cadets; they're not going to whisk me off to war or anything."

"Don't talk about it, dearest, just kiss me."

* * * * *

While Richard was enjoying heroism's rewards, his brother was finding a four legged friend.

"Cute little bugger ain't he?"

"Yeh, and if you keep feeding him like that, he'll be a fat little bugger and all," Charlie Clayman complained, eyeing the chips enviously. "Pass 'em over here if you don't want 'em."

George pushed the plate across the wine blotched tablecloth. Oeufs and pomme frits; nothing tasted quite like them; well worth a Franc, including roll and coffee.

"Here, look at that," he chuckled, enticing the dog to snatch the penultimate frit in mid air, turn a somersault and land, beg-poised in the sawdust. "Should sign him up for the old Test Match."

"Huh," Charlie grumbled. "Him behind the wicket and you at silly-mid-off."

"Now there's a thought, a wicket-keeping whippet. That'd be one for the record books."

"Which is exactly where he'll end up if he follows us."

"Nah, not where we're going; dogs ain't that daft."

There was a battle brewing; all the signs were there. Oranges and chestnuts had appeared in the rations; staff officers had been buzzing about like bees. Any day now the men would be formed up on three sides of a square and reminded of the regiment's proud tradition and of what a good show they were going to put up.

"No more, boy," George showed the dog his empty palms before wiping them on his trousers. "Any more of that vin rougy?"

They'd tried the byrrh first time out to find it wasn't beer at all and that, according to Charlie, "that that was, was all froth and no bollocks."

"It's van," Charlie corrected him.

"No it ain't, it's 'vin'. It says so on the bottle, see?"

"Yeh, but they pronounces it van."

"Well, they would, bloody Froggies; never did know how to spell. Put bloody silly marks all over everything to tell you how to say it and still they get it wrong." George filled his glass. "Anyway, it's better than that blank bloody stuff, pure ruddy vinegar, that."

"Not if you put some of that grenadier in it."

"Dah, makes it all pink. Still, eggs was alright. If they had a decent drop of stout, this wouldn't be a bad place to spend the duration."

George rocked contentedly back on his chair, bumping the man behind in a fruitless rummage for Woodbines.

"Sorry, mate."

"No harm done."

"Don't know how they cope," he continued his search, "just the two of 'em, all

69

on that little stove and all. None too shabby, neither, the older one."

"Give over; you're a married man," Charlie reminded him.

"So? I can look, can't I? Lend us a fag, Charlie."

"Ask the bloody dog."

"Dah, you don't smoke, do yer chum?" George patted the sleek head. "Reckon he is a whippet? Oh, ta."

"Well he certainly ain't no poodle," Charlie said, taking a cigarette for himself, lighting both, then extinguishing the match with a mouthful of smoke. The 'none too shabby' waitress came to collect the plates. "Mercy, Madam; trez bons."

"Hark at you," George smiled, "You wanna watch it, mate, or they'll be mistaking you for a pooloo and packing you off to old Papa Joffrey."

"Bugger that," Charlie protested. "It's bad enough on a shilling a day. Them poor sods don't get tuppence. Don't know how they manage. Anyway, it's poilu."

"Nah, you're wrong there. The way they honk it's gotta be pooloo."

"Pfah, gotta get myself another pipe, these things you smoke are bloody chronic," Charlie grimaced, spitting out a strand of tobacco.

"What d'ya mean, *I* smoke? You bought 'em. You sure you looked everywhere?"

"Yeh, had me whole pack apart. Someone must've nicked it. I always keeps it here, see," Charlie tapped his side pocket. "Could'nt've fallen out; never has done before."

"Well, there's always a first time."

"And a last, if I catch the bugger."

"Well it wasn't you, chum, was it," George coochie-cooed the dog. "Noooo, 'cause you got nowhere to hide it, have you?" His joie de chien was lost on his compatriot. "Oh, come on, Charlie, buck up. You can always buy another."

But it wouldn't be the same, and George knew it. Charlie would never admit as much, but his upside-down pipe had become his talisman.

"'Scuse me, mate," said the man George had bumpsadaisied. "Did I hear you say you'd lost a pipe?" He reached into his pocket. "Wouldn't be one of them upside-down jobs, would it, like this one?"

"Well fuck me sideways," Charlie cried. "Where'd you find it?"

"Over by the bogs. Must've fallen out while nature was taking its course. I'd give it a good wash if I was you."

George passed it on, making sure to wipe his fingers on the dog's mangy pile.

"I was gonna hand it in," the man continued, "but thought better of it. The old Adj. is alright, he'd pick up a pound note and give it straight back, but I wouldn't trust that corporal of his no farther than I could throw him."

"Bit like our sergeant. Thanks, mate." Charlie polished the bowl on his sleeve. "Can I buy you a drink?"

"Don't mind if I do."

"Mam'selle?!"

* * * * *

With Richard elevated to the status of deity, Laura's popularity at the Priory knew no bounds. Still she wore no pin. Others began to copy her, until pin wearing became 'bad form' and its once omnipotent matriarch a dowager of bad taste. Whether Joanna Hetherington liked it or not, Laura now set the trend.

At the Grammar, Richard's reputation was no less lofty. On Laura and Scott's urging, he told his parents about his cadetship, arguing that, if conscription were brought in, the experience he was gaining could save his life. He would also stand a good chance of being an officer with all the benefits of rank.

His father saw the sense in it and was justly proud of his son's medal, but his mother was inconsolable. Distressful days were to pass before recrimination capitulated to the tears of repentant motherhood.

Although excused duty, Richard continued to drill his squad. Academically, his main frustration was his inability to hold charcoal or paint brush. Recognising the boy's talent, his Art Master loaned him books of his own to study in class. In these his fledgling Reynolds found aspects of art otherwise denied the adolescent student.

His initial reaction to the female form was one only to be expected, but the mastery of brushstroke, the subtle tones, even in sepia, the different techniques employed to capture beauty, innocence and sensuality, soon absorbed him. He longed for the day when he would glorify Laura as Velasquez had glorified his Venus, or Ingres his 'Grande Odalisque'. He was honest enough with himself to acknowledge that his aspirations were as carnally motivated as they were artistically so, however, when he eventually found the courage to voice them, it was with all the pseudo justification of the artist. His flaming cheeks betrayed him.

Laura teased him mercilessly, playing on the weakness of man as only woman can, until he took refuge in a sulk and stomped off home, angry at his ineptness, angry at his sexuality's insistence on making a fool of him.

That night Laura sat at her dressing table, deep in contemplation. In the wake of his heroism she had vowed to deny him nothing. She'd experienced few qualms over their maturing intimacy, but this? In an age where modesty was no stranger to the marital bed, her fantasy of baring all in conjugal darkness had been enough to water the tangled roots of moral conflict. Now the sheer depravity of presenting herself, not in darkness but in light, not in passion but in unmitigated passivity, tied that tangle into a stomach churning knot, inducing a charge so shameful as to be inadmissible even to herself.

But how could nudity be sinful, or even posing for that matter, she asked herself. If Richard's books were anything to go by, some of the most revered paintings in the world were of nudes, even those of the Madonna. She'd never heard anyone label the classical painters or their models sinners. Therefore the sin had to be in the motive. If the endeavour was strictly artistic, surely there could be no sin?

But were her motives pure? Were they not also driven by that overpowering eroticism which, in the honesty of meditation, she could admit to feeling? Was this the carnal lust, the satanic wickedness of her mother's preaching?

She remembered, as a child, being thrashed by her mother for running bath-naked into her father's arms. In the mirror, her long suppressed resentment surfaced. If, as an innocent, she could be guilty, what hope had she now? The truth stared back. She was what she was, she felt what she felt. She was searching for justification, but for whom? For herself? For her mother? If God was all knowing and all seeing and the thought was as guilt laden as the deed, she was already past redemption.

Fury incited her to rip off her nightdress, to bare body and soul before her mother's uncompromising Almighty. Still her conscience crippled her. But why? He would see nothing he hadn't seen before.

She sank back on the velvet stool, scarlet in blasphemy. But, if nakedness was natural, surely God intended it to be so? Biblically the fig leaf was the mark of the sinner, nakedness that of the innocent, that was the whole imagery of religious art. The question remained; if she posed for Richard would she be doing so as the Virgin Mary, or as Mary Magdalene?

She'd gone full circle. The intellectual gave way to the practical. Whatever the rights or wrongs, the whole idea was impossible. When would they get the chance; on their weekly walk home from Sunday school? Profanity upon profanity. No, she would appease him with the all-encompassing compromise, perhaps when they were married.

Her father's tread brought the knock of normality, the silhouette of worldly truth. A goodnight kiss and she was alone to make her peace with her Maker and her mother's memory.

CHAPTER ELEVEN

George rose from the trench at the sound of the whistle, the double rum ration in his belly churned to acid. Once more he faced death in the sweat-soaked uniform of fear.

The past few days had been hell. He'd tasted gas. There'd been ample warning, rumours had abounded, prisoners taken who'd been only too eager to tell all and escape the area. But G.H.Q. had known better. It was all 'subterfuge, meant to promote panic and cover the enemy's true intent,' the decree had come down. 'The reported employment of teargas against us last October, and of a deadlier vapour against the Russians, has been fully investigated and found to be inconclusive.'

"Besides, the use of gas is against the Geneva convention," George's officer had assured him.

And then it had come, a greenish yellow cloud, drifting across no-man's land from cylinders placed in the German lines days before, waiting for the right wind conditions. The French had been the first to suffer and had broken before it. Then it had been turned on the British.

They'd had no protection. There'd been nowhere to hide. Fifteen feet above, the air had been clear; at ground level the chlorine had stripped the lining from men's lungs, making each breath a searing intake of agony in the hours' long struggle against drowning as, starved of oxygen, the lungs filled.

George had been lucky. His company had been out of the line. Wearing improvised masks of flannel and lint, soaked in urine from the latrines, they'd moved forward to retake the lost ground.

The countryside had been yellow, petrified cattle and pigs adding their agony to the death throes of men. For the lucky ones, the storm of high explosive and shrapnel had ended their bestial torment, for others it had only increased it.

The trenches had been clogged with retching wounded, desperate to get away, their faces green, their wheezes bubbling through the bloody froth that oozed from their lips. The only way forward had been over open ground, and so the company had advanced, suffering the conventional consequences. But, coughing, spluttering, barely able to see, they'd retrieved most of the position, losing two thirds of their number in the process. George had suffered a dose of gas, but not enough for hospitalisation. His lungs had burned, he'd coughed up a little blood, but he'd remained on his feet. Within twenty-four hours he'd been returned to duty.

Now they'd been ordered to recover the remaining ground, although even sergeant Hollis could see they were better off where they were.

"Bloody typical," he'd moaned. "Nice bit of ground, dry as you like, and they want to send us back into that sodding mire. Bloody geraniums, they've got no idea. If just one of 'em would get off his arse and get his boots dirty, he could see for himself."

"Too busy licking the General's," Charlie Clayman had said.

"Boots or arse?"

"Both."

Through the fog of battle George could see the German wire, some hundred yards ahead. The enemy had been given time to strengthen his defences and the short barrage laid down by the decrepit British field guns had made no impression.

Bullets whistled by, as he sidestepped the dead and wounded. Some had lain there since the first assault, days before. Shellburst after shellburst re-tossed their offal, impregnating the smoke with its gangrenous stench.

A hand anchored itself to George's puttees. He knew him well, this ashen faced boy from Hayfield whose legs and loins had been torn away. The fingers held firm, disembowelling the torso as George dragged it along in blind horror. Then, ten yards ahead, the earth erupted and his mantrap was sprung. Winded, half blinded, he stumbled into the smoking crater.

Charlie Clayman was close behind.

"Jesus Christ! Fuck this for a game of soldiers. Thank Christ the wind's in the wrong fucking direction, that's all I can say. You alright, mate? George?"

George forced himself from the brink. "Seen Hollis?" He gasped.

"Have I fuck. Probably carted himself off as a gas case, skiving bastard."

"There ain't no gas."

"Exactly."

A lump of shrapnel sizzled into the pool forming at George's feet.

"Nice here, init? Friendly like," Charlie grinned, but all George could see was that boy's stricken face, until Sergeant Major Parks muddied the water.

"On your feet, fuck you! What the hell do you think this is, a bloody boxing match? There's no resting in-between rounds here, you mangy bastards. Now move!"

The enemy wire was twenty yards ahead and, beyond it, the trench, spitting flame. In one of those queer quirks of fate, George saw the hand grenade coming, like a vision, through the swirling smoke.

"Down!"

Muck and mud showered over him; a clod thumped him on the head. When he looked up, he saw Parks leaping over the dead and wounded that bridged the steel brambles.

"Come on!"

George would never forget his tumble over the wrecked parapet, the timeless panic of being flat on his back under a raised bayonet, nor the bewilderment in the wielder's eyes as Charlie's blade struck first.

"Get this trench sorted out! They'll be coming over soon as they're organised," Parks cried.

Forty had made it of the two hundred who had set out. Feverishly they reversed the firing step, piling bodies onto the old parados for cover.

"Seal those flanks."

As soon as the German artillery adjusted its sights, shells rained down, blowing a lance corporal clean out of the trench and decapitating the last surviving officer. Suddenly the torment ceased.

"Look to your fronts!"

The Germans rose from their support lines and the men let fly, emptying clip after clip, until their barrels were blister hot. The Vicker's cooling cylinder boiled, threatening to fracture.

"Mark your targets. Take care of that fucking machine gun, it's the only one we've got."

The attack was beaten back, leaving a swathe of wounded, but nothing could be done for them; exposure meant certain death.

"Will they come again, Sarn't Major?"

"Do cows shit?"

Four times the Germans came, their machine gunners raking no-man's land to prohibit relief, while their artillery pounded the trench, lengthening its trajectory when the infantry counterattacked. By dark, the defenders were down to a blood-soaked sixteen with barely a bullet between them.

"Where's the bloody reinforcements," George heard the sergeant Major grumble.

"Maybe they ain't coming," Charlie frowned.

"Dah, 'course they're coming," George told him.

The Sergeant Major scrambled over to them, trailing bandage from his mangled left hand.

"I need a runner, Clayman, and that's you."

Charlie looked apprehensively at George.

"Woods is signaller, Sarn't Major, he'd be quickest."

"Not with a bullet in him, he wouldn't. Find the Colonel, tell him the situation. We've got to have support or we're done for. Now, off you go, and be quick about it."

George offered his hand.

"Keep your head down, chum."

"Tell Betty... well, you know."

"Hold on, Sergeant Major; runner's here," someone warned.

"All right, Clayman, as you were."

The runner staggered along the trench. "Message from Battalion, Sarn't Major," he gasped. "You're to withdraw."

"Withdraw? What the fuck does he mean, withdraw?" George asked incredulously.

"That's enough of that, Bowden," the Sergeant Major snapped.

"Sorry, Sarn't Major," the runner regained his breath. "No reserves. All to the north. This was a bluff. Can't support you."

"Jesus Christ!" George exploded.

"Private Bowden!"

The Sergeant Major's anger was not aimed at him, George knew that. The man had known every feature of every face now ground into the mud or staring blankly to the heavens. Still his iron will held.

"You heard what the man said. Let's be having you."

75

* * * * *

Sheffield Wednesday beat Chelsea 3-0 in the Cup Final. April turned to May. The Dardenelles campaign and the sinking of the Lusitania dominated the headlines, along with horrific reports of a Canadian infantryman being crucified by the Germans, but the sinking of H.M.S. Recruit off Clacton and the Zeppelin raids on the coast, common gossip in the village, remained classified.

"Makes you wonder just how bad that Yarmouth do was," Arthur Bowden posed the question over a pint in the Barley Mow, after reading a blow by blow account of a similar air raid on Southend. "Must've been pretty drastic for them to hush it up."

"Old Simpkins from Rayntree, he's got a half-brother up there, reckons half the town ended up in the sea," Amos Crutchley confirmed glumly. "And what about our Yeomanry over yonder? Old Withers says they darsen't put that in the paper; all but wiped out, and all because the bloke in charge didn't know his arse from his elbow. I don't know. Mind you, nice about that Cardiff girl, giving her skin to that officer. Amazing what they can do nowadays. Not that I'd fancy wearing someone else's skin. Don't seem right, somehow. I mean, you wouldn't be you, would you?"

"Better than looking like that bloke I saw in Elmsford the other day. Turned my stomach just to look at him, poor sod. Fancy another?"

"Go on, then."

While Joe Crutchley, nineteen at last, took himself off to the Army, the recruiting drive continued. Posters were affixed to every tree, gatepost and barn, marches organised, meetings held. In opposition, the Brotherhood Movement campaigned against the war, claiming that the boys were being uselessly slaughtered. Indignant at being pressured, the farm workers ripped the posters to shreds, causing Arthur Bowden to examine his special constable's conscience one night, when he caught a saboteur red handed.

"Here, what do you think you're playing at?"

He grabbed the man by the scruff of the neck, only to find that it wasn't a man at all, it was the Vicar's sister.

"Miss Soames!" He let go at once. "I'm sorry, Miss, but I thought... "

"Yes; they're Gregory's," she indicated her trousers. "They're more practical for this sort of thing."

"But, you, Miss? Well, I don't know what to say."

"No, nor do I, officer. I suppose 'I arrest you in the name of the law' would be most appropriate. After all, I can hardly deny it." Ruefully she raised a handful of rent poster.

"But why, Miss?"

"I believe in God's word, Mr...?"

"Bowden, Miss."

"I believe in God's word, Mr. Bowden; 'thou shalt not kill.'"

"Well yes, don't we all, but..." Arthur was not about to embroil himself in

76

theological argument. "Does the Vicar know what you're about?"

"I'd rather not say, if you don't mind. You see, there's another commandment for that."

"The two of you aren't mixed up with this Brotherhood lot, are you?"

"I don't mean to be pedantic, Mr. Bowden, but there's only one of me."

"Well, are you?"

"Not exactly. I suppose you could call it a matter of conscience, if a woman is allowed such a thing where war is concerned. I think it's wrong, that's all."

"Well we've got to stand up for what's right, Miss."

Again the philosophical smile.

"So, do you summon a black Maria with your police whistle or shall we walk along to constable Johnson's?"

"I really don't know, Miss, bless me if I don't." Arthur scratched his head. Arrest the Vicar's sister? He'd never hear the last of it. "Look, if I let you go, will you give me your solemn word you won't do it again?"

"God's work is never done, Mr. Bowden."

'I'll take that as a yes, then,' Arthur mused. "Then let's just say it is for tonight, shall we. Now you hop off home, before I change my mind."

"God bless you, Mr. Bowden."

"And you, Miss Soames."

* * * * *

The eighteenth of May dawned bright and clear, accentuating the emergence of blossom from bud, woman from child. Laura smiled smugly at herself through her wardrobe mirror; in her blue blazer and ribboned hat, she looked and felt a picture of prettiness. It was Richard's birthday.

"We don't want to be late," her father called.

"Coming!"

Richard was sitting astride his bike at the Bowden gate, demonstrating his newly restored right arm. The bone had knitted rapidly and De'Ath had relieved him of plaster and sling the previous evening.

Laura gave him his present, biting her lip with exasperation as he painstakingly unpicked the knot and unfolded the wrapping paper. Inside was a Parker pen, gold nibbed and engraved with his initials. He beamed delightedly. She squirmed with satisfaction.

"It's from both of us, but I chose it."

"Now stow it somewhere safe and come on, otherwise you two will end up in detention, and I'll be out of a job," her father hurried them up.

The morning was hot and humid. Like the Grammar, the Priory maintained a strict dress code, nothing could be discarded, not a slip, not a stocking, however warm the weather, however hard the ride. Laura arrived at the gates flushed and perspiring.

It was a good day, almost a pre-war day; she received an eight for her English test, and even managed a seven in French, much to her own amazement. At four o'

77

clock she met Richard by the school gates and they headed home under a threatening sky. By the time they reached Hayfield thunder was in the air and gaining by the interval. They rode, hammer and tongs, for the mill and the shortcut through the fields, but the rain beat them to it, splattering the footbridge as they ran their bikes across.

"Head for the willow!"

They just made it. The lightening forked, the heavens opened. They dumped their bikes and brushed themselves off, he teasing her about beating the rain, she contending that she'd saved him from drowning, until the downpour's awesomeness prompted them into each other's arms.

A droplet splashed onto Laura's nose. They laughed; their lips met.

"Happy Birthday dearest."

As Laura rested her head on his shoulder, a stunning realisation gripped her. The willow's leaf laden vines bowed to the ground on all sides. Beyond them, the rain was like a lace curtain. They were completely isolated and alone. Trepidation drained the blood from her face. Fate had provided the circumstance, but could she find the courage?

She broke away.

He couldn't hide his disappointment. "Is anything the matter?"

"No." She forced a smile. "Have you got your sketchpad with you?"

"Yes, why?"

Her first, hastily formulated condition was met. Her nerves jangled.

"Show me. I want to see what you've been up to while my back's been turned," she granted herself a reprieve. If the rain kept up, then...

Moodily he unstrapped his satchel. "I'm sure there's nothing you haven't seen, I haven't drawn anything for weeks, you know that."

She did, and she could also read his mind. Why was she wasting such precious time? Her stomach tightened; she scanned the pages distractedly.

"Who's that?"

"It's a bad copy of a Goya," he huffed.

"She's quite pretty, I suppose, in a peasanty sort of a way."

"Not as beautiful as you," she heard him conjure from the depths. The compliment escaped her. She had been counting to sixty over again. Her self-imposed deadline was expiring; the demon inside her was persistent; 'The rain won't last forever. I dare you.'

Her heart thumped; her fingers trembled; 'fifty nine, sixty;' the moment came. She double-checked their seclusion. Her next words would be irrevocable.

"I've... I've got a special present for you," she croaked. "But you mustn't look, not until I tell you."

"I won't look," he sulked.

"You've got to promise. No peeking; you must shut your eyes and keep them shut."

Morosely he promised.

"All right, then."

Steadying herself against the willow's bark, she shed her shoes and reached under her smock. "Are they shut?"

"Yes!"

The bow on her bloomers slipped into a knot. Her fingers refused to grasp, to grip. Desperately she glanced over. His eyes remained closed, too piqued even to be curious. At last the ribbons gave.

"Now can I look?"

"No!"

She trod cotton, her heart palpitating her to the verge of paralysis, as she lifted her underclothes over her head and rolled down her stockings, almost overbalancing as they caught on her toes. Her breath became a whimper. There was no going back now. Instinctively she shielded herself.

"All r...ight."

His eyes opened and a fearful exhilaration gripped her. Hesitantly she let her hands fall. She was shivering, scared to distraction, but she'd dared to be naked in front of him, before the world. She basked in his rapture.

"It's all right, really it is. You can draw me, just as you always wanted."

"But if someone comes...."

Her breath juddered, and not just from fear. Her conscience rebelled. It was all going horribly wrong; she needed him to pick up his pencil, to validate her justification.

Then his arms were round her and his words as tender as the love in his eyes, as his own vulnerability. She felt no embarrassment when he instinctively glanced down, no shame, no inner conflict. Even when they parted and he took up his sketchpad, her intoxication was not that of the deviant, but that of being at one with nature, conscious of the air's caress, the roughness of the tree's bark, the sheer joy of nudity.

A droplet kissed her collar bone; she followed its trail down a body that seemed strangely impersonal. She felt like stretching up; she wanted to waltz. Yet to feel his eyes upon her was to feel her stomach tauten, her nipples tingle, her thighs moisten.

The light began to improve, the rain to ease. Anxiety eroded his concentration. It was too dangerous, he said, it was a popular path.

The leaf-filtered sunlight danced seductively over her skin. She didn't want to get dressed.

"But if someone comes," he repeated his warning.

As petrifying as the possibility was, she almost wanted it to happen. "It's your only chance." The words tumbled from her mouth.

He re-applied pencil to paper. The insect world resumed its sunlit chatter, birdsong filled the air. Alert to every sound, every distraction, he couldn't get it right. Still she egged him on, tipping the scales of discovery, until chance reached the very gates of certainty to which her daring had chained her.

A pair of heavy boots clumped across the footbridge, marking time to a tuneful whistle. Richard crouched low, waving her down, but Laura's demon held her. The whistler neared; the wet grass swished against his stride.

"Keep still!" Richard mouthed.

The vines' impenetrability melted away. Laura saw corduroy flicker through the foliage, a swinging sleeve, a rolled neckerchief, Mr. Clayman's profile. All he had to do was turn his head.

Her sight spangled, her heart pounded. Surely that, alone, would give her away? And then he was gone and she was reeling against the willow's bole.

Richard scrambled over, reaching for her draws. Inhibition rallied her.

"It's all right, I can manage."

He tripped over the cycle frames in his panic to shove his sketch pad into his satchel. By the time he'd disentangled the handlebars, she was dressed.

"Is it... on... st...raight?" She stuttered through a mouthful of hat pins.

"It'll do," he told her.

She held the bikes, while he double checked the path. The coast was clear. They broke cover.

High in the eaves the Miller smiled.

- CHAPTER TWELVE -

As soon as he got home, Richard went to his room to carefully extract the sketch from his pad. His mother had a habit of delving into his satchel, complaining that he never showed her anything. He stared at his inadequacy, for inadequacy it truly was against the perfection imprinted in his mind, retracing the sweep of her shoulders, the symmetry of her pert breasts, the dimple of her navel, the curve of her hips into the soft sacred shadows, until he came to the broken point of panic and her fear seared into his soul. His degeneracy had driven her to within a whisper of ruin. Would she hate him for it? Would this be the end? Was this how he returned such love? His self-respect evaporated, his lust wilted in condemnation.

If Laura remained a nervous wreck, it was not the epilepsy of self-depredation which convention may reasonably have demanded, but a legacy of elation that beggared her recoiling moral conscience. She'd felt fear before, but she'd never tasted the intoxicant that daring distils from its compound, made all the more potent by her nearness to discovery.

However, as the days passed, she found the episode's impact was not solely sexual, it encompassed a deeper liberation which, after tea with Sarah Jameson, a new girl at the Priory, advanced Laura's interest in women's suffrage to passive support.

Sarah's mother was something of a praetorian when it came to emancipation. In 1910, she'd left Natal and her apathetic husband, a disappointing antithesis of his swashbuckling namesake, to take up the cause, arriving in England just in time to join the 'Black Friday' protest in Parliament Square against the failure of that November's 'Conciliation Bill'. A crack on the head from a policeman's truncheon had only hardened her ardour.

After three years of bombings and despoliation in London, she'd moved to Elmsford to breathe fire into the local lodge, only to find Elmsford's recently elevated Cathedral unworthy of the fuse wire, and the town devoid of art treasures. Nevertheless the recreation park's pagoda had gone up in flames and Hettie Jameson before the Beak. She'd escaped gaol by a whisker, only to demonstrate against the declaration of war from the dock and be promptly rearrested. Hettie was the only person Laura knew with inside knowledge of a police cell.

"And every time she gets arrested, I have to change school," Sarah had moaned.

Hettie could see no reason why women should be denied the vote. "The problem is, far from advancing the cause, the war has quashed it," she told Laura. "Our esteemed leader goes on recruiting drives. A thousand suffragettes have gone to France, more fool them. Most galling of all is the government's about-turn on employment. We can get all the jobs we want, now; men at the front, women in the factories. They tell the men their jobs will be safeguarded, but can you honestly see any employer honouring such a commitment, after investing millions in new machinery a child could operate? I think not. Women are far cheaper to employ, we work harder *and* we don't pour half our pay down our throats in pubs. Do you know, as many working hours are lost to drink as they are to sickness, even with a war on?

But that's beside the point. The vote is the vital issue. If women had had an equal say in 1914, this country wouldn't be at war now. The sooner we get it, the sooner it will end. And I say this for men's sake, too. For all those who fear for their re-employment if they enlist, there are just as many who wouldn't go at all, given the choice. And still there are women who say, "go." It's unforgivable. I, for one, have no wish to sign a man's death warrant by stepping into his work shoes, however seductive the wages. Thank God for Sylvia Pankhurst. She, at least, sees the War for what it truly is, a criminal waste of lives."

If Laura found Hettie's arguments confusing, she grasped their one essential. If women had the vote, they would end the War. For, surely, no wife or mother in their right mind would willingly send their menfolk off to fight?

She had only to look at her own reactions to the Pin Brigade's persecution and Richard's cadetship to find an unpalatable answer.

* * * * *

The casualty figures mounted; further reports of commanders' incompetence filtered through. By the beginning of June, all those likely to volunteer, approximately half those eligible, had done so; the remainder would have to be compelled. There wouldn't be enough manpower to bring in the harvest, women and children would have to be employed.

"I don't mind the boy lending a hand, but not my Beatty. I haven't worked like a cart horse all my life for her to go slaving in the fields like some flaming diddycoy. Let's see the high and mighty get their hands dirty for a change. My wife's got a home to run." Arthur Bowden set out his stall.

Southend suffered its second Zeppelin raid, London its first.

"Paddington Station's been raised to the ground," the rumour went round the village, until a letter arrived from a girl in service in Bayswater.

"Whitechapel it was, Mrs. Endicott says. Got a letter from her Faith. Reckon it'll be our turn next," Amos Crutchley wagered over a pint.

"Best dig myself a cellar and fill it with ale; at least I'd die happy," Arthur Bowden mooted, only half-jokingly.

At the Grammar school, the military disasters at Gallipoli fuelled the staffroom debate. Chapman, with the aid of a map, had outlined the strategy to his class, a far-sighted one, in his view, which, by taking the Dardanelles and subsequently Constantinople, could knock Germany's ally Turkey out of the War, establish an ice-free supply route to Russia and a base for a future thrust through Austro-Hungary to Germany itself.

His pupils had been impressed, but not Blundell, the Cadet Captain, whose blinkered vision, like that of British High Command, extended no farther than a war of attrition on the Western Front.

"But why keep butting the beast head-on when we can deal him a death blow in the flank? And just think of the effect our beating the Turks would have on the Empire. Our stock would rise in leaps and bounds," Chapman had appealed to his colleague's imperialism.

"Not if, by knocking on their back door, we let them through our front," Blundell had parroted the Army line. "No, my dear chap, to beat the Hun we must have a preponderance of men at the critical point, not halfway round the bally world on some fools' errand."

'If only to ensure that the last man standing is on the right side,' Chapman had groaned to himself.

However, for once, G.H.Q. had been politically outmanoeuvred. The 'fools' errand' had been Churchill's, Admiralty Supremo, and he had forced it through. At least he would live to regret it, unlike the tens of thousands who would reap the whirlwind of High Command's reticence and resultant incompetence. After months of folly and fiasco, the only ably executed part of the entire operation would be the dead of night withdrawal. Churchill would be relegated to a Colonelcy on the Western Front. It would take him a quarter of a century to restore his credibility.

* * * * *

As June progressed G.H.Q. finally lifted the lid on the Munitions Crisis. Argument had raged between High Command and Government for months; now the acute shell shortage provided the perfect scapegoat for the disasters of the spring, along with the diversion of vital supplies to Churchill's 'Turkish adventure'. Heads rolled; David Lloyd George took over the Ministry of Munitions. Under his motivation, the problem would be solved, not least by the employment of women.

As Scott had predicted, a profusion of camps had sprung up in and around Elmsford during spring and early summer, to guard against invasion, air raids and espionage. The town was a major centre of war industry, as was Rayntree, ten miles to the northeast along the high road that meandered through Ashleigh.

It was an espionage scare that found Arthur Bowden bumping along on the back of Amos Harris's milk cart one morning. He had just opened his yard when a fellow Special raced in with news of a spy seen wheeling his punctured pushbike along the Rayntree road. Harris had offered him a lift back to Ashleigh, but hadn't been understood. According to Harris, the man's accent was thick and foreign and, if that wasn't suspicious enough, he'd been relieving himself by the roadside.

Harris's horse thundered after the suspect as fast as his tired old legs would carry himself, the cart and the Keystone Cops clinging to the churns for dear life.

The infidel hove into sight.

"Whoooaa," Harris hauled on the reins.

The men jumped down. The horse snorted relievedly, bewhinnying his woe that he hadn't been put out to pasture years ago.

"And where might you be going?" Johnston the village bobby demanded of the miscreant.

"Rayntree?" Came the hopeful, completely alien reply. Even the man's clothes reeked of foreignness.

"And where you come from?" The constable enunciated, incorporating every inflection of terror a self-proclaimed descendant of Eric the Norse could conjure up.

The accused could only repeat, "Rayntree."

"I think you'd better come with us."

As, with malice aforethought, authority advanced, the man dropped his bike and backed away, jabbering excitedly.

"He's German right enough; hark at that! Grab him lads!"

The specials converged on the guilty, carrying him, kicking and screaming, to the cart.

"Watch him lads, watch him," the Viking advised, standing back as a flying fist caught Arthur in the eye. It could have been anybody's, but the prisoner got the blame, adding assault to the charge sheet.

"See if he's got any papers on him," Johnston instigated a search of the foreign pockets.

"Says here he's Belgian."

"Belge! Belge!" The man cried.

"Belge, my arse," Johnston snarled. "Belgees talks French; there's one in Elmsford market, and he don't sound nothing like him. That's German he's talking, or I'm a kipper. One of them submarines must've landed him. You've only got to look at them papers to see they're forgeries, and none too clever ones at that."

"What about his saddlebags?" Harris piped up. "There might be a bomb."

"Take care, lads," Johnston volunteered, re-tying his bootlaces. "Don't want the bloody thing to go off."

Gingerly the bravest bent over the bike.

"It's ticking right enough."

"Alright, leave it where it is," their leader ordered. "Hop on, you lot. Arthur, you and Harry stay put and don't let no one near it. I'll send to Elmsford for the army."

The old horse staggered.

"Hold her steady, Amos!"

"Her's an 'im."

"He won't be if he has me off."

"Trot on!"

The horse bowed its weary head and took the strain.

"And keep your distance," Johnston cried, posing over his prisoner like a custodial Woden.

Two hours later, a military escort negotiated the backed-up traffic. The ticking was coming from a clock, en route to its Rayntree owner after being restored to working order by the spy, a Flemish clockmaker from the refugee camp in Elmsford. The village would never let 'Kipper' Johnston, the parish Viking, forget it.

* * * * *

84

While Arthur Bowden was nursing his black eye, over in France, his son George was about to 'suffer the consequences' of crossing Sergeant Hollis once too often, and all over a sleeping bag he'd found tucked away in a dugout and refused to relinquish.

"It's against regulations," Hollis had told him, wanting it for himself.

"I got Lieutenant Johns' permission," George had checkmated him.

His comeuppance had been an intelligence stunt, guiding an officer across no-man's land to eavesdrop on the enemy.

"Knows the lay-out like the back of his hand," Hollis had volunteered him.

"Well he ain't having my fleabag, and that's that," George railed to Charlie Clayman, as he prepared to slip over the top. "If I don't come back, it's yours, Charlie. And if you don't want it, burn the bloody thing."

Suitably mollified, he crabbed and crawled across the divide, freezing at every 'pok' of a flare pistol, sniffing out any gangrenous pile.

"Makes one feel rather like Gulliver over Lilliput, what?" the officer whispered in his ear.

The trench they were making for had been British. George had helped dig a latrine for it before the position had been overrun. The sap to it had been stoved in by a shell and it had been abandoned, but, if enough of it remained, it would make the perfect listening post, if it wasn't an outpost already, occupied by the Germans.

The depression of an obliterated communication trench offered an approach. The workings were still there, and seemingly in fair order.

'So why leave it unmanned?' George wondered. It made no sense.

They slid into it, but instead of setting up shop, the officer moved deeper into the sap, forcing George to follow. The sap deepened into a tunnel, properly propped, under the German wire. George swallowed hard. The danger signals were plain to see. Still he followed his leader. The man knew best, better than best, he was an intelligence officer. Then voices from the next traverse turned his legs to jelly. It took all his willpower not to bolt, to hold the torch's pinprick light steady, while the officer took notes. Surely the fool must have realized the sap was in use, a passage into no man's land?

His cold sweat turned into a torrent, as confirmation from behind brought a challenge from ahead. A password was called. They were caught like rats in a trap.

The officer pushed past. George heard him draw his revolver.

'He's got to be joking,' his incredulity shrieked, before a deafening report fused him to the earth. His ears rang with shots and confusion, until, just as suddenly, silence fell, wired with terror, pregnant with anger and agony. A German voice called.

"Camerad!" George employed the only German he knew, "camerad!"

Each syllable caught on his teeth. His crawling limbs could barely hold him. "Camerad, camerad," he desperately repeated. He sensed alien body odour. His voice dried to a croak; his whole face quivered; then the torch in his hand leapt back to life, shooting its beam into terrified eyes. A bayonet gleamed.

Hay carting began on June 22nd, though, with few carts and fewer horses left after the army's latest requisitioning, it lacked the atmosphere of old. By July, pea picking was proving to be the year's big money earner with families making as much as ten shillings a day. However, an extra pound or two were of little compensation for those with relatives in the Essex Yeomanry, of whom there'd been no news since the long lists of those 'missing' had been published in April.

"If they're all dead, why don't they just say?" Arthur Treadwell protested to Arthur Bowden.

"Don't despair of him yet, Arthur. Your boy could still be a prisoner, just like our George," Bowden bolstered his own hopes as well as Treadwell's. The telegram had come. George had been posted missing in action. "There's none more bloody-minded than that Kaiser; probably keeps the names back on purpose."

"I hope you're right, Arthur; I do bloody hope you're right."

- CHAPTER THIRTEEN -

"The patient in room fourteen has not been secured, Sister. Please see to it."

"Directly, doctor."

The patient in room fourteen had been on her best behaviour today and sister Frampton had felt constraint unnecessary. However, doctor's orders were doctor's orders. She strode purposefully down the corridor, calling for a nurse to fetch a straightjacket.

She hated this job. The patient would resist; the patient in room 14 always resisted; often she had to be sedated; and those eyes; even among such brethren, their despair pierced the soul.

Ahead, the door to room 14 was ajar. Frampton quickened pace. It was always kept locked. The doctor was new here, a locum, but surely he'd relocked it, the protocol was cast in stone.

The room was empty.

'Dear God.'

All outside doors and windows were open at that time of the morning for airing purposes; there was no telling where the patient might be. They would have to search the grounds, there would be an enquiry, and Frampton knew exactly where the blame would fall.

The nurse arrived with a straightjacket.

"Quickly, nurse; you go this way; I'll go that."

The instruction had barely left Frampton's lips, when a scream rent the air. It came from outside. Clinging to the bars, Frampton looked down from the corridor window. A distraught auxiliary was running across the lawn.

Taking a parallel route, Frampton arrived in the entrance hall to find the girl weeping in matron's arms.

"It's the patient from room fourteen," Matron said abruptly. "She's impaled herself on the railings."

* * * * *

Fretful days preceded Richard's Summer Camp, as stress over George revived his mother's recrimination. She cried, she remonstrated, she twisted and turned the psychological screw.

Although Richard did his best to hide it, inevitably it was a depression shared, and, when he finally moped off to Camp, Laura found her conscription as assistant supervisor on the Sunday School Outing less irksome than, otherwise, it might have been; anything to alleviate the gloom.

The last parish cart horses took the strain and the brakes trundled off on the eight miles of winding Essex back lanes to the tiny estuary town of Merdon, with its modest fun fair, boating lake and paddling pool, the nearest thing to a seaside resort within travelling distance. It was a rare fine day for the summer of 1915 and the troops training in the area were out in force, swinging along to 'Pack up your Troubles' and 'Tipperary'. Laura, looking very Gainsboroughesque in her wide-ribboned hat, turned whole platoons of heads, but she was too preoccupied with the children to appreciate the attention, as they flirted with disaster, precariously reaching out to brush the overhanging leaves and cup butterflies.

At last they arrived to the stampede inspiring sight of two navy gunboats tied up at the jetty.

"Is them battleships?" A wide-eyed little boy asked in wonder.

"Don't be daft; destroyers. Don't you know nuffink?" His mate told him.

Laura led the girls to the Ladies' Bathing Huts. Few had proper costumes, even fewer could swim, the river at Ashleigh was far too shallow and weed choked for anything but paddling, and a daytrip to Clacton was the stuff of dreams. Nevertheless, soon all were thrashing about in the pool, while the Vicar kept watch from the Anglican safety of a deck chair.

The boys played to the gallery and it wasn't long before Laura had to wade to the rescue, suffering the pain and embarrassment of a tiny tot's limpet grip as she carried her to the bank.

Next came the Boating Lake, where the Reverend did some rowing and the more piratical Drakes some ramming, rampaging around in their paddle boats to volleys of rage from the agitated attendant. Laura sat out the confrontation with the landlubbers, daydreaming of Richard and a punt on the Cam, until the custodian saved his armada from complete destruction with a horn fracturing "Come in now, Vicar, your time is up!"

A pious apology was followed by lunch at the brakes, dispensed from two huge hampers packed with pies, sandwiches, cakes, lemonade and ginger beer donated by the Parish Ladies and plundered by the gulls when the 'whoop, whoop' of the departing gunboats sent the children scampering to the promenade.

With 'Rule Britannia' sung and the picnic cleared away, the Vicar dispensed the Christian shilling and they all flocked to the Fair.

"Miss, miss, I've lost my sixpence."

"Jimmy Coombes took my place on the roundabout, Miss, and I was there first!"

"I need the privy, Miss."

"I've hurt my knee."

"Waaaaaaaah!"

After two hours of toilet duty, grazed knees, lost fortunes and squabble settling, shepherd and sheepdog penned their dissenting lambs into the brakes and they started for home. They met only one army column en route, resting by the roadside. A chorus of suggestive approval, which Laura shrugged off with a smile, spurred the Vicar into an impromptu, rut-warbled sermon on the sins of vulgarity from the back of his brake, until a pothole deposited him back on his perch.

'Get yourself some sea legs, Vicar,' some wag cried.

It was an ill omen. As they lumbered along, pits and potholes took their toll on queasy tummies. The sickly breath of the mite on Laura's lap wafted nauseously up her nostrils. They pulled into Ashleigh not a moment too soon.

That evening Scott and Laura dined at the rectory, where the Vicar sang Laura's praises to the hilt. In normal circumstances, Scott would have been highly gratified, and he would certainly have asked after Miss Soames, the Vicar's sister, apparently called away urgently. As it was, he was barely able to focus. He'd been notified of Marian's death; suicide the asylum had said.

She'd looked awful on his last visit and been under sedation. He'd been warned that she'd taken a turn for the worse, but he hadn't been prepared for death.

As he walked Laura home in the fading light, each flashback became a conscience racking recrimination. If he'd insisted on leaving London earlier, could he have saved not only his first child, but Marian's sanity? God, how he'd regretted his weakness. But what was past was past, his memory, both mercifully and unmercifully, allowed only transient regression. Whatever responsibility self-reproach heaped upon his shoulders, reality lifted and placed in perspective. There was nothing he could have done to save Marian from herself. He'd tried everything, finally risking and losing his daughter's life in his efforts to appease her. From every standpoint, however guilt instilling, her release was nothing but merciful, probably more merciful for Marian than sanity could ever imagine. At last, it was ended, the lie was now reality; Marian was gone.

He patted the hand resting on his cuff. Thank God Laura was spared the truth, and thank God she had Richard. If only the War would end and ensure the boy's survival. He remembered their tiff at Easter. As stable as she was, she was her mother's child. If anything happened to Richard, who knew what effect it would have on her? The possibility that Marian's madness might be hereditary was Scott's worst nightmare.

* * * * *

The following day it was inherent temper, rather than apparent insanity, that sent Elizabeth Bowden storming across the road to remonstrate with the boys from the Industrial School. They'd pitched their tents in the stubble field opposite, a last minute substitution for the promised cow pasture, to which the White's prize bull had stubbornly refused to relinquish the grazing rights. They were now fanning the smoke from their camp fire like errant Red Indians.

"Here, do you mind; I've got washing out back! What the hell do you think you're playing at?"

"Blimey, she's bonkers," a voice piped from the shrinking pack.

"Cooking fire, missus." The bravest stood his ground.

"Cooking fire? What about my washing?"

"Sorry, missus, but we gotta get it going, Mr. Quiller's orders."

"Well you won't do it with that," Elizabeth scowled, kicking the tinder. "Where did you find it, in a pond? It's wetter than my woollies. The wood's got to be dry!"

"Don't do that, missus; it's all there is, honest, we looked everywhere."

The appeal came too late. Doleful eyes watched the embers die.

89

"Took us all morning to get that going. Now we ain't gonna eat. Mr. Quiller said. Ain't that right, you lot?"

The gallery of long-faced lost souls ebbed Elizabeth's anger. She grimaced into the cauldron of miscellaneous inedibles.

"What you got in there anyway?"

"That's our dinner."

"God bless your stomachs."

"Beef stew."

"You could've fooled me. Smells worse than them dung divers," she indicated the cause of her first complaint of the morning, four leapers still standing at punishment attention by the malodorous midden mound. Picking up a ladle, she plumbed the depths. A lump of rancid skirt bobbed through the surface slime, along with a gross of maggoty carrots, pulled straight from the ground.

"You're supposed to take the tops off first and scrape 'em. Then you cut 'em up, see; same with the meat; it'll never cook like that."

"We didn't know missus. 'Sides, we 'ain't allowed a knife without Mr. Quiller being here," the spokesman pleaded.

"Anyway, it'll never cook now," another moaned.

The last dregs of Elizabeth's dander drained. Whatever the poor little sods had done wrong, they deserved better than this. For half of them probably their only crime was being orphaned, as she had been herself.

"So where is this Mr. Quiller?"

"Went down the village, missus. Smithy got caught nicking at the store. He's gone to sort it out."

'Bloody worcesters! Better lock the doors tonight.' Elizabeth's alarm bells diminished her compassion with their portentous clang. Nevertheless, the urchins had to eat and charity might prove a better insurance policy than aggravation.

"Look, bring it inside and I'll see what I can do. You two take a handle each, and mind you don't spill it on my nice clean floor!"

* * * * *

While the Borstal boys squatted round the camp fire that night, ging-gang-gooleying 'the best stew we've ever had,' Arthur Bowden sat at his kitchen table bemoaning the National Register.

"More ruddy forms. Christ, they'll be logging our bowel movements next."

"Really, Arthur," Beatrice objected.

"Well... They've got all our birth and marriage certificates and whatnot; what do they need this for?"

"You don't reckon it's to do with this conscription, do you Arthur? That's what Mrs. Beasley says."

"You haven't been listening to her, have you? Christ, I'd've thought you had more sense, mother, after the trouble she caused them Crutchleys. Young Joe would never've signed up if it hadn't been for her, so Amos reckons. Says he'd all but talked him out of it 'til that bloody old cow stuck her nose in. She should keep

90

it out of other people's business."

"All the same, I'm worried, Arthur, really I am. Our family's done enough. They can't take our Richard, he's all we've got left."

Beatrice's lip quivered.

"Come on now, mother, don't upset yerself. Our George is a tough old bird. Missing don't mean dead, not by a long chalk."

"Oh, Arthur!" Beatrice sobbed.

"Now, now, old girl, he'll turn up, you see if he don't. Anyway, conscription or no conscription, the boy's not old enough. Most likely it's rationing, especially with women on it and all."

"But the boy, Arthur; can't we just say we never got one?"

"What, when it was hand delivered?"

"Well just leave him off, then. If they're asking who's living here, they can't know, can they?"

"There's a twenty pound fine for doing that, and three months hard labour. And if it is rationing, what'll we do then? There'll be barely enough for two, let alone three. Besides, even if they don't know he's here, they'd find out soon enough; your friend Mrs. Beasley'd see to that. Why you consort with that woman, I'll never know."

"I don't consort with her, we speak, that's all. It doesn't hurt to be civil."

"I wouldn't give her the time of day, if it was me, but there you are. They wouldn't have a fine if they had no means of checking. We've got to be sensible. When was he born?"

"Eighteenth of May nineteen hundred," Beatrice lied.

- CHAPTER FOURTEEN -

They gathered at the Jameson house. The slogan was simple: 'Women Unite! Stop the Slaughter!' Laura and Sarah had been on their knees all afternoon painting in the hand-ruled letters. Twenty posters would have to suffice. Something had to be done to restore the nation's sanity, and quickly; the previous week forty thousand women had marched through London in support of the war, demanding a part in it.

Hettie's planned rally had been voted down; none but her had been prepared to stand up and be counted in a daylight demonstration; dead of night had been the condition of the dedicated. Even so, the turnout lived up to disappointing expectation.

They left at intervals, just after twelve, each pair concealing brush, adhesive and sedition under their voluminous clothing. Hettie would have preferred a later start, but again she had been outvoted; instead she would have to rely on a moonless night and the blackout to preserve the proclamation for the morning masses. For her part, despite the added risk of an alerted constabulary, she would wait.

Sarah had succumbed to sleep just after one. Laura, absorbed in stories of Africa and Mrs. Jameson's activist days in London, had shown more stamina. Nurse Frost, the only one with a plausible excuse for being out so early, was due at three. She didn't arrive. Hettie knew she couldn't do the job alone; even with two it would be difficult. Laura had been entrusted to her care, to involve her was out of the question, but to fail was equally unthinkable. She would have to try, or her credibility would crumble. It wasn't just a matter of pride, it was the survival of the movement itself, a factor which Laura was quick to glean and argue with all the fervour of a racing pulse.

Conviction versus responsibility: the ticking clock decided in conviction's favour. They roused Sarah, whose, "do I have to?" dissent, in the honesty of semi consciousness, extended only to her own recruitment. In Sarah's case the cause had long been a lost one.

"Yes, you do. Now hold this." Cursing her husband's lethargic genes, Hettie held her arms up while twenty feet of banner was wrapped, corset-tight, around her. "Phew, I can hardly breath!"

"You look like Mrs. Rawlinson," Sarah ridiculed both her mother and their obese neighbour.

"Oh, come on Sarah," Laura cajoled her. "Think how many lives could be saved if women would only do something."

"It's silly. No one's going to see it. They'll have it down before the milk arrives."

"Then stay here; we'll manage on our own," Hettie snapped.

"Oh, all right," Sarah capitulated.

Elmsford was a town of few alleyways, London Road a fareway of few bends. They detoured to avoid the hospital, wherein the berated Nurse Frost was performing emergency heroics of a different kind, taking the narrower and darker Molesham Street.

"Sarah! Look where you're going," Hettie whispered over a clipped heel.

"I'm sorry! I can't see a thing."

"Sshhhhh! "

In the pitch blackness only the clump of a policeman's boot or the flash of his torch would alert them to danger; a lightfoot would be on them in an instant. They groped their way across the Regency bridge and into the wider High Street.

"Look out!" Hettie hissed, ducking the girls into a doorway.

The thin beam of a masked lamp brushed the gutter by their feet. Pedals and wheels whirled by. The danger passed.

"They can't have found the posters. They'd be hulla-ballooing all over the place if they had," Hettie reasoned. "Come on."

Cold shop windows clung to Laura's touch, glossed wood, coarse brick.

"Damn!"

"For pity's sake, Sarah!"

"I've trodden in something."

"I told you to watch where you were going," Hettie scolded more Sarah's continuing incalcitrance than her inattention.

"How can I, when I can't even see my feet?"

"Come on Sarah, we're almost there."

Laura's words seemed of little encouragement.

"It's all right for you, you haven't got dog poo all over your shoes."

With Sarah 'pohing' every step, they crept into the spit and sawdust shelter of South Street, probably the town's oldest and certainly its most notorious thoroughfare, lined with Coaching Inns, stables and tack shops from a bygone era, barely wide enough for two Broughams to pass, its black oak beams impregnated with hops, barley and horse leather. Here, ale and blood had been spilled in equal pints for centuries. Even at four in the morning the murmur of brag players could be heard from behind closed doors.

At the top sat the Square, with the Corn Exchange, commandeered as a servicemen's recreational centre and temporarily renamed 'Soldiers Hall', on one side, the Shire Hall on the other and the Cathedral a stone's throw behind, as, to its right, was the Police Station. It was the perfect platform.

Hurrying on, they unfurled Mrs. Jameson in the murky shadows of Soldiers Hall.

"Now what?" Sarah asked, as her mother delved under a pile of refuse.

"Now this." Hettie produced a coiled rope and two paint pots, hidden there late the previous evening.

"What's that for? I refuse to paint the whole stupid town!"

"Sarah, please! Now be careful, the lids are loose. Take one each and follow me."

They stole into the square. For the first time, Sarah's truculence was tinged with trepidation. A lamppost loomed.

"Now put that down and hold this."

Handing Sarah the banner, Hettie uncoiled the rope and, with awesome expertise, hooked it over the lamppost's barely discernible stanchion with one throw.

"Well done," Laura breathed.

"Now you two haul me up like so," Hettie demonstrated, after knotting an end round her waist.

"Mother, don't be ridiculous, you'll break your neck."

"Sarah, stop procrastinating and hand me the banner. Let me see, I want... yes... this end." Draping the folds over her shoulder, Hettie set herself at the lamppost. "All right, now pull me up, but slowly, one hand and then the other; and whatever you do, don't let go."

"This is madness," Sarah moaned.

Hettie had shinned halfway up before the girls took the strain, garrotting the breath out of her as she spiralled into space.

"Let her down, Laura, let her down!" Sarah panicked.

Hettie flapped her arms in the negative, riding out the revolutions until she could grab the pole.

Laura couldn't fail to be impressed. "Bravo!"

"Now girls, gently this time, gently!"

Up Hettie went, with Sarah's anxiety heightening by the equal inch.

"Someone's bound to come, I know they will."

"Sarah, I'm nervous enough as it is," Laura pleaded.

"She'll get herself stuck up there and we'll all be arrested. Mother Superior will crucify us."

"Don't be silly."

"Well, you get thrown out of three schools in three years and see how you like it. Oh, I do wish she'd hurry."

"Quiet, Sarah! Now hold it there." Hettie scissored herself to the upright and began tying.

"It's useless! Look at it; a child of five could reach it," Sarah grumbled on. "One omnibus and the whole thing'll be..."

A resonant tread echoed her into silence.

"Stay still!" Hettie hissed.

Laura knew the sensation well; Sarah was bristling like a petrified cat.

The footfalls grew louder, seeming to come straight for them, then faded down the High Street.

"All right, now let me down, but gently."

Laura could feel the tension in Sarah's grip.

"Slowly Sarah, slowly."

At last Hettie trod solid ground.

"Phew, that was close. Now for the next one."

"Mother, you can't! We'll be caught for sure."

"We'll just have to be quick, that's all. It's no good as it is; now come on."

Hettie had paced and re-paced the span over the past week; twenty feet exactly from lamppost to lamppost. The birds were beginning to stir; dawn was an urban horizon away. It took her three goes to get the rope over the stanchion; again the girls took the strain. It was as if they were lifting the night with every heave. Roof tiles and windows became clearly visible.

Triumphantly Hettie tied the final knot.

"Right, now down."

Sarah's coordination had passed the point of compliance. She let go with a rope burned yelp, leaving Laura to soar into the air against Mrs. Jameson's plummeting counterweight, until she, too, lost her grip and succumbed to gravity in a parachute of skirts.

"Mother! Laura! Are you all right? The rope slipped; I couldn't hold it; look at my hands!"

The fallen rose, bruised but intact.

"Stop gibbering girl and get the paint," Hettie scowled, freeing herself from the rope.

"But my hands, they're burnt!" Sarah blubbed. "And anyway, what do we need paint for? The stupid thing's up; lets go!"

"Just do as I say."

Hettie scanned the square for signs of detection. Sarah brought the paint.

"Now you take this lamppost and I'll take the other. Aim as high as you can and give it a good dousing, then empty what's left round the base. We must stop them from climbing it, understand? Stand clear, Laura, I don't want you getting paint all over you. Right now, Sarah, give it a good swing... and mind the banner!"

Given Sarah's nerves, it was never going to happen; paint and pot sailed from her grasp to land with an alarming splash and clatter five feet from the target.

"Go, you two, go!"

The girls ran for their lives, leaving Hettie to complete the job to the hollow hoot of a police whistle.

With the hue and cry, it was plain they would be lucky to make the bottom of South Street, let alone all the way home. Hettie herded them back into the shadows of Soldiers Hall, intent on cutting through the cattle market and doubling back to the Cathedral. They would have to cross Market Street and Queen Street, in full view of the square, to get there, but it was their best chance.

Surviving a close call among the market stalls, they lifted their skirts and sprinted across each byway. The Cathedral gates were open; ducking from headstone to headstone they reached the House of Truth undetected. There the evidence came to light. Sarah's shoes and dress were paint splattered, Hettie's coat the same.

"You'll have to change with me," she ordered, taking her coat off and wiping Sarah's shoes with the sleeve. "And please don't argue."

Turning Sarah's dress inside out to hide the marks, Hettie squeezed into it. She would have to leave the girls there. If she stayed, they would have no chance; caught in the company of the infamous Mrs. Jameson? Guilty as charged. The sooner she diverted the constabulary's attention the better.

"Beckwith; you understand? Beckwith," she told them, giving them a false name and address before hurrying down the aisle.

"But what will I say?" Sarah wailed.

95

"You'll think of something."

Hettie crammed her paint stained coat under a back pew and was gone.

"We can always claim sanctuary," Laura smiled.

"That's not funny Laura. What a mess. Why I ever let her talk me into this, I'll never know; and, as for you, she had no right, no right at all. What are we supposed to do now, pray?"

"Well we're in the right place for it. Look out!"

"Sweet Jesus, hear our prayer..."

Hobnailed boots fell on flagstone, ringing out the hour of judgement. A dark presence approached, a reverential cough.

"Excuse me Miss, but could I ask what you're doing here?"

Sarah was first in line, her tears real, her face grief stricken.

"I'm sorry, Officer?"

"It's a bit early for worship, Miss."

"My brother (sniff) was killed last night (sniff), at least (sniff) we got the telegram last night. In Flanders (sniff); he's dead," she blubbed with complete conviction, ending with a distraught wave of the hand.

As awesome as Mrs. Jameson's gymnastics had been, Sarah's theatrics impressed Laura more. She was biting her lip trying to produce a tear.

"And you, Miss?"

Laura felt her cheeks flame. She fixed her gaze on the hassock in front of her. "We're sisters."

"I see, Miss. I'm sorry, but could I ask your name?"

"Beckwith," they answered in apocalyptic unison. Laura felt the cold metal of handcuffs snapping round her wrists.

"And have you been here all night, Miss?"

"I, I don't know when it was, Officer," Sarah sobbed. "No, not all night; I don't think so. What time is it?"

"It's getting on for five thirty, Miss."

"I'm sorry, Officer, but I can't..."

"Just one more question, Miss. Have you seen anyone else?"

Sarah shook her head. Laura sensed the man's compassion. 'Dear God, was he convinced?'

Then a harder step fell; a gruffer voice growled.

"Alright, Harry?"

Their interrogator gave a tactful nod. "Bereavement in the family."

"No one else been in?"

"Don't look like it."

"Best check the pews, just in case. Might be someone hiding."

Laura cringed. They would find Hettie's coat. There was no alternative.

"Someone did come in... a little while ago. They sat over there." Laura discovered her acting potential at last. "I, I don't think they stayed long."

Sarah looked at the Iscariot in hand shielded horror.

"When was this, Miss?"

"Oh... not long ago, I don't know exactly. Why, is something wrong, Officer?"

"Harry, here a minute," echoed down the aisle. Hettie's coat was in Constable Gruff's hands.

Whispers cut through the Gothic reverberation; "No more than schoolgirls;" "lost their brother;" "said someone came in;" "wouldn't know the score;" "we've got to be sure." The prosecution approached the dock.

"Is this anything to do with you, Miss?" It was Constable Gruff with Exhibit A.

"No, I've never seen it before," Sarah sobbed.

"It must have belonged to the lady who came in," Laura offered.

"This lady; did you see her, Miss?"

"No, I just caught a glimpse. But I'm sure it was lady, at least, I think it was."

Constable Gruff scowled. "I think you'd better come with us."

"I'm sorry, Miss, but there's been an incident. We'll just see you safely home, have a word with your dad. Where do you live?" Said Constable Kindly.

Hettie's instructions evaporated in fear. Laura looked to Sarah for guidance, only to find her memory similarly parched.

"Please, Officer, my poor mother...."

"I'm sorry Miss, but we have to check. Where did you say, Miss?"

Laura walked in a daze, each paving slab a step to the scaffold. What would her father say? Richard? The Bowdens? Damn Sarah. What on earth had possessed her to give her real address? She hadn't said what number in London Road, but they'd find out soon enough. Hettie's instructions had come back to her in a flash, Dempster Street, 87 Dempster Street, home of the real Mrs. Beckwith, but by then Sarah had opened her big mouth.

She looked at her friend and immediately felt remorse. Sarah had wanted no part in this. Now here she was, in it up to her neck, struggling to keep her mother's skirt from falling round her ankles.

Laura dared not glance at the Square. Was the banner still there?

A milk cart rattled in the distance, a whistler brought Clayman and the willow to mind. What price her daring now?

A dray was replenishing the cellars of South Street; she felt the eyes of the leather aproned hauliers upon her.

"Nice cop, Constable. Nice to know we can sleep safe in our beds."

"Masters at disguise, them Germans. Wouldn't mind catching one of them myself."

"Button it, you two," Gruff growled.

The call came halfway down the High Street.

"We've got her, Fred! It was that Jameson woman. Paint on her skirt, the works."

Laura's heart sank with all hands.

"Like this you mean?" Gruff cried, holding Hettie's coat aloft. "She dumped it in the Cathedral. These two saw her do it."

"You'd better bring it along, though it don't make much odds, she's copped to everything," the messenger called back.

Laura grasped the situation in an instant. "Does that mean we can go, officer?"

She turned all her vulnerability on constable Kindly. "I'm thinking of our mother, well, you can imagine; and even if it was whoever that man said, I didn't see her clearly enough to be of any use."

"What do you think Fred?"

Constable Gruff shrugged. "Suppose name and address'll do for now, just in case. I'm going back with the coat."

Sarah had already told the officers 'London Road'; a false house number was easily given, though it took a panic attack to remember their fictitious name.

"Well, that seems to be about it, ladies," Constable Kindly said, pocketing his notebook. "Might as well see you safely home. Can't be too careful nowadays, some odd types about, especially at this time of the morning."

"Oh, really there's no need, constable."

"It's no trouble, Miss."

He'd walked them past the hospital and into London Road, before Laura's last ditch appeal, 'for our mother's sake,' finally persuaded him. "It's just down there."

"Of course, Miss."

They were home and dry, or so Laura thought, until Sarah's vengefulness filled her with horror.

"Please tell that Jameson woman that I hope they lock her up and throw away the key. It's no more than she deserves."

The constable stopped. "So you know her, then?"

Laura's glare was met with defiance.

"I should..."

"Oh, not personally," Laura cut in. "Our father's always saying what a nuisance she is. That's all. She lives up the street. Anyway, it's nothing to do with us. Thank you again for seeing us home, constable, good night."

Taking Sarah's arm, she hurried her away.

- CHAPTER FIFTEEN -

Camp exorcised Richard's stress-induced summer cold and he returned not only intact, but in uniform, promoted Sergeant, the highest rank attainable by a cadet. He'd also been allowed two shots with a long barrelled Lee Enfield. The cadets had been lucky to fire a rifle at all, some men had gone to war with only five shots under their belts. The unexpected recoil had sent his first attempt wildly astray, while his second had hit the target a bruised shoulder left of centre. Nevertheless, it had been a rewarding two weeks, a distraction from the familial anxieties that resurfaced to mar his train-trip home. He was a true boy when it came to trains, but, as the engine pulled into Elmsford, the romance of steam evaporated in apprehension.

Waiting on the platform, Laura was also on tenterhooks. Hettie's paint had proved effective and the banner had survived long enough to make the local Chronicle's front page. Only the dependence of a daughter had saved Hettie from gaol. Sarah had been summoned to attend the hearing. In school uniform, hair pigtailed, and going boss eyed behind pebble glasses, she'd had a heart stopping moment outside the courtroom when Constable Gruff had walked by, but she'd got away with it. Even so, Laura dreaded a similar encounter.

Yet, at this first sight of Richard in uniform, that fear was as nothing. Had the Army claimed him? She flew into his arms, oblivious of his embarrassment.

"Down the steps, at the double! Form up in the forecourt, column of four!"

There was no time for explanations. Desolately Laura wheeled her bicycle in discipline's wake, peering through the Grammar gates, while the cadets paraded before their headmaster, all the while telling herself that Richard couldn't be in the Army, that he would have had to have volunteered and he'd promised he wouldn't, and, anyway, he was too young; they couldn't take him, they just couldn't.

Three cheers interrupted her paranoia. The boys were dismissed. Her eyes followed him to the bike sheds, then watched the entrance for what seemed an eternity, until he emerged in school cap and blazer. Her relief was palpable.

"Sorry I was so long," he said. "I thought I'd better change for mother's sake. She'd go berserk if she saw me in uniform."

"Never mind your mother, what about me? You nearly gave me a heart attack. I thought you'd joined up. You haven't have you?"

"Of course, not. You are silly sometimes."

"But the uniform?"

"Oh, I've just been promoted, that's all. I'm still a cadet, just a bossy one. Come on, I've got some spare pocket money, I'll treat you to tea."

Over sparsely buttered scones, they exchanged the vagaries of camp life and the Sunday school outing.

"It was a real hoot," Laura told him, "especially at the boating lake. And you'll never guess what; I stayed at Sarah's one night and her mother got arrested."

She'd rehearsed her lines over and over. It was same story she'd told her father, of how she and Sarah had been tucked up in bed, oblivious of the goings on, until they'd woken next morning to find Hettie's bed hadn't been slept in. She was pretty certain her father had swallowed it, although he'd still banned her from having anything to do with either Jameson.

"It's a bit harsh, especially on Sarah; I'm the only friend she's got."

"He's probably right, though. You don't want to get tarred with the same brush," Richard took the bait.

There had been no word of George. Laura reached across the table.

"Let's pray he's all right."

They took the Mill track home, pausing by the willow to remember the risks they'd taken. A dragonfly zipped across the water; a beautifully marked kingfisher scanned the undercurrent for its afternoon snack.

"I wish it were raining," he told her.

"Ah, but you haven't got your pad," she teased him. "Seriously, darling, do you think they will bring in conscription?"

"Hopefully not. Even if they do, I've still got another year, yet; even Chapman thinks it can't last that long, purely on economic grounds."

"But what if he's wrong?"

"We'll just have to see."

"You could always take religious orders and lock yourself away in a monastery or something."

"But then I wouldn't see you. Simpler if I just hide under your bed, or in it."

Laura squirmed at the thought.

"Really, Richard Bowden, sometimes I'm sure that's all you think about!"

Smugly, she mounted her bike. With Hettie Jameson's message still coursing through her veins, his guaranteed survival was once more Laura's prime concern. His life was more precious than any sense of shame, she told herself, although, just a few months earlier, her theory had hardly withstood the test.

"Come on. Your mother will be going frantic."

At the Bowdens' house, far from frantic, they found Beatrice in euphoric mood. Elizabeth had had news. George was alive, a prisoner in northern Belgium. Notification in hand, she'd grabbed the children and rushed to Arthur in his yard and then on to Beatrice, who'd immediately sent her back to the village to buy cans of George's favourite things for a food parcel, while she made him a fruit cake and a meat pie. If she wrapped them well, they should keep.

That night Arthur broke out the remains of the Christmas brandy. However long the war lasted, one day George would come home. For the Bowdens, it was the happiest night of the War. In Beatrice's case, it needed to be; the following morning Arthur would find himself faced with a five pound fine for the errant date of birth entered for Richard on the family's National Registration form.

With the warmth of Richard's parting kiss on her lips, Laura lay wide-awake, longing to see him as he had seen her, to sleep in his arms, to wake beside him. Most of all, in her rose scented Utopia, she wanted his baby.

But it was a future that this first sight of him in uniform suddenly and materially threatened. The comforting buffer of years had all too soon become only months. What if the war wasn't over by next spring? Until today, it had seemed inconceivable that he would go, that they could be anything other than fate's favoured children. Now that confidence had been fundamentally shaken.

She'd heard that true belief could work miracles; now she was learning that the faintest doubt holes its cast iron forever. No matter what plug she forged, drip by drip faith's power drained into the trough of a new reality.

Had she, at that moment, been able to sink into his arms, her faith may have been restored. But that contentment was a dream away, a dream which the war's ever lengthening shadow was carrying into oblivion.

She woke next morning with a new sense of purpose. However, by the time her father came down to breakfast, the sum total of two hours' strategic thought was an ill temper aided and abetted by her monthly curse. For a whole week fate teased her before, by way of recompense, playing the fool.

With troops now stationed in the area, many villagers had taken to locking their doors when they left the house, and the Bowdens were no exception, which is how a bedraggled Richard came to arrive on Laura's doorstep one morning, locked out.

Bowden and Son had been re-plumbing a riverside property. With the pump cut off, Richard had gone to the river to fetch water for the cement. Crouched like a frog on the precipitous bank, he had dangled the bucket in the water then hauled it in; its counterweight had done the rest.

He'd trudged home, taking every duck and dive possible, only to find himself face to face with Mrs. 'Po face' Beasley, ambling along the heavily nettled, briar protected path that any lesser mortal than Morton Stanley would have avoided like the plague. What she was doing there even God could only guess.

"Oh, you're all wet young Richard," she observed, eyes gleaming with gossip worthiness. "Looks like you fell in the river."

"It does, rather," he smiled over gritted teeth.

"Tch, well there's a thing. Does your mother know?"

"No doubt the entire village will by sunset."

It was hardly subtle. It hit Mrs. B. right between the eyes that hardened on impact.

"Here, you're dripping all over the path. I've got to walk through there. It's bad enough as it is without you making a bog of it."

Given Newton's law, he wasn't sure where else he was going to drip. His temper frayed.

101

"Yes, I'm afraid I've left the whole of Ashleigh underwater; you'd best go round Eastleigh way."

"Pah! Facetious young pup! Children today. You wait 'till your mother hears about this, she'll soon wipe that smirk off your face."

"I'm sorry, I didn't mean to cause offence," he apologised in jowl-glowing indignation at his demotion to child.

"Ah, bit different now, isn't it? Taste of the strap, that's what you need young man." The scowling Beasley barged past. "You should show more respect to your elders. If that's what education does for you, I'm glad I ain't got none. Should've been our Tom; I said so from the start." The jealousy of years brandished its resentment. "At least he minds his manners, which is more than can be said for you!"

Richard was left dumbfounded. It had never occurred to him that anyone harboured a grudge over his scholarship. And where on earth had the old hag picked up 'facetious'?

"Bah, silly old faggot."

"Richard, what on earth happened to you? You're soaking!" Laura didn't wait for an answer. "Look, you'd better come round the back." As much as she loved him, she couldn't allow him to flood the hall.

In the kitchen she ordered him out of his wet things while she fetched a towel and some of her father's clothes. When she returned, only his socks lay in a pool on the tiled floor.

She handed him the towel, commiserating while he vigorously rubbed his matted hair, then ran his fingers through to restore a soupçon of vanity.

The moment came.

"If you stand there like that much longer you'll catch pneumonia."

He reached out for the clothes.

"You can hardly put them on over the top, Richard."

"No, I suppose not."

Bashfully he divested himself of his sopping shirt and vest. Their replacements remained in Laura's grasp.

"Let me see you."

He paled; his stomach visibly tightened.

"You are seeing me."

"You know."

"You can if you want, but I'm not exactly an artist's dream."

"Let me be the judge of that," she grinned softly. "Besides, it's only fair."

"It's hardly the same."

"Richard, please."

She'd left him no room for manoeuvre. Hesitantly, awkwardly, he unfastened his trousers.

"I can't. It's not the same for men. I'm not in a suitable condition," he blurted.

"Richard!"

Bashfully, he peeled down his trousers and pants to expose his complete embarrassment.

But how beautiful he was. She'd heard men were ugly. It wasn't true. She absorbed his shoulders, his lightly muscled chest, his smooth, hard stomach, his masculine legs and proud genitalia. Yes, he was truly, Byronly, beautiful.

Tilting her head, she enticed him onto her lips. His hands sought. She moaned provocatively, indenting his back with eager encouragement. His heartbeat against hers was electrifying, his hardness against her stomach magnetic, the power that pulsed in her palm astounding. She immersed herself in how it would feel inside her, how it would ever fit inside her, and then the pulse surged and his mouth crushed hers so hard she thought she would suffocate.

"I'm sorry; I'm so sorry," he breathed in her ear.

It was almost a sob. She didn't understand. Fervently she kissed his face; "it's all right, it's all right." Then her hand brushed the truth and her eyes widened in wonder. It took all her willpower not to look.

"It's what's supposed to happen."

"But your dress."

"Dresses can be washed." 'Besides it's a skirt,' she smiled smugly to herself, basking in the proven power of her attraction.

The wonder still lingered that afternoon, when Laura wrung out her skirt over the kitchen sink. She had seen the seed of life. The girls at school had talked endlessly about it, about what it looked like; now she knew.

Through the window the garden was sunlit. The birds were singing, the insects buzzing about her father's flowerbeds. How she yearned to be under the willow, to feel the warm sun on her shoulders, the breeze against her skin. This end of the garden wasn't overlooked; the empty fields stretched away to the horizon; the road was quiet. Dare she?

Fear fostered bravura, bravura the challenge. Nerve tight fingers unhooked her catches. She inched open the door. All remained clear. Tremulously, she stepped out of her clothing and into daring's fulfilment, luxuriating in being, once more, at one with nature, naked under the sun, naked to the wind, naked under the clear blue sky. One day she and Richard would make love like this, she promised herself, nothing could be more perfect.

- CHAPTER SIXTEEN -

For the remainder of the holiday Richard helped his father convert the Hollands' surplus bedroom into a bathroom, a luxury only the manor, the doctor's house and the vicarage had previously boasted. The boiler would be serviced by a hand pump in the garden, connected to the house by piping. Bowden had repaired such systems before, but never installed one. Richard researched the latest developments and helped draw up the plans. At drainage Bowden was a past master.

After two weeks of toil, the bath was brought in the supplier's new motor van. With their best horses requisitioned by the Army, many of Elmsford's tradesmen had motorised. Even Truelove, the village Baker, was giving up his nag in favour of the 'infernal combustion engine,' as Richard's grandfather still called it. Truelove's ancient assistant was to be the driver, much to the community's consternation. Old Agnew had proved himself something of a liability with the horse and cart; heaven only knew what dangers lay ahead when he was let loose with an automobile. Delivery had been promised by September. The villagers waited in trepidation.

In the middle of August two more village boys were posted 'missing, believed killed.' Word also came of the departure of an Essex Battalion for the Dardanelles, among its officers, Squire Stafford's son.

* * * * *

"Warsovie befallen! Warsovie befallen!"

"What the hell's up with them?" George Bowden wondered, wiping the grimy prison pane with his sleeve. "You don't reckon it's over, do you?"

"Nah," Sarson assured him from the next bed. "Probably found a cure for the pox, or the Kaiser's fucking haemorrhoids. Here, Loughy, you've got an inkling; what are they on about?"

"From what I can make out, they've taken Warsaw."

"Walsall? That's in fucking England, init?"

"No, this one's in Russia or some bloody place, Poland, I think."

"Poland? Christ, with a name like that they're welcome to it; sounds like a right shit hole," George remarked.

"Well that's rich coming from a bloke who's had his hand up more flues than Oscar fucking Wilde," Sarson wisecracked. "Call yourself a bloody turd burglar; you want to get across that parade ground, mate, and sort out that fucking cesspit; bloody thing stinks to high heaven. It's a wonder we ain't all caught rabies."

"Shows how much you know. You get rabies from rats."

"So? The buggers can jump, can't they?"

"Run a mile, more like, with your bloody arsehole hovering over their heads," Lough grinned.

"Least they could put something round it. Making us perch like that in front of them women, and us shitting our guts out like a load of fucking cattle at bleeding Smithfield, it's fucking disgusting," Sarson grumbled. "Filthy fucking bastards."

Dysentery was rife, its stench awful and unremitting. At night the sick bay was awash with it when the single latrine bucket overflowed. Still George preferred using the pail to the pole, a degradation he would risk fouling himself to avoid, even if the women working in the fields did affect merciful disinterest. He clenched his sphincter and changed the subject.

"Actually, my mate got bitten by a rat. Got in his pack. Almost had his finger off. Trigger finger it was, too. Pulled it back before he realised, silly sod, otherwise he'd've been well out of it. Rat'd scarpered before he got the gumption to stuff it back in."

"Bit like our old cook," Lough told them. "Chopped half his bloody hand off when they told him he was for the firing line. Scared shitless, he was, silly bugger."

"It's a wonder he didn't face a firing squad," George said.

"Couldn't prove it, see. I mean, how many butchers do you know with a full set of five? Mind you, if the Brass Hats had tasted his cooking they'd've shot him for sure. Nigh on poisoned the whole bloody Company, what with his rat bloody stew. Said it was rabbit. 'Not with a tail like that it ain't,' I told him."

"Cor, what I wouldn't give for a decent bit of stew," Sarson savoured the memory. "Pity about that pie of yours, George."

Beatrice's meat pie hadn't survived the journey. George had ripped the packaging apart to find it, 'higher than a pigeon with piles,' as Sarson had put it. The fruitcake had fared better. The tins had lasted a day, the peaches going to the guard for the loan of his jack-knife.

"Must've been the kidney," George groaned regretfully. "Still, with them so happy, maybe we'll get a bit of meat today."

"Only chance of that's if the cow jumped over the fucking moon and you jumped after it, cleaver in hand, which, with your fucking leg, would be a bit of a minor miracle."

"Just sharpen that cleaver," George laughed, happy that he could laugh. If instinct hadn't spun him on his axis, the bayonet thrust at him in the German trench would have plunged into his stomach instead of his thigh.

Even so, things had been touch and go. He'd been dumped in a schoolhouse with a hundred others and left for days without food or water. By the time the order had come to march to a transit camp, his leg had swollen to elephantine proportions. His comrades had carried him most of the way, a five day hike on empty stomachs. And still the wound had been ignored. The only treatment he'd had was the field dressing he'd applied himself. One after another, he'd watched similar cases go gangrenous. When, finally, the doctor had seen him, it hadn't been a moment too soon.

"A bit of proper cabbage would do," Sarson said. "Instead of all this sauer-fucking-crap they keep dishing up. Might even plug up the old bung hole for a day or two."

"Sauerkraut is cabbage," Lough told him.

"Well, you could've fooled me; thought it was fucking wood shavings. What do they do, piss on it?"

It was a marination too near the truth for George to contemplate. "How come you speak German then, Loughy?"

"My granddad taught me. Came from Hamburg; he was a sailor, see. Met my nan in the Albert docks and ended up living in Bethnal Green."

"Christ, he must've been desperate," Sarson cackled.

"Do you mind, that's my family you're talking about," Lough protested.

"I meant Bethnal Green."

"Well, it's better than bloody Bermondsey. There's nothing wrong with Bethnal Green what a bulldozer wouldn't cure. Best housing in London, according to old Peabody, ain't that right, George?"

"Dah, no use asking him. Built half the bloody borough and he's never heard of the fucker, have you Georgie boy?" Sarson ribbed him.

"Can't say as I have."

"That's 'cause you're a cowpat, see. Still, it's better than being a fucking Froggie. Why we teamed up with them fuckers I'll never know. Call 'emselves cooks. Christ, there was a bugger back in Funky Villas what couldn't even fry a fucking egg. All runny on the top, it was, and crusty as me old granny's knickers on the bottom, fucking thing. I told him straight, 'if you can't cook a proper egg, don't cook one at all, one arm or no fucking arms."

"Tell you what, though. It's a bloody good job my old granddad changed his name and took my grandma's," Lough continued. "The old baker in the next street had his shop burned down from under him, when war was declared, and he'd been there half a century. Nice old bugger, too, he was, from Vienna originally. Lost everything and no one lifted a finger, not even the bloody Fire Brigade. Lucky to get out alive."

"It's a wonder they ain't done the same to Buckingham Palace," George aired his eavesdropping on the origins of English royalty.

"Do what?" Sarson rose to the bait.

"German through and through, our royal family."

"What are you on about, Bowden? Course they're bloody not. They're descended from Queen Victoria."

"And what was she, if she weren't German? Had been for centuries, her lot. Even the present Queen was Princess of Tek before she was wed, and if that ain't German I don't know what is. One of them Georges couldn't even speak English."

"And there's another one here speaking a right load of bollocks. Christ, what are you, Bowden, Oliver fucking Cromwell risen from the dead? If what you say was true, old Squiffy would've locked 'em up for the duration."

"Ah, but he's sworn to secrecy, see; they all are."

"Oh yes, George, right, George. Well, you obviously didn't take the oath, did you."

"You may laugh."

"Too bloody right," Sarson dug his heels in. "English to the bone, our royal family, salt of the earth."

"Well even you must know that Albert was German; and he's the present King's father."

"Grandfather, mate, grandfather, just like Loughy's, and he's as English as they come."

"That's different."

"No it's not. Now if you was talking about that Battenberg bloke, I might agree with you. How they ever put him in charge of our navy, I'll never know. But, as for the rest, you're talking out of your arse. Here, come on, Loughy, you've stood guard at the old palace often enough, tell him," Sarson appealed for Lough's Coldstream support.

"Freezing me bollocks off in a sentry box hardly makes me privy to their innermost secrets, but, as it happens, I do know a bit about it. My old man was a right one for royalty; got a map of all the crown heads of Europe stuck on the wall; made us learn them off by heart, god rest his soul."

"So?"

"Well, truth be told, George ain't far from wrong. They're all connected, one way or another. Queen Victoria was descended from the Hanoverians on her father's side and the Saxe-Coburgs on her mother's; she married Albert, who was a cousin on her mother's side, and so on and so forth. The only one what ain't been German is Queen Alexandra, who was Danish, if memory serves me right. Actually, if old Victoria had stopped at one, Kaiser Bill would have been our next in line, his mother being her first born. Wouldn't have been no war, then; either that or we'd have been fighting for the other side. Makes you think, don't it?"

"Christ," Sarson cried, "it's a bloody conspiracy!"

- CHAPTER SEVENTEEN -

August 17th. had been a busy plumbing day for Bowden and Son. How Richard wished they had a bathroom of their own; he would have liked nothing better than to relax in a nice hot tub instead of making do with a wash-down in the sink. Having wolfed down his cottage pie, he wandered along the lane to spend the evening with Scott and Laura.

Scott had said he might be late, but as seven stretched to eight and his cold salad withered in the pantry, Laura began to worry. Eight became nine, nine nine-thirty. The lovers went into the lane, searching the fading light for the pinprick glimmer of Scott's cycle lamp. The minutes ticked by; they kept their vigil; then Richard heard a dull rumble he couldn't place, until the gears were re-engaged and the truth thunder-clapped through the clouds.

"Good grief, it's a Zeppelin."

He scanned the sky, but saw nothing until the breaking moon caught the long, panatela shaped airship over to his left.

"There it is! It seems to be circling."

"Look, Richard, over there."

Across the valley someone was driving hell for leather towards Elmsford on full beam.

"What an idiot," Richard seethed, turning his attention back to the airship.

Again, the clouds obscured his view. The throbbing engines picked up a gear, roared to a crescendo, then began to fade.

"It seems to be moving. It must be following the car."

'BANG!'

The galvanised bath rattled against the outhouse wall with the force of the explosion.

"Richard? Laura?" It was the boy's mother. "Thank God you're alright!"

His father was close behind. "That'll show them buggers what moan on about the blackout. Pardon my French. Where's your dad?"

"He hasn't come home," Laura told him. "I'm so worried."

"What do you think it was, dear?" Beatrice asked.

"Your guess is as good as mine. Look, you stay here with young Laura, mother. I'll go down the road aways. Maybe he's had a puncture or something."

"I'm coming, too," Richard said determinedly.

"Do be careful, Arthur!"

Bowden and son fetched their pushbikes and set off along the back road, two whitewashed cycle lamps and memory their only guides to the ruts and potholes. On reaching the highway they rode side by side, widening their field of vision, until an agitated Amos Harris, on special constable duty, called them to a halt at the parish boundary.

"Oh, it's you Arthur," he sighed relievedly. "Thought you was another one of them blooming motors. Who's that with you?"

"It's the boy," Bowden identified the bough-shadowed phantom. "You haven't seen Scott come past this way, have you?"

"Scott? Can't say I have. Just some bloody lunatic in a car, lights full on, driving like his tail was afire. I waved him down, but he drove straight through me. Scared the life out of me, he did. Just before them Zeppelins came over. Reckon it weren't no coincidence. I rang through to Elmsford on that old catraption there and reported him. Must have been a spy, they reckon, showing them buggers the way. Reckon I was lucky, he could as like as made a hand of me. I'd take care, if you're going up there, don't know what might be lurking."

"Maybe you'd better stay with Amos, boy," Bowden suggested.

"Not likely," Richard told him. "Besides, I ride this road every day; I probably know it better than you."

Still the boy's lips dried to parchment as they pedalled through a blacked out Hayfield. A mile from town, he caught sight of a murky figure.

"Mr. Scott, is that you?"

"Who's that?"

The voice was unmistakable.

"It's Richard," the boy answered. "My father's with me."

Scott wheeled his crumpled bike into view. "Some ruddy fool ran me down."

"You weren't the only one," Bowden commiserated. "He nearly had Amos Harris and all. You hurt?"

"Oh, scratches and bruises, nothing serious, but he's well and truly put paid to my bike. The sooner I get a car the better. Did you see the Zeppelin?"

"Yeh, following the motor, they reckon," Arthur said.

"Wouldn't surprise me; damned near blinded me with his headlights. I think they dropped something over by the factories; there was one hell of a bang."

"We heard it from home," Richard confirmed.

"Oh this is useless. I don't know why I'm bothering." Scott rattled his mangled spokes.

"You was bloody lucky, if you ask me, state of that," Bowden told him. "He must've run right over you."

"Actually it was a tree that did the damage. I rode headlong into it trying to avoid him."

"I'd dump it, if I was you. You'll never ride that again."

"Never a truer word, Arthur. Oh well, it was a good bike while it lasted." Scott hauled the buckled frame into the ditch. "Daresay some rag and bone man'll find a use for it."

"Make a shell out of it and give them buggers a dose of their own medicine," Bowden grumbled, unbuckling his saddlebag from the carrier. "Here, you take Richard's bike. You hop on the back of mine, boy, and mind your feet in the wheel."

The full story emerged over the following days, relegating the latest bulletins on the

'Brides in the Bath' murder trial, then in progress at the Old Bailey, to the village's verbal inside pages. The Zeppelin had dropped two bombs on Elmsford, the first landing by the ballbearings works, leaving a sizeable crater in the adjacent waste ground, the second smashing through a two storey house to lodge itself, unexploded, in the parlour floorboards, missing a sleeping child by a whisker. More bombs were said to have hit the outskirts of London, although nothing appeared in the papers.

"Keeping it quiet, ain't they; don't want the old Hun to know how close he came," Kipper Johnson confirmed.

"Pity the buggers didn't carry on and drop a parcel on them silly pillocks in Parliament," Amos Harris commented wryly.

The riddle of the speeding car was never solved. Vehicle and occupants, person or persons unknown, had disappeared without trace. Scott's reference to owning a car, however, proved more substantive. He'd clinched an order to supply hut sections to the army, the previous month. His reward had been a directorship and a suitable rise in salary. He'd been late that night due to some rudimentary driving lessons.

The following weekend he gladly suffered the indignity of wobbling into Elmsford on Laura's bike to drive home in a smart, second hand tourer of his own. Heads turned as he pootled proudly through the village. Harold Scott was coming up in the world.

* * * * *

By September, the forthcoming British offensive was common gossip.

"Christ, if Uncle Tom Cobley knows about it, surely the bloody Kaiser must do, and all? The next thing you know they'll be putting the whole caboodle in the paper, dates, times, everything old Jerry needs to know," Bowden moaned, turning the pages of the Star over his bread and cheese.

"You shouldn't read at the table, Arthur. It's not manners," Beatrice reminded him.

"What? Oh, right dear," he read on regardless. "Bloody hell, says here that Marie Lloyd and that lot was making three hundred quid a week before the War."

"Must be a mistake, dear. Thirty, maybe, but not three hundred, not even the King gets that. And do mind your language."

"Well, that's what it says here. Down to eighty, now, apparently. Still more than most of us makes in a year, two for some. I should've been on the boards, your old dad always said so, 'specially when I toppled that old lavender cart of his over the garden path that summer. Do you remember that?"

"Must've been thirty years ago, Arthur."

"Yeh, suppose it was. Talk about fun and games. Must've been nigh on six months' worth. I'll never forget your old mum's face, when he shovelled the lot over her prize petunias with the Vicar standing there."

"Yes, Arthur," Beatrice grimaced, reading 'Zeppelins; the Star's £8,500 free Life Insurance Fund' and 'Free compensation for Zeppelin damage,' from the folded front page and wondering what she'd get for the yard and Arthur in it. "I'm sure we don't need reminding. Are you going to eat that pickled onion?"

"No."

"I'll put it back in the jar, then."

"Best blooms she ever had; won prizes, they did. Oh well," Arthur returned to the stage. "I bet there's plenty of poor blighters over yonder what'd gladly swop what they're in for for a bit of clodhopping at the Hippodrome."

"Let's just hope there's an end to it this time," Beatrice prayed.

* * * * *

September became October; the battle of Loos played itself out, the British turning their first use of gas on themselves instead of the enemy in a classic case of blind, against the wind, obedience. By the middle of the month fifty thousand had fallen.

At home the locust of dismissal visited by Lady Alice upon Cyril Tate turned into a plague as the area's landowners followed the example of the Prudential and other big City firms, by firing all men of enlistment age into the path of Lord Derby's recruiting drive.

As October progressed, many of those who had responded to Kitchener's call the previous year were given leave. So far, only the first one hundred thousand 'K's had seen active service; the majority's turn to take the test to destruction was still nine months away. Paradoxically, many who had taken the King's Shilling after them and been drafted into Regular or Territorial battalions, had already seen action; some were already dead. Now the final 'class of '15' were being prepared for the slaughter, their number boosted by the recent sackings.

Scott was forty-two, Bowden in his fifties. But Scott, despite his traumatic life with Marian, looked younger than his years. He hadn't completely dismissed the idea of remarrying. Both professionally and socially, his confidence had enjoyed a considerable boost recently, but first he would have to find the right woman, and he had scant time for that.

'Perhaps, when this beastly war is over,' he contemplated the future, before Marian's astral accusations corrupted further fantasy.

In November the Rayntree munitions works installed new, easier to operate machinery, taking on a predominately female workforce, among them girls of superior social status keen to 'do their bit' while the men they displaced were taken for cannon fodder. Whatever deference they expected, they would find TNT no respecter of class distinction; their washing water would turn as blood red, and their skin as canary yellow, as that of their common workmates.

Winter set in, mild as it was; even the flies returned to buzz about in the unusual clemency. By the end of the month, Lord Derby's recruiting drive had ended in failure. In early December all able-bodied men were required to take a medical, whether enlisting or not. The farm lads had got their way. It was the prelude to conscription.

- CHAPTER EIGHTEEN -

Friday December 10th, 1915:

'On Saturday last, the County Ground witnessed one of the most thrilling climaxes to the school soccer season in some years, when Elmsford and Brentfield Grammars contested the Tindal Cup,' Scott read from the Elmsford Chronicle. 'Kicking off in difficult conditions...'

"Actually it was like Merdon mudflats," Richard told him.

'... Elmsford sustained an early setback when their centre forward was forced to leave the field...'

"That's bruiser Bates; he was knocked senseless."

'... Mindless of the weight of the waterlogged ball and the added impetus of the trajectory, he attempted a header...'

"He didn't 'attempt a header' at all; not even Bruiser's that stupid. He went to trap it and got shoved in the back. It landed on his bonce like a spongy cannonball."

'... He played bravely on...'

"Staggering about like a poleaxed ox..."

'... until a mishap in the Elmsford penalty area led to Brentfield scoring...'

"It was from a corner. Diggers went up to catch it and Bruiser barged him into the back of the net, thinking he was up the other end. That's when Igor took him off."

'Despite the disparity, the ten men of Elmsford resisted stubbornly, and, as the game progressed, began to gain the upper hand...'

"All thanks to Igor's cross-country running. We hated it at the time, but it paid dividends in the end."

'With fifteen minutes to go, a cross-field ball found the Elmsford inside left...'

"That's me."

'.... unmarked in the Brentfield penalty area.'

"I was completely surrounded."

'... A clever chip found the net...'

"Well at least he's got that right."

'Soon after, the return of Elmsford's centre forward sealed Brentfield's fate, again with the assistance of Elmsford's inside right...'

"Left! Who wrote this?"

'... who, finding a firmer footing down the flank, ran the entire length of the pitch before crossing for the centre forward to

112

side-foot home.'

"It hardly tells the story. You should have seen old Bruiser, charging down the middle, scattering clods like a raging bull. I have to admit, it wasn't the best of crosses. If the mud hadn't held it up the ball would have gone straight to the goalie. As it was the two of them collided head on, Bruiser poked out a boot and it dribbled over the goal line. I don't know how he stayed upright, I really don't; cracked half his teeth; his mouth was a real mess."

"Well, well done, that man, and well done this man, too," Scott clapped Richard on the shoulder.

* * * * *

Beatrice started at the apparition pressed against the windowpane, then cowered as the shading hand lifted, allowing the sunlight to pour into the temple's deep indentation. The spectre moved on. The rap was no louder than that of a cigarette on its box. Beatrice hid behind the door, hoping he hadn't seen her. The rapping persisted.

"Who's there?"

The answer was barely audible.

She asked again more forcefully.

"It's Billy," the whisper raised itself to a croak.

"Billy? Billy who?"

"Billy White," the voice hissed urgently.

Billy White had gone off to war with George. His brother Herbert had been the first reported missing. Beatrice lifted the latch.

Billy's face was like a crudely restored tapestry, the eyes stepped, the left of glass, staring blankly from a ravine which seamed the cheek and lifted the upper lip into a sneer. Where the ear had been there was only a ragged remnant; the jacket's left shoulder sloped unsupported; no hand protruded from the left sleeve.

"Billy?" Beatrice fought desperately to contain her revulsion.

"Ssshhh!" Billy warned, lifting a finger to his lips. "You gotta speak soft in case they hear."

"In case who hears, Billy?"

"Them Germans, of course." Billy looked furtively round. For all its disfigurement, his face was that of a child.

"But there's no Germans here, dear."

"They don't have to be near. They can hear for miles. Is your George in?"

"George? No dear, he went off to the war with you; don't you remember?"

"Oh." Billy looked puzzled. "I thought he'd be home by now. Charlie ain't there, neither. Are they hiding, d' you think, like our Herbert?"

"No, dear, George is a prisoner," Beatrice sniffed, looking away.

"You mean the Germans've got him? Oh, that's not good. I'd better go and fetch him back. Can't leave him with them, rough lot them Germans, there's no telling what they might do to him. Which way did they go?"

Beatrice couldn't hold back her tears.

113

"Now, don't you fret none, Mrs. B, they can't've gone far. Did they take him to the village, do you think?"

"Yes, Billy," Beatrice sobbed. "I expect that's it. Perhaps you should ask Constable Johnson, he might know."

"Oh, don't wanna do that," Billy shook his head. "George might be in trouble."

"He's not in any trouble, Billy. I'm sure you should."

"Nah. I'll fetch him back, Missus, you leave it to me."

* * * * *

While Bruiser Bates was suffering the dentist's drill, Sir John French, Commander in Chief of the British Expeditionary Force, was scoring an own goal of his own.

"Heard the latest, Harold? French is resigning. It's all hush-hush, of course, but he's going for sure; Loos was the last straw."

Scott closed the door to Colonel Simpson's office.

"But that despatch of his in the Times placed the blame squarely on Haig's shoulders. Surely, if anyone's to go, it should be him, after all, it was his show. The way it read, French bent over backwards to lend him support."

"Do take a seat. Well, that's just it; apparently he didn't. According to Haig, far from releasing the reserves as stated, notwithstanding that they should have been under his control from the start, French actually withheld them at the critical moment, and when they did finally arrive on the scene, it was too late for them to be of any effect. Condemned to pointless slaughter, so the official report says, or words to that effect."

"But Haig must have known that when he committed them."

"There's the rub. If French had used his noddle, he could've hung, drawn and quartered him on that admission alone. Instead he's put his own head in the nose and handed Haig the lever. Well, let's face it, Haig's been angling for the top job all along. Given his connections, it was only a matter of time."

"Just how close is he to the King? One hears so many rumours."

"Very; his wife's a lady-in-waiting; they go riding together. In fact, it was his horse that threw his majesty, when he went over last October. You must have read about it, it was in all the newspapers. Highly embarrassing for Haig; that kind of thing can ruin one's chances. Archie, my nephew, said he'd never seen him in such a state. He's on his staff, you know, helps with his correspondence and what-have-you. He said Haig devoted more diary space to that than he did to the entire battle of Loos. Filled his private papers with it; wrote reams to his wife."

"Well, with all due respect, if his majesty's bruised backside means more to him than the needless slaughter of thousands, I can't say I'd be turning somersaults to serve under him."

"Well, there you are. I'd prefer Plumer, myself. Hamilton was always Kitchener's choice before this damn Dardenelles fiasco, though I don't suppose it makes much odds, whoever moves the pieces, the pawns will bear the brunt, it's the nature of the game."

- CHAPTER NINETEEN -

In the week before Christmas, Bowden tightened the last tap on Scott's new bath and stacked the boiler. Impressed by Holland's bathroom conversion, Scott had commissioned his own. By the time Richard went round that evening, the pipes were singing.

"If you two are going to go on about conscription all night, I'm going to bagsy first bath," Laura announced, reappearing an hour later in her dressing gown.

Richard could have warmed his hands on Scott's embarrassment.

"Your turn," she told her father, nonchalantly. "Shout when you're done and I'll make the Horlicks."

"You'll make more than that, young lady. You'll make yourself decent, and you'll do it now," Scott fumed.

"But I am decent."

"Well, I'm glad you think so. I'm sorry, Richard, but I must ask you to leave."

"Oh, really," Laura huffed.

"I'll see you out," Scott ignored her.

"Go round the back," Laura mouthed over her father's shoulder, clandestinely pointing the way.

The key was turned, the bolts rammed into place. Richard's stomach churned; conscience and apprehension shivering his spine. What on earth was she playing at? If her father caught him lingering by the back door there'd be hell to pay.

Still he followed his libido. Through the back window he could hear Scott scolding Laura's immodesty. Then all went quiet. Upstairs, a door slammed. He heard water being drawn, Scott cough.

The latch lifted, the door opened and Laura stood there, haloed in hob light. Her robe was loose, the invitation irresistible.

* * * * *

That Christmas Richard gave Laura a ring, a single sapphire he had been saving for since summer. It matched her eyes. It wasn't an official engagement, even the lovers knew that, but it was intent enough to cause Scott a sleepless night, as Marian's disgruntled ghost made its presence felt.

Had he been parentally negligent? He thought back over the years. That first summer after Marian's stroke had been the key. He'd been only too grateful to the Bowdens for taking Laura under their wing. He could hardly have left her on her own, and full time help had been simply unaffordable, he'd barely had enough to pay the cleaning woman. His only alternative, to send Laura back to smog-bound London to live with her grandparents, had been unthinkable.

But one summer had suddenly become a whole adolescence. Heaven only knew what miseries these past years would have held for the girl had her mother recovered, but, even so, shouldn't he have adopted at least a modicum of Marian's aloofness, made some sort of effort to substitute the Bowdens for people more socially suited? He'd had the connections, the Vicar had always been sympathetic, so why had he held back? Could he have been pandering to his own social insecurities to Laura's detriment?

He had to admit the possibility, but even if that were true of the intervening years, he suffered no such complex now. The most recent truth was simply that he'd been too preoccupied with work to consider the social benefits his elevation offered Laura. Was it not his duty, even so belatedly, to introduce her to her peers, to at least open her eyes to the alternatives, before it was too late?

But what was he saying? His own origins were hardly manorial, his education hardly Etonian. Richard's schooling and prospects, particularly in Elmsford's 'Old Elmsfordian' environs, easily matched his own, and socially, if he had cause for concern with the Bowdens, he could entertain no prospective embarrassment in Richard's case. Even with Arthur and Beatrice, the class gap had no fundamental meaning. There was no embarrassment in honesty, only in the fiction of social superiority; if Marian's megalomania had taught him anything, it was that. Besides, if it weren't for the War, he would still be an undermanager; a cut above maybe, but still way down the pack.

Yes, the War; he was no Jung or Freud, but wasn't that the crux of it, his fears for Laura's sanity should anything happen to Richard? As things stood, the boy was sure to be called. A broadening of Laura's social horizons might at least provide some sort of buffer should the worst befall. Unquestionably, he could not allow them to marry. There might be a child. Should Richard lose his life, or be crippled for life, what then?

But would the decision be his? He trusted the boy implicitly, but male restraint had its limits and he was seeing worrying signs in Laura, parading around in her dressing gown for one thing, and her association with that damnable Jameson woman for another. And even if she didn't take matters into her own hands, what if the war dragged on and on, would it be right to deprive them, or to ask them to deprive themselves, of love's fulfilment?

Such complex issues were, thankfully, not his immediate concern, but his daughter's rebellious streak most certainly was.

* * * * *

Soon after Christmas the doctor confined Laura to bed with a bad cold. On the first two days Mrs. Creswell, Scott's new daily, was there to fuss over her; by the third, she, too, had caught the infection and Laura was alone when Richard arrived. The bedroom fire glowed in the grate, the clock was on their side.

For the first time in their young lives they shared the love nest of a bed. Her thighs held him, her sex kissed his manhood, yet, even in their ecstasy, they kept to their covenant. How much more incredible would the ultimate union be? They had reached consummation's final milestone.

And so the dark descended, drawing December to a close. As the clock chimed in 1916, the families raised their glasses round the fire, but would dawn bring victorious peace, or were the violent winds that had battered the village for the last few days an omen, would it be a daybreak to disaster? It was no time for resolutions, only prayers.

- CHAPTER TWENTY -

January saw more men invalided home and on leave. These were franker about their experiences than their 'Old Contemptible' predecessors, telling tales so horrifying that some accused them of putting it on, things couldn't possibly be as bad as they said. Few expressed any eagerness to return to the fray, two ensuring their discharge by accidental discharges of their own, one into a hand and one into a foot.

"It was a complete accident. He was cleaning his ruddy rifle and it just went off," Tilly Seaton told Elizabeth. "Doctor says he might lose his hand; now he wouldn't do that on purpose, would he? Anyway, he's done his bit. They should make them others go, them lot skiving in the factories and what-have-you."

But even when 'them lot in the factories' were called, only a third would be found fit enough for front line service, forty one percent receiving the lowest classification, C3, thanks to childhood malnutrition in the world's richest country.

The villagers also griped about recent Government pleas to economise, particularly in light of the small fortune Prime Minister Asquith had lavished on his daughter's wedding the previous November. Village opinion was adamant; "if Asquith and his kind forked out just one tenth of what they've got stashed away, there'd be no need for economies."

In an effort to curb drunkenness, round-buying in pubs was outlawed, a decree which had Amos Harris up before the beak for treating his wife to a Port and Lemon in Elmsford's 'Dog and Gun'. It cost him a nine shilling fine; it could have cost him six months in gaol.

"Sorry state of affairs when you can't even buy your own missus a drink," Arthur Bowden complained to Kipper Johnson in the Barley Mow.

"Well something's got to be done, Arthur. Bloody factory workers are more drunk than sober. Never win the war at this rate."

"Halve their pay, that's what I'd do with 'em," Arthur Treadwell chipped in. "Can't spend what they haven't got. Christ, if I drank the way they do I'd be broke in a fortnight. Fill her up, Alf."

"Our worst enemy, drink, so Lloyd George reckons," Amos Crutchley added his sixpen'th. "Worse than them Germans and Austrians combined."

"Well he should know, the drunken git. I bet his missus don't buy her own, or whoever he happens to be canoodling at the time. And what about that bloody wedding? Old Squiffy have a barman there, did he, charging all and sundry? 'Here you are, Lady Asquith, that'll be one and six?' Dah, it's bloody ridiculous," Bowden moaned on.

"Ridiculous or not, it's the law, Arthur, and it's our job to uphold it," Johnson reminded him. "If the King can do without, so can we. Changing the subject, did I tell you about that Mrs. Ridley, from out Belsham way? Government sent her a telegram saying her husband was badly wounded in France and that they'd pay for her to go and see him. Told her to take the telegram to the nearest police station and they'd give her the money."

"I read something about that in the Daily News," Treadwell said.

"I thought you were a Mail man," Bowden queried, "conscription and all that."

"Well I was, but after what they said about Lord Kitchener, I had a change of heart."

"But the News is dead against conscription."

"So's the Star, and you still read it."

Where conscription was concerned, Bowden's head and heart pulled in opposite directions. "So this Mrs. what's-her-name, what happened, then?" He returned to Johnson's story.

"Well she turned up at the station. I didn't know nothing about it. So I checked with Elmsford and apparently it's right. Anyway, I didn't have no money, so I sent her there."

"And did they give it to her?"

"Oh yeh; and she went. Paid for somewhere to stay and everything. Mind you, her husband died soon after."

* * * * *

On January 27th, the Military Service Act was passed, conscripting all unmarried men between the ages of eighteen and forty one. A three week conscription period would come into force on February 10th. At the beginning of March the men would have to go. The poster offered each man two courses, but little option:

(1) He can **ENLIST AT ONCE** and join the colours without delay;

(2) He can **ATTEST AT ONCE UNDER THE GROUP SYSTEM** and be called up in due course with his group.

 If he does neither, a third course awaits him:

HE **WILL BE DEEMED TO HAVE ENLISTED**

Scott had escaped the cut by a year, although his widower status would have saved him until May, when married men would be included. John Wilkinson, whose family farmed the land to the north of the parish, was also exempted, having married in December; however, his twin brother, Albert, had been posted notice. Neither had volunteered previously, in deference to their father's wishes.

Joshua Wilkinson's property bordered the Manor, and the ownership of a four acre strip had long been disputed. His family had farmed it since the early eighteen hundreds, when it had been leased, in perpetuity, to his great-great-grandfather for dragging one of his Lordship's ancestors unconscious from a burning barn. However, no written agreement had ever existed. When his present Lordship had inherited the estate, the maps had been unrolled and the discrepancy discovered.

Discounting Wilkinson's story as 'unfounded folklore', his Lordship had ordered the original boundaries re-consolidated. But those were Joshua's most productive acres, to lose them in years of lean harvest would lead to hardship, whereas their loss to his Lordship's balance sheets would be paltry by comparison.

Battle had been joined. Joshua had torn down the new Manor fences and erected

119

his own, only to have them torn down in turn. Tit for tat reprisals had followed, until, one summer, the Estate had let Wilkinson plant the acres unhindered, only to plough the ripened wheat into the ground before it could be harvested. Court orders had been obtained; Wilkinson had ignored them and been heavily fined. Unable to pay, he had been sent to prison.

Already suffering from bronchitis, his wife had insisted on driving the trap through a bitter winter gale to visit him. Pleurisy had developed. With two weeks to serve, Wilkinson had begged for remission. It had been refused. Finally, the doctor's repeated pleas on the family's behalf secured Joshua's release two days early. With neither coat nor transport, he had walked the five miles home through a raging blizzard. He had been half-dead on arrival; his wife had passed away an hour before.

From that moment on, Joshua had hated the aristocracy and the establishment with a vengeance. As he saw it, the greed of one and the collusion of the other had robbed him of his wife and livelihood. Theirs was not his England. 'Those thieving bastards and them toadies what lick their boots,' were responsible for the war and they could fight it; neither he nor his sons would lift a finger in defence of a regime he detested. He had burned Albert's conscription papers and all the warnings regarding non-compliance that had fallen through the letterbox. Finally Kipper Johnson was ordered to take the boy.

Denying any such papers have been received, Joshua cursed and swore himself into an altercation, condemning Johnson as a traitor to his own kind and forcing him, broken lipped, from the door. Securing the bolts, he loaded his shotgun and awaited Kipper's reinforced return.

It came three days later. The Army had been called out, together with the village's Special Constabulary, Arthur Bowden amongst them. The Officer banged on the door, ordering Wilkinson to open up. He was answered from the bedroom window by Joshua's shotgun.

"I told you lot before, you ain't having him. Now get off my property."

"Don't be stupid, man," the Officer shouted up. "The boy has to come by law. He'll be back this afternoon, it's only a preliminary examination, but he has to come."

Arthur Bowden groaned. The authorities had picked the wrong man for the job; his demeanour and accent represented all that Joshua despised.

"And who's law might that be?" Wilkinson sneered. "I ain't giving him up to the likes of you. Go and get himself killed, while your kind sit on your backsides safe at home? You must think we're barmy. Stole my land and put me behind bars you may have, but you ain't making a hand of my boy like you did my missus, and that's a fact. Now get back in that bloody motor of yours and tell that to your bloody superiors."

"Don't be an ass, man. If you do not co-operate you will find yourself in serious trouble. I cannot leave here without your son. I have my orders. No one means him any harm, but he has to come. Hand him over now and no further action will be taken, I promise you."

"It'll be the end of him, that's for sure," Joshua cried. "I've heard all your promises afore; your kind foul the air with your promises. What about my land? We had the lord almighty's word on that and where did it get us? Oh, no, promises from you ain't worth a pig's fart. Now, if you don't get off my property, what's left of it, I'll blow your bloody head off, and that is a bloody promise."

Arthur saw Albert by his father's side. He knew the boy didn't want this, he'd told Arthur as much in the pub, and, judging by Joshua's annoyance, was saying the same again. Wilkinson pulled the window to.

"Just a bit of patience, that's all that's needed," Arthur murmured. "Let the boy talk him round."

But the officer's patience was at a premium.

"Wilkinson, we haven't got all day. Open up and let's put an end to this fiasco," he bellowed.

The window swung open again. Joshua levelled his gun. "I'll put an end to you if you don't bugger off. Tell him, Arthur, I mean what I say."

Arthur knew Joshua wasn't joking. It was time to speak.

"Josh, you won't right the wrongs of the past by killing anyone. Think of the boy. You don't want to see him in prison. Every man here's got a son out there doing his bit. It ain't right that Albert should let the others do all the fighting."

"So why ain't he over there, that pompous bastard, mouth so full of other people's plums he can't even speak proper. I got nothing against you and yours Arthur, if your boys want to go and get themselves killed that's their business, but my Albert ain't going and that's an end to it, not for you, not for him, not for the bloody king himself. It's their war, Arthur, they started it, let them go and fight it and good riddance to 'em, that's what I say, we'd be better off without them. Now clear off, the lot of you."

"Open the door, man," the Officer fumed. "If we have to break it down, I won't answer for the consequences."

"You'll answer, right enough," Joshua assured him. "You'll answer to him up there 'cause I'll blow you to bloody kingdom come."

"All right you men, break it down," the Officer ignored the threat.

Joshua cocked both barrels.

"This is madness," Arthur heard Albert cry. "I ain't gonna see you hang, dad, not on my account."

"Come back here. Do you hear me? Watch them John!"

Joshua abruptly left the window. Seconds later, a shotgun blast filled the air.

Arthur ducked, others dived for cover. Silence reigned, then John's voice cried from the door.

"I'm opening up, I'm opening up!"

Albert lay on the floor, his shirt ripped, his body bloody.

The men approached warily.

"For God's sake help him," John cried. "Dad came chasing after him and the bloody gun went off. He didn't mean to shoot him, I know he didn't."

Arthur climbed the stairs. Joshua was halfway up, motionless. The splintered banister rail confirmed John's story. Joshua had always been proud of his feather-light triggering.

"Give us the gun, Josh," he said softly.

There was no response. Carefully he eased the weapon from Wilkinson's grasp. Below, the officer pronounced Albert dead.

John fell to his knees, but Joshua face remained petrified. The party was halfway to Elmsford before his tears watered the recriminatory desert to which his soul was now consigned.

CHAPTER TWENTY ONE

Conscription; the word gnawed at Beatrice Bowden as relentlessly as the rats gnawed the fallen in Flanders. She knew for certain now that, barring a miracle, Richard would have to go. After nineteen months of war, there was no sign of respite, let alone peace. She and Arthur had struggled all their lives to give their children a decent upbringing. Two had already been sacrificed for the nation. The third, thank God, was assured survival. Now her last son's life, the son whose achievements filled her with such pride, was to brave the loaded dice of destruction.

She knew the odds. Of the five who'd gone off with George, only Charlie Clayman remained unscathed. The one lifebelt to which she clung was that Richard would be an officer; perhaps they'd take more care of officers. Had she known that the highest casualty rate of all was among junior officers, that the life expectancy of a subaltern averaged two to six weeks, depending on battles, she would surely have drowned.

Had it been a matter of voluntary enlistment, she would have used every weapon in her maternal arsenal to make him shun the call to arms, but the decision was no longer his. All she could give him now was a mother's love. In his presence she adopted a mask of normality, in private she shed copious tears.

It was in angst-ridden solitude that Laura found her one Saturday. Unable to compose themselves, each spoke with the unshackled honesty of emotion.

"If only we were older, if only we had just a few months together, a few weeks even," Laura sobbed.

Her tears watered the onus of age.

"But you have my dear, he won't be gone yet."

"No, I mean, we've waited so long, and now this. I know we won't marry, I heard them talking about it. My father's afraid in case anything should happen. But I don't care. When it was just a question of school, of waiting until the right time; but he might be killed."

"Oh Laura. He's only trying to be sensible. What if there was a baby?"

"But I want Richard's baby, more than anything in the world. We could marry; there's still time."

"But, my dear, you're far too young."

"I'm nearly seventeen; other girls marry at seventeen, even younger."

"But think of the responsibility. God forbid that anything should happen, but if it did."

"But, don't you see, that's why. At least a part of him would live on."

Beatrice could see where this was leading and any thoughts in that direction had to be nipped in the bud.

"Look, I've never told anyone this, but there was a boy, once, long before I met Mr. Bowden," she confided. "We was very much in love. I love Mr. Bowden, don't get me wrong, a woman couldn't wish for a better husband, but I loved that boy more than words can say. Only kids we was, even younger than you. He gave me a ring, a silly thing really, he won at the fair; I've still got it somewhere, upstairs. But then he got sick and, well, I never thought I'd get over it..." Memory wandered from the point.

"Would you, had you have known?"

The question was shocking in its directness, and its implications.

"Laura, we was children."

"But would you?"

"No!" But Laura's forthrightness shamed Beatrice's self-righteous pretence, leaving only avoidance. "No, it doesn't bear thinking about. Look, he'll come through all right, don't you worry about that. Then you'll have all the time in the world." Discomfort apart, she could no longer contemplate her son's death.

Long after Laura had left, Beatrice remained well-deep in memory. Even now, after all this time, the past came flooding back. She understood how Laura felt, with a compassion beyond sympathy. She pictured her lover's child grown in his image and her grandchild, another Richard or perhaps even a girl, and a smile broke through her tears. Perhaps, just sometimes, it was right to let the heart rule the head.

* * * * *

The tree stood tall against the grey sky, its winter ermine no less majestic than its scarlet summer cloak.

The war news had been bad, although the Official Bulletins never admitted as much. Gallipoli had been evacuated and the Germans had attacked the French at Verdun, starting an offensive and counter offensive which would last the entire year and claim half a million lives. From the normal weekly wastage of men in their thousands, new names appeared on the Grammar's Roll of Honour, names Richard knew: Arlot, his old House Captain, Jennings, the fastest bowler he'd ever seen, and Cummin.

How they'd pulled Cummin's leg over that name and how he'd played up to it, from the day he'd first entered the classroom to the aftermath of puberty, when the mere mention of his name would provoke a snigger.

At seventeen, he'd lied about his age and enlisted. Others had done the same, only to be recaptured by grief stricken mothers, but Cummin had got through. Now he would be 'Cummin' no longer, although the spirit of the joke would be reincarnated with each new generation, embossed on the Roll of Honour.

Boys were already being called as they came of age. In a few weeks it would be Richard's turn to wheel his bicycle through the main gates for the last time. He would miss the old place; he'd loved it from the very start, the imposing, red, Victorian brick, the Georgian sandstone annex, he would miss it very much, it was all so much a part of him, the him that he had become.

He continued to stare out of the window, contemplating the future in the tree's frozen bark, until Fotheringay's cough brought him back to Bunyon and academic reality.

All through the day the snow continued to fall. Neither Scott nor Laura had braved the elements that morning; by four o' clock the road to Ashleigh was reported impassable.

"We'll put you up in the dorm," Richard was told. "Is there any way of contacting your parents?"

"Our neighbour, Mr. Scott, has a telephone."

Richard stood beside his housemaster, listening to the crackle of Scott's voice, a spirit in the hallway reaching out to Laura.

Homework followed tea, supper followed homework, bed followed supper. He found the borders' quarters more homely than he'd imagined, and warm in the extreme. The radiatored dormitory was a far cry from his own igloo of a bedroom, where his breath frosted the window. Unable to sleep, he opened his eyes. The blackout curtains had been lifted after lights out, allowing the moonlight to fall between the beds, each regimentally marked by an epic of glorious empire.

Farther along, someone broke wind; another was adenoidilly snoring. Richard, too, silently flatuated. The pungent gas wafted up, outflanking his defensive puffs. 'Phaaahh!' He was a boy who valued his privacy when it came to bodily functions. He'd always hated school loos; even at camp he would risk a hernia to choose his moment. His bowels now reminded him there was no time like the present.

He slipped from the blankets and tiptoed to the door. The handle creaked; no one stirred. Stealthily, he crept along the corridor. He'd been shown the nearest lavatory, but he couldn't remember which door it was. He didn't want to walk in on his housemaster, or matron, and certainly not on his housemaster shagging matron. He chortled at the scene and settled on the downstairs cloakroom.

The stone steps were like ice blocks under his feet. The wind, gusting through the quadrangle, chilled him to the bone through his borrowed pyjamas. Wrapped in his hands, he hurried along, hopping over the snowdrifts blown between the columns.

The cloakroom was unlocked. Before he could draw breath a startled whimper muted his gratitude. Instinctively he reached for the light switch. Two terror stricken third formers met his gaze, cowering in the corner, erections drooping in the glare of discovery.

Shock and incredulity pre-empted his disgust. He blinked repeatedly, but they were still there, their distress mounting by the second. But he knew these boys. What the hell should he do? If he raised his voice the game would well and truly be up.

"Get out of here," he hissed with all the repugnance he could muster.

They fled, ashen faced, leaving him in judicial confusion. Physical responsibility, command of a situation when the course was clear, these he had learned, but this? One word from him and they would be expelled in disgrace, perhaps hounded for the rest of their lives, even to suicide. He knew it went on, but, until now, it had impacted him no more than fiction.

He sank onto the slatted bench. How lucky he was that he'd always had Laura.

Way back in the summer wheat of infancy, he and three others had indulged their curiosity, but he had never touched another boy, nor another boy him. Strange, when he looked back on it, bum baring had been the dare. And these were boarders with no female contact at all, unless one counted matron, whose motherly obesity and sprouting facial mole, it had to be said, hardly promoted heterosexuality. Who was he to pass judgement? It was probably just a phase they were going through, even simply a shared enlightenment; it wasn't as if they'd been buggering each other. But, God damn it, he was a prefect, he had to do something.

His stomach reminded him of his original intent. Finding the cleanest cubicle, he emptied his bowels and crept back to a conscience-beleaguered bed.

* * * * *

Far across the channel, George Bowden was shivering under his single prison blanket. His clothes were nothing but rags and he never took them off, to do so was to freeze to death. He still had his boots, a godsend compared to the sabots issued to those without. Frostbite was common, chilblains taken for granted. His wound, although healed, ached with the cold.

He'd learned not to huddle round the stove. The derisory fuel ration wasn't enough to heat a saucepan, let alone a man's body. Still some stuck their fingers and toes into the flames for the few minutes a day the fire lasted and suffered the gangrenous consequences.

The food was getting worse and, consequently, the dysentery, lethally so for Lough, whose guts had suffered the added corruption of appendicitis.

"Thank your British Navy," the Camp Commandant had told them, vilifying the blockade, which was already proving to be the Allies most effective weapon of the War.

Now the prisoners were to be taken to Germany itself. Surely there conditions would be better. In any event, they couldn't be worse, George reasoned. But, once there, he would have no chance of escape. One or two had already tried, only to be recaptured before they reached the trenches, not that anyone had any real notion how to get through them.

George's own plan had been to get to Holland, but, with his leg stiff and sore with the cold, notwithstanding that no one knew exactly where Holland was, he'd decided against it. Even if he'd made it and then made it back to Blighty, what then, a pat on the head and back to the front? Whatever the hardships, he was better off where he was.

His mind wandered over the water to his family in Ashleigh. He pictured the scene, the children in their beds, Elizabeth by the fireside. How did that song go; 'keep the home fires burning?' Tears welled in his eyes and he abruptly shuttered the magic lantern. He missed them so much it didn't bear thinking about.

Unfortunately, George was the last thing on Elizabeth's mind at that moment. Had he known the truth, his sentimentality would have evaporated in fury. Elizabeth's home fires were definitely aflame, but it was a Midlands private stoking them, rather than any wifely yearning.

The profusion of camps that had sprung up in the district during the preceding six months had brought an abundance of trade to Ashleigh and a number of locals had set up shop in their living rooms and parlours. Pubs were also doing a roaring trade, serving far into the night, as the men either dodged the 10pm curfew or sneaked back after lights out.

Private Jones, however, was a teetotal Baptist, who preferred to invest his meagre remittance in bullseyes, his addiction to which had saved George junior's life. Leaving the shop one day, Jones had snatched young George from the path of Agnew's van, riding the radiator with the boy in his arms until the old codger had piled into a snowdrift, yards further on. Young George had been badly shaken. Jones had taken him home; Elizabeth had taken it from there.

Had it been left to virgin Jones, nothing would have happened, but Elizabeth's frustrations would not be denied. She'd taught him all the things that pleased her most, although she missed George's masculine dominance and staying power.

It was that potency she pined for now, as Jones arched prematurely into ecstasy. She lay back, consoling herself with the recuperative powers of youth, while she contemplated her fantasy of two Tim Joneses in the same bed, a fantasy her cousins had fulfilled in a hayloft one summer's night, before George had come on the scene. Now one was dead and the other doolally, what was left of him.

'Poor George,' she indulged her conscience, ruefully admitting that he'd been better than all of them combined, before mitigating her guilt with his stupidity in joining up in the first place. Anyway, what George didn't know wouldn't hurt him. Tim arrived in the dead of night and left before dawn. As long as she was careful, no one would be any the wiser.

While Jones was retracing his snowprints and George was battling hypothermia, halfway between Charlie Clayman was sitting cross-legged on a ground sheet, belly full of chapattis and feeling appreciatively pukka.

His battalion was out at rest.

"Rest? Bloody hell. If this is their idea of rest, I'd hate to try one of their works' outings," he'd joked the first time. George had been with him then. Nothing had changed since. Reveille at six, roll-call at seven, breakfast at eight, then inspections and drills; dinner at one, training 'til tea, then again 'til supper, then two hours off to blanco the brasswork reburnished every morning after a night up the line on carrying parties, which, this time around, was every night.

Returning in the small hours, he'd followed his nose to a group of Pathans squatting round a campfire, pattercaking dough in their swarthy palms. They'd been surly at first, but he'd won them over, initially with his impression of a Rajah and then, faced with a dagger, another of Grimaldi. Now, with his hunger satiated, it was time to established his warrior credentials.

He rummaged his pockets for his collection of memorabilia; a bullet he'd dug from the heel of his boot, a shard of shrapnel that had lodged in his pack, various watches, epaulettes and insignia he'd looted from dead Germans.

"If they catch you, they kill you," he was warned.

"Not if I kill them first," he boasted bravely.

"You kill?"

"One or two."

"And this you take?"

They seemed singularly unimpressed.

"Yeh, well I've got one of them spiky helmets, and a few other bits and pieces besides, belt buckles, scabbards, that sort of thing. Can't carry 'em all. I could've had a machine gun, too, captured one single-handed, but I'd nowhere to put it, see."

"This for children," his assortment was dismissed. A hand reached into the folds of a shawl. A necklace was dangled before him. "This for warrior."

It took Charlie nonplussed seconds to discern that the string's adornments were human ears.

"For wife," the Pathan grinned dervishly.

The chapattis rose in Charlie's gullet.

"Jesus Christ! You're a bunch of bloody savages!"

* * * * *

The cold snap continued into March, keeping Arthur Bowden busy with burst pipes and Elizabeth snug in her lover's arms. But, as the snows melted, so her luck ran out; the Midlands were moving on to make way for the Cameronians. Totally cheesed off, she determined to make her last night with Jones a memorable one. By four in the morning he had barely enough energy left to swing his legs into his long Johns. Elizabeth extended a teasing foot. Even after such a night, the raw recruit refused to lie down. Jones ignored it, pulling the wool over his aching buttocks.

"Spoilsport," she teased him.

They were down in the kitchen before seduction finally prevailed.

"You'll get me shot," he told her, as she enticed him onto the table.

Out on the Rayntree road the two Arthurs, Bowden and Treadwell, were calling it a night. Armed with the new flashlights that had become all the rage since January, they'd been trudging the country lanes for the best part of four hours, pointlessly as far as Treadwell was concerned. Bowden agreed; no spy would be abroad on a night like this; the flood water was deterrent enough. They were more likely to apprehend an errant carp.

They'd whiled away the time discussing Wilkinson's impending trial. Bowden had been called as a witness. He felt desperately sorry for the man; after all Joshua had been through. Homeward bound, he was still compiling his evidence when he noticed a glow coming from Elizabeth's kitchen.

'Funny,' he thought. 'Not like her to break the blackout, not at this time of night. Hope nothing's up.'

Stealing down the path, he knocked lightly and lifted the latch.

The sight of Tim Jones' shirt-tail flapping rhythmically between Elizabeth's flailing legs was not for the faint hearted.

"What the hell's going on here?"

"Oh my Lord!"

Yanking up his trousers, Jones sidestepped arrest, grabbed his greatcoat and skidaddled into the darkness, leaving Elizabeth spread-eagled across the table.

"Dad?" She gawked at her father-in-law.

Arthur's first thought was of rape, but the circumstances spoke for themselves.

"For God's sake cover yourself, girl!"

"Please, dad, the kids'll hear."

"Perhaps they should hear. Perhaps they should know what kind of baggage their father married," Bowden roared, slamming the door closed.

"Please, Arthur, please," Elizabeth begged, pulling her dressing gown around her.

"Do yourself up, I said!"

"Alright, alright."

Arthur continued to seethe, while she did as she was told.

"Well, what now?" She released the pressure valve.

"You tell me. You, of all people. I never thought it possible."

Elizabeth shrugged. "We're all human, Arthur."

"And what about our George, rotting away in some damned prison camp, while you carry on with the likes of him? What the hell do you think you're playing at, woman?"

"I'm sorry, Arthur. It just happened, that's all."

"What do you mean, it just happened? Things like that don't just happen."

Elizabeth frowned.

"Well, do they?"

She had no answer.

"If I'd known what kind of girl he was marrying, I'd never have let him do it."

"And exactly what kind of girl is that, then, Dad? Hey?" Bowden had touched a nerve. "I've been faithful all my life. This is the first time I've done anything untoward. Good God, I'm a married woman, I need a man."

"And any man will do, is that it?"

"No, that's not damned well it, and you know it. Tim saved young George's life. That bloody fool Agnew would have run him down, if it hadn't been for him."

"So?" Bowden sneered. "Rewarding the bloody hero, was it? Don't make me laugh."

"Well, with George gone, what was I supposed to do?"

"You're supposed to wait for him, that's what; not throw yourself at the first Tom, Dick or Harry what knocks on your bloody door."

"It wasn't like that, Dad, truly it wasn't. Tim's the only one what's been here. Anyway, I don't suppose George's been no angel, what with all them French girls and all."

"Don't be so bloody ignorant, woman. It's a war they're fighting. More likely to

129

get a bayonet in his guts than his end away with some French tart, and damned near did. He was bloody lucky to get out of it alive. Or do you suppose they supply them with whores in them there prison camps? Suppose you'd be the first to volunteer, if they did."

Elizabeth's hand raised in fury. "Don't you dare call me that."

"Oh no, I forgot, whores charge for their services, the likes of you do it for nothing."

The hand shaped into a fist, then fell. A flurry of tears doused the flames.

"And don't come none of that m'larky with me, young lady; I'm not one to fall for that kind of game."

"Please don't tell him, Dad; it'd break his heart, I know it would."

"If you knew that, what the hell did you do it for in the first place?"

"He never would have known. I couldn't help it, Dad, really I couldn't. I do love him, I do."

"Couldn't help it? Course you could bloody help it."

"He didn't get it in, honest he didn't," Elizabeth grasped at straws.

"Well if that ain't getting it in, I don't know what is."

"No, no, it wasn't what it seemed. I wouldn't have let him go all the way."

"Well, you got funny ideas on how to stop him."

"Honest, Arthur, it was just a bit of larking about, really it was."

"Well, that's what you say," Bowden muttered.

"Look, dad; you're the only one what knows. It'll never happen again, I swear it. Please don't tell no one."

"Well, I don't know."

Had Elizabeth left it at that, all may have been well. Instead she reverted to proven tactics; repentantly, she took Arthur's hand.

"I'm really sorry, Arthur."

The seduction in her eyes was unmistakeable.

"You fucking whore!"

She sprang at him, claws drawn, but his anger was steely, his grip like iron. He wrestled her to the floor, sapping her strength, until, with a contemptuous snarl, he flung her aside and stormed out.

Halfway down the stairs, the children stared through the banisters.

- CHAPTER TWENTY TWO -

Richard sat in his classroom, struggling with the secrets of Shakespeare. Despite his impending call-up, Joscelyn was determined to cram as much knowledge into him as time would allow, in the hope that, should he survive the War, a university scholarship might be possible. However, for weeks his concentration had suffered the slings and arrows of reneged responsibility, as he'd let slip every opportunity to take the locker boys aside and read his own riot act. Each sighting only exacerbated his loathing, both of them and of his own weakness, and this morning's had been no exception. The self-accusatory arrows were raining thick and fast, martyring the bard and prompting Fotheringay's tongue to unloosen its own bolt.

"Mr. Bowden, may I remind you we are engaged in Hamlet, not a Midsummer Night's Dream. Now will you please pay attention."

"Yes, Sir; sorry, Sir."

* * * * *

Back in Ashleigh, old Agnew was loading Truelove's bakery van with a clearer conscience. He hadn't been to blame for the incident with young George, nor for Mrs. Dick's cat. Both had run out in front of him. Besides, he'd missed the boy.

Now widespread flooding had made some roads impassable. Nevertheless, the bread, like the Pony Express, must get through. Stashing the last tray in its rack, he closed the door and swung the starting handle. The engine spluttered into life. He smiled proudly, hauled his ageing frame aboard, let-go the handbrake and applied the throttle. The spinning wheels muck-sprangled the yard, until, having dug themselves starting blocks, they propelled him headlong through the gate. A hard right, a slewed back and he was trundling towards the ancient stone bridge.

"Get over!" He cried at the apparition of Amos Harris's milk cart.

The old horse reared; Harris reined him in.

"He should be in the knackers yard; he's a danger to life and limb!"

Harris's reply was drowned in acceleration. Every rev was needed for the gear-grinding gradient out of the village.

From the brow it was level ground for the next uneventful mile or so. Agnew settled into song, whistling 'Take me back to dear old Blighty', a new ditty he'd picked up from the soldiers in the Barley Mow, segueing into 'Oh! Oh! Antonio'. His lack of dentures affected his performance somewhat, but didn't detract from his musical pleasure, nor from his gummy enjoyment of the Chelsea Bun that filled the interludes.

The treacherous 'Belsham Bend' awaited him, an 'S' bend at the bottom of a vale, complete with ford-spanning bridge, Agnew's daily dose of danger and excitement. The swollen stream flashed briefly over the one in four hedgerow. Agnew's eyes glinted, his mittened knuckles gripped the wheel, his foot hovered over the accelerator. Plank rattling speed was essential for the climb out of the final curve.

Too late he saw the flood water. Forsaking the handbrake, he braced himself, caught the throttle and sent the van aquaplaning into the deep waters of disaster, snorting steam like a sinking Dreadnought.

Perched on the hilltop above, the windows of the White Hart opened onto the catastrophe. Ten minutes later Agnew was sitting, blanket-wrapped, in front of a blazing fire, up to the gills in river water and embarrassment, but, otherwise, none the worst for wear. That afternoon, his van was towed from the river and back to Ashleigh. As it passed the Barley Mow, the regulars exacted their pound of flesh.

"Bin swimming, old 'un?"

"Reckon he thought he was driving one of them there submarines."

"Up periscope!"

For weeks Agnew would be hailed the village authority on submersibles and, above all, advanced driving methods in the wet.

* * * * *

The floodwater subsided, leaving its muddy residue to the cleansing showers of April. The first conscripts were called. Some had been excused through occupational indispensability; a few had been rejected on health grounds. Had Joshua Wilkinson only known it, his son Albert's flat feet would almost certainly have exempted him. Instead the boy was dead and Joshua was facing trial for manslaughter.

In mid-March rumours were rife of a German landing at Harwich. The bugles called the newly arrived Cameronians from their tents, but they remained in their quagmire of a camp; Beatrice's nerve nutrient was returned to its draw.

Then, on the night of March 31st, three enormous explosions shook the village, followed soon after by the throb of Zeppelin engines. Later, fainter explosions were heard from the south-west.

The raiders returned shortly after midnight, hovering overhead 'like a load of ruddy railway engines letting off steam,' as Scott complained to Laura, huddled in his arms.

Next morning, Richard arrived with tales of Rayntree's destruction. Scott despatched his last piece of toast and rose from the breakfast table. "Well let's see for ourselves, shall we? Today's my day off. Fetch your coat, Laura. You can leave the plates."

In Rayntree's outlying fields, earthworks were being dug that looked, for all the world, like mass graves. Scott drove grimly on. At last the town's roofs and spires came into sight.

"It's all right," Laura cried.

"Thank God," Scott sighed. "Perhaps it was an April fool after all, young Richard."

"I doubt it, not coming from constable Johnson," Richard called from the back. "An awful lot of people have fallen for it, if it is."

132

"Point taken."

The traffic into town was nose to tail, the lanes packed with sightseers. Scott edged his way through, just managing to avoid the heaps of shattered glass swept up in his path. Along the High Street, a burned out stationer's shop still smouldered.

"Five people killed. First bomb dropped dead on eleven by the Town Hall clock, there, timed to the second. They reckon it weren't no accident," a spy-catcher told them.

"What's all the digging for, out on the Elmsford road?" Scott asked.

"Trenches. The whole town's going to take to the fields every night in case they come again. It was five this time, it could be five hundred next."

"Move along, there, move along," a policeman waved them on.

There was little more to see and nowhere to park. "Oh well, now we're out, we may as well make a day of it," Scott decided. "Fancy a spot of map reading, Richard?"

Lunchtime found them in a particularly picturesque village Scott had been told about, famed for its brimstone past.

'The Witches Brew' welcomed them with a blazing fire.

"Did they really used to burn witches here?" Laura whispered, as they waited to be seated.

"So they say," Scott confirmed.

"Then she'd better not sit too close to the fire," Richard grinned, nodding towards a wizened old woman by the hearth.

"Table for three, Sir?" The waitress seemed friendly enough, not at all covenous.

Trade was brisk, the better seats were already taken. She led them cronewards. A broomstick revealed itself, propped against the wall behind her.

"I hope she didn't hear you, young Richard, or you'll be a frog in no time," Scott warned.

"Just don't hop into my soup, that's all," Laura smirked.

A young woman was sitting alone by the window. She smiled familiarly as they passed.

"Why, Miss Cooper!"

"How are you, Richard?"

"I couldn't be better. You know Laura, of course, and Mr. Scott?"

Scott's memory was taken by surprise. This wasn't at all the plain Jane school mistress he remembered from Laura's brief sojourn at the village school.

She offered them her table. "I was just leaving."

"Nonsense, you haven't finished your soup," Scott protested.

"I've had sufficient, thank you Mr. Scott."

"Surely we can share?"

The ritual played itself out. The schoolteacher moved her hat and scarf. Scott took the chair beside her.

"Well this is a pleasant surprise, I must say," she told them.

133

"I assure you, the pleasure is all ours," Scott returned the compliment, conscious of a gleam in Laura's eye. The waitress came. "Soup for four, please, and take this one away, it's gone cold; entirely our fault."

"Oh, please, no more for me, Mr. Scott."

"Come, Miss Cooper; another bowl of soup won't hurt, particularly on a day like this. I must say I admire your choice of watering hole. I haven't ventured this way before."

"No? I come here quite often; they do excellent cream teas."

Scott had seen that smile before, at the village fete, when she had linked the children's hands for the very first time and sent Marian into madness.

"It's a long way to come for a cream puff."

"Not really, Mr. Scott; I'm an avid cyclist, the exercise does me good."

"Turning a steering wheel's about all the exercise I get nowadays. That's mine, out there," he found himself boasting.

"Oh, really, daddy; he used to cycle a lot, Miss Cooper," Laura reddened her father's cheeks.

"Did you hear the air raid last night?" Scott asked. "They hit Rayntree you know. We've just been over to see."

"I thought of going. Is the damage severe?"

The scene was described, the story of the town hall clock related verbatim. "Five dead."

"Dear God, where will it end."

"In victory, one hopes."

"Then let it be soon."

The soup arrived. Scott held court; Miss Cooper held her own. Scott was impressed. He wondered why so educated and attractive a woman had never married. She wore a mourning ring, but that could be for a relative, or simply a keepsake. Whatever the reason, he found her maiden status comforting. This was a woman he would like to know better; how to achieve that intimacy was his conundrum.

He asked if he might smoke.

"Oh, daddy, do you have to? Say no, Miss Cooper, or he'll pong the place out," Laura embarrassed him again.

"Actually, I think a pipe rather becomes a man." The teacher nipped Scott's vexation in the bud.

Inevitably the conversation returned to the War. Miss Cooper's brother was still in training, she told them. He'd enlisted soon after the outbreak.

"He says it's terribly boring, the same old routine, day after day, although the bond between the classes is tremendous. His best friends are a dustman from Rayntree and a bank manager from Brentfield. Who would have thought?"

"We played Brentfield at soccer last term," Richard went off on a tangent.

"Did you win?"

"I should say so, and with only ten men for most of the match."

"If only the war could be won so easily. Henry's only fear is that it might be over before he gets there. For my part, I earnestly pray that it is. Too many young lives have been lost already and for so little gain."

Scott sensed a personal tragedy. "I understand this place is steeped in witches and warlocks and what-have-you." He lightened the mood.

"Actually, local folklore is something of a hobby of mine," Miss Cooper said, her melancholy lifting. "Legend has it that the original owner of this place was hung from that tree over there for dispensing a potion to a pregnant woman, whose baby was subsequently born deformed."

Scott found himself blushing. Surely, 'with child' would have been more tactful? But then, he supposed, he was behind the times. "Really? I thought they used to burn witches?"

"Oh no, Archbishops and heretics, especially in Mary's reign, but witches were generally hung."

"Didn't they make them put their hands in boiling water and horrible things like that?" Laura asked.

"Trial by ordeal; yes, that too. Ducking was most prevalent around here, although it was hardly ducking as we know it. The cruellest thing was that, if, by some miracle, the accused survived, it was deemed to be yet further proof of their guilt. This was Matthew Hopkins' old stomping ground, the infamous Witchfinder General. I believe mention of witches can still be found in the church records."

Laura insisted on looking. Scott signalled for the bill.

It was a beautiful little chapel with its square tower and Perpendicular windows, built a century or so later than Ashleigh's own parish church. Its stone effigies and oak carvings had suffered, as so many had, at the hands of the more fanatical apostles of seventeenth century Puritanism, bringing Miss Cooper back to Matthew Hopkins and his torture chamber in Colchester castle.

"We've been learning about the siege there. It was the last one of the Civil War, or, at least, the last major one," Richard took the opportunity to impress. "The Royalists held it for weeks before the Roundheads starved them into submission. My history master says musket balls can still be seen in the walls."

"Didn't Boadiccia raze Colchester to the ground in Roman times?" Scott stretched his memory, determined not to be outdone.

The vestibule was open. There they found the leather bound volumes. The style and grammar and the fading of centuries made the handwriting difficult to decipher; however, one or two heavily scored entries and another scratched out completely hinted of legendary evidence.

"Look," Laura tugged Richard's sleeve, "I'm sure it says 'Gurny'. Could be one of your ancestors; seventeen something or other. Perhaps they're buried in the churchyard. Let's go and see."

Scott seized the moment. "We'll meet you back here. With you out of the way, we might have a chance of perusing this thing ourselves. Unless, of course...?"

"No, really; I'd like to study it in more detail," Miss Cooper assured him.

That night Scott lay awake, reflecting on Agatha Cooper. He'd lashed her bike to the back and given her a lift home. He guessed her age at thirty two, purely on the grounds that she'd been Richard's school teacher, although she looked younger. Even if he was right, the age gap was considerable. Could she ever be attracted to him?

He thought back to his time with Marian. They'd known such little happiness. For the best part of his adult life, he'd been as good as celibate. He'd never been the kind to seek solace in the arms of a prostitute or a clandestine affair. A girl in his London office had shown him every encouragement one Christmas, but, other than a prolonged kiss under the mistletoe, he hadn't pursued it.

Throughout Marian's illness, through the years of pretence, he'd worn the mantle of widower while entrapped by the living truth. Even had he met someone else, marriage would have been impossible. But now he was free and his circumstances had improved beyond all expectation.

The first thing on his agenda was to find a new home, the primary reason for his tour that day. As a director it was his duty to entertain, and he could hardly do so in his current house. Being a widower had eased the pressure, but he couldn't excuse himself indefinitely. There were also ghosts to lay, those from the past and, more sombrely, perhaps from the future. God forbid that anything should happen to Richard, but, if it did, the effect on Laura would be devastating.

In another six weeks or so, the boy would be called up. As close as they were, she would need more than a father to soften the blow should the worst befall, and who better than Agatha?

Again he contemplated the broadening of Laura's social horizons. The Mayor's soirée was coming up. He had planned to take her, but what a golden opportunity it would be to impress Agatha. It was a pity he couldn't take them both.

He shut his eyes and pictured Agatha beside him, his prospective bride, house-hunting in the Bentall. A new wife, a new home, a new life; he'd been alone too long, it was time he remarried before the world passed him by.

He returned to the age gap. She was nearer Laura's age than his own, but, if he could establish a friendship, she may learn to love him; after all, he was fast becoming a man of means.

The Zeppelins came again that night, this time saving their bomb-loads for London. Gun flashes were seen in the vicinity of Brentfield, but to no avail. There seemed to be no effective defence against them except the weather.

Laura watched the monsters float slowly by, their gondolas plainly visible in the moonlight. How the guns could miss them she couldn't fathom.

"Barbarian's," she hissed, through gritted teeth. "What kind of men are they that can drop bombs on innocent people? I wouldn't miss, if I was shooting at them."

In Elmsford gaol, Joshua Wilkinson also stared out at the sky. Even if he stood on his wooden stool, he could only just reach the window's iron bars. He longed to look out on the town and the fields beyond, but the sky was all he could see. By coincidence, he had been given the same cell as before; on Monday he would stand in the same dock, before the same judge.

'They' had killed his wife; 'they' had stolen his land; 'they' were responsible for Albert's death; 'they' should be in the dock, not him. How the sanctimonious bastards would gloat. Well, he'd deprive them of the pleasure.

Stepping onto the seat, he pulled out the carefully measured length of braided twine he had secreted in his pocket, placed its noose round his neck and tied the end to the bars. He had nothing left to live for.

His mouth dried, his vision blurred. Commending his soul to God, he breathed out, held his nerve and kicked the stool from under him.

The pain was immediate and excruciating. He clawed at the noose, desperately stretching his legs to stop the agony, but his boots could only brush the flagstone.

The twine scored deeper; blood spilled from its abrasions. Joshua's tongue filled his gaping mouth. He felt his eyes bulge, his face swell. He thought his lungs would burst, his heart explode.

He reached up, tearing his fingernails in his frantic attempts to grip the window ledge. He no longer wanted to die. He'd thought it would be quick. Even this he'd got wrong.

He jerked his body with all his might, praying it would break the twine and end the torture, but it only plaited tighter, until it reached its zenith and uncoiled him wildly into the wall.

His head struck the brickwork; his sight blanked, his senses swam. A hole opened under him, a well to the underworld into which his innards were draining. He felt his whole being fall; then a cloak rose up and he sank into it, leaving his mortal remains to settle like a lapsing clock, head tilted towards the iron door, eyes set accusingly to stare out his incarcerators in the cold light of day.

CHAPTER TWENTY THREE

Arthur Bowden's problems multiplied; barely a month after he'd caught Elizabeth red-handed, she was seeing a Cameronian. As secret as she'd kept her affair with Jones, this latest fling was common gossip. He hadn't mentioned it to Beatrice, she had enough to worry about, but it could only be a matter of time before she heard, unless she already knew and was keeping it to herself.

Beatrice aside, the children worried him most. They may be only babies now, but village memories were long and playground tongues vicious. Besides, young as they were, they weren't blind, and innocence had a voice of its own. If someone didn't put a stop to it, what on earth would happen when George came home? Divorce? Murder? Whatever the outcome, it wouldn't be a happy one and the children would suffer most. He was at his wit's end; if being caught in the act hadn't cooled Elizabeth's ardour, he doubted the effectiveness of further confrontation, but he had to try.

"The only one they've seen me with is you, Arthur, on top of me that night and me half out of my clothes, trying to fight you off. They was watching through the banisters. So I'd be careful what I say, if I was you. Believe me or not, people'd sure as hell believe them."

He left without a word, slamming the door behind him.

* * * * *

Why her father had insisted she came, Laura had no idea. Even if he had dashed her hopes of a cosy twosome by telling the Bowdens about the soirée, she would still rather be with Richard. Boring old fuddy-duddies, boring old wood, boring old war, boring, boring, boring, and as for that Jeremy character and his gushing mother!

The worst of it was the drip wouldn't leave her alone. "Can I get you a cordial, Laura?" "Another vol-au-vent, perhaps?" "Do you play tennis? I'm awfully good at it, I even beat Godber and he's school champion." "Can't wait for a bash at the jolly old Boche. My brother's on divisional staff, you know, but I rather fancy the flying corp, myself." "Perhaps we could make up a foursome, you know, doubles and all that." "Have you ever dissected a frog?"

Ghastly. His father wore the regalia of Mayor; the room was littered with aldermen and bigwiggery. Laura was impressed in a way. Her mother would have been in her element. However, as illustrious as the gathering was, she'd met no 'Lady' this or 'Baroness' that, not even a knight as far as she could tell, not even a Stafford. The residence was imposing enough, though.

"I say, Laura, you must meet my aunt."

It was him again. She looked to her father for salvation, to find him deeply embroiled in his latest tale.

"Those trenches at Rayntree; complete waste of time. Gave the whole thing up after the first night. Councillor Ridley told me the people made such a din they may as well have had a brass band playing under a lime-lit placard saying 'bomb here'. The general consensus seems to be that the place got bombed by mistake. The Boche got lost, heard the town clock strike and simply let loose. But here's the rub...."

To interrupt him was impossible. Groaning inwardly, Laura let the chinless wonder lead her away.

"Aunt Cloe, this is Laura."

Laura recognised the drip's aunt immediately; the woman was slower.

"Haven't we met before, my dear? Your face seems familiar."

They had, at Hettie Jameson's, the night of the Tindal Square banner escapade.

"I don't believe so, unless you have some connection with the Priory. Actually, Mrs. Jameson's daughter is in my class there. You know, the suffragette?"

"Ah." Laura watched the penny drop. "Perhaps it was there. I do visit occasionally; I know one of the sisters. I hear you're going to play tennis with Jeremy, here. I do hope you win."

"Hang on, Aunt Clo, you're supposed to be on my side," her nephew objected.

"I'm sorry, Jeremy, but we women must stick together, must we not, Laura?"

"Absolutely," Laura confirmed. "Although I'm no Dorothea Chambers. I rarely play at school."

"Nevertheless, I shall expect you to put up a good fight. We can't allow these men to have it all their own way. Well, my dear, I shall hope to see more of you." Aunt Cloe looked suggestively at Jeremy.

'Over my dead body,' Laura thought, consigning herself to zombiedom for the rest of the evening.

"Young Jeremy seems to have taken quite a shine to you," Scott commented on the drive home. "Invited you to tennis, I believe."

"Oh, daddy, he's such a drip. In front of his mother and everything, I could hardly say no. I'll make my excuses."

Scott chuckled. "Well, I don't see the harm. You're young, you should get out more, make new friends."

'Make new friends?' Laura frowned. What did he mean? "I'm quite happy with the friends I have, thank you very much."

"But you seem to have so few of them. It wouldn't hurt to broaden your horizons, nor young Richard, for that matter, you're far too reliant on each other."

Laura couldn't believe her ears. Her resentment was instantaneous.

"Then perhaps I should invite the drip over. I'm sure the two of them would get on like a house on fire."

She watched her father fume at his ineptitude, her perception and impertinence, his own treachery and hypocrisy.

"Don't be ridiculous. All I'm saying is it wouldn't hurt to have a friend or two. Richard'll be gone soon. What then? You can't just hibernate, and if you think you're going to consort with that damnable Jameson woman, you've got another think coming!"

"On the contrary," Laura came back at him, ignoring the Jameson slur. "If the friends you so obviously have in mind are anything like that slimy toad, I think I'd rather hibernate. I couldn't have been more bored if I'd stayed at home reading Mrs. Beaton."

"Damn your insolence, girl. I'm your father and I'll thank you to respect the fact. Whatever you may think, I have only your best interests at heart."

"If you did, you'd let me marry Richard."

"Let you what? For heaven's sake, you're still at school!"

"I'm seventeen, nearly."

"You're sixteen and you'll damned well do as I say! Damn the War!"

* * * * *

While Scott and Laura drove on in silence, Jeremiah Gurny was downing his first pint at the Barley Mow in weeks. He'd contracted influenza back in February and been close to joining the ancestors Richard and Laura had traced in the church ledger. At eighty three he could still do a day's work and enjoy his Mild and Bitter.

The pub was packed, his haunt, the tap bar, overflowing with soldiers.

"What's them, then?" He asked Joe Petty, the Blacksmith some four years his junior.

"Them's Cameroonians, Jem; Scotsmen."

"Well, I can see that, can't I."

"What you ask for then?"

"Huh," Gurny shrugged, returning to his dominoes, "no wonder I can't understand a bloody word."

He was about to make his next move when a roar of ribald laughter tuned his ear to the Highlanders' drawl.

"Yu on about that floosie o' yurs, Jamie?" A burly corporal asked.

"Aye, she's a reet goer, that she is," Jamie answered. "Likes a drop of the hard stuff, and no mistake."

"She a widow or what?"

"Husband killed at Wipers, so she says. Two bairns and all. Tits like yu wo' nay believe."

"Yus wanna be careful, laddie, or yu'll be marchin' up the aisle wi' a ready made family an' another on the way," the corporal advised him.

"Och, there's nay chance o' that," Jamie said confidently. "All she wants is a wee bit o' comfort once in a while."

"Aye, well it would be wee in yur case!"

"She's no complainin'; purrs like a kitten. Can't get enough. Och, Elizabeth, my angel, wrap your thighs round this." Jamie thrust out his sporan to raucous approval.

'Elizabeth?' Gurny hadn't cracked every word, but he'd got the gist of it. His skin prickled, his cheeks flushed. Common as the name was, there was only one Elizabeth in the village who fitted the description. He found confirmation etched in Petty's embarrassment. He struggled up.

140

"No, Jeremiah, no!"

The heavy handle of Gurny's walking stick hit Jamie full in the groin, sending him screaming to his knees.

"That's my family you're talking about, you bastard," Gurny yelled, shaking with rage. "There's my grandson, rotting away in some damned prison camp, while you're here taking liberties with his wife. I'll bloody kill you, you bloody swine!"

Only Amos Harris's cudgel-arresting grasp saved the Scotsman's head.

"That's enough, Jeremiah, that's enough!"

The bar hushed; Jamie groaned on the floor.

"Yu had nay cause t'do tha'," the corporal turned on Gurny, whose Essex brogue had been as equally unintelligible to the Scots.

"Alright, alright," The landlord elbowed his way along the bar. "We'll have none of that or I'll ban the lot of you."

"We weren't doin' nuthin'," the corporal protested. "We wuz just sharin' a wee joke, when this auld man ups and hits our Jamie in the balls for no reason at all."

"No reason?"

It needed Harris, Petty and 'Mine Host' to restrain Gurny.

"Alright, Jem, that's enough," The Landlord ordered. "Leave this to me."

While Scots and villagers squared up to each other, the Landlord pulled the corporal aside and explained the facts of the matter.

"He did'ne know, honest he did'ne. He never wud have got involved, if he'd've known tha'," the Scotsman told Gurny. "He owes yu an apology, reet enough, but he's in nay condition to give it. Honest, he did'ne know."

"What apology, Jock?" An irate comrade demanded.

"I'll tell ye later. Just help him up, will ye, it's time we wus leavin'."

"But, Jock, I've just ordered a pint."

"Then leave it!"

Slinging Jamie between them, the Scots trooped out.

* * * * *

At the far end of the village, Elizabeth sat drowning her sorrows. Jamie was late, too late.

"Damn you, Arthur," instinctively she laid the blame at her father-in-law's door. "How the hell did you find out? Well, just you say something, just you try. You wouldn't dare tell my George; you wouldn't bloody dare."

She drained the gin bottle and looked at the clock. Twenty past one registered through the haze.

"Where the hell is he?"

The clock ticked on, each swing of the pendulum a doleful knell.

"Sod it." The gin was gone.

She reached across the table. The lamp refused to meet her. She stretched farther, lost her footing and crashed to the floor.

Cursing and swearing, she scrambled up, snatched the lamp by the handle and lunged for the stair rail, hauling herself up step by step, until a missed toehold sent her into pivotal confusion. The lamp clattered down the stairs, spilling oil and broken glass. By the time her sozzled brain could react, the fiery fuse was rushing up to meet her.

Suddenly she was fear and panic sober, but as fast as she stamped out one step another ignited. Flames licked at her dress, more steps caught light, then the paint on the struts, then the banister rail.

Clambering up on all fours, she raced along the landing.

"Wake up, kids, wake up, Young George, Doris!"

Dragging the children from their beds, she carried them, kicking and screaming, through the conflagration and out into the night.

"Get next door, boy, tell 'em to come quick. You stay here, Doris, and don't you move."

Legs scorched, her skirt smouldering, Elizabeth filled the nearest bucket from the garden pump and ran back into the house. The water evaporated in a cloud of steam; the staircase blazed. Face blackened, limbs blistered, she staggered out.

"Mr. Wright's coming," Young George cried from the gate, but it was already too late; the house, one of the few in the village still boasting a thatched roof, was soon an inferno.

* * * * *

While his home burned, George Bowden was rattling across the German border, one of sixty crammed into a cattle truck, back to flea-bitten back, side to lousy side, warmer than he had been for months among the lolling heads. He'd started the journey against the slats, hoping to catch some air and a glimpse of countryside. Racked by kidney pains, he'd soon wished he hadn't.

'Better the fug than the frost,' he thought now, with only cursory pity for the fool who'd swopped places with him. 'It's every man for himself, as the captain said on the Titanic. Anyway, it was him that asked.'

He raised a saturated buttock. No food or water had passed the prisoners' lips for forty eight hours; still the dysentery spilled from the bucket according to camber, eddying around boots and backsides.

"Like pigs in shit," George muttered; "pig's in fucking shit." But, however widely he flared his nostrils, he couldn't smell it, not anymore.

He'd lost the feeling in his leg hours before, but if he got up to stretch the whole pack would concertina closed and he would end up back at the slats. Anyway, it was better than cramp, better than kidney pains, better than Wipers; anything was better than Wipers.

'Christ, I hope Charlie's alright. Mind you, if anyone's got a nose for keeping out of trouble, it's him,' he comforted himself.

He and Charlie had come up in a cattle truck the first time out. There'd been forty to a wagon then, with two full bales of straw to cover the boards. Three days it had taken, from Le Havre to 'Pop'. A snail could have crawled faster. They'd jumped down to crap, that's how slow the train had gone, and taken their dixies up to the engine to beg boiling water.

When the old puffer had finally got going, the men had climbed onto the roof, two at a time, taking turns to chuck handfuls of chippings at the insulators, high on their poles, the others cheering each time someone shattered the glass. But, when their turn had come, Charlie had held back with one of his 'funny feelings', and a good job he had, for the next man up had got his neck half severed by a cable the prop man had missed.

And then there'd been that fracas over the old woman's washing, laid out behind the lines.

"She's bloody signalling the enemy, telling them where that battery is, over there. I've heard tell of it before," Charlie had remonstrated, trampling the bedsheets into the mud in his haste to snatch them up.

The old hag had been livid. There'd been one hell of a slanging match, no interpreter needed, brought to an end at the point of Charlie's bayonet.

"Let's hop it, before the fireworks start," he'd said, after he'd driven the old hag back into her house.

George had laughed like a drain, but, ten minutes later, the shells had come screaming over, bang on target. They'd gone back when it was all over. The house had taken a direct hit. The woman was nowhere to be found.

"Serves her bloody right," Charlie had grunted.

Memory wandered on to 'Hellfire Corner,' to the Whizz Bangs and Handcuff Kings crashing over the cross-roads to hell, to the Woolly Bear that had ripped the working party to bits like a giant flail, with Charlie shielding them both under a sheet of corrugated, not that it would have saved them.

George remembered the gas, the bull, the barrackroom banter, of sharing a September sunset in a front line trench, looking homewards over the parados like a couple of kids; of 'suffering the consequences' for getting drunk and disorderly, twenty eight days field punishment, tied to a cartwheel for two hours a day, all pay and allowances stopped, thanks to that bastard Hollis. There'd been hell to pay at home; Elizabeth had threatened divorce, until Charlie had sent her his savings, saying they were George's.

Yes, they'd been through a lot together, him and Charlie; they'd even shared their first fuck, Winnie Truelove, the village bike, behind her father's bakery. She'd had terrible breath, as if she'd been chewing manure.

"I won't let you unless you kiss me," she'd insisted, clamping his tool between her legs.

She'd been through the whole village before she was sixteen, including little Jimmy Ruthers, the half-pint hunchback who'd died soon after. Rumour had it she'd even been behind the old verger's heart attack.

'God help her husband,' George concluded, allowing the train to sway him back into limbo. 'And thank God for my Betty.'

* * * * *

Elizabeth's burns proved superficial, however nothing survived of her home except smoke blackened walls and charcoaled furniture. There was no alternative; she and

143

the children would have to move in with the Bowdens.

For Richard, their arrival was a nightmare. In essence, he'd been an only child, George had been well into his teens when Richard was born; he had never suffered the patter of infant feet and the seemingly constant caterwauling that accompanied them.

To cap it all, Scott's new social calendar meant that Richard and Laura were spending more time with the Bowdens, and Elizabeth was ever present.

Even when Scott was home, Richard sensed an atmosphere that, for some inexplicable reason, seemed to revolve around him. On the surface everything appeared to be normal and Laura assured him it was, but still his gut-feeling belied his logic's insistence that, if there was any friction, Scott's obvious, if discreet, courting of Miss Cooper was the cause.

The one plus that had come out of the fire was that it had put an end to Elizabeth's philandering, and, if Richard was called up, having the children about would be a boon to his mother, although his father seemed far from happy about the situation. He went to the pub most evenings and otherwise kept out of Elizabeth's way.

- CHAPTER TWENTY FOUR -

By Easter Sunday, April 23rd, Richard, although too tired to attend Church, had returned from his last cadet camp, Laura had celebrated her seventeenth birthday, and Spencer Stafford had come home from the War. Wounded at Gallipoli, he'd been dragged from heaven's door by the agony of repeated surgery. After recuperative weeks in a fussy, freezing Scottish nursing home, he'd been given leave and, with rumours of a summer offensive already rife, had requested immediate active service.

His father stood beside him, belting out the hymns with thanksgiving gusto. Stafford senior was something of an enigma, his present Lordship's first born out of wedlock. His housemaid mother had resisted an abortion, agreeing only to emigration after the convent birth in return for a guaranteed future for her son. The boy had been fostered to the estate's then managing agent. After his Lordship's accession, he'd been made steward and installed in the Manor. The relationship was no secret; both within the family and locally, Stafford was expected to inherit the Ashleigh estate.

Spencer had arrived unannounced the previous evening, thankful to find his mother and sisters in town for the weekend; he had been dreading their pity. He avoided his father for the same reason, retiring early and rising just in time for Church. He needed to go; he needed to find whatever ghost of a God still remained. Instead he found distraction.

"Who's the girl, Pater, the one in blue?"

"For heaven's sake, Spencer, we're in the middle of service," Stafford hissed.

"No matter," Spencer muttered. But it did matter; he knew her. While the congregation attended the Vicar, he delved into his memory's deepest recesses. She was a village girl; that was it; she'd gone to school at the Manor. He'd snapped her with his first box camera, the day he'd taken the class photo. She'd been a child then, and he'd been at Caius, but still she'd made an impression. There'd been some fuss about her mother, dropped dead or something at the village fete. Well, she'd certainly lived up to expectation; she was damnably pretty, not that he'd be of any use to her now.

He bit his lip in suppressed rage. Blood was a familiar taste. They'd managed to poke his intestines back, a miracle in itself, but there'd been little they could do for his genitals. He could pass water without much pain, but sexually he simply didn't exist.

"Oh, God," the words escaped.

"What?" His father asked.

Suddenly the little parish church felt unbearably claustrophobic, like the ether impregnated cabin of the Britannic, the hospital ship that had brought him home from Mudros. The building began to rock, as on a turbulent sea. He had to get out.

Pushing past his father, he paced down the aisle, conscious of heads turning, of the Vicar stopping in mid-sentence. The door was open; he ran out.

Footsteps ground the gravel behind him, compounding the pulsing in his ears.

"Good God, man, what on earth's got into you, making a fool of yourself like that? Remember your station," his father admonished him.

"Oh, my station, is that what I've got to remember? Well, which station would you like, Pater, Liverpool Street, Victoria, Charing Cross, Marylebone? You see, I remember them all."

"Don't be so childish. And kindly look me in the eye, when I'm talking to you."

"Well, which bally station, Pater?" Spencer obliged. "Chunuk Blair, or is that too ruddy far for you? You'd know the place if you saw it, if anyone here ever saw it, the hills around are covered in poppies, amongst less agreeable morsels. Didn't know the old Ottoman grew poppies, did you? Biggest beggars known to man. They make opium out of them; dulls the pain."

Stafford raised a despairing hand. "Please, Spencer. How could you do such a thing, in the house of God, of all places?"

"God?" Spencer questioned bitterly. "Oh, yes, praise be to God. God the Merciful, God the Almighty, God whose incompassion surpasseth all understanding."

"You don't know what you're saying."

The strains of 'Oh God, our help in ages past' reverberated through the leaded east window. Spencer turned towards it, raising his voice in mock worship.

"For what we have received, and for what we are about to receive again, may the Lord, in his infinite mercy, make us truly bloody thankful."

"For pity's sake, pull yourself together, man," his father pleaded.

"Why? Do you think He'll hear me? Not much chance of that, Pater. Sing louder, brethren, don't you know He's stone bloody deaf. Can't hear a damned thing, not even the bloody howitzers!"

"God sacrificed his only Son that we might live," Stafford asserted heatedly. "You're being blasphemous, Spencer, and I won't have it, do you hear?"

"Well we're the sacrificial lambs now. It's a wonder He knows where to put us all. Besides, so did some of those in there, but I don't hear you singing their praises, I don't see you kneeling in their damned parlours offering up a prayer to the great god White or Truelove, or whoever it is who actually bakes our daily bread."

"Don't be ridiculous," Stafford exploded. "I won't be a party to this."

"Ah, but you are, you see, we all are, all party to God's great covenant. Although, come to think of it, He managed to resurrect His Holy Ghost; cunning that; would that any of us could enjoy so miraculous a recovery."

"Really, Spencer. Do you honestly believe God wanted this?"

"Well, He hasn't put a stop to it. Tell you what, do you reckon they're having a dingdong up there, and that's why? You know, 'thine will be done' and all that, Christ versus the fallen angel, only we do all the fighting down here in case one of the old archangels blows a hole in Heaven by mistake? Can't have that, can we, a hole in bloody Heaven, nowhere to go when the time comes? No, we definitely can't have that, we'd have nothing left to live for, and I know how that feels, bloody awful."

At last Spencer crumpled. His father reached for his shoulder. Spencer shrugged him off. His father tried again.

"Come on, old chap; let's get you home."

Hiding his face in his hands, Spencer allowed himself to be led through the lych gate and into the waiting Vauxhall. His father took the wheel, leaving the chauffeur at his prayers.

* * * * *

For Laura's birthday, Scott organised an Easter Monday mystery trip, inviting Agatha and Richard along for the ride. His courtship was proceeding encouragingly, although it was far too early to pop the question. Besides, there was Laura to consider. If the Mayor's soirée had ended in resentment, what bitter rebellion would the irony of him marrying, especially so impulsively, unleash?

Parking the car at Elmsford station, he herded his party aboard the 9.45. The line was congested with military traffic and it was an hour and a half before the train pulled into Liverpool Street.

"How can anyone think up here," Richard called above the clamour, adding, "or see," as the locomotive engulfed him in steam.

Scott watched the boy's eyes widen at the head-spinning height of the Great Eastern Hotel, heard his involuntary whistle, when he took in the concourse's massive canopy and, from the elevated walkway, the platforms themselves, covering an area of six football pitches or more, reducing rolling stock to toy dimensions and the scurrying crowd to automaton ants. Near conscription age or not, the boy was still a boy.

Scott led the way underground. 'Westbound' wasn't much of a clue for a girl of seventeen, bubbling with the excitement of a ten-year-old.

A rush of warm air became a rumble, the rumble a throaty roar. The train thundered in, acrid with the coagulation of overheated electrics and oil.

"In you get," Scott grinned at Richard's awe.

The train lurched forward, almost depositing Scott in Agatha's lap, then trundled on, from darkness into daylight, then darkness again, through Moorgate, Aldersgate, Farringdon Street, King's Cross, Gower Street and Portland Road to Baker Street, disgorging and engorging humanity en route.

"Alight here, please," Scott joked in the jargon of the transport service.

They climbed the stairs into the blinding sunlight.

"This way."

The sign emerged, some hundred yards ahead, above the bustle of Marylebone Road.

"Madame Tussaud's!" Laura squealed.

The queue shuffled forward like a geriatric caterpillar. It took them twenty minutes to reach the turnstile.

Boer generals, De Wet and Botha, were the first to catch Richard's eye, along with buckskinned 'Buffalo Bill', without whose feats no schoolboy annual would be complete. Scott instantly recognised George Bernard Shaw, Agatha's favourite

147

author, although the French notaries remained as anonymous to him as the heroes and heroines in Grand Hall Two were familiar; Nelson, Wellington, Drake, Mary Queen of Scots, and the giants of English literature, Shakespeare, Dickens and Sir Walter Scott.

"Do I glean a family resemblance?" Agatha teased him.

"Regretfully, not," he had to admit.

Dan Leno smiled out at them, W. G. Grace knocked Richard for six and Tom Thumb titillated Laura. 'Small enough to hide under your skirt,' Scott was about to tell Agatha, before the innuendo stilled his tongue.

The diminutive Lord 'Bobs' was next, vanquisher of the Boers, along with Sir George White, whose dithering, according to colonel Simpson, had led to his besiegement in Ladysmith for a great part of that War, a fate shared by Baden Powell at Mafeking. Many stirred the patriotic conscience, but the effigy of nurse Edith Cavell, so recently executed by the Germans, captured the emotion.

The American Presidents lined the way to the suffragette Pankhursts, Kenney and Lawrence, to whom Laura paid rather too much homage for Scott's liking. He silently cursed 'that Jameson woman' and moved her on to the nation's hierarchy, Admiral Jellicoe, French, the sacked Field Marshal, Haig, into whose hands Richard would soon place his life, and finally the King and his cabinet. With the exception of the towering Kitchener and the corpulent Marshal Joffre, the French Generalissimo, they all seemed so small, so blank. Could the men, like their effigies, really be so devoid of feeling?

England's rulers through the ages held court in Hall Three, the Normans and Plantagenets, the Tudors and Stewarts, through to the tableau of the great Victoria herself. More unfamiliar faces followed, until Scott found himself face to face with the Kaiser.

He'd seen him in the flesh at Queen Victoria's funeral. He and Marian, newly wed, had been in the crowd. The Warlord's uniform was splendid, his face imperious, as it had been then. 'Strange, the things one remembers,' Scott thought.

He moved on, past the marble busts and relics of the Napoleon rooms, to the Chamber of Horrors, with its murderers and traitors, its torture tableaux and guillotine, the cell door from old Newgate and Crippen, its star attraction.

Self-accusation shivered his spine; Marian's agony contorted every death mask.

"They should've put Haig and that lot in here. What say you, Albert?"

"Nothing wrong with our esteemed generals what a whizz-bang wouldn't cure," an amputee answered from his crutches. "Get old Kitchener out there, that's what I say; he'd soon sort things out. It was him in the Sudan, and him what did for the Boers in the end, while Bobs took all the credit."

"As long as they don't bring back that bloody fool Buller."

Shrugging off a protesting 'I say!' from a eavesdropper, the hospital blues led on into the Hall of Tableau and the Children's Gallery, an antidote to the preceding exhibition of man's inhumanity to man. Even so, Scott was glad to feel the sun on his face.

"I think a spot of lunch is in order."

The Bank Holiday eating houses were packed; it took fifteen minutes to find a table. Lamb chops were followed by ice-cream, ice-cream by the bill.

"Where to, now?" Laura wanted to know.

Scott's answer was back to the bowels of the earth, this time via the novelty of the escalator to the Bakerloo line. Mindful of Richard's artistic bent and of Laura's loss of faith, he'd chosen the National Gallery as the perfect peace offering. Once inside, youth and maturity went their separate ways, arranging to meet at the entrance in two hours.

Richard wandered the galleries, awestruck by the painters' sheer genius, the depth of colour, the radiance, the magnitude of their endeavour. The size of the canvases had been beyond his previous comprehension. Rubens, Botticelli, Leonardo, Rembrandt; his own efforts paled into schoolboy perspective.

The Gainsboroughs were stunning. He stood before the landscape portrait of Mr. and Mrs. Andrews, totally absorbed. It was in the sky, in the sheer brilliance of the sky. He could have stepped into the canvas, breathed its air, walked the meadows, felt its sun on his face.

And then he saw it, the Velasquez, the Rokeby Venus. He'd never dreamed he would see it.

"It's a miracle they managed to restore it," he heard someone say, learning how a Suffragette had slashed it before the War. He stared at it incredulously. What he wouldn't give to paint Laura like that.

"She's a little on the plump side, don't you think?" His subject broke the spell. "And not at all pretty, judging by the reflection. It's a wonder she didn't break the glass. That must be why he painted her with her back turned."

Richard allowed himself to be clawed away into the Constable Gallery. Here was a landscape he knew well, 'The Haywain' and 'The Cornfield', painted just a day trip from Ashleigh, then the more alien 'Weymouth Bay' and 'Salisbury Cathedral'.

As with Madame Tussaud's, there was too much to take in. He could have spent a whole day simply absorbing the Velasquez, let alone the Rubens' and Botticellis', 'Landscape with the Chateau de Steen', 'Mars and Venus'. Leonardo's 'Virgin on the Rocks' had, quite literally, taken his breath away. And there were all those he had only glanced at, Hans Memlinc, Holbein, Goya, Bruegal, even the Turner sunsets he'd almost missed on the way out. He hadn't touched a paintbrush for some time; now he wanted to do nothing but paint, to paint the fields, to paint the skies, to paint Laura in a sunlit landscape.

Braving the pigeons in Trafalgar Square, the group followed the fleet down the Mall to gaze at the seat of the most powerful empire the world had ever known.

"It's big and everything, but it's a bit plain, isn't it? With that netting on its head, it looks like it's ready for bed," Laura derided Buckingham Palace's protective mesh.

"It's to catch any bombs that might be dropped," her father explained. "There was a similar one over the National Gallery, if you noticed."

"Really?"

They rested in St. James' Park. The spring flowers were in bloom; daffodils, crocuses. Westminster's wildfowl patrolled the lake's edge in small flotillas, on the lookout for scraps.

"Come on; let's feed the ducks." Laura pulled Richard up.

"What with?"

"Well, look at them then."

"Make the most of it; it'll be full of army huts, soon. They're going to drain it to put the Zeppelins off the scent." Scott repeated yet another of Colonel Simpson's state secrets.

They sauntered down to the water's edge. A military band struck up, calling the Bank Holiday promenaders to the pagoda with the ever popular 'Soldiers of the Queen'.

Nearby, a whining urchin pulled at his mother's skirt.

"Ma, Ma! Sid's eating a worm!"

"Sidney!"

A slapped leg brought a siren of a wail that continued all the way to the bandstand to send the cornets into discord.

Laura longed to feel the cooling breeze on her skin. 'No one batted an eyelid at the nudes in the gallery, least of all Richard,' she fumed. But her jealousy was momentary. He'd worn his cadet's uniform. He had to be boiling under all that serge. She pictured him stretched naked on the grass. He was so beautiful without his clothes.

'One day,' she vowed, 'one day.'

Scott and Agatha remained on the park bench. To Scott, it was as if the past three weeks had been decades. They still hadn't kissed romantically, yet each day he loved her more with a maturity that belied retrogressive infatuation or the sexual repression of years. This was a woman for all seasons, but was this the moment? Should he make hay while the dichotomy of war, which had already gifted him so much, almost as if in bottomless reparation, still shone, before the boys came home?

He took her hand.

"Agatha, I hope you won't think me too forward, I know we haven't known each other long, hardly any time at all in fact, but... would you ever... well, what I mean is, it would make me the happiest man in the world if you would consider... I don't mean immediately, but... dare I hope?"

Agatha bowed her head, lost in mourning ring memories under beige summer glove.

Scott cursed his impulsiveness, his total stupidity.

Her grip tightened; her eyes met his, tearful and tender.

"Yes," she said, simply.

Scott rounded off the outing with a private box at the Savoy. Richard had never been to a theatre, not even Elmsford's own Regent; he couldn't believe its opulence, nor the cost of the box, listed in the programme. Four guineas would feed the Bowdens for a month.

The production was H. B. Irving's 'The Barton Mystery'. The great man was playing 'Beverly - a drunken psychic.' Richard also noted the name of the 'Maid', Psyche Le Mesurier.

"Very apt," he joked, opening an outlet for the day's accumulated excitement. From the moment Irving stretched out his hands and uttered the legend, 'All is dark...', a proem he repeated ever more melodramatically with every revelatory tour de force, Richard saw the funny side. The darker things got, the funnier they became, until his hilarity spluttered forth, prompting a communal 'sssssshhhh' from the white-faced followers in the stalls.

Laura contracted the disease. The occupant of a neighbouring box cast his monacled indignance in her father's direction.

"Behave, you two," Scott growled.

"All is dark..."

It was asking the impossible. From the line's first reprise in Act Two, hilarity did battle with gnawed lips, pinched cheeks and bitten tongues right through to the final curtain.

"I thought people wore evening dress to the theatre," Laura tested her father's temper in the taxi to Liverpool Street.

"Bad form nowadays," he told her brusquely. "Khaki's the thing. Isn't that right, Richard?" Facing backwards in the bucket seat, Richard could only nod, nauseously. "It's just a pity the two of you couldn't have behaved with a bit more decorum."

Outside the station the newsboys were hawking their wares: "Revolution in Ireland, read all about it!"

Scott snatched up a paper.

"Good God."

"Is it serious?" Agatha asked.

"It would appear so. They could be hanging 'Traitor' round your Bernard Shaw's neck by morning," he revealed the gene pool of his daughter's jealous trait. "Come on, we'll miss the train."

However, not even insurgency could dampen their day.

"Do you think he'll propose?" Laura whispered, snuggled up to Richard in the back seat of the Bentall, while Scott saw Agatha to her door, their betrothal still an unshared secret.

Drawing a deep breath, Richard held out his hands and boomed in his best Irvingesque, "All is dark..."

"Sssshhhh!" Scott and Agatha hissed from the porch.

CHAPTER TWENTY FIVE

"Hello, it's Miss Scott, isn't it?"

Laura turned into Spencer Stafford's genial smile. She'd driven into Elmsford with her father to buy Richard a birthday present.

"I'm sorry; of course, you wouldn't remember; Stafford, Spencer Stafford." He touched the peak of his cap. "From the Manor?"

Laura had recognised him instantly, but she'd hardly expected the opposite, let alone that he should know her name. He looked tall and handsome in his officer's tunic, riding britches and Sam Brown belt.

"Oh yes, Captain Stafford," she acknowledged maturely, before a tactless, "you were at Church on Sunday," put her back in pigtails.

"Ah, yes," Spencer cleared his throat. "Couldn't stay, I'm afraid; bit of trouble with the old war wound."

"I'm sorry, nothing serious I hope?"

"Oh no, nothing at all, really. I'm back to the battle soon; next Monday in fact, unless they send me off to Ireland, of course."

"Yes, it is rather worrying."

"From what I gather, we've got them bottled up in the General Post Office. It shouldn't take long to flush 'em out. Doesn't bode well, though; the last thing we need is an uprising in our own backyard."

"Quite. Well, good luck, wherever you go."

"You're most kind."

The conversation had reached its natural conclusion, but he seemed in no hurry to move on.

"Fine weather for the time of year."

"Yes, very pleasant," Laura agreed, now both femininely and socially flattered. Conversing with a captain, and a Stafford at that, held a certain, egotistical 'Je ne sais qoi'. It would only take one Priory blabbermouth...

"Meeting anyone, or on a lonely shopping excursion?"

"The latter," she told him, "a birthday present."

"Family, friend, or someone you can't abide but have to buy for, like a crabby old aunt or some such?"

Again his familiarity surprised her. "Friend," she laughed politely, adding a little bashfully, "special friend," as if to put the record straight.

"Oh, I see. Look, I'm going your way, may I offer my assistance? My sisters tell me I'm an excellent shopper; apparently I have a knack for picking the right things."

Laura could find no grounds for excusal; the proffered arm all but forbade it. After all, he was a Stafford, his etiquette inbred and reliable; he wouldn't have offered had it been improper. It would be unrefined to refuse and, besides, he was amusing and there was something rather sad about him. He was returning to the

War soon; what harm was there in accepting? It might even cheer him up. She wasn't doing anything wrong.

Nevertheless, she checked for witnesses, as she took his Captain's cuff.

Since Easter Sunday, Spencer had stabilized his emotions with whisky. Then he had seen Laura. Time had been too precious for social propriety, forward had been the only way, although he didn't quite know to where.

"What sort of thing are you looking for?" He asked.

"I don't really know. Something special; he's going off to war soon."

Spencer had rather hoped her 'special friend' might be a 'she'. Still, what did it matter? Her tone precluded a man on leave, which meant the lucky beggar was either coming of age or otherwise being conscripted. If he was coming of age, what did that make her, sixteen, seventeen? His sister Mary was seventeen; there couldn't be much in it.

"Officer?" He asked without condescension. He'd soon learned to respect the men under his command.

"Yes; at least I assume so. He's a cadet at present."

'Cadet' was more of a clue, although nowadays it could easily mean a pleb from a grammar school OTC. Spencer had been out of touch socially, but he hardly thought Sandhurst or Woolwich, not for a village girl, however pretty. The distilled poison of his predicament seeped onto the canvas. Whoever this boy was, he envied his virility.

"Then it must be something to remember you by, and if it can be of some practical use, so much the better." 'Like a bullet proof jockstrap,' his sarcasm fed his self-pity. "Does he smoke?"

"No, not at all. He might have a cigar at Christmas, but that's all."

"Well, he will do. Everyone smokes in the army; there's often little else to do. Relieves the boredom." 'And settles the nerves,' he added to himself. "Perhaps a cigarette case?"

"Perhaps."

"A handy thing to have. Keep it here, you see," Spencer tapped his breast pocket, "over the heart; been known to save a man's life." 'Doesn't do much for one's balls, of course, but that's another matter,' he kept up his mental momentum.

"Is it really so bad?"

"I'm sorry, I didn't mean to alarm you. No, not at all; not much chance of getting bumped off, as long as one's careful."

Her forced smile quickly faded.

They stopped in front of Ward's Outfitters.

"A good pair of boots, now there's the thing. Sturdy boots are a must in the trenches."

"But surely the army supplies boots?"

"Good Lord, no. An officer's boots are his own, bad form to wear regulation. I get all my kit here. First class man, old Wardy."

Laura looked less than enthusiastic.

153

"No, I suppose it's hardly the thing."

They wandered on from window to window, but nothing caught her eyes.

"I'll tell you what; how about a watch, one of these all weather numbers with a luminous dial?" The inspiration came. "They're all the rage. You can have it engraved on the back. Damned useful things. I have one myself. I can't tell you what a godsend it is on dark winter nights. Flash a torch and one's likely to get drilled, but with one of those, telling the time's a doddle. He'll love you forever, I guarantee it. It will be a constant reminder."

She agreed to look.

"Stephenson's is the place."

The doorbell tinkled. The manager advanced in time honoured subservience.

"Captain Stafford; this is indeed a pleasure."

"The young lady is looking for a watch, Mr. Stephenson."

"Actually, it's Hitchcock, sir," the manager reminded his valued customer, as he always reminded him, smiling unprepossessingly at the girl over half-moon spectacles. "Charmed, I'm sure. Mr. Jeffries, a chair for the young lady."

An acne-faced youth brought the gilded podium. Hitchcock produced the presentation trays, excusing the afflicted from the vicinity with a "thank you, Mr. Jeffries," lest the boy's eruption-ripe acne should explode over the merchandise. He'd had his eye on it all morning.

Perfection beckoned in the second from the left, top row, third drawer. It was simplicity itself, a circular gold frame on a silver casing, its white face marked with Arabic numerals and modestly inscribed, 'Longines'. The skeletal hands were coated in radium, much to the detriment of the painter's health, so it was rumoured in the trade.

"An admirable choice, Miss, if I may say," Hitchcock beamed, extolling its 'limited edition' virtues. The watch had been a special order, sadly annulled by a sniper's bullet. He had been living with the loss ever since.

The captain ushered him out of earshot to discuss terms.

"Of course, Captain Stafford, of course."

He returned to the counter. "I believe it is to be engraved?"

"Oh, yes," the girl collected herself. "But I need to know..."

"Come and look at this," the captain forestalled her indiscretion.

Hitchcock had eavesdropped on such conversations a hundred times; "Look, I'd rather you left the financial arrangements to me; it would be just too embarrassing." "But I don't know if I can afford it." "It's already taken care of, I have an account here. Now, if you'd care to compose the inscription, we'll find the nearest coffee shop and let them get on with the engraving." "But Captain Stafford..." "Don't worry. Everything will be fine, I promise you."

Hitchcock had pencil and paper waiting. It would be ready within the hour.

In Friar's tea rooms, the waitress poured.

"Cream, Sir?"

The coffee was whitened, the bill left. Spencer toyed with his spoon, absorbed by the creature sitting opposite. He was happy, actually happy. This girl was like an elixir.

"How clever of you. It was a wonderful suggestion," she beamed. "Now, you must tell me how much it is."

"Look, won't you allow me?"

"Oh, but I couldn't. It's a present, you see."

"Well now it's two presents, from me to you and from you to him, whoever he is."

"But we hardly know each other, Captain Stafford; it wouldn't be right."

Even her middleclassness amused him. And he felt something else, a need, a rivalry.

"My dear girl, we may never have been formally introduced, but I've known you since you were that high;" he held out his hand. "I even have the pictures to prove it."

"You do?"

"Indubitably I do."

He watched her puzzle it out. Her smile was like a sunburst.

"Oh course; the school photo; it was you."

"There, so you see, our acquaintance is practically lifelong. Anyway, it's such a small thing. You must say yes, I'll be terribly hurt if you don't."

"Please understand, I don't mean to be ungrateful, but I couldn't possibly," she pleaded.

Why was he doing this? He could see it in her eyes. It was a question he was asking himself. He had no conscious ulterior motive. Disability notwithstanding, he would love to get her in front of his camera again, preferably as naked as nature intended, but that wasn't the reason, the fantasy was unworthy. He was doing it simply ... because.

"Look, I'll be gone in less than a week. It would mean so much to me, a bit like treating one's favourite sister. Honestly, I'm no Sudanese slave trader about to whisk you off to the Kasbah or what-have-you, not that one wouldn't be tempted." Suddenly revelation was imperative, impulsive. "You see, I couldn't have my evil way with you if I tried; I've been incapacitated in that regard since Gallipoli."

There; he'd admitted it. 'You fool,' his self-pity screamed in its death throes, then the struggle was ended and he felt at unprecedented peace. But how could he have spoken to her of such things? She was a complete stranger, almost a child.

"Please forgive me. I'm afraid I've embarrassed you. I shouldn't have..."

"Oh no, Captain Stafford; I didn't know. I'm so sorry. Is there nothing they can do?"

In her reaction was a maturity beyond her years, in her concern a depth beyond the superficial. This was no child, this no stranger. Her aura embraced him. 'God, if only....'

"No, I'm afraid not. So, you see, really, it would simply give me the greatest pleasure to buy it for you, that's all."

"But how can I ever repay you?"

"You already have," he grinned, "you've made my whole morning. Well, I'm glad that's settled. The coffee's cold, I'll order another; we have plenty of time. Don't worry," he tapped his nose. "It will be our secret."

* * * * *

Scott met Laura for lunch. She was looking extremely pleased with herself.

"You found something?" Scott smiled.

"A watch," she announced. "I found it in Stephenson's. It's perfect, daddy, absolutely perfect."

"Stephenson's, eh?" Scott raised an eyebrow. The Jeweller had enjoyed a lucrative morning. He thanked providence they hadn't bumped into each other. "Must've been expensive. Are you sure you had enough?"

"More than enough, thank you. Do look."

"Oh, it's a pity to spoil the wrapping. Describe it to me."

"Well, it's solid silver, with a gold frame and it even glows in the dark!"

"Good Lord, whatever will they think of next?" Scott handed it back. Luminous it may be, but, on her allowance, hardly solid silver. "I'm sure he'll love it, my sweet. Pocket or one of those new fangled wristlet contraptions?"

"A wrist watch; it's got a strap and everything, and I've seen the perfect present from you, a pair of boots. Officers have to supply their own boots. They're brown and they lace up at the front; proper trench boots."

"I thought cavalry boots were all the rage?"

"Oh, no; they went out with the Ark."

"Colonel Simpson still wears them."

"Yes, but Colonel Simpson's an old fuddy-duddy."

"Well, you'd better find out his size from Mrs. Bowden. Look, I've... er... I've asked Miss Cooper to dine with us tonight."

"Oh, daddy, don't be so stuffy. Her name's Agatha. She'd be most hurt to know you called her 'Miss Cooper' all the time."

"All right, Agatha then," he acknowledged affably, taking a list from his pocket. "Anyway, I thought we might spoil ourselves, have a drop of wine and whatnot. Would you mind seeing what you can find, then meet me at the office, say about four? Here's some money. I've asked Mrs. Creswell to do the cooking."

The employment of Mrs. Creswell was no slight on Laura; Priory girls were not expected to cook. She looked down the list. "Smoked Salmon? French cheese? My, we are pushing the boat out."

"Yes, well, it doesn't hurt, once in a while. We'll invite young Richard, if it's not too late; perhaps we'll play crib. Four o' clock, then?"

* * * * *

Spencer rendezvoused with Laura, as arranged, and they shopped, he, flouting regimental rules, carrying the bags from store to store, until three irreverent recruits

156

decided to play army convention at its own game by doubling back and forth along the High Street, forcing him to acknowledge their salutes. After dropping one parcel and squashing another, he decided enough was enough.

"Hey, you!"

They took their conscription in good heart, following like native bearers from emporium to emporium. The only thing unavailable was the wine Scott had chosen.

"I'm sure he'll find this one most palatable," Spencer came to the rescue.

By four o' clock he and Laura were firm friends. He walked her to the Timber Yard and ordered the bearers to deposit the bags in the back of Scott's car, before dismissing them with a florin. He turned to Laura.

"Now, are you sure you can manage?"

"There's nothing to manage. You've been so kind; I don't know how to thank you."

"It was my pleasure, absolutely. Look, today's been such fun, I was wondering, would you care to come up to the house for tea or something, before I go, bring back memories of your childhood and what-have-you?"

"Not all pleasant ones, I'm afraid," Laura said sadly.

"Really, I'm sorry to hear that."

"My mother..."

"Oh, how stupid of me; of course," Spencer remembered. "Well, perhaps a picnic, then, how's that? Just the ticket."

"I'm not sure my fiancé would approve."

"Oh; I didn't realise you were actually engaged. Yes, I do understand," he affected to confess, playing on her sympathy with downcast eyes, while cursing her lack of sophistication. "But, surely, tea wouldn't hurt?"

The ploy worked.

"All right, then."

"Oh, jolly good. Let's say Friday, about three?"

"Three would be fine."

"Oh, I am pleased. Well, I'd better go and retrieve my motorcycle. I left it with the stationmaster, poor fellow. Hopefully he hasn't mistaken it for army ordnance and put it on a train to Timbuktu. Until Friday, then?"

"Friday," she nodded.

"Who was that?" Scott asked, when he joined Laura at the car.

"Captain Stafford from the Manor; you know, the Squire's son? He was going to introduce himself, but I knew you'd be in a hurry. I hardly recognised him; I hadn't seen him in ages, not since I was at school there. It was nice of him to remember. He commandeered three men to carry the groceries, officer's aren't allowed, you see. It was a real hoot. I felt like Mrs. Curtis in 'King Solomon's Mines'."

Scott was impressed; to have a Stafford carry her bags rather put his social efforts in the shade.

"So, that's young Stafford, is it? Taken bad at church, wasn't he?"

"Yes, but he's all right now. He's leaving for France next week, or perhaps

Ireland, he's not exactly sure. Ready?"

The news negated further enquiry; Scott's mind was on the evening ahead.

"Well, you know what they say, can't keep a good man down."

Even so, he looked on his daughter, if not in a new light, in a more illuminating hue.

- CHAPTER TWENTY SIX -

The dinner went off perfectly. To Laura's immense relief, her father didn't mention Spencer, even when he complimented her on the wine. Richard would have been unbearably jealous; he'd sulked for days over the 'drip' episode; she wished she'd never told him. However, her resentment rose like bile, when, with Agatha by his side, her father announced their engagement.

Its residue fermented when her father drove Agatha home, dropping Richard off on the way. Laura didn't begrudge her father his happiness, if anything, she felt guilty at her tempered response, but she couldn't help contrasting the freedom of her elders with the fetters inflicted on youth. It wasn't fair to charge her father with betrayal, but it was that very feeling which now possessed her and, perversely, focused on Richard.

Why did he have to be so sensible all the time? Why couldn't he demand that they marry? She was seventeen, lots of girls married at seventeen. It just wasn't fair! Why couldn't he, just for once, cast responsibility to the wind? He could have sneaked back tonight, her father would be ages yet. Why was it always left to her to take the initiative?

It was then, as if on contradictory cue, that Richard appeared on the doorstep. He had sensed her depression. She fell into his arms.

"Oh, Richard, why can't we marry, why?" She sobbed.

"We will, my darling, we will."

The implicit future tense was tantamount to treason.

"No, Richard; now; I want to get married now," her frustration cried.

"Oh, Laura, you know it's impossible."

She gloried in his caress, but it wasn't enough. She wanted to lie with him for long hours in naked togetherness in their own marital bed.

"Stay with me tonight."

It wasn't a conscious plea of emotional blackmail, only of desperation, a desperation that quickly grasped the logistics. He had been given a key since being locked out. The Bowdens would be in bed, so what did it matter what time he slipped back?

"You can hide in my room until father's gone to bed. He'll never know, honestly he won't."

"But he's bound to hear us."

"Not if we're quiet. Oh, please, Richard..."

The boy sat on the edge of Laura's bed, fidgeting with his thumbs. He knew he'd be caught, he just knew it. Was this how he repaid Scott's trust? He couldn't go through with it, it was too risky. He rose; the front door opened; he lowered himself back on the bed, quiet as a mouse.

"I'm home," he heard Scott call.

"In here," Laura answered from the kitchen. "Cocoa?"

"Yes, please."

The die was cast. The boy swallowed hard. Despite the mildness of the night, he began to shiver.

Laughter filtered through the floorboards, easing his nerves. Scott had been a different man since meeting Miss Cooper. His eyes were brighter, a smile came more readily to his lips, he looked years younger.

They must be talking about the wedding, he figured, allowing his mind to wander through the lych gate and down the aisle, until footsteps on the stairs startled him back to the present.

"Are you coming up?" Her father's proximity set his heart thumping.

"I'll just clear away," he heard Laura call.

"Goodnight, then. Check the back door, will you? I've seen to the front."

"Goodnight."

The landing boards creaked. Richard's eyes boggled; dear God, Scott was coming in! But the door that opened wasn't his door. His breath escaped in a rush. He heard the lavatory being used, a tap being run. He could sneak out now and Scott would be none the wiser; but he sat, riveted.

Again doors opened and closed. He heard Scott's shoes clump to the floor, coat hangers clatter, bedsprings squeak. How on earth was he going to escape without being heard?

Lighter steps fell on the stairs. Laura took longer in the bathroom.

"Goodnight."

"Pleasant dreams."

And then she was there, a goddess cast in lamp-lit relief. The flame died, cloaking her in black velvet. Richard heard the latch click, sensed her beside him. His skin prickled, his buttocks tightened, his manhood rose. She opened the curtains and stood before him, a trembling foal in the faintest light. He enfolded her, scarcely daring to breath, scarcely daring to believe that the world was his.

She slept childlike in his arms, a picture of sweet contentment. He'd lost the feeling in the crook of his arm, the pillow on which her beauty rested, but he didn't care.

They'd made love in silent slow-motion, the daring of their predicament intensifying their ecstasy. The sensation still lingered. Her wet sex bathed his leg. She had almost lost control, smothering her cries at the moment of release, yet, still, fear and conscience had forbidden them the ultimate union.

A pale glow haloed the horizon. Across the landing, her father was snoring.

He kissed her tangled hair. "Darling, I've got to go."

His whisper barely roused her.

"Hm? No," she complained, tightening her hold.

"Laura, you've got to wake up." He loved her more desperately than ever.

She squinted. "It's still dark."

"Sssshhh! Really, it's time."

"You don't have to go yet."

"Yes I do."

"Oooh," she moaned. "It's not fair."

He sat up and rubbed the circulation back into his arm.

She draped herself over his back.

"Come back to bed," she yawned.

God, how he wanted to, but it was impossible.

She slumped sulkily onto her pillow, then arched up again, throwing her arms around him.

"I love you, Richard Bowden."

Scott's snoring eased them down the stairs and into the hallway's disorientating darkness.

"Mind the chest," Laura breathed too late.

"Aahh!"

While Richard hornpiped round the hall, the ululations from above stuttered and stopped. Every creak of the floorboards amplified Laura's apprehension.

"Stay still," she hissed.

At last, Scott's adenoids sounded the all clear.

"Come on."

She led Richard blindly into the kitchen, softly pushing the door to behind them before opening the blackout curtain.

"That was close," he breathed, letting out an involuntary 'ouch' as he eased his shoe over his throbbing toe.

"I told you to be careful. It's not broken is it?"

"I'll survive."

Noiselessly, Laura slid back the door bolts and lifted the latch, only for the hinges to groan in petrifying complaint.

"Go," she hustled him out.

"I love you."

"I love you more."

A last kiss and he left her, heading for the garden fence.

"Is that you, Laura?"

She flew into the hall. Lamplight flickered down the stairs. Her father's dishevelled head peered over the banister.

"Yes, it's only me. I couldn't sleep. I thought some milk might help."

She cursed her nerves. She sounded like a lesser-spotted wood warbler.

"Are you all right?"

"Yes. Something must have woken me; probably an owl or something."

Her father nodded. "As long as you're all right." In his sleepwalking state he seemed easily satisfied, if not totally unobservant. "Where's your dressing gown, girl? Really, you should take more care."

"I'll only be a minute."

"You're sure you're all right?" He sounded like a drunkard.

161

"Yes," she grinned up convincingly.

"See you in the morning, then."

Scuttling back to the kitchen, she bolted the door and turned the key.

* * * * *

Richard climbed the stairs on tenterhooks. His mother was a notoriously light sleeper. Dawn had broken before he finally succumbed to sleep. Within the hour he was being shaken awake.

Breakfast was porridge, a village fad since the Cameronians' arrival. He spooned it down robotically, thankful that Elizabeth and the children were late risers. A cold wash and a brisk walk to the yard cleared his head, although, all day long, he remained preoccupied with the stomach churning risks he'd taken and his longing to take them again. However, when evening came it offered only frustration. Scott wasn't seeing Agatha. Richard was home shortly after nine. His parents were already in bed; Elizabeth had stayed up.

"You're home a bit previous, aren't you?"

"I needed an early night," he told her, emphasising the fact with a gaping yawn.

"Well I'm not surprised, time you came home last night, or should I say this morning. No need to ask what you was up to young man."

His security was shaken.

"What do you mean?"

"As if you didn't know. Don't come the old innocent with me, my dear, I'm not your mother. It's a wonder she didn't hear you, the noise you made coming up them stairs; it was enough to wake the dead."

He slumped dejectedly into his chair.

"Don't worry, I won't tell on you. It's good to have a healthy young man about the house. Just mind you don't get caught, that's all."

He was too tired to argue. The truth was the truth; she knew and that was that.

"Besides," she grinned, "you was only doing what comes naturally, like you nearly did with me that time."

He'd long forgotten that Christmas and he'd hoped she had done the same.

"Come off it, Liz, nothing happened."

"Could've done though. I seem to remember you being eager enough, and no mistake."

"Liz, I was drunk, we both were, I don't even remember."

She sidled onto the arm of his chair. "Oh, I think you do. I was more gone than you and I remember alright. 'Course, we could always pick up where we left off."

She fondled his hair; her cleavage brushed his cheek. He turned away irritably.

"Don't, Liz. Look, you're in enough trouble as it is."

"And so might you be if I was to say summat. Besides, one good turn deserves another. Maybe I could teach you a thing or two, keep that Laura of yours happy."

"I don't think she'd have anything to be happy about, do you?"

"Well, I won't tell her if you don't," she breathed, teasingly circling his crotch with her fingertips. "Come on, boy, you know you want to."

162

"Stop it, Liz, it's not funny."

She cut the radius.

"He seems to like it alright."

"Give over, Liz, please."

She giggled. "Oh, come on, bit of fun won't hurt."

Her tongue dipped into his ear. His complaints lacked any consonant or vowel of conviction. He was barely aware of anything, until he found her breasts bared before him, full and firm, burgeoning with temptation.

"You like them, boy, don't you? There's none better in the whole village."

She reached for his fly buttons. Despite his guilt, despite the stupidity of letting himself be seduced, the battle was lost.

"Don't, Liz," he moaned, but made no curtailing move.

"Just this once, then I won't tell on you, I promise."

Her practised fingers eased him into surrender; her flesh tantalised his lips.

"That's nice, boy. Bit harder... yes... like that."

He filled his mouth with her ripe nipple; his hands sought.

"Mmmmm," she oozed. "Nice and big, just like my Georgie." Her head dipped. "Let's see how he tastes."

He watched in astonishment as she closed her lips around him, then her words crashed through his rapture like an express train.

"No!" He threw himself from the chair. "This isn't right. Tell whoever you like, I don't care. You're my sister-in-law, for Christ's sake!"

Elizabeth's incredulity turned to angry humiliation. She struggled into her dress.

"I don't know what's wrong with you Bowdens, really I don't."

"What's wrong with me is that I let it get this far," Richard fumed, buttoning himself. "What's wrong with you, God only knows."

"Well, hurrah for you, mister bloody righteous."

"What's going on down here?" Mrs. Bowden was at the door in hairnet and curlers. "You'll wake the whole house."

"Nothing," Richard spat, glaring contemptuously at Elizabeth. "I'm going to bed."

"Have you been trying it on with him, you hussey?" Beatrice railed at Elizabeth, after Richard had gone. "If you have, I'll..."

"We had a disagreement, that's all. He'll get over it."

"You'd better make sure he does." Beatrice had the last word.

Upstairs, little Doris started to cry; she'd been easily provoked since the fire.

'Christ Almighty,' Elizabeth seethed, heading for the door in turn. 'Chance'd be a fine thing!'

- CHAPTER TWENTY SEVEN -

Laura set off for the Manor just after nine, taking the footpath across the meadows and over the footbridge. The hedgerows hummed with insect activity, the burgeoning nettles, burdocks and dandelions danced in her slipstream. However platonic the circumstance, she should never have accepted Spencer's invitation, nor gone shopping with him; and, as for letting him pay for the watch, what ever had possessed her? What had seemed innocent before the lovers' night of passion, now instilled guilt. The note was in her purse; there had been no time to post it; she would slip it through the letterbox. She hoped the money was enough; it was all she had.

She was just emerging onto the main road, when the roar of a motorcycle checked her progress. She knew instinctively it was him. Spencer braked and lifted his goggles.

"Miss Scott! What a lovely surprise."

"Captain Stafford."

"You haven't forgotten this afternoon, have you?"

"No, I..." Laura's tongue tied itself in knots. She felt like a miscreant caught in the act.

"I'm so glad; the family are dying to meet you. How do you like my steed? They've taken all the horses."

She was lost. She could only force a smile.

"Well, must dash, Pater's expecting me and I'm late already. See you at three, then."

'Damn!' Laura watched her excuses accelerate away. Why couldn't she have told him? Her heart sank.

The afternoon was warm and fine and Laura forewent the discomfort of a coat. Already suffering from conscience, etiquette now added to her apprehension. The Priory had prepared her for society, she'd sailed through the Mayor's soirée, but tea with the Staffords was entirely different. Although she'd been to school at the Big House, she'd never been a guest there.

She felt the first spots of rain as she passed the gatehouse. She hurried on. Halfway to the house, the heavens opened. She ran for all she was worth, but by the time she reached the Doric portico, she was drenched. Her hair, her best summer dress! She could have cried. It was as if Thor himself had cast his bolt. Why hadn't she told Richard? After all, Spencer was only a friend, there was nothing for Richard to be jealous about, nothing to hide.

The April shower drew away as suddenly as it had come, leaving the paddock glistening.

'Thank you very much," she groaned. "I can't go in looking like this."

Resigned to a sodden tramp home, she was heading down the steps, when the door opened behind her.

"There you are. I was afraid you might be caught in the... Oh, I see you were."

It was Spencer. Glumly, she turned to face him. He was walking towards her, umbrella in hand.

"Yes. I'm afraid I'm rather wet."

"Never mind, we'll get you dry in no time. Hawkins!" He called for the butler. "Come in, come in."

"Oh, but I can't." She couldn't meet the Staffords looking like this.

"Don't be silly, of course you can; you must, before you catch pneumonia."

She pictured Richard in her kitchen, similarly soaked; she had coaxed him out of his clothes with those self-same words. It was a conspiracy, she shouldn't be here, but the gods were leaving her no option.

She squelched into the hall. The spindly-legged epitome of the ancient retainer appeared.

"Hawkins; I'm afraid the young lady is soaked through. Ask Mrs. Avery to rustle up some dry clothes, there's a good chap."

"No, really Captain Stafford," Laura protested.

"You can't sit around dripping like a tap. Apart from anything else you'll ruin the furniture."

"This way, Miss."

Hawkins led the way up the restoration staircase, his arthritic knees crackling like dried twigs. At any other time Laura would have felt like royalty; today she felt like a herring. 'Please God, don't let anyone see me,' she prayed.

"If you'd care to wait in here, Miss, Mrs. Avery will up directly."

Sanctuary at last. The room, unused for years, had seen better days. The trim of the emerald drapes was a sunbleached aquamarine, the floral wallpaper in direct window line faded. The mahogany furniture sat with the discretion of a trusted friend round the threadbare Persian carpet. It was a pleasant room. The last fleeting cloud scudded across the sky; sunshine poured through the tall French windows. Laura smiled, the room smiled back.

A knock on the door heralded Mrs. Avery, a stout woman in her fifties, towel in hand.

"Oh, my dear, you're dreening." She waddled to Laura's aid. "Let's get you out of those wet things before you croak."

Laura was glad of the 'croak'; one more accusatory 'catch pneumonia' and she would have surrendered herself to Constable Gruff.

"I haven't seen you, oh, must be some five years or more," Mrs. Avery chattered on, helping Laura out of her dress. She had, of course, in church, but that didn't count. "My, you've grown." She felt Laura's underwear. "No, they'll have to come off, too, dear, can't walk around in those."

Mrs. Avery seemed to have a disconcerting obsession with active assistance.

"Oh, they're not too bad," Laura shied away.

"But you can't wear them, dear, good gracious no." Mrs. Avery looked horrified. "Oh, you mustn't mind me; I've seen enough nakedness to last me a lifetime. The upper classes don't dress themselves, you know; that's what servants is for."

Still Laura hesitated.

"Well, put this on, then," the housekeeper passed a Chinese robe from the wardrobe, delving deeper while Laura peeled off under it.

"Don't think we'll find anything in here, these were all Miss Daphne's things. She's a mite fuller in the figure than you, more so now, with a baby on the way. Miss Mary's more your size. Shan't be a mo'. This place could do with a lick of paint," she tutted on the way out.

Laura wandered into the sunlight, allowing its warmth to highlight the farcicality of her predicament. It was all some ungodly joke, or godly, as the case may be. Well, it served her right.

Through the window the manor's arbour glistened. She was completely shielded; she could stand there naked and no one would see her, but, today, that would be tempting fate too far. Instead she contented herself with sun-kissed fantasy, until she heard the rustle of Mrs. Avery's skirts.

Under normal circumstances, there would have been no question of a village girl being introduced to the family, however illegitimate the branch. As it was, Mrs. Stafford had found her diary full. Squire Stafford's overriding concern, however, was the impact the girl might have on his son, particularly given her looks, although he had to admit that Spencer's mood had improved remarkably since he'd met her. Stafford only hoped the boy didn't suffer a polar reversal.

When he joined them for tea, his fears multiplied. The lilac and rose combination she was wearing, if a little on the large side, suited her well. Her hair cascaded in curls; at close quarters, her mouth was the definition of sensuality; her eyes, alone, were enough to melt the heart of any man.

'If only I were younger,' he lamented, complimenting her on her outfit. "I believe our Mary has one just like it. I'm sorry she's not here to meet you; she and her mother had a prior engagement."

They talked of Laura's time at the Manor School, and inevitably of her mother's stroke.

"Sad, very sad; during the coronation fete, wasn't it? Which reminds me; that scholarship boy, the handyman's son, is he doing well, do you know?"

Richard's reported progress registered no more than a tick in an inconsequential credit box. Stafford's mind was on Spencer. He seemed quite like his old self. Even when they touched on the War, he didn't react adversely. Stafford's fears faded. If the girl made Spencer happy, so be it. Come Monday, the poor chap would be back at the front; whatever solace she could afford him was gratefully accepted.

After twenty enjoyable minutes away from Estate affairs and the latest invasion scare, Stafford finished his tea and excused himself.

"Yes, he's not a bad old stick," Spencer conceded over replenished cups and more cake.

The conversation turned to the future. Laura asked his plans, once the War was over.

"Well, I don't really know." He'd long discounted the concept of a future. Now, just perhaps, he was beginning to regret his suicidal impulse to return to the front. "There's always the estate, of course, but photography's my real craving."

"Really? I've seldom had my picture taken," Laura told him. "Once, when my mother and sister were alive, and school photos, of course, but then you know about those, at least some of them."

'A sister?' Spencer didn't ask, he was otherwise engaged. A barely holed button had popped open on her blouse. He caught a tantalising glimpse of bare flesh, the discernible curve of a breast. His fleeting coffee house fancy revived. He would love to get her in front of his camera, and more.

"I've been studying the art for some time," he gathered himself, crumbling Madeira cake. "I enjoy it immensely. I lose myself in it." He could hardly embarrass the poor girl by telling her she was exposed, but it was difficult not to look. "You should let me take your picture sometime. Photographs are such wonderful things; one can capture a moment, a memory. Nice to look back on when one's older."

"Perhaps, when I don't look like a drowned rat in someone else's clothes."

'And out of them?' He teased himself, instinctively looking again, as she lifted her cup.

"But yours is such a natural beauty; it should be captured for posterity."

His eyes flicked up, catching her catching him. She looked down. He looked away, crudity's child caught at the keyhole.

The cup rattled in her saucer. She flushed. The charade had to be ended, yet equally preserved. He searched for an escape route.

"I say, would you like to see some of my work? I'll go and fetch it; shan't be a mo'."

When he returned, the button was fastened. He sat beside her, wishing it wasn't, willing her to reciprocate his invitation to "be my guest," when he handed her the album.

She browsed, seemingly absorbed, from his first snapshots of friends and retainers, to the class photo and studio portraits, landscapes and still-lifes, then some of Gallipoli, the warships in the bay, the troops in the trenches.

"Not this one." He reached over with a covering palm. "It's definitely not suitable for young ladies."

"Oh, don't be silly," she proclaimed her maturity.

"No, honestly; the men aren't decent."

He turned the page, only to have it flipped back when he took his hand away.

"Well, don't say I didn't warn you."

But he found any embarrassment purely his own; the nudity of the men bathing in the sea didn't seem to shock Laura one bit.

"Are there others?" She asked, reaching the end.

Should he show her? The tantalising glimpse of her breast, her open-mindedness over the bathers, the shortage of time, all prompted him. He may never get another chance. The identity of his sitters would be safe enough; she would never have met his sister Mary or Lady Alice, and, even if she had, in their get-ups she wouldn't know them from Eve. The opportunity was too tempting to pass up. Besides, what had he got to lose?

"Well there are, but I'm not sure I should show you; they're of a type which, well, not to put too fine a point on it, some people might take exception to, although I don't see why. When it comes to the human form, it seems paint and canvas are one thing, the camera quite another. It's a load of rot, if you ask me. We're both trying to capture the same thing, the painter and I."

"Yes, I can see that."

His pulse quickened.

"Well, there you are. Personally, I regard them among my best work. I keep them in the dark room, away from prying eyes. If anyone saw them, well... Few have your acuity."

"Oh, do let me see."

Suddenly he was unsure. Would the pictures adversely colour her perception of him? Did he care?

"It's terribly dusty in there."

He led the way, damning himself for his chicanery. Even now he could act the dunderhead and pretend he'd been misconstrued. He had other pictures far more shocking, of the bloated dead at Chunuk Blair, of the skeletal hand sticking out of the dugout wall, of half a head, thick with flies, its brain baked black by the Turkish sun. But he didn't need to be reminded and she didn't need to see.

He opened the studio door. A cloud of dust rode the thermal currents from floor to skylight.

"I'm dreadfully sorry. I don't allow anyone in, you see. I haven't used it for yonks, not since the war, in fact. It was our playroom, when we were young. I remember riding a horse in here once and Mrs. A. going berserk. I'll ask her to give it a good going over. The dark room's through there. You'll find it a bit cramped; it used to be our toy cupboard."

It was bigger than he remembered, big enough to shelter a whole platoon. He brushed the cobwebs from the electric desk lamp and rummaged among the piles and paraphernalia.

"Ah; these are they." He wiped the portfolio's cover with his sleeve. "Now, are you sure?"

He hadn't seen the erotica for years. It offered him nothing. But then he was hardly likely to find his own sister arousing, or lady Alice, for that matter, nude or not, he reasoned. Yet in its sharing was the baring of his loins, both in their past potency and their present deformity.

Laura's profile stood proud against the single light source. Her absorption was pulsating. He wished to hell that her button would come loose again, that her whole damned outfit would fall apart.

"These were taken before the war, of course. I could do much better now. The turbans and whatnot look rather silly. You don't think them... well, you know."

"On the contrary, I think they're quite beautiful."

She could hardly have given him more encouragement.

"I'm so glad. Though, as I say, I've improved immeasurably since then." Would she? He felt like a lecher. "A study of you would put these to shame."

The blood rushed to his cheeks, charged with a self-condemnation made all the more acute by the blood that effusively rushed to hers. Her silence was more censuring still. His courage failed him. He cleared his throat.

"Yes, well, perhaps we should be getting back; it wouldn't do to set tongues wagging."

He snapped the book shut and returned it to its hiding place.

"After you."

Each retraced footstep resounded with his crassness, each vacuum it left with his cowardice. Why hadn't he asked her outright? The answer was simple. That first session with his sister and Alice had been a spontaneous prank more of their own, one-upmanship instigation, than his. It had been all he could do to stem their hysterics while he clicked the shutter. This would have been entirely different. Whatever happened, he had to see her again.

"Look, joking apart, why don't you sit for me, a portrait for your intended? Such things can be a great comfort in the trenches. Of course it will have to be tomorrow, or I won't have time to develop them; as you know, I leave on Monday and God only knows when I'll be back."

He cast his eyes in mourning, prompting another self-accusation of slyness.

"It's too much to ask," she smiled nervously. "I'm sure you'd rather spend what little time you have with your family."

"On the contrary," he assured her, "I can think of nothing I'd like better and no one with whom I'd rather spend my last hours here. It would mean more to me than I can say; please say you will. What is it, Hawkins?" Spencer damned the man's timing.

"The young lady's clothes are dry, Sir."

"She'll be with you directly."

Hawkins waited, too hard of hearing to take the hint.

The clock was striking five when Laura returned.

"I really should be going."

"Will you come tomorrow?"

She looked almost fearful.

"There's nothing to be afraid of, I assure you. The camera won't bite."

"If I do, no one must know, you must promise me."

There was a tremor in her voice, a wildness in her eyes that stopped him in his tracks. She couldn't mean...? No, he was reading too much into it. She must be afraid her fiancé, whoever he was, would blow his top if he found out. But he would find out anyway, when she gave him the photographs. Oh well...

"You have my word. Until tomorrow, then?"

- CHAPTER TWENTY EIGHT -

"Damn! Damn! Damn!"

Even as the Manor gravel crunched beneath her feet, Laura cursed this mad Alice who popped up in Spencer's wonderland. The last thing she'd meant to do was see him again, as if once wasn't enough. She could have died when her blouse had fallen open, all thanks to Mrs. Avery's inability to find suitable underwear. The pink slip had swamped her and the white vest had shown through.

But other forces had been at work, those same forces that had possessed her under the willow, producing a rush so potent that it had left her dumbstruck. And thank God it had, because he hadn't meant that kind of thing at all, just a portrait, he'd said after, and for Richard.

Even so, she'd said no and meant it, until she'd gone to change and, through the window, a lopped, lonely oak had rooted her justification in Spencer's sacrifice, both past and probably future.

But what about Richard?

In Spencer's company her guilt seemed so baseless and Richard's undoubted jealously so childish. There was nothing between her and Spencer; how could there be? Why didn't she just tell Richard? She would have to tell him. One word from Mrs. Avery and it would be all round the village. And if she did? She imagined the scene.

It was all so stupid. She wasn't doing anything wrong. Good Lord, the poor man was incapacitated. Even if she posed for him like Richard's precious Rokeby Venus, it would be no more a betrayal than Richard's obsession with the damned thing.

Suddenly she was back to the biblical, back to the pros and cons of artistic justification. Brush or camera; surely Spencer was right, the motive and principal were the same, purely hypothetically, of course.

While Laura reassured her moral conscience, the Eve in her rested under the apple tree, salivating over its irresistible ambrosia. Yet, even if she buried this reality beneath the sod of sophistication, even if she discounted it as some reactionary legacy of her mother's mania, even if she took refuge behind the window dressing of artistic patronage, the entire argument was immaterial. The prevalent truth was that, from the moment she'd met Spencer, she'd been compromising the total trust of her relationship. For Laura, virgin though she remained, the age of innocence was past.

That night, she sought desperately to atone for her fall from grace, but each reciprocated endearment only exacerbated her guilt, forcing defence to the fore. By the time her father donned his motoring cap to drive Agatha home, dropping Richard off en route, she'd argued herself round. In two or three days Spencer would be gone; she would see him just once more, for the portrait. She would tell

Richard, but later, when she gave it to him. Besides, she'd had no opportunity and to tell him now would spoil the surprise, not to mention risk a row, not only with Richard but with her father for not asking his permission to go to the manor in the first place.

Whatever kind of compromise it was, it condoned her silence while confirming her fidelity.

Richard could give himself no such leeway. This time alcohol offered no mitigation for allowing himself to be seduced, and he could hardly claim pity as the instigator. However passively, it had been as much his doing as Elizabeth's; blackmail was only an illusionary peg on which to hang his excuses. The deed had been done, the consequences had to be faced, it weighed too heavily on his conscience. He needed absolution.

He waited at the Bowden gate, defying the deceitful common sense that bade him enter, until Scott's tail lights disappeared round Clayman's bend. Trusting to love, he headed back.

The world exploded in Laura's face; pain, disillusion and anger racked her. Why? How could he? His blurted excuses sank like stones to the bed of her distrust, heightening the floodtide of distress. He loved her? How could he possibly say he loved her after that?

He said it had gone no further, that it didn't mean anything. She pictured the scene and almost vomited.

He tried to hold her; she pushed him away; the very memory of his touch was as repugnant as the sight of him.

He swore it would never happen again. She didn't believe him, she couldn't believe him, her belief in him had floundered on the iceberg of infidelity. And she had been worrying herself sick about Spencer?

He'd kissed her earlier. How dare he kiss her after that? How could he sit there all night pretending? She purged her tongue, disgustedly rubbing away the corruption of those Judas lips.

She snatched the ring from her finger, the locket from her neck. How contemptible they were, these tokens of treachery. She could cast them aside as easily as he had cast their love aside, she needed no reminders.

Those parting tears, those empty words, 'I love you, Laura. I will always love you,' how they tore into her heart, how her grief burst through the breach to break upon the rocks of pain.

"Love? What love, Richard?"

That night, Marian's lips impressed themselves on Laura's brow. Yet it wasn't the sorrowful kiss of consolation, nor the damning kiss of religious retribution, which left its mark, Laura was too stable to be receptive to the founding father of her mother's madness. It was the kiss of vengeance.

And so she plotted, too consumed with retaliation to realise that the means were merely the negative of the justification she'd sought all along.

Richard hadn't gone home, he couldn't go home. He'd stumbled his way to the weir to stare into the fathomless black waters, turbulently re-churning the self-contempt in his soul, the acidic void in the pit of his stomach.

The rush of recrimination rang in his ears, the bewilderment, the blame, the destruction, all poured out the tragedy. His head sank, his eyes closed. How could he have let it happen? How could he have hurt her so much?

"Please, God, no! It meant nothing, Laura, nothing!"

His love had never been stronger, never more agonising. He tortured himself with her distress, contrasting her virtue with his irrefutable sin, his Adam exposed for the serpent he was. Richard, the hero? Some hero.

He cursed the day Elizabeth had come to stay, he cursed George for marrying her; most of all, he cursed his own stupidity. If only he could turn the clock back, if only, if only. Now all was past redemption.

The moon sheltered behind a cloud. The wind gusted through the newborn leaves. He looked over at the willow, aweep in remembrance. How fragile she'd been, how she'd trembled, how much she'd trusted him, trusted in their love, and he hadn't been able even to trust himself. Trust was the key, the very heart, lost forever, leaving only this carcass of contempt.

He dragged himself along the river bank, instinctively surefooted on the path he'd trodden from infancy, a path that, now, led only to wasteland. 'Like coming home' he'd heard of love; five minutes of madness had destroyed its very foundations, swept away even its dust.

"Laura! Oh, Laura!"

He stared across the fields at the silhouette of sadness that was her house and drowned in her heartbreak.

"Laura!"

Nothing else mattered, nothing else had ever mattered.

A rat plopped into the water along the riverbank. A bat flew by. Soon the roses would bloom again, the white roses, which had so epitomised their love. How painful, now, the memory of that unblemished past.

* * * * *

The morning light played on Laura's eyelids and she experienced a moment of semiconscious contentment before reality clamped her in depression's vice. Today those once precious white roses wound up from her soul like choking bellbine. She screwed her face into the pillow and crushed them with all her might, casting them back into the abyss. Still their thorns stuck fast, yet another cruel reminder of the pain he had inflicted. She despised them as she despised him as she despised the world.

172

Her father was up and about. He, too, was a traitor. He'd been working every Saturday since Easter. She willed him to leave; she didn't want to see him, she didn't want to see anyone.

She buried her head under the blankets, fuelling her hatred with images of Richard with Elizabeth, until the click of the front door latch carried her to the landing to watch the car pull away, careless of the morning chill, careless of anything; if anyone saw her through the window, so be it. Spencer would see more, much more.

She rekindled the boiler and took a lukewarm bath. She would let Spencer take his pictures, the more the merrier, completely naked, if he liked, then she would show them to Richard, she would rip his heart out with them, as he had done hers. If only Spencer could be in them too, doing to her what Richard had done with that bitch Elizabeth.

She scorned breakfast; she had no appetite for food, only vengeance. Eleven o' clock, Spencer had said; by the time her hair had dried, the hour had come. Taking a tip from Mrs. Avery, she wore nothing under her dress except stockings and bloomers.

But would she still have left the house with that same sense of purpose had the extent of her vengeance not been gauged and governed, however subconsciously, by Spencer's impotence?

The studio remained exactly as Spencer had left it eighteen months earlier. After breakfast, he brushed off the cobwebs, burned the coating of dust from the lamps and loaded his camera. He'd been hoping for sufficient natural light, but the sky was overcast. Short of film, he'd fired off only two preparatory shots.

The hour between ten and eleven dragged by. The women were home. His father's favourable report had aroused their curiosity. Introductions would have to be made. He would have to shoot a roll of portraits in any event to avert suspicion, especially that of his sister Mary who'd already raised an eyebrow. That would leave just one roll.

Laura's forced smile hid little; as soon as Hawkins announced her, Spencer knew something was wrong. There was an air of untouchability about her. Yesterday she'd been so open; today she was a stranger. Had she had a tiff with her boyfriend, a family quarrel, or was this a nervous reaction at the hour of reckoning, the defensive armour of refusal, or even attack? Had she seen through him? Were these the eyes of mistrust, of despisal? He wished it were yesterday.

The introductions seemed interminable. Laura handled herself well, he thought, demonstrating the modesty that had so impressed his father. Yet, today, even that modesty seemed compromised. At last, reminded of her social calendar, his mother excused them, adamant that he must show her the results.

He ushered Laura into the studio.

"I came in earlier and prepared everything," he said.

He felt like a criminal awaiting the denunciation of the prosecution, the hatred of those blazing blue eyes. But how could he reassure her without compromising himself? He almost wished his sister were there to pre-empt the accusation, to disclaim the truth, instead of halfway to Elmsford.

"You'll find some powder over there. It may be best if you use some, the lights are very strong you see."

He would take his time, put her at her ease, wind the clock back to Wednesday.

"Just a dab or two should do the trick. It's in the box on the left."

He busied himself with his apparatus. When he finally looked across, he had to gulp back his incredulity. Her shoulders were bared, stripping away all pretence, leaving Spencer, the lecher, naked in the spotlight. His ears burned; self-denial quivered on the brink to be snatched up by the eagle claws of lust.

"I'll, er, I'd better lock the door," he croaked.

When he turned again, her dress was folded over the chair, the sweep of her pale back broken only by her bloomers. She was dabbing her cheeks in the dressing table mirror, her breasts in full reflection.

"I've never used powder before. I don't know how much to put on."

He went over, feeling like Satan.

"Not quite so much; look, like this."

Her nipples were flushed and proud, their treasure but a breath away.

"That's better, you just need a touch." His voice broke like an adolescent's.

"Should I take off my shoes?"

The question sounded absurd.

"Yes, er, whatever you prefer," he blurted, upsetting the powder as he returned the puff to the oval box.

He took a couple of badly needed breaths.

"Well, I think we're about ready. If you'd like to step this way."

She was a lithe Aphrodite, yet yielding with the seduction of Delilah. He wanted to sink to his knees, to rest his tortured brow on her belly, to succour his sorrow on her ripe, jutting teats.

He dragged himself to the lens, which was now his masculinity.

"If you'd care to rest one hand on the cupola; that's it, not too far, and stand perfectly still."

Her beauty was breathtaking. His hand shook. He pressed the shutter and wound on.

"Now look slightly to your left. And again."

Yet, as magnificent as her body was, as much as his lens rapaciously devoured its sexuality, in her eyes Spencer found only a daunting defiance, which reduced him to juvenile servitude and each frame to mere erotica.

Self-deprivation was a hard pill to swallow, but so, too, was this transformation of Faerie Queen into King's whore. He had to get his Laura back, before the illusion was lost forever, before his only memory of her was her despisal and the future his own.

"I can ask no more. Truly. You've been wonderful."

It was quite all right, she said. Did he know the Rokeby Venus? Surely he must. She saw he had a couch; there was even a mirror. She didn't mind, really she didn't.

If her initial preparedness had stunned him, this confirmation was more stupefying still. Had he been wrong all along? Was this, after all, the real Laura? Even whole, he would have been a eunuch.

Stomach wound aching, he hauled the chaise longe into position and reset the lighting. When he looked back, she was completely naked. A confusion of instinct and reality, need and impossibility racked him. His useless loins screamed at their impotence, his lust tore at the bars.

The distraction of meeting the family hadn't broken Laura's resolve. One snapshot of Richard with Elizabeth and the fuse of vengeance had flared full flame. Yet still it had taken all her willpower to break stage-fright's hold.

How her heart had pounded, how her ears had rung, how she'd trembled, and how she'd revelled in the eyes that had drunk of her fountain; 'Are you watching, Richard, are you watching?' And, when the camera had feasted on her floodlit pores, how it had focused her obsession, how it had magnified her elation, how each click of the shutter had fed her frustration, until she'd drowned in its cup and cast all inhibition aside, too consumed with her mission to notice Spencer's bared and bleeding soul, until it had broken before her.

Covering herself, she'd followed him into the darkroom to catch the sobbing shadow, for him of the man he used to be, for her of the hate that had brought her here. She had done this. As the full realisation drained reprisal's venom, she'd at last shed the reptilian skin that had proved so impervious, to find her fulfilment in the Laura he needed so much.

The full implications of what she had done only hit her in the sad, twilight solitude of her bedroom, with a delayed reaction that set her head reeling, as the serenity of the last act gave way to the insanity of the first. What had she done? The disgrace of it all. What must Spencer think of her? And her father! If word ever got out, if anyone saw the pictures! To ruin her own life was one thing, but to ruin his? He would never survive the scandal, they would have to move away, to leave everything he had worked so hard to achieve, his whole future with Agatha. Oh, God, dear God.

Her whole world hung on the gossamer thread of Spencer's discretion. But how could he respect her after that? And even if he said nothing, what about the pictures; what if one of the family pried into his things when he was away; what if he were killed? Dear God, why hadn't she thought of these things before? What had driven her so blindly on?

That night was one of the worst of her life. She found the strength to tell her father of her rift with Richard, but how could she say more?

She found sleep as impossible as redemption. Supported by her insomniac's face, she excused herself from Sunday Service on the premise of a headache. How could she face Spencer? How could she face Richard? How could she face God? While the faithful prayed for peace, Laura, racked with her own folly, prayed for her own miracle.

When Spencer telephoned, shortly after lunch, Laura's joy compounded Scott's astonishment. His immediate notion, remembering their shopping excursion, was that Spencer was behind her break-up with Richard. Thinking back, she'd been rather too reticent, rather too eager to dismiss the subject. He gave her no such leeway now.

The admission that she'd been seeing Spencer, that she'd been to the Manor, far from succouring his social ambitions for her, further disconcerted him. She'd said nothing of the arrangement, nothing about having her picture taken; and there was an invasion alert on; if she'd left the house at all, she should have left word; she'd directly disobeyed him.

The proof of his parental laxity stared him in the face; and more. Was it possible he didn't know his own daughter, that, despite her previous antipathy, she'd seen her chance of advancement and, forsaking Richard, grabbed it? Was there more of Marian in her than met the eye?

No, it was inconceivable. But, if it was only the friendship she claimed, why so secretive and why so overjoyed at a mere phone call?

Later that afternoon, Spencer arrived with ten photographs of her, each taken against a classical background. Scott's anger had hardened. The man had acted like a bounder, he greeted him disagreeably, yet, despite his annoyance, he had to admit Stafford had captured her well; too well, in fact; each print was a portrait of sadness. What the devil was going on?

He renewed his inquisition after Spencer had gone. Whatever Laura's feelings may or may not be for her precious captain, Scott wasn't stupid enough to believe that a Stafford would marry a Scott. There came a point where the social rungs ran out with the balcony still high above. If Laura wasn't careful, she'd end up a laughing stock with her reputation in tatters. Besides, if the rumours about young Stafford's injuries were true, even if the man was serious, any marital relationship was out of the question. But did Laura know? Scott certainly hoped not, but, then again, what if she didn't?

The embarrassment of an explanation was a daunting complication he preferred to defer, satisfying himself with the certainty that nothing untoward could have happened. Which left friendship as the only explanation; what other motive could young Stafford have?

Laura's adamant denials and firm defence finally convinced him. But what about Richard? The boy had obviously found out and taken umbrage, Scott concluded. If the hussey had treated him as she had her father, whether or not she'd meant the photographs to be a surprise, the boy had every reason to be upset, but he would be a fool to let a few snapshots come between them on any permanent basis and he certainly wasn't that. Time would be the healer.

Spencer had passed Laura the second package when she'd seen him to the door. She'd slipped it behind the hall's oak chest, ready to retrieve when the interrogation she knew was coming gave her the pretext to storm up to her room. He'd given her all twelve shots. There was a note.

"My dearest Laura,

I have never felt so indebted to anyone in my entire life. You will always be in my thoughts and in my prayers and I hope that, God willing, one day we shall meet again. You have given me so much to live for, so much hope with which to face the future. You are truly the most remarkable person I have ever met. These are the only prints, the negatives are enclosed for your safekeeping. I promise, no one will ever know.

With deepest affection,

Spencer."

She thanked God and Spencer for her deliverance, yet, with the evidence securely in her grasp, the tone of the note and her fury over her interrogation waylaid her previous resolve to destroy the damned things at the first opportunity. The clarity was astonishing; there she was in all her glory, yet even her most wanton poses failed to shock her, and that failure fuelled her anger. The pictures weren't enough. Richard should have been there, she should have made him watch.

Not enough? This all-consuming thirst for vengeance had led her and the father she loved so dearly to the very gates of ruin. She had jeopardised everything for what? To make Richard suffer? She wouldn't send him the pictures and she knew it, she'd always known it. Then why? To ease her own suffering? Perhaps. For Spencer? She doubted it. For what, then? Simply for her own gratification? Why now, faced with the proof of her degeneracy, did she feel no shame? Her eyes were not those of the seductress but those of the sadist, and for that she was sorry, the studies deserved better; but, morally, any regrets she had were subject only to her public exposure and there was no longer any fear of that. The biggest shame of all was that Richard had let himself be seduced by that bitch Elizabeth. If it hadn't been for him, nothing would have happened.

Laura looked into the mirror, her eyes again reflecting the hatred captured by the camera. Now the same Alice lived on both sides of the looking glass.

- CHAPTER TWENTY NINE -

Richard spent the weekend in his room on the pretext of homework and squealing children. The very sight of Elizabeth sickened him, yet he said nothing; rows and recrimination wouldn't win Laura back, and, besides, if he'd been able to call a halt when he had, why not earlier? For his passivity, he had only himself to blame.

On Sunday afternoon, the roar of Spencer's Norton sent George Junior scampering to the gate, closely followed by his mother, whose running commentary did nothing to raise Richard's spirits. What the hell was Stafford doing, calling on the Scotts?

Lumber was his father's verdict; "must be tying up some loose ends for his father before he goes over yonder."

Even so, Richard was racked with jealousy.

As for Elizabeth, her part in the break-up never entered her head. 'Maybe her father found out about the goings on and put a stop to it. That'd explain why he came home early that night, and why he acted the way he did,' were her self-consoling thoughts on the subject.

Beatrice Bowden found the whole thing incomprehensible; they'd been so much in love, and to happen now, with Richard's call-up barely two weeks away? His cheeks were sunken, his eyes sullen. In this frame of mind, what chance would he have? The very will to survive was missing.

As night fell and Richard's misery deepened, Beatrice determined to speak to Laura. Arthur forbade it. "It's his business, mother, and his alone. He wouldn't thank you for interfering. If he wanted to do something about it, he'd go round. Now you just leave it alone."

And there it was left.

* * * * *

The days passed, the Dublin Rising petered out and the Military Service Bill was extended to include married men, but, like the Zeppelins which had reappeared that fateful Spring, these momentous events passed the lovers by as they drowned in depression.

School and his prefecture offered Richard distraction, while the tree, bough-laden with spring leaf, whispered words of poetic wisdom. No, Richard Bowden was not dead, he was as alive as his love was undying. His emptiness was the selfish void of need, even greed, for her love. True love demanded no such necessity, it carried no conditions. Still, his heart bled.

Over at the Priory, Laura took refuge in the logic locker. What she had or hadn't done with Spencer had no bearing on the ending of her courtship, that had been solely Richard's doing. In fact, the goings-on at the Manor were all Richard's fault, his and that bitch Elizabeth's.

Even in its superficiality, her anger was a tough layer to crack, particularly when it constituted her protection from her own underlying depravity, which, with Spencer out of sight, she put determinedly out of mind. She had the photographs to remind her, but, as she used them only as an antidote and, on occasion, an incitement to her masochistic jealousy, they seldom pricked her conscience.

Sarah Jameson was her sole confidante; if Joanna Hetherington and her cronies found out that she and her precious Richard had separated, Laura's life wouldn't be worth living. However, Sarah's advice went distinctly against the grain. In Sarah's view, painful though Richard's betrayal was, his confession and the devastation it had wrought only proved the depth of their love. Laura owed it to him and to herself to give that love a second chance.

Laura could see the sense in the argument, even the truth, but it was an unacceptable truth. If she shut her eyes, she could still see Richard with Elizabeth, the hurt was still there. But then, in unguarded moments, she'd feel the pain of being apart; she'd look for him at the school gate, wishing the whole awful business had never happened, until resentment and revenge would once more consume her. Then, how she would want to taunt him with the photographs, how she would want to watch him squirm.

Spencer was a secret she kept even from Sarah.

But as Sarah's words took effect, so the flaws became cracks and the cracks became canyons. Why had she done it? Even if she could forgive Richard, he would never forgive her, and to keep it from him would be impossible. Love's last rites had been enacted, not by Richard's hand, but by her own.

* * * * *

At the Manor, Hawkins memory of events had barely stretched to breakfast, while Mrs. Avery's integrity, born of a lifetime of service, ensured that any downstairs tittle-tattle remained downstairs. It would have taken Sherlock Holmes himself to deduce more than civility in her nodded acknowledgement of Laura at Church the following Sunday, although Stafford's raised hat raised congregational eyebrows to Scott's credit; "hobnobbing with the gentry now."

Like Richard, Laura refused to discuss their separation; the merest mention was enough to send her into hibernation, any prying certain to induce a scene. Scott was nearing his wit's end. She was fast becoming the Laura of his worst nightmares. The deeper her depression, the keener he deduced Marian in her, more so because, in place of melancholy, there was bitterness.

Another week of unremitting misery went by. Laura excused herself from church, refusing to capitulate as she had the previous Sunday. Richard was also absent. Scott had a word with a frantic Mrs. Bowden. The boy's birthday was just days away; if he went off to war with things as they were, as much as Scott shared Beatrice's fears for his well being, he feared for Laura's sanity, especially should the worst befall. What on earth had come between them? Spencer was Scott's only clue.

Well, if Laura wouldn't talk about it, perhaps Richard would. If this was a case of petty jealousy, it had gone too far.

He walked Beatrice home, hamming up an excuse about collecting some of her homemade pickle. Richard made a reluctant appearance and agreed, even more reluctantly, to 'a quiet word'.

Ten minutes of gentle cajoling achieved nothing, but at least the boy hadn't flown off the handle. Scott decided to take the bull by the horns.

"If all this is about Spencer Stafford, there's nothing in it, you know."

He was met with startled incomprehension.

"Stafford? What's it got to do with him?"

Scott was thrown completely. The boy didn't know.

"Oh, nothing, nothing at all."

He watched the abacus of Richard's hurt pile twos on twos by the brainstorming second. He'd well and truly let the cat out of the bag. Some kind of explanation was necessary.

"He took some photographs of her, that's all. I thought perhaps you'd found out and got the wrong end of the stick. They were meant to be a surprise. You heard about his wounds, I suppose? Dreadful, truly dreadful. Fancy never being able to marry."

Even put so delicately, it was far too obvious and embarrassingly out of character.

"Richard, what on earth came between the two of you?" Scott tried the outright question, the last ditch attempt.

"I'm sorry, Mr. Scott, I'd rather not talk about it. It's over and that's all there is to it."

There was nothing more to be gained, only to be lost. Scott had come on a mission of mediation; instead he'd only fanned the flames.

"Look..." But further mention of Stafford was more likely to set the last plank of the last bridge ablaze. He'd made a complete cock of it. "If you ever feel like talking, you know where I am."

* * * * *

On his birthday morning, Richard was summoned to Joscelyn's study.

"Have you received your military papers, Bowden?"

"No, Sir, I left before the post."

"Oh, I see," Joscelyn frowned. "Well, I feel it my duty to warn you that, when you do, they may not contain the summons you may, quite justifiably, be expecting. Despite your notable achievements, your lack of social credentials disbars you from a commission. I'm sorry to put it so bluntly, but there it is."

Richard was stung. Since overcoming the bigotry of his first term, his social status had been a forgotten factor.

"I must admit, it's something I'd scarcely considered," Joscelyn went on. "I trust that your prefecture is testimony enough of my personal appraisal, and, may I say, no boy has deserved the distinction more. Nevertheless, the authorities take a different view."

Richard blanched. The rope had never been more frayed, the chasm more fathomless. Why had the entire world suddenly turned against him?

"However," Joscelyn continued, stroking his whiskers. "All is not lost. On your past showing, the colonel of the Essex regiment has agreed to consider you for a commission, conditional upon you passing an examination, as though rising from the ranks. I trust you'll pardon my alacrity in accepting the opportunity on your behalf."

Relief and gratitude shone in Richard's eyes. It wasn't purely for pride's sake that a commission was necessary. Ever since the Wilkinson episode, his father had adopted a 'them and us' attitude, along with others in the village. Richard had cited himself as the exception. To have been denied a commission would have been more than a bitter pill, it would have destroyed all faith.

"Now, you will need this." Joscelyn passed Richard an envelope. "It contains a letter to the effect I've described. You must hand it to your conscription officer, and for goodness's sake don't lose it or you'll end up in the ranks."

Richard couldn't thank his mentor enough. For once, a chink of warmth appeared in Joscelyn's armour.

"My boy, it is no more than you deserve. A word of advice, though. It may be prudent to keep your origins to yourself where your fellow officers are concerned. The better part of valour is discretion; remember that."

"I'll do my best, Sir. I would do nothing to dishonour the school."

"Of that I have not the slightest doubt. However, with the Big Push expected shortly, the war may well be over before you complete your training. And not before time, I may add. I know you boys are biting at the bit, but, personally, I preferred the world the way it was. Well, good luck to you, Bowden."

In the classroom, Chapman signed off the Stuart line of succession with a flourish and turned from the blackboard.

"Enter, Mr. Bowden; resume your seat. Now gentlemen, the present conflict..."

The history master, too, was in optimistic mood at the prospects of the much anticipated summer offensive. With the Germans so heavily engaged at Verdun, where would they find the strength to combat the might of Kitchener's New Armies? Perhaps, despite all his misgivings, the war would soon be brought to a successful conclusion. He'd fervently prayed so at morning assembly, and would do so again that night by his bed, for he, too, had received his conscription papers.

* * * * *

Heartened by Jocelyn's news, Richard spent that birthday evening half expecting Laura to appear, to give him the second chance he had so beseeched God to make her grant him. It was not to be. As darkness fell, he slouched off to bed.

Along the back road, Scott softly lifted the latch on Laura's door. She was sitting forlornly on her counterpane, clutching Richard's present. An hour earlier he had urged her to put aside their differences and wish the boy a happy birthday, warning her that it may be her last chance. But his prompting had only stimulated her stubborn refusal. He'd left her to cool her temper. Now he took her in his arms.

"I'm sorry, my darling, I didn't mean to bully you."

She buried her head in his waistcoat.

"Was it Spencer?" He asked gently.

"No. I mean yes. I... I don't know what I mean," she sobbed. "It's me; it's everything. I want to die."

He longed to tell her everything would be all right, that it wasn't the end of the world, but, for Richard, it soon could be. With that in mind, perhaps it was wiser to leave things as they were.

"It just wasn't to be, that's all."

"Oh, daddy, I've been so stupid...."

- CHAPTER THIRTY -

On May the 21st. Daylight Saving was introduced, causing mayhem in the village, when some stubbornly kept to old time while others changed to new.

"Don't know if I'm coming or going. I turn up at one place and they tell me I'm early; I go to the next and they tell me I'm late," Arthur Bowden complained.

"Same on the farms," Amos Harris commiserated, "and in some of the shops. Don't know when to deliver the milk, buggered if I do. I mean, what's the point, if we're going to change it all back come October?"

"Bad enough not knowing what day it is, let alone what hour," old Joe Petty muttered, rewinding a century and a half of village resistance to the Gregorian calendar. "Lost twelve days then and never got 'em back. Far as I'm concerned they can stuff it."

June's events were even more seismic. The losses at Jutland shook the nation's faith in its navy, Fort Thiaumont and the town of Fleury fell to the Germans, the high tide of their Verdun offensive, Roger Casement was sentenced to death for his part in the Irish Uprising and Lord Kitchener was drowned in HMS Hampshire, en route to Russia.

Then, throughout the final week of June, village windows rattled to the thunder of distant guns. The Somme offensive had begun.

On July the 1st, untouched by the debacles of the previous two years, Kitchener's new armies lumbered forward, gift wrapped for slaughter in steel helmets and shiny tin patches, humping sixty six pound pack loads. It would be a cakewalk, they'd been told, the enemy had already been pulverised. Walk on.

The Germans, subjected to the greatest bombardment the world had ever known, emerged, half crazed, from their bombproof shelters dug deep in the chalk, to vent their spleen on the pack mules. Over fifty seven thousand felt steel's sting on that first day, by the 14th, another one hundred and sixty thousand, while the French, already steeped in death at Verdun, donated a further fifty thousand from their dwindling reserves.

And still censorship sort to deceive the public. Banner headlines boasted of victory over maps enlarged to make each paltry yard gained seem like a mile. However, the hospital trains arriving in London, nose to tail, told their own story. By the end of the month the telegrams were catching up. The flower of the nation had been scythed in its prime, ploughed into the ground like so much compost. Percy Cudlip, Arthur Holland, Ronald Petty, Harry Seaton and Henry, Agatha Cooper's brother, had all gone west. As with every town and village in the country, Ashleigh mourned en masse, and still the fighting raged.

* * * * *

Beatrice stood sweltering under the awning of 'Cyril's Cycle Shop', while Elizabeth went in search of ginger beer. It had been a long walk from Ashleigh, but they were right by the roadside, they would get a good view. To left and right, as far as the eye could see, soldiers lined the highway like khaki hedgerow. As yet, they were stood down; later they would be clipped to regimental perfection. However, for Beatrice this was more than obeisance, it was a pilgrimage.

"Here you are. 'Fraid it bubbled over a bit." Elizabeth handed her the sticky bottle. "Miss Cooper's got the kids down there aways, and there's a whole row of field cookers dishing up the mens' dinners, so he can't be expected yet awhile. One of them was tipping out the water and half the tatters with it. Just wiped them off, he did, and put them back in the pot. You should've heard the language."

"Not in front of the children, I hope," Beatrice objected.

"Oh no, they're further on. Soup, they're having with big chunks of meat in it. 'Any to spare,' says I. Well, I don't have to tell you what they said, cheeky so-and-sos."

"They just carried one off from down there," Beatrice redirected the conversation. "Heat stroke, it must've been."

"Not surprised. Some of them have been standing there since first light, apparently. Someone said one of them had died. Silly not to let them sit."

"Apples, bananas!" A vendor cried from his bike.

"Where'd he get bananas from?" Beatrice wanted to know. "Haven't seen one of them since war was declared."

"State of 'em, he's had 'em ever since; black as the ace of spades, they are. Here, look at them, all dolled up to the nines," Elizabeth nodded towards two Land Service Leaguers across the divide. "Who the hell do they think they're trying to impress, toffee nosed bit... you-know-whats."

"Quiet, Elizabeth, they'll hear you."

"Don't care if they do. We do our bit, too, you know," she raised her voice. "Just don't make a song and dance about it like some people!"

Beatrice grimaced; the offended flounced off. A scruffy dissenter defiantly wheeled his bicycle down the middle of the road.

The ranks stirred, then the order came, "At ease!"

The sun arched into another hour.

"Taking his time, ain't he?"

"Elizabeth," Beatrice protested, "that's the King you're talking about. I'll mind you to show some respect."

"Well, he should have been here by now; it's past three. Don't know as I can stand here much longer, my arches is aching something rotten."

"I expect he's got held up," Beatrice excused her sovereign while silently cursing Arthur's 'old time' obstinacy, how ever illogically.

"I'll ask one of them officers," Elizabeth said, heading across the road.

'And I bet I know which one,' Beatrice grumbled under her breath. 'She's been eyeing him up all morning. Look at her, like a cat on heat. Might as well rub herself against his leg and have done with it.'

Flirtatious laughter floated back. "Won't be long, now, mum. I'm just going to pop along and see how the kids is doing."

184

'Trollop. Don't know why George married her, really I don't,' Beatrice scowled, as her daughter-in-law swaggered off, hips swaying like a heifer's.

"'Scuse me, lady."

A little boy was tugging at her skirt, bearing a stool twice his size.

"Me mum says would you like to sit?"

"It's all we've got, I'm afraid," the proprietoress smiled apologetically from the cycle shop doorway, "but you're more than welcome, you've been standing so long."

"Oh, that's very kind of you, dear; if it's not putting you out?"

"Not at all. I daresay you could do with a cup of tea and all, couldn't you?"

"Oh, no, I'm fine, really I am."

"It's no trouble, the kettle's on."

"Well, alright, then; thank you kindly."

"Sugar?"

"Are you sure?"

"Yes. Don't take it, myself. Does me teeth in."

The cup was brought.

"Well, he's picked a nice day for it."

"Yes," Beatrice agreed, savouring the infusion of tea, bicycle oil and tyre rubber. "Bit too nice for some of them poor beggars; been carrying them off regular, from up there. Still, suppose it's worth it. It's not every day you get to see the King. Husband off at the War is he?"

The lady nodded. "He's in Arabia. Sent him off to fight the Turks. Missed the Dardenelles by a whisker, thank the Lord."

"I hope they do the same with my boy. Don't want him going over to France, not with what's going on over there. He's training at the moment. He's going to be an officer," Beatrice found herself boasting. "His brother's already a prisoner. He was in the territorials. Two weeks a year, it was meant to be. That's his wife that's with me."

"Well at least you know he's safe."

"Yes, there is that; though we still worry."

"Well you would."

The military stirred again; the officers were on the move; commands were barked and re-barked. The men drew themselves up in double rank.

"He's coming, mum!" Elizabeth called, hurrying back.

"Atten.....tion!"

The click of a thousand heels hushed even the birds into silence. It was as if time itself was standing rigidly still. A motorcycle came into view, flying the Royal Standard, and then a second and, behind that, a green, open topped Vauxhall tourer, pennants fluttering.

"It's him, mum, it's him!" Elizabeth cried.

Beatrice focused her entire being on her sovereign. He was in uniform, leaning forward behind his chauffeur, his left hand resting on his knee, his right mechanically rising and falling to the peak of his cap. She drank in the etched forehead, the cavernous eyes, the hollow cheeks, the greying beard. The blood drained from her face, all hope from her soul. She was looking, not at death, but at its certificate.

And then he had passed. There'd been no cheering, no anthems; a funeral procession.

"That was General French beside him, I've seen his picture," Elizabeth announced.

Beatrice was still holding her cup and saucer. She flushed at her irreverence. The lady from the bike shop took it from her with a melancholy smile.

"I'll fetch the kids; silly them going back with the school at this hour," Elizabeth decided.

The bands struck up, the regiments moved off, the locals wended their way home.

- CHAPTER THIRTY ONE -

Richard stared out at the ripe Essex corn, homeward bound on ten days embarkation leave, his training cut short by the losses on the Somme. The Swan Vesta flared between his fingers. He lit his cheroot, sending a pall of smoke curling up, to be vacuumed through the vent of the soot-speckled window. Officers travelled First Class; still he'd suffered ticket inspectionitis.

The train pulled into Brentfield; not long now. Laura would be at the station to meet him. She'd been there on the day he'd left; he'd seen her tears from the window and had fought his way to the carriage door.

He fingered his watch's gold band, then its silver casing. She'd thrust it into his hand as the train had pulled away. One of the orderlies, a jeweller in civilian life, had identified both maker and metals. Richard wondered how on earth she could have afforded it, even with Scott's help.

They'd written in the interim; there were no secrets now.

He'd battled to come to terms with her infidelity. He wouldn't know the outcome until he saw her, until he held her in his arms. God, how it had hurt, how it had wrenched his heart apart. Disowned, revenge had leapt from her confession to dance to the mute agony of his heartbreak. Once invoked, it is seldom denied. Only numbness had eased the pain; it still did. All that had been sacred was flawed; to touch her would never mean the same again.

Damn! Against all argument, all reasoning, nausea prevailed. It was his fault; his weakness had been the catalyst. But if his five minutes of madness meant nothing, how could Laura's mean so much? The answer was stark and simple; he had been seduced; whatever her justification, Laura's had been a full frontal affair of her own instigation.

The train slowed; he was on the wrong side. Pulling his valise from the rack, he negotiated the tangle of legs, unhooked the leather fastener and let the window fall.

She was standing by the exit, prettier even than he remembered, yet curiously unattractive.

He turned the door handle.

There was no race into each other's arms.

"Hello."

His voice sounded as hollow as the pit of his stomach. Her reply was barely audible. Their eyes met, hers betraying temerity, his betraying nothing. He couldn't loosen contempt's stranglehold. He wished she hadn't come, he wished he hadn't told her, he wished he'd never loved her, then it would have been so easy to forgive, to forget, to take her in his arms.

She reached for his sleeve. He couldn't respond. Her hand slipped away.

"Is your father here?"

"He's waiting in the car."

Solemnly, they walked down the stairs. He showed his pass at the barrier; she handed in her platform ticket.

Scott welcomed him home, telling him to sling his bag in the back while he cranked the starting handle.

Richard filled the back seat, confining Laura to the front. At least, in the back, he couldn't see her face, just the contours of her cheek, her neck, her thin shoulders. 'She's lost weight,' he thought dispassionately.

He wanted to see the photographs, to see just how much of a whore she'd made of herself. In his hardened moments, he'd even found their existence masochistically stimulating. Yet it was more than that, it was a desire to see the proof of her harlotry, to destroy the fantasy forever.

They sped home, the open top unable to dispel the all-pervading gloom.

Scott pulled up at the Bowden gate.

"Thank you for the lift, Sir. Laura;" Richard touched his cap.

Laura couldn't look at him; she could only nod. Her hurt gave him cruel satisfaction.

From the house he heard his mother's joy, sensed his father's pride.

"Goodnight to you, Richard," Scott said glumly, setting the car in motion.

He couldn't sleep. He found some of Gurny's Elderberry wine in the cupboard and helped himself, wishing he'd bought some Scotch. Officers drank Scotch; he'd been baptised on his first day in the mess. Thereafter, taking Joscelyn's advice, he'd kept himself to himself, unable to meet the financial demands of a military social life. He settled himself in the kitchen, periodically refilling his glass.

"Is that you, Richard? Are you alright?"

Elizabeth's whisper came as no surprise; he'd heard her footsteps on the stairs.

"Have a drink, Liz," he offered. "Hail the conquering hero."

She closed the door quietly behind her.

"Whatever's the matter?"

"Nothing's the matter; I just fancied a drink, that's all."

"You shouldn't be drinking like that at your age."

"You didn't say that when you got me drunk that time."

"That was different, it was Christmas."

"Oh, what the hell does it matter when it was, it's all the same now, all in the past, over and done with." He slumped in his chair.

"It's that Laura, isn't it? Whatever happened between the two of you, you was so much in love?"

"Funny, really. You happened. I told her about the night you tried it on."

"You did what? What'd you do that for? You trying to get me in trouble? We never done nothing, you know that."

He ignored her indignation. "Don't I just, but it was enough. I should never have told her, but there you are. You're not drinking, here."

"I don't want none," Elizabeth sulked.

"You don't?" He affected surprise. "Huh, the worm turns."

"Beg pardon?"

"Nothing," he grunted.

Elizabeth relented. "Surely she's not still holding it against you?"

"No, she decided to hold it against someone else instead," he cackled bitterly.

Elizabeth didn't catch on. "What, me you mean?"

"No, Liz, not you. I meant... Oh, it doesn't matter." He couldn't be bothered.

"Well, what then?" Elizabeth persisted.

"She went with someone else," he said irritably, hoping, now, she would shut up.

"Laura? I don't believe it. She's having you on, trying to make you jealous."

"Please yourself," he told her dolefully. "Now, can we drop the subject? Just please don't tell anyone; it's bad enough as it is."

"'Course I won't tell anyone; I don't go shooting my mouth off like some people. 'Cept I don't believe it. She wouldn't; she loves you too much."

He poured himself another drink.

"Did she go all the way with him?"

"What's the difference?"

"Well, if it was only a bit of groping, well, that's different. I bet you groped a few in your time, me included, 'cept that was more me than you," she admitted.

"It may seem all right to you, Liz, but it's not the same, it'll never be the same."

"You're asking for bloody miracles, you are. Good God, isn't a girl allowed one mistake in her life?"

He couldn't argue. His vision was beginning to blur, his speech to slur. "What the hell does it matter now, it's finished."

Elizabeth snatched the bottle from him.

"Now you listen to me, Richard Bowden. You go round there tomorrow and make it up with her, do you hear? You can't throw it all away over a piddling little thing like that. Swallow your stupid pride, for once. Men. I'll never understand them, I'm sure I won't."

"Be like you, you mean? Fuck who you like when you like and bugger the consequences," He hissed sarcastically.

"I couldn't help it. And you mind your language! I'm not proud of it. It's hard for a woman when she's used to someone like my George."

Richard said nothing.

"Look, I'm sorry if it's me what's to blame. If you want me to talk to her, to explain..."

"Thanks, Liz, but I think you've done enough. Besides, it's too far late for that."

"You don't know that. You've just got to put it behind you and get on with your lives. You still love each other, for Christ's sake; that's what counts."

"Easy for you to say," Richard moped. "But I can't; I've tried. It's just impossible. I can't touch her."

He didn't want to talk anymore. He levered himself up.

"I'm going to bed."

He clumped up the stairs; his door banged behind him.

Below, a tear spilt onto Elizabeth's cheek, and then another. For the first time since news of George's survival, she cried.

Richard slept late and woke with a hangover. It was past ten before he stumbled down to breakfast. His mother's fussing irritated him. He wanted everything to be normal, but then he supposed this dull distemper was normality now. He forced a semblance of a smile for her sake. She would have been up early, baking the bread so it would be warm from the oven, just for him. He could sense her chiding herself for not realising how tired he would be.

"Bacon and eggs?" She asked.

"Just the ticket. Father gone to the yard?"

"Yes, no peace for the wicked." The old adage sounded stale. "Actually, he's over at Eastleigh, working on Mr. Scott's new place, ready for the wedding. Elizabeth's taken the kiddies down the village; thought you might like some peace and quiet. School holiday, see."

Laura had told him about the wedding. He even knew his father was doing the renovations to Scott's new house.

He plonked himself down at the table, with no appetite at all, until the first mouthful hit his taste buds. The eggs were cooked to perfection, not like the frazzled abortions they dished up in the mess.

His mother locked him in a bear hug. The food fell from his fork.

"It's nice to have you home."

His aversion to physical contact was all encompassing. A stifled grunt was his only response. She let go.

"Don't mind me. Eat your breakfast while it's hot."

He could hear the hurt in her voice.

"Looked like a good harvest from the train," he made conversation.

"Yes, but I don't know how they're going to get it in, what with all the men gone. Us women'll have to do it, they say. There's a parcel of land girls coming, volunteers from the city, though how much they knows about farming the Lord only knows. We was asked if we could have one here, only, with you coming home, I told the Vicar we wouldn't be able to manage. No room, see, what with Elizabeth and the children."

"When do they start arriving?"

"Oh, tomorrow or the day after. Laura's volunteered, I hear, along with some of her school friends..."

Richard refused to rise to the bait.

"... And Elizabeth and me are going to do our bit, though your father's none too pleased about it. But I told him, someone's got to do it."

Richard found the news disturbing. An infestation of women would seriously impair his abject misery, and that realisation suddenly alerted him to the pettiness of his self-pity. He hadn't been able to indulge himself at camp for the simple reason that it would have been met with the contempt it truly deserved. He'd slipped into it on the journey home, settling into a state of comfortable depression to play on the sympathy of the only people who cared enough to tolerate it.

Immediately his mood lifted. He carried his empty plate to the sink. His mother was preparing vegetables.

"You're the best," he told her, kissing her cheek.

* * * * *

Laura had risen early, she didn't like to be in bed when the home help arrived; eight o' clock was late for Mrs. Creswell, who was usually there to cook Scott's breakfast. Her husband had worked in the fields from dawn to dusk before his call-up. Her eldest son was also with the colours, while her second would be eligible in November. She'd been barely sixteen when she married; Creswell, himself, was still only thirty nine. With a third son and two daughters, Laura couldn't imagine how the woman coped.

Together they made up the spare room. Sarah was staying for the harvest. 'As long as she doesn't bring her mother,' was her father's only condition. When Richard had written of his arrival, Laura had cursed the arrangement, but now it hardly seemed to matter. She fought back a tear.

"There, she should be comfortable enough." Mrs. Creswell plumped up the pillows.

"I'll make some tea," Laura volunteered, heading for the stairs before her emotions made a fool of her.

Alone in the kitchen, she wound back the clock to May. By the time she'd plucked up the courage to knock on the Bowden door, Richard had already left for the station. She'd cycled furiously after him, dropping her bicycle on the station steps to sprint down the platform and thwart, or perhaps court, fate.

Through the torturous weeks since, she'd prayed that, as soon as they saw each other, everything would be all right. How forlorn had been that prayer. His frigid eyes, his icy words; she'd shivered in his coldness. They'd been closer through their letters, while a hundred miles apart.

She'd received a letter from Spencer that morning, his second from France. She wished the affair had never happened, but it wasn't his fault, he was one of the kindest men she'd ever met. And, anyway, if Richard professed that his sordid goings-on with Elizabeth meant nothing, why couldn't he accept his own argument, especially when what she'd done was paltry by comparison?

Her frustration rose and, with it, her temper. She was angry with herself, angry with him, angry at his stubborn stupidity. She poured the water into the pot, agitating the leaves.

"Is that tea ready, dear?" Mrs. Creswell bustled in, haloed in dust particles. "Thirsty work in this heat." She sat at the table, fanning her face with her apron while Laura poured. "Reckon you'll be sorry to leave here, won't you?"

"Oh, I don't know; it hasn't been the happiest of homes, with mother's passing and everything. I like the new house. Mr. Bowden's over there, now, doing the alterations."

"Well, stands to reason, don't it, what with you and young Richard. Came home last night, didn't he?"

Mrs. Creswell seemed well informed.

"I'm not too sure about that, Mrs. Creswell." Laura passed a cup.

191

"No? I thought you was going to the station to meet him? Thank you, dear."

'How on earth did she know that?' Laura wondered. "Oh, yes, he's home all right."

"Oh, we all have our ups and downs, dear; it'll be alright, take my word on it," Mrs. Creswell assured her, slurping her tea straight from the saucer.

Laura smiled through her misery. Were there no secrets around here?

Mrs. Creswell left at twelve. Laura ran a bath, tepid to the toe, cold against her ankle, and arctic when she took the plunge. Gradually her body adjusted. As with the sea, it was fine once she was in.

How often had she lain there, wallowing in fantasy? Nowadays she needed no cold bath to cool her ardour. Since Spencer, and particularly since her confession, desire had deserted her. It was as if she were going through a penitent cleansing process.

Again she played the 'if only' game; if only Elizabeth's house hadn't caught fire; if only Richard hadn't gone home early that night; if only Spencer hadn't caught her on her way to the Manor; if only, if only, each as tangible and reversible as the soap in her hand, the days and hours in-between as breakable as the water's surface.

She lay back, allowing the ripples to lap into oblivion, until a knock on the front door turned time into a tidal wave.

"Who is it, please?" She called from the landing.

"It's Richard!"

"Just a minute!"

Her bloomers stuck to her wet calves. In desperation she kicked them off and reached for her robe. Her hair was a mess, but there was nothing she could do about it now.

"I'm sorry. You caught me in the bath," she excused herself at the door.

"Funny time to be having a bath."

"I'd been helping Mrs. Creswell with the housework. Look, come through."

In the kitchen she offered him tea. He asked if he might smoke.

"Smoke? Yes, of course." She remembered Spencer's words; 'everyone smokes in the Army.' "I'll fetch an ashtray."

"So, does your char come every day?"

"Most days; normally she'd do it on her own, but Sarah's coming for the harvest."

"Mother said you'd volunteered. And you're moving?"

"Yes, after the wedding. I'm sure I told you. You'd love the new house; it's as old as the hills, full of oak beams and lattice windows and this huge Inglenook fireplace."

"Look Laura, about yesterday... I... I don't know what got into me. Can we start again from scratch?"

"If you like. Only, I'm not sure I quite know what scratch means."

"I mean just forget all this bad stuff ever happened. What we had was so special. I'm sure it's still there. It is for me, anyway. I love you, Laura."

192

"Oh, Richard."

Laura fell into his arms. He had to take her now, he had to; through love's fulfilment the past would be exorcised.

But Richard's words were not reality, as much as he willed them to be; nor was his lust all obliterating. Even as he knelt over her, even as she gave herself, in its very driving force lay its backlash. Each kiss, each caress only invoked the nightmare, re-energising his hatred, fouling his mouth, until revulsion forged his tongue into saw edged steel.

"Is this how it was with Spencer? Was he in uniform, too?"

"Richard, don't, please don't..."

"You whore!"

Through her distended eyes, he watched the bayonet sink into her soul. In their devastation his gargoylic face reflected back, satanic in triumph, and then the thunderbolt struck and her agony shattered him. What had he done?

He'd never known remorse until this moment. He leaned over her in desperate repentance, but she was far beyond reach. He sank back on his haunches, then slumped to the floor, his head in his hands. It was all so clear to him now. Until that moment, it had all been a game, its outcome never in doubt, its wounds, however painful, superficial. Now he had struck the mortal blow.

He begged her again, but she could only beg him, in turn, to, "go, please go!"

He stumbled home. The house was empty; his mother must have gone shopping, or perhaps to the Gurnys.

The grandfather clock ticked off each memory as he stood in the hallway, bags packed. An hour ago he had been part of it, now he felt like a trespasser, as if goodbye, itself, was a memory.

'Recalled to my battalion. I love you both...'

He propped the note on the kitchen shelf, against the coronation mug he had won at the fair all those years ago, when he had first held Laura's hand and even her sorrow had been like the sun, innocence to ashes, dreams to dust.

He left like a fugitive past the drooping white roses. Might there still be a chance? Even the deepest wounds can heal, if one learns to live with the disfigurement.

'Go, please go!'

All hope was lost.

He continued down the cinder path and over the back fence, too distracted to notice the blood red poppies bidding goodbye in the breeze. In the desolation of Flanders, their brethren would remind him of home. Few roses grew in hell.

PART TWO

- CHAPTER THIRTY TWO -

Richard took the footpath through the fields to join the main road just short of Hayfield. His hand rose perfunctorily to return a salute outside the tea shop and again on the outskirts of Elmsford; on he sloped to the station.

The train was packed with servicemen. Squeezing past to a first class compartment, he threw his bag into the luggage netting and took the one spare seat. A captain slept by the window, remnants of youth in his rest-relaxed face belying the grey in his moustache.

It was easy to tell the leave men, they carried a resignation and looked a generation older than those green behind the gills, although for some the difference was no more than months. It was a sufferance Richard found easy to emulate, until suppression failed him and his thoughts returned to Laura.

The thread of their letters had been too frail to stand the strain of reunion. If ever they loved again, it would be a knot of a different coil that bound them. Soon Sarah would be there to comfort her. She'd need a friend.

Richard hadn't had a true friend since Joe Crutchley and dear old Frank Cudlip, his childhood partners in the 'triumvirate of terrors', as the old Vicar had dubbed them. He wondered what had happened to them, 'Crutch' and 'Cudders'.

'Cudders?' God, how pompous it sounded; how they'd rib him if he called Frank that. 'What ho, Cudders, old fruit!' At school and at camp he'd got used to 'cad', 'bounder', 'wallah' and any amount of '...ers', the language of his peers and brother officers, with the odd 'bastard' and 'bugger' thrown in for good, blasphemous measure. He'd even been called 'Bodders' himself, his first sign of acceptance.

Both Joe and Frank had volunteered, he knew that, Frank when he was underage. Frank's father had asked Richard to write to the authorities, explaining how Frank had lied about his age and that his father wanted him back. Some major in the records office had written back, saying, as far as the army was concerned, Frank was the age he'd given on enlistment. Wouldn't it be funny if they ended up in his platoon, the terrible trio together again, wreaking havoc on the enemy?

The vision unmasked his charade of implacability. He replaced it with the window, superimposing apparitions of Ashleigh onto the countryside's surrender to the marshalling yards and soot blackened brickwork of outer London. He pictured his mother finding his note, but it was too late now. Perhaps it was better this way; a face to face farewell didn't bear thinking about.

He thought of school, of the classroom and his empty desk, of the Georgian annex and the Assembly Hall. Would he bathe, once more, in the translucent magnificence of the 'Lives of Great Men', or spend a tranquil moment in the tree's shade, or would his be yet another gilded name on the Grammar's Roll of Honour?

Despite the heat, a shiver ran down his spine. The tree; he'd walked past it, oblivious in his dejection. He shut his eyes and embraced it in apology.

When Scott came home, he buckled under the head hammering intensity of Laura's misery. The season of her depression had cast more than a shadow; it had eclipsed his whole world. He'd tried to contain it, but the facade was beginning to crack. Agatha was mourning her brother, killed on the Somme, but, if anything, the tragedy had brought the couple closer. It seemed somehow immoral that their love should offer so much while Laura was suffering such heartbreak. It was a guilt complex compounded by the resurrection of Marian's aura and the sense of betrayal, however unjustified, that Scott's love for another engendered. In Laura's ever deepening distress, Marian's ghost was almost tangible.

Scott had arranged to meet Arthur Bowden at the new house in Little Eastleigh to discuss the work in progress. It was obvious that Laura hadn't left home all day; he had to get her out of that damnable atmosphere, even if it meant forcing her bodily through the door.

To his relief, she came quietly. His heart went out to her as they passed the Bowden's house. He'd let her meet Richard at the station alone, hoping to see them emerge arm in arm. But, if his hopes had been dashed, hers must have been shattered.

He picked up Agatha en route. Laura forced a smile.

The byway to Little Eastleigh was no more than a rutted country lane, wide enough for passing only where field entrances allowed. From the overhanging horse chestnuts and oaks, the cawing and cooing crows, rooks and wood pigeons did battle with combustion, but their world looked as lost to Laura as her own, its verdant canopy merely a compactor of the hopelessness reflected in Scott's mirror.

The Grange, originally a farmhouse, dated back to the fifteen hundreds. At the turn-of-the-century, the land had been sold off, leaving the house and two acres. The previous owner had landscaped the grounds; now Arthur Bowden was converting the old carriage stables into a garage, complete with gravel driveway, courtesy of the nearby pits.

The oak-beamed edifice was as picturesque as the roof the thatcher, brought out of retirement, was lovingly restoring with bundles of fresh reed and willow pegs. Below, a club-footed gardener was reclaiming the lawns and flowerbeds. The fragrance of freshly cut hay mingled with that of summer flowers.

'It would be impossible not to be happy here,' Scott concluded as he applied the handbrake. Once they'd moved in, Laura's mood must improve. He and Agatha already reflected that happiness, even in the sadness of her brother's death. If only Laura and Richard could patch things up. Still in the dark as to the cause of the rift, he instinctively damned Spencer Stafford to hell.

While Bowden took Scott on a tour of inspection, Agatha followed Laura into the house. The work was on schedule, Bowden needed no prodding from Harold and, consequently, Harold none from her. They'd plumped for a September wedding; the house would be ready in ample time.

The lintel was low; the thick oak door weather-beaten, opening onto a hallway which divided the ground floor. The house boasted two reception rooms, study, dining room and kitchen, with an upper storey of five bedrooms and a new bathroom, serviced, as at Harold's house in Ashleigh, by a hand pump in the garden. A narrow staircase led from the kitchen to the servant's quarters in the eaves. Before the war servants in such a house would have been the norm, now their accommodation was earmarked for a nursery. Not surprisingly for a teacher of infants, Agatha wanted lots of children.

She found Laura in her chosen bedroom, staring out at the back lawn, fully fifty yards square and hedged on all sides, with fields to the left and walled vegetable garden, orchard and a dilapidated greenhouse to the right. Ashes and oaks liberally marked all boundaries, aided by a stream to the north. She knew how Laura had longed to share it with Richard.

"It'll be all right, you'll see." She gave her a hug. "Just give it time."

But there was so little time. She loved them both; they were still children to her, despite Richard's commission and the physical love that, to whatever extent, they surely shared. In that regard their relationship was far more advanced than her own. She loved Scott, but she wasn't, as yet, in love with him. However, that would come; her rescuer from old maidenhood deserved nothing less.

The casualty figures spoke for themselves and her subconscious had been quick to read between the lines. With potential brides already outnumbering eligible men two to one, the conflict's survivors, if it ever did end, would be spoilt for choice, and, at a staid twenty eight, Agatha was no Elizabeth Bennet. She just thanked God that Scott, if not quite Mr. D'Arcy, was no Reverend Collins.

They strapped Arthur Bowden's bike to the back and gave him a lift home. Elizabeth ran out to meet them.

"Dad, Mum's in a terrible state. Richard's gone, called away. You'd best come."

The blood drained from Laura's face. Her eyes glazed.

"Get her home, Harold, quickly," Agatha whispered, lending her support.

Laura had recovered long before the doctor arrived. "She must build up her strength," he told Scott and Agatha. "Get her to eat more, she's as thin as a rake."

That night, under a vow of secrecy, Agatha took Laura's confession. It was plainly not the whole truth, but the overburdened boughs of sorrow told enough of the story; to expose the roots would be to dig too deep.

"I wish it hadn't happened, but I was so angry I didn't care. Besides, Spencer needed someone and there was only me. There was never anything between us; he was more like a brother."

Agatha could have reminded her that siblings didn't usually indulge in physical intimacy, even to the limited extent implied by Laura, but to bandy words would have been unworthy. She understood the motivation and the advantage she imagined Stafford to have taken of it. She also knew the agony of unrequited remorse. She, too, had spurned the love of her life in comparable circumstances; he'd gone off to war and been killed at Festubert.

197

Had Richard still been there, that understanding would have prompted her to do all in her power to heal the breach, if only to save Laura's sorrow the added requiem of regret. But he had gone, as surely to his death as her own lover, leaving damage control her only option; she must convince Laura that the past was the past and that a future beckoned beyond the heartbreak, to cushion her against the greater grief to come.

"These things happen, my dear. I know it doesn't seem so now, but you will get over it. You'll meet someone else and love him every bit as much, even more. And there's so much you can do, nowadays. When I was your age, the best a girl could hope for was nursing or teaching. The world is different now and changing by the day. There'll be women in parliament soon, you mark my words. Who knows, we may even have a woman prime minister one day; it might even be you."

Laura smiled at the outlandishness of the suggestion, but the underlying message seemed to sink in. Simply, no one else had truly accepted that the relationship was ended and, therefore, neither had she, Agatha reasoned. They'd sympathised with her sorrow and suffered her self-pity. Over the next few days Agatha allowed no such indulgence. By Sarah's delayed arrival, Laura was on the mend, and there Agatha, preoccupied with wedding arrangements, was content to leave it.

* * * * *

Richard arrived in London with nowhere to go. He wasn't due to report for another six days. Having found his way to Victoria station, his final point of embarkation, he stood, forlorn, on the concourse.

"Lost, are we, sir?" A porter asked.

"Pardon? Oh, no, no. Waiting for someone."

He played out the charade for another five minutes, gathering his thoughts, looking at his watch, Laura's watch. Finally he wandered out into the street, supposing he'd better find somewhere to stay. An hotel presented itself. A smartly dressed man was booking in. The price of a room was displayed behind the desk. He quickly left and found another in another street, shabbier but half the cost. There was a woman behind the desk, rather than a concierge. He took his key and went to climb the stairs.

"Not that way, dearie; that way." She pointed to the basement stairs.

A jug, basin and misted glass covered the ring marks on the room's battered chest of drawers. He drank some water, laid on the bed and slept.

Next morning, he caught the bus to Trafalgar Square and the National Gallery, hoping against hope that Laura would find him under Velasquez's Rokeby Venus. He repeated the vigil the following day, until memories turned to mayhem and hunger led him onto the streets. Staring at a menu in a restaurant window, he suddenly found himself being hauled through the door by a complete stranger, a full lieutenant, obviously the worst for drink.

"Hello young wart. My name's Keller, but you can call me Jimmy. Now you must come and join us. We're all completely blotto, but never mind that. There's someone in here who's dying to meet you. Says you look sad. You look all right to me, but that's women for you. Waiter! Another glass. Who's round is it?"

"Yours," his table companions cried in chorus.

"Oh, damn. And another bottle! Sit down, man, sit down."

A girl made space on the bench. Richard squeezed into it.

"I'm Elspeth," she introduced herself.

He didn't want to be there, he didn't want to be part of their drunken camaraderie, but he had no idea how to extricate himself. "Bowden, Richard Bowden," he completed the formalities.

"Then I shall call you Dickie Bow," she smiled flirtatiously, refashioning his tie.

"My God, where did you learn to do that?" Keller cooed. "Never offered to do mine. Must have been a manservant in some previous existence, skeletons in the closet, and all that. What are they eating over there? Looks like pig's afterbirth."

"James, you're disgusting!"

A honking motor horn alerted Richard to the hubbub of city traffic. It was outside and he was definitely inside, in bed, his shirt and tie loosened at the neck, his stockinged feet perspiring uncomfortably under the counterpane, but, he hadn't the foggiest idea of how he'd got there or what his trousers were doing hanging over the tainted brass bedstead.

Painfully, he raised his head. The room, drably rose in the evening gloom, was completely unfamiliar to him. At the foot of the bed, a Victorian wardrobe stood solidly against the wall, flanked by a well-travelled sea chest and an ancient commode, both bearing copper scuttles replete with dried flowers. To his right a pale pink chaise longe buttressed an oak tallboy, while, to his left, a gilded dressing table sat between two profusely draped townhouse windows, like something out of Madame Bovary. From the door's sentinel hat stand to the Aladdin's laundry basket by a screened off corner, it was a room caught on gender's cusp.

He leaned forward. The room span, making him cling to the bedclothes. At last, the islands and elephants of the watermarked ceiling slowed into focus. Leaky pipe or spilled Chamber Pot from the floor above? Pupils, grey matter, humour and hangover gave up the challenge.

The next time he opened his eyes the room was in darkness. A wedge of light spread across the floor. His head had cleared a little and Elspeth's soft, enquiring voice wasn't quite the surprise it might have been. He made a show of sitting up.

"It's all right," she told him, leaning over the bed to stroke his temple. "The others have gone; we're quite alone. You had quite a skin-full."

She was older than him, perhaps twenty-two or twenty three, with wavy brown hair pinned back to emphasise her high cheek bones and dimpled cheeks. From her hazel eyes, her nose sloped to a classical precipice over lips made fuller by a subtle coating of gloss.

"Did I make a terrible fool of myself?" He asked.

"Not at all. We were all pretty merry. It was Jimmy's last day; the others have gone to see him off."

He remembered Jimmy, but his recollection of the others was a blur of unfamiliar faces.

"I'm sorry," he apologised, "I've kept you back."

"Oh, that's all right, I hate goodbyes. I shall miss him though; he's a true life and soul of the party type, is our Jimmy. By the way, he's my cousin, in case you were wondering. This was his flat; now we share it."

Her conviction precluded further apology. "Oh, my head," Richard moaned.

"I'll get you some coffee."

When Elspeth returned, Richard was asleep, innocent to the point of infantile. She would let him rest; he'd spoken of another four days leave before he'd slumped into her lap. At least he hadn't been sick.

She leaned over and kissed his forehead.

"My poor little Dickie Bow. Why must they take them so young?"

CHAPTER THIRTY THREE

"You look glum, Arthur."

"Our boy's gone over yonder. Sent him home for a week's leave then called him back the very next day. His mother's beside herself. Lost two of his brothers fighting the old Boer. The Germans've got the third. If anything happens to this one, I reckon I'll be committing her to the grave and all, either that or a mental home. Whole streets of 'em lost, whole towns, even, and still it goes on."

"Well, there you are, Arthur, there's nothing the likes of us can do about it, though there is something you can do for me, or rather I can do for you, if you'd care to take a look."

The Elmsford contractor led Bowden into the house.

"Christ, you'd've thought a bomb had hit it."

"Precisely, Arthur. That's what you get for letting to the Army. Not that they gives you much choice, mind; fair game if its empty, they reckon, and there's many that are since them Zeppelins've been coming over. Still, you'd've thought they'd've looked after it a bit better than this. I've got a parcel of them to do up, some in this state, some a damned sight worse. What do you reckon?"

"Well, of course I can do the job, but I can't start for a week or two, I've already got something on." Arthur stepped onto the door, laid like a duckboard over the floor's splintered joists. "I'll need a carpenter. How much did you say they was paying?"

"Army's offered the owner twelve quid. I ask you. This alone's got to be twice that, and the upstairs the same. There's hardly a board left intact, ripped them all up for firewood, door jambs, the lot, and half the stairs. As for the cupboards, well, you can see for yourself, just ripped them off the wall, even the karsy out back. I told her, it's a good job she moved her furniture out or they'd've had that and all, poor old biddy. Don't suppose you know her, do you, old Mrs. Hubbard? And don't laugh, I've heard all the cupboard jokes I can handle. Nice old girl, but she's certainly no Rotheschild, so do the best you can."

'Yeh, so you can pocket the difference,' Arthur thought caustically.

"Tell you what, do a good price on this and there's a couple more I can put your way. Speaking of which, this job you're doing for that Scott bloke from the timber yard..."

"How'd you know that?"

"Word gets round. Wouldn't mind having a word with him, would you, see if you can't wheedle a bit of timber out of him? Well, you can see what's needed. I'll make it worth his while, tell him, and yours, of course."

"Not much likelihood of that, Horace. Straight as a die, our Mr. Scott."

"Well, it's worth a try. Even a bit of discount would help, what with things the way they are. I'm paying half as much again as I was before the War, as must you be."

Where inflation was concerned, Arthur could fully sympathise. "Well, I'll see if there's any leeway on price, but, as for the other, there's no way, and, to be honest, I wouldn't like to put him on the spot, us being friendly like; it wouldn't be right."

"That's what friends is for in my book, Arthur, but then you always was too straight for your own good. Anyway, see what you can do, hey? Tell him I know where I can lay my hands on a bit of extra petrol for that motor of his, if it helps. Meantime, give this place the once over and tell me how much."

* * * * *

Richard stood with the recruits crowding the stern, wrapped in emotion's greatcoat. It was farewell to everything he'd ever known, everything he'd ever loved, all faded into the gloom with the last flickering harbour light. He'd never felt so alone, as much a number among the numberless as the identity discs around his neck.

"You should put them on immediately, Sir, and takes especial care of them," the wheezy Quartermaster Sergeant at Southampton had told him. "Without them you could be anybody, Sir, with them only yourself."

The metal was stamped with name, rank, regiment and 'C of E'. With them had come a field service notebook, a gas helmet, pistol ammunition for Richard's Webley Mark V, prismatic compass, gravity clinometer and a bandage. He hoped he would never need the bandage, or the gravediggers the discs.

Consternation was growing over a red light that was trailing them.

"Thank your lucky stars she's there. That's our escort, that is, destroyer most like," an old sweat said reassuringly. "We won't get scuppered while she's about. Now, who's gonna try his luck on the old mud hook?"

The weather was set fair for a profitable night. Like 'Kitty Nap', 'Brag' and 'Pontoon', 'Crown and Anchor' was outlawed, but, nevertheless, an army institution. For the men it was, at least, a distraction from the privation of bedding down on the open deck with nothing but a lifebelt for a pillow and a greatcoat to keep out the cold.

The gamblers gathered round. Richard turned a blind eye, gazing up at the funnel smoke evaporating into the night sky.

"What bloody Albatross?" Someone wisecracked.

The ship rolled. It was time to turn in; he'd been a landlubber all his life, mild as it was, the swell was beginning to affect him. He sidestepped down the companionway and searched for cabin number six.

The tiny rectangular compartment was in darkness; the other subalterns were asleep, or pretending to be. Richard got his bearings, shut the door, groped for the frame and hauled himself onto the empty upper bunk, bumping his head on a roof rivet in the process.

Lying down helped quell his queasiness, although it wasn't exclusively sea induced; all that lay ahead played its part, along with the boyhood he had left behind. In the darkness they were there again, Laura, his home, his family. He blanked them from his mind, turning to the barely opalescent porthole - Richard through the looking glass.

He'd bidden aurevoir to Elspeth in her Jermyn Street flat, two doors from the restaurant, having moved in with her the morning after. She'd paid for everything, the dinners, the theatre, the whisky, even his cigarettes. The last round in the restaurant had left him penniless. He'd paid her back in kind, staggering onto the train in a state of near collapse. As she'd said, she hated goodbyes, she hadn't come to the station.

Elspeth; his weary loins stirred at the thought. What an incredible woman, a joy to be with; she'd lifted him to new heights, indeed, made a man of him. His only gripes were that her incontinent cat had peed over his tunic and her insistence on calling him 'Dickie Bow'.

If it hadn't been for Laura, he might have imagined himself in love with Elspeth, but, as unbelievable as the experience had been, he would have forgone every last second just to hold Laura in his arms and hear her say she loved him. But that was impossible. If ever again he trod the river path home, he wouldn't find her in the little house that had witnessed the blissful revelations of adolescence, their clandestine coming of age.

The thought filled him with sadness. But home is where the heart is and that would always be with Laura. For all the ecstasy they offered, Elspeth's arms would never be more than a halfway house.

After five hours of abortive dozing, Richard was up with the gulls on the gunwale to watch the ship glide past wharves terraced, house high, with supply crates to dock in what appeared to be the heart of Le Havre. The men trooped down the gangplanks straight onto the 'Place de la Gare', fringed with Tamarisk trees and already bustling, like some sketch come to life from his French primer.

He took in the tall windows, the wrought iron work, the old men in their berets and blouses, the women in seemingly compulsory black, skirts brushing the cobbles. But no textbook could have prepared him for the all-pervading ether of French tobacco, fish guts and the inadequacies of Gallic plumbing, lightened only by the alluring aroma of freshly baked bread.

In the marshalling yards, a huge locomotive shunted into its couplings. Even its steam smelled different.

"Quite a beast," someone said, before it let out such an incongruously castrato 'toot toot' that its waiting cargo collapsed in hysterics.

The men were herded into cattle trucks labelled 'Hommes 40, Chevaux 8 (en longe)'. Richard thought he would rather be a horse. A slat-seated carriage accommodated the officers. Social separation had never been more marked, nor prime British buttocks by journey's end, reached after a ten-hour crawl from siding stop to siding stop. Even a Major had peed from the door.

Amiens? Richard's hunger pangs turned to palpitations. He was supposed to be going to Rouen.

"And you've come from Le Havre? Christ, you could've walked it in less time than it takes to crap. It's practically the same place," the R.T.O. told him.

He finally arrived twenty-four hours late, posted missing, presumed drowned.

"It used to be pretty lively here before the Somme," a subaltern welcomed him, when he sat down, bleary eyed, to a breakfast table of bleak faces next morning. "Now it's a ruddy mausoleum."

The congealed porridge and cold, fat-frazzled bacon did little to raise his spirits.

Across the aisle, a couple of freshmen began biting at the bit to get to grips with the Hun.

"Stupid bloody schoolboys," a manic depressive, returned to duty before his scars had healed, railed at them. "There's nothing heroic about being blown to bits, laddie, nothing poetic about a bullet in the brain or a lump of shrapnel in one's guts, unless one happens to be Rupert bloody Brook, and he died of ruddy dysentery. Damned cretins."

"All right, old man, they're not to know," a companion tried to quiet him.

"Well, someone's got to tell 'em; these damn 'blood and guts' base wallahs sure as hell won't, they've never been within ten miles of a front line trench." He turned back to the rookies. "If your name's not listed, be thankful; your turn will come soon enough."

Richard's came after two weeks of watching men come and go, with nothing to do except complete the 'Last Will and Testament' in the back of his pay book, swot up on his Infantry Training Manual and take advantage of some target practice. He was to proceed to Amiens and, from there, pick up his battalion in reserve, somewhere near Beaumont Hamel.

It was night when the train pulled in. The men tumbled from the trucks. Those back from leave made their own way; the new blood formed up in platoons by the trackside. Richard found the Transport Officer, the same one who'd sent him back to Le Havre a fortnight earlier.

"I'll be with you in a moment," the R.T.O. grumbled, storming down the platform to remonstrate with another novice, struggling to organise his milling mass. "Get those men in order! We haven't got all day!"

The subaltern blushed. Richard felt desperately sorry for him; he was being shown up in front of his men. His sergeant came to the rescue, barking out the appropriate commands. The platoon formed up and marched to the exit.

"Now, what can I do for you?" The R.T.O. returned, still hot under the collar.

"I'm looking for the Essex, Sir; somewhere near Beaumont Hamel, I was told."

"Then what are you doing here, man? You should be in Albert."

Richard had been here before, metaphorically speaking.

"They told me Amiens, Sir."

"Huh; too late now, the ruddy train's gone. Beaumont Hamel, you say? Well you'll have no trouble finding it, that's for sure. Those ambulances are going up, ask one of them to take you."

It was a long, bumpy, fug of a ride from Amiens to Albert, a straight road of petrol fumes, dried blood and body odour. Even leaning, breath bated, into the driver's thick, Geordie accent, 'why-aye' was all Richard could decipher above the throb of the engine and the rattle of empty stretchers. As nausea crept up on him, he

204

reverted to the door, nodding on cue, until, at last, he found himself retching into the outskirts of town.

The driver pulled up at an aid station, said something unintelligible and got out. An orderly approached.

"This is as far as she goes, Sir."

"I thought he was going to Hamel."

"Not this one, Sir, but you'll find plenty that are, trucks, limbers, take your pick. The sand pits is what you want."

After a recuperative cup of First Aid tea, Richard hitched a lift on a limber, thankful that mule sweat was more nostalgic than nauseous, as the animals picked their way through the masonry-strewn streets.

"Full to the rafters with scrap iron," the driver told him, nodding towards a row of warehouses. "Owned by some rag and bone millionaire. And up there, that's the old Madonna, that is. They says that when she topples the war'll be over," the man continued his guided tour, nodding again at the statue of the Madonna and Child perched at iron-rodded right angles from the cathedral's shattered tower, silver rather than gilt in the moonlight.

Richard stared up. It seemed impossible that the Mother of Christ hadn't fallen and taken her infant with her. It was almost as if God had frozen her in the act of casting him down.

"Not much chance of that now; out of range since we pushed 'em back; more's the pity," the driver bemoaned. "Good baths, mind; a sort of greenhouse affair built on the back; water comes at you from all angles."

Out of range or not, the guns were clearly audible. Their volume increased as the limber cleared the urban ruins and headed into the abyss beyond.

"Now I know how Christian felt," Richard said.

"Sorry, Sir?"

"Pilgrim's Progress, John Bunyon."

"Oh, I see, Sir. Not much of a reader myself; never quite got the hang of it."

"How near are we to the front?"

"It's over there aways," the driver nodded vaguely eastward. "Only it's not so flat down here, not like Wipers. Up there you can see the Very lights for miles. Don't want to go up there if you can help it, Sir, right shit hole, if you'll pardon my French. Up to the bloody axles, even in summer. Here's better; chalk see; though it's none too clever neither, when the weather turns."

A chain of flashes broke over the downlands, like an electrical storm over petrified sea-swell. Their thunder followed.

"Someone's copping it," the driver said glumly, joining the conveyor belt of trucks, limbers, ambulances and wagons, nose to tail in both directions, the outgoing bearing the tools of destruction, the incoming the human testimony to their efficiency, each flanked by a chain of khaki clad humanity, those going up spick and span, in good order, those coming back dirty, dishevelled, ragged, exhausted.

"Care for a smoke?" Richard offered.

"Shouldn't really, Sir, ammo in the back," the man said, dipping into the proffered pack. "Still, won't do no harm, long as the old redcaps don't nab us, hey?"

Cupping the cheroot expertly in his palm, he took a deep drag.

"Cor, right bloody gaspers, these. Bit different to the old Woodbines," he managed to wheeze, before degenerating into seizure.

"Sorry, I should have warned you."

The driver waved away the apology, choking on the upshot then spitting it over the footboard.

"You'll have to excuse me, Sir; never been the same since the gas."

Richard asked about Beaumont Hamel. "My battalion's near there. The R.T.O. seemed to find it vaguely amusing in an odd sort of way."

"Ah, well near is about as far as anyone's got to that place. Half the bloody Army's up there having a go; lost the other half trying. Just can't shift them. You'd think they'd call it a day and find some other way round. I mean, they've got the whole of bloody France to choose from, why keep hammering away at the same old spot? But there you are; reckon Haig must know what he's doing. I hope to Christ someone does. I thought the whole idea was to wipe out the bloody enemy, not our-bleeding-selves."

The conversation lapsed. The dust rose, the road worsened. Richard hadn't ridden a wagon since his last childhood harvest; he suspended his backside over the mercilessly hard postilion.

"It takes a bit of getting used to, Sir. It's murder if you've got piles."

The convoy trundled on.

"You did say sand pit camp, Sir?"

"That's what I was told."

"Well we're almost there. Now, if you jump off at the next corner and take the track off to your left, it'll lead you straight to it. I'll slow down a bit to give you a sporting chance, but, if I stop, there'll be hell to pay from behind; Handcuff King Corner, they calls this; not a place to linger."

"Handcuff King?"

"It's a Jerry shell, Sir, like two smoke rings; you'll find out. Rip a team to shreds and us with it. Right, now you tell me when you're ready and I'll haul them in."

"Ready."

The driver pulled on the reins.

"What's the bloody hold up?" Immediately the cry came.

"Alright! Keep yer hair on! Good luck, Sir, good luck."

The limber picked up speed, leaving Richard to mull over the maze of tracks which lead off to the left.

"eenie-meenie-minie-mo......"

He kept to the widest. Twenty minutes later he stumbled into the row upon row of bell tents that constituted Sand Pit Camp.

"No, no, no, they've told you all wrong," the duty officer told him. "The Essex are ruddy miles away. Pointless trying to find 'em in the dark; first time out, no guide, you're as likely to end up having breakfast with the boche. If you take my advice, you'll bed down here for the night and try again in the morning. You can get your hair cut while you're about it; can't have a mane like that going into the trenches."

CHAPTER THIRTY FOUR

"Thank heavens that's over." Laura collapsed, sore backed, in the parlour, after a hard fortnight's harvesting. "Next time I'll volunteer for factory work."

"Did you see that boy hanging over the railings? Dirty little tyke," Sarah said. "Someone should tell his mother. I didn't know where to look."

"Oh, I think you did."

"Well, it was hard not to. I'm sure he was doing it on purpose."

"Not at his age."

"Well he obviously knew what it was for. Do you know who he is?"

"Just some boy from the village," Laura lied, knowing exactly who he was - young George, Richard's nephew. "I'm sure Sister Rowena will see far worse, where she's going. Imagine, her a nurse, and in Russia of all places."

"I know. She'll faint at her first sight of a man's do-da."

"Look who's talking."

"I didn't faint."

"No, but you turned a considerable shade of purple."

"Actually, I've been thinking of joining the VADs. It's pointless me trying for university. Even if I pass the exam, mother doesn't have the funds and it's no use asking father, he's firmly convinced that ignorance is bliss where women are concerned. Half the brain capacity, you see; what goes in comes out half baked. He calls my mother 'the wildebeest'."

"Do you miss him?" Laura asked.

"Not really; he was always out on the veldt or down some mine or other. He writes occasionally, and there's the allowance, of course. If it wasn't for that, mother would be up the proverbial creek without a paddle. Mind you, if he knew what she and her friends were up to, he'd cut her off without a penny."

"Why, is something in the offing?"

"Oh, I keep out of it. All I'll say is there's been some strange comings and goings recently. If she tries another stunt like that stupid banner escapade, they'll lock her up for sure."

"It wasn't stupid."

"Yes it was; it was totally useless."

Laura didn't argue the toss; she was more interested in the present.

"You must know something."

"No, and nor do I want to. I'm fed up with being sworn to secrecy. In fact, I'm fed up with the whole stupid thing. It's time I did something for myself. At the moment I feel like some piece of left luggage, or worse still, a travelling trunk being sat on by my mother."

"But by joining the VADs, don't you think you'd be supporting the War?"

"Oh, please, Laura, not you, too. You sound like mother and her 'higher conscience'. No, I don't think that, not at all. I'd be supporting the men who have to fight it, and there's a considerable difference."

"They could refuse to go."

"And what then? If you want to stop the fighting, Laura, you've got to stop it on both sides, and, to be honest, I don't see the kind of support you and mother claim, in fact, rather the reverse. At that rally last year, forty thousand women marched in favour of the war, not against it. Mother's anti-war brigade couldn't muster half that many, not even a quarter. Anyway, you were all for nursing yourself, at one stage."

"That was then."

"Well I'm sorry, Laura, but I have to do something. I know I can't go overseas, you have to be twenty three to do that, but I'm sure there's plenty I can do here. Anything's better than staying with mother. I wouldn't say anything on purpose, of course, but there's always a chance I may let something slip."

"So you do know something."

"No."

"Oh, come on Sarah."

"No!"

* * * * *

Richard struggled along the battered communication trench, tin hat bobbing uncomfortably on his cropped scalp. "M.O.'s orders," the barber had told him. "it makes dressing head wounds easier."

Flies swarmed all around, but, with much tastier morsels of mankind to pursue, spared him their aggravation. What amazed him most was the quiet. He wasn't in the habit of walking along ditches, but, other than that, he could have been in the middle of the Essex countryside. Except in Ashleigh's green and pleasant land you didn't hear peculiar whistling sounds and have to duck for cover.

The shell exploded some way ahead. Instinctively he peeked over the top and saw its dissipating smoke, his first hostile encounter. He waited for more, but heard nothing except a distant boom and the dry rattle of a machine gun, similarly far off.

Gathering himself, he continued on, conscious of a strengthening malodour. He'd been told he would smell the front long before he got to it.

'How much bally farther,' he wondered, turning into yet another empty traverse, not that he minded, it was like dragging his heels on the way to the dentist, convincing himself the ache had gone.

His mind marched from the dentist's chair to the parade ground and the thousand and one things that had been drilled into him. He could remember them now, but would he remember them under pressure? More to the point, would he hold his nerve?

And just what had they thought of him at training school, tutors and cadets; and what would his fellow officers and men think of him now? Would they find him out? It should be no one's birthright to be obeyed, particularly on the evidence of some of the upper class arses he'd met, but, for better or worse, that was the system, everyone in his place, which begged the question, was he in his? Many of the men coming under his command will have been out longer than he'd been a

209

cadet; some may even be Boer War men, like sergeant Baron from cadet camp, fighting for the flag when he'd been in nappies.

Each insecurity led him deeper into the labyrinth, until all vacillation was flattened from him by two cursing stretcher bearers, barging past with their cargo of misery. He caught a glimpse of a mashed face, half an eye hanging. He held his stomach until the bearers had rounded the traverse, then doubled over in revulsion.

'ZIP, THUD!"

"Jesus Christ!"

He flung himself flat, muscles tensed against the red hot bullet about to bury itself in his back. It never came. He became conscious of birdsong, of melodic normality. His head ceased to spin, his ears to ring. He scuttled under the bulwark, staring back at the bullseye where his brain had been. He'd felt its wind, he'd felt its ruddy wind! He shuddered.

'Get a grip, for God's sake.'

A series of deep breaths steadied him. A swig of water moistened the grit grinding between his teeth. He wiped the coagulated dust and bile from his lips. Whatever safety the earth had to offer, this was no place to linger.

He scampered on, nose in the dirt, following the contours of the trench like a bowl-headed beetle, until he found a pair of boots barring his path. Puttees wound up too symmetrically to be anything but a sergeant's.

"And where the hell have you come from?" He was asked officiously.

He got to his feet, scanning his tunic for tell-tale vomit stains. All had been neutralised by a thick coating of chalk dust, along with his insignia. He brushed himself down, praying for nonchalance.

"The Sand Pits, Sergeant."

His accoster looked mortified. Despite the new uniformity of officers and men, no more piping on the cuffs, no more jodhpurs to mark the Germans' targets, to mistake an officer was beyond the pale. He came to rigid attention, staring straight ahead, as if trying to span his gaffe.

"Beg pardon, Sir, I didn't realise you was an officer. All I saw was a tin hat, Sir!"

"That's quite all right, Sergeant, at ease."

"Sir!"

Still the man stood ramrod straight.

"At ease, Sergeant; no offence taken," Richard assured him. "Where can I find the C.O.?"

"The C.O., Sir? He's down there aways. Private Short!"

A second man separated himself from the sandbags.

"Escort this officer to the command post. And none of your lip, understand?"

"Lip, Sergeant? Me, sergeant?"

"Yes, you, Private Short; now hop to it."

"Yes sergeant. If you'd care to follow me, Sir."

In each bay a sentry sat on the firing step looking out into no-man's land via a rudimentary periscope, an angled mirror attached to a pole. Other men were squatting, more were tucked into funk holes, some sleeping, some brewing tea on Tommy Cookers. None saluted, in the line that duty was excused unless directly reporting to a superior.

Richard could sense them sizing him up. His guide asked for permission to speak.

"Lose your footing, did you, Sir?"

The man's familiarity was tantamount to insubordination. It was no wonder the sergeant had warned him to button his lip. Nevertheless, pride demanded an answer.

"Actually I was dodging a bullet."

"Yes, well it's a wonder you got through at all, Sir. Jerry's had a fix on that stretch for the best part of a week. We spend half the night building up the parapet, then over comes the morning hate and we're back to square one, gap the size of Watford; perfect for snipers. No one moves along there in daylight 'cept if it's an emergency."

"Well, luckily for me, his aim was a bit awry today."

"See any stretcher bearers, Sir?"

"Yes, they got through, too."

"Pity the poor bloke on it. Face like that, it would've been kinder to prop him back up and let 'em have done with him."

"Had he been out long?"

"Couple of weeks. Didn't know him well. Well, it doesn't do, does it? Cor, you was lucky alright. That bugger's had three this past couple of days. Wouldn't mind being in your mob; that kind of luck rubs off."

It was a welcome boost to Richard's confidence.

"What's your name again, private?"

"Short, Sir."

"Are you usually this familiar with your officers, private Short?"

"Familiar, Sir? Me, Sir? Lord love us no, Sir. Only speaks when I'm spoken to, me, Sir; regulations. Not far now, Sir. Now, don't mind the C.O.; he may seem a bit grumpy, see, on account of the last show, but he's a good man to have on your side when the going gets tough." Short lowered his voice. "For a man without none, he's got balls, I'll say that for him. Officer reporting, Sir!" He called into the chasm.

Spencer sat at his desk, a kitchen table salvaged from a flattened farm cottage and cut down to size. Beside him his adjutant sifted through paperwork. In the corner, a signaller sat on a camp chair, hunched over a D3 telephone. It was a comfortable dugout, as dugouts went, bigger than most, timber lined and furnished with a proper bed and a war torn armchair, also salvaged.

The replacement stumbled down the earthen steps.

"Second lieutenant Bowden reporting for duty, Sir."

"All right, as you were."

How many fresh faced young subalterns had presented themselves in just the same manner and how many had died within days? Spencer was past pity, past sadness, resigned to the inevitable, and tired beyond belief.

He took the subaltern's papers. 'Bowden;' the name meant nothing to him, he had too much on his mind to invoke adolescent memories of apple scrumping plumber's sons, or to introduce himself.

"Straight from training camp, Bowden?" The adjutant asked.

"Yes, Sir."

"How long?"

"Six weeks, Sir, but I was in the O.T.C. before that; got my War Office Certificate 'A' last Easter, Sir."

"Oh, a man of experience," Spencer commented dryly. "Well, at least you're an officer and we're damned short of those. You'll find Sergeant Wilmot in the next bay. Get him to take you along to Mr. Langham. We'll talk again when you're settled in."

"Yes Sir."

"Alright.... Bowden," Spencer checked the name. "Dismiss; and do smarten yourself up; doesn't do to set a bad example."

"Yes, Sir, sorry, Sir; I had a bit of an accide...."

"Dismiss Lieutenant."

'B' company was entrenched on the far left of the position. The sergeant left Richard by the steps of its command post. The fug of stale tobacco smoke, tea leaves and guttered candle wicks thickened as Richard descended.

"Lieutenant Langham?"

"Yes, old boy. Would you mind, you're in the light."

Richard moved to one side, allowing the daylight back onto the page.

"Shan't be a mo'," Langham continued to read, "and do stand down; none of that seniority stuff here."

He finished the paragraph, marked the book and swung his legs from his makeshift bed. "Now, what can I do for you?"

His accent was everything Richard had been dreading, steeped in that self-assurance which came only from a lifetime of obeisance, from butler to the batman he summoned like a dog after Richard had explained himself.

"Care for some char? You have to take sugar, it comes in the milk. Awful stuff, really, but there you are. Unless you prefer it black, of course."

"No, no; the more the merrier."

"Tea for two, then, Corporal Smith. Dump your stuff over there," Langham indicated an age-stained palliasse on wire netting slung between upturned ammunition boxes. "It's not exactly a four poster, but you'll find it more comfortable than the camp variety. I made it myself in a moment of madness. This one too."

'Had it made, more like,' Richard mused, hanging his helmet on the vacant nail. "So, the Captain's in command, is he?"

"'Acting Major, actually. The colonel's gone down with gout and major Fallows is on leave, thank God; he's a stickler for paperwork. At least Stafford let's a man rest."

'Stafford!' The name dropped on Richard like a Minnenwerfer. He remembered

212

private Short's words; 'for a man without none, he's got balls.' But it couldn't be, it just couldn't be. The man had looked so old.

"You wouldn't happen to know his first name, would you?"

"Stafford's? Spencer, Percival. 'Sunday Pictorial' the men call him on account of the damned camera he's always carting about. Completely against the rules, of course, but the colonel turns a blind eye. Why, some kind of acquaintance?"

- CHAPTER THIRTY FIVE -

Richard was still absorbing the Stafford bomb-blast, when a German salvo added its own sixpen'th, cascading chalk into the mug of tea Langham's batman had just brought him.

"Right on cue. I'm sure the bloody boche have some kind of tea detector," Langham told him. "Not far off; sixty yards, I'd say. One becomes a pretty good judge of these things after a while. It doesn't do to duck unnecessarily in front of the men."

Outside, someone called for stretcher bearers.

Langham reached for his helmet. "Not again."

Two bays down, the sentry's periscope had been sent hurtling into no-man's land, along with the holder's forearm.

"That's two today," Langham moaned. "Completely put me off my tiffin."

How Langham could think of his stomach at such a time, other than trying to keep it down, Richard couldn't begin to comprehend. The stretcher bearers tied a tourniquet above the shattered elbow and carted the donor off, still conscious. "Got me a proper Blighty one. That's me out of it," he cried stoically through the pain. News came an hour later that he'd died of shock on the way back.

Stand-to came at dusk, historically, with dawn, the most likely time of attack. Beyond the parados, the sunset was magnificent, the plaintive evensong of the nightingale poignant, yet mocking in its immunity.

The ration party came up in the darkness with its dixies of bully beef and ration biscuit stew.

"We all share the same menu," Langham explained. "Food parcels from home are left in reserve, at least in this part of the line; more important things to carry up. Serves a dual purpose, the stew, sustenance and constipation; makes visiting the bogs a less frequent necessity, unless one has dysentery, of course. Favourite target, the old latrine, excrement flies all over, along with the innards of any unfortunate occupant. That's what happened to that chap you bumped into coming up. Landed on the lip, well, just short, over in Petherill's section. Nice chap, Peverill, you'll like him; Oxford Blue."

"Is there much dysentery?"

"Not really. The men get it, mostly, though I have known the odd officer to be sent down with his bowels hanging out of his trousers. It's the flies, you know, and the water, of course. There's a stream to our left, contaminated to hell and strictly off limits, but still the men use it to fill their flasks.

No, I'd give the jakes a miss, if I were you. Better a bully beef tin in the privacy of the old dugout. There's thousands about; just hang 'occupied' on the old gas flap and toss it over the top on completion. By the way, that tin of Maconachies is your emergency ration. Keep it safe. Compared with the ruddy Fray Bentos it's quite a treat and apt to go missing."

214

The wind changed direction, adding a peculiar sickly sweetness to the unremitting stench of open cesspits, chloride of lime and body odour.

"What's that smell?" Richard asked, afraid it might be gas.

"Putrefaction, old chum," Langham told him matter-of-factly. "One ceases to notice it after a while. It's a devil of a stink when the weather's really hot. There's a bunch of stiffs out there, been there for weeks; some in that stream I told you about. Can't get 'em in, too risky."

"You mean ours?"

"That's right."

"And we just leave them there?"

"'Fraid so. Unless, of course, stinker Jessop's back; they carried him off in more bits than a Meccano set, but, if anyone's immortal, it's that man; not even God would have him, and certainly not Satan, he'd starve the whole ruddy inferno of oxygen. Never known a man to whiff so. I mean, we could all do with a bath, but Jessop - worse than the foulest camel. So," Langham returned to the afternoon's unrequited question, "you know our illustrious Captain, do you?"

"Not really, his father's our local squire, that's all." Richard was answer-ready; still it stuck in his gullet. "He caught me scrumping manor apples when I was a boy, although he obviously doesn't remember, if, indeed, it's the same Stafford," which he had no sour doubt it was. "He's aged a millennium, if it is, I didn't even recognise him. I'd be grateful if you didn't say anything."

"Mums the word, old boy, though you'll find him hard to avoid, when the C.O. gets back, he's our company commander. No, it's definitely the stiffs," Langham concluded. "You may have a point about gas, though; wind's coming from the east, better be on our guard. These things are gas gongs, by the way;" he knocked lightly on a shell case, hanging lantern-like from a prop. "There's one in every bay. If you hear one being hammered, get your gas hat on pronto.

Yes; Stinker Jessop; if ever there was a contest between the whiffy living and the fetid dead, that man would win hands down. Lord what a pong. Oh well, may as well get you started. Not much to do tonight, just some parapet to mend and a bit of revetting upstream. Pity about Aimes, that chap who lost an arm. He was a good man. County cricketer, you know. Not any more."

Darkness fell. Langham left Richard in his sergeant's care. Under the stars, Richard stared out into no-man's land's eerie moonscape, devoid of vegetation, scattered with the debris of war and wire entanglements, only a cemetery of splintered trunks denoting where once had been a copse or a wood, truly the Slough of Despond.

"Makes you think, doesn't it, Sir," the sergeant said. "Just a few weeks ago all this was green fields full of poppies and cornflowers. Even had larkspur growing in the trenches. First time out is it, Sir?"

"Yes Sergeant."

"Well, if you don't mind me saying, Sir?"

"Not at all, Sergeant."

"Well, it's safe enough poking your head up at night, but I wouldn't try it in the daytime, likely to get it blowed off; in fact, it's a dead cert."

215

Richard smiled. "So I discovered on the way up."

"Yes, heard you nearly copped it. Boys reckon you was dead lucky. Never been known to miss before, a real dead-eyed Dick, that one. We still haven't spotted him. Thought we had, in that wood over yonder, if you can call it a wood. Got the old gunners to give it a going over, but next day he was at it again."

How providence spawns reputations. In the act of vomiting, Richard had become 'Lucky' Bowden. Such luck rubbed off; such luck bred confidence.

A flare soared, throwing the devastation into stark relief.

"Now, if you're out there on a working party or what-have-you and one of them things goes up, just stand stock still, they're not likely to clock you if you do that. One false move and you're a goner, along with any that's with you."

The night wore on, the watch ended. Richard negotiated the gas curtain. Down in the dugout, candlelight flickered over Langham's sleeping face, half-housed in a poetry book. A pile of magazines lay toppled by his bedside, Tatler, Punch, Town Topics, The Bystander. Over his head three Kirchner pin-ups posed provocatively, the same three Richard had seen on barrack-room walls.

Immediately he saw Laura posing for Stafford. He snuffed out the candle and image together and lay on his bunk. He'd let Langham rest; he'd be going out again soon. He checked his watch and Laura was there again, etched into the luminous dial. Her watch, Stafford's company; the god of irony must be belly laughing himself into convulsions, he scowled.

He must have dozed off, for the next thing he knew damp paws were pattering across his face, followed by the drag of a fat, clammy tail.

"Ugh!" He leapt up, thrashing his hair and clothing.

A match flared, Langham peered over.

"What the hell's the matter?"

"A rat or something; it just crawled across my bloody face!"

"Is that all," Langham groaned dispassionately. "That's something else you'll get used to. Just don't get bitten by one, that's all. I forgot to tell you, if you've got any edibles, hang them from the ceiling, it's the only safe place." He relit the candle and sat up, yawning into his hands. "I'm sorry, you must be tired, I didn't think. Boche are quiet for a change, you might as well make the most of it."

"No, it's all right, you probably need it more than me. I couldn't sleep anyway."

"Well, if you're sure." Langham swung back with a sigh. "Wake me if you need me. Leave the candle when you go out; rat deterrent; it also prevents them from eating the damned thing."

Richard wandered along the line, familiarising himself with the layout, almost tripping headlong into the latrine. A swarm of angry bluebottles rose up. He flailed his way back to the front trench. Rats, flies, death and destruction; picturesque Picardy completed its introduction. The quagmire of Flanders still awaited and the final sacrament, his baptism of fire. But he had other preoccupations, Laura and, above all, the hand of fate that had marked his card for Spencer's pack.

- CHAPTER THIRTY SIX -

In the early hours of September 3rd, Harold Scott lay star-gazing in his bed, consumed with the change in Laura. Physically, Sarah's stay and the harvesting had had the desired effect and she was a picture of health. Mentally she'd become a different person, one whose callousness increasingly reminded him of his first wife. Yet she had none of Marian's religious mania, none of her bitterness and guilt; he'd even caught her skipping next to naked between the bathroom and her bedroom one morning. Marian would have been mortified. Agatha had asserted it was just a phase she was going through; he hoped to God she was right.

He was about to plumb the depths of Hettie Jameson's evil influence, when the drone of aero engines had him racing to the window. He saw nothing until a huge explosion sent the bewildered birds screeching up into its brilliant halo. The bomb had dropped due north, in the vicinity of Little Eastleigh.

"The house!" Scott reached for his clothes. All his hopes, all his dreams, his new life with Agatha, its therapeutic effect on Laura, all destroyed by a German bomb?

"You bastards," he yelled through the window. "You utter bastards!"

Laura burst in.

"What is it, Daddy?"

"It's a bomb! The ba... they're bombing the house!" Nothing else mattered.

"Wait for me, I'm coming, too!"

A police roadblock beat them to it.

"Sorry, Sir, there's been a bomb."

"I know there's been a bloody bomb! Let me through, damn you, my house is up there!"

"Sorry, Sir, my orders are to let no one through 'til the danger's past."

"The danger is passed, damn it, they're bloody miles away by now. Now, get out of my way."

Scott revved his engine towards a serious altercation. It was Arthur Bowden who saved the day, arriving on his bike, throwing Scott back to the night of Elmsford's first air raid, when he'd been run down by 'person or persons unknown,' later rumoured to be showing the airship the way, and Bowden had come searching for him.

"Arthur, thank God. Tell this man to let me through, would you?"

The constable took some persuading. "Well on your head be it," he finally agreed.

The barrier was moved. Bowden left his bike and climbed into the car.

It was too dark to see much. The bomb hadn't fallen on the house, but in the next field. The concussion had shattered the windows, but, as far as Bowden could tell, the structure was intact.

"Take more than a Jerry bomb to flatten this place," he said, slapping the lintel. "Solid as a rock, that; the Kaiser ain't been born what could shake them

217

foundations."

"Thank heavens," Scott breathed. "Well, there's nothing more we can do tonight. Do you think you could pop over in the morning and give it the once over?"

"Well, I'm tied up in Elmsford at present, but I'll see what I can do. An hour or two shouldn't hurt."

"I'd appreciate it, Arthur."

"Consider it done. By the way, thanks for that bit of wood the other day."

"Think nothing of it. Can I offer you a lift home?"

"Won't sleep no more tonight, not with all this kafuffle. Wouldn't say no to a lift back to my bike, though."

"Of course, of course."

* * * * *

Richard had little time to acquaint himself with the trenches of the Somme, after just twenty four hours the Battalion moved to rest huts in Acheux Wood, from where, after a seemingly ridiculous exercise of route-marching two platoons, Langham's weighed down with full, sixty pound pack loads and Peverill's not, with the object of gauging which fared better, it entrained for Poperinghe and the Ypres sector. The two-day crawl ended outside the terminus. The smell of burning drifted back.

"Looks like Percy's been up to his old tricks. It's a complete mess up there," Langham reported from the window.

"Excuse my ignorance, old boy, but who or what is Percy?" Peverill asked.

"It's a bloody great cannon, biggest ever made. Took it off a battleship. Ruddy inaccurate, but when it does hit the mark it leaves a hole the size of lake Windermere. It's famous up here."

"Remind me to bring my yachting cap next time."

"Looks like we're getting out."

Richard was the last to jump down. Levers protruded like broken teeth from the blackened jaws of a signal box. Farther along, the rails twisted crazily over a gigantic crater, belly full of a mangled shunter. Richard pursed his lips. Another few minutes and it could have been their own engine coughing its last on a bed of shattered rolling stock.

The men formed up by the trackside, company by company. The officers' horses were de-trained. Stafford's mare dropped dung in Richard's path.

"By the right..."

They marched from the outskirts into town and beyond. Camps, dumps and field hospitals filled every field, leaky tents and huts aligned guy rope to guy rope, pane-less window to pane-less window, wretched hardship to a noviciate from home, but, judging from the comments in the ranks, untold luxury to those from the trenches.

"Looks like it's Little London for us," someone said cheerily on their way into Ouderdom. "Bloody lovely. All mod cons, canteen, the works."

218

They missed out on the huts, bivouacking in an open field, training by day and carting all the accoutrements of trench warfare to the firing line by night. Richard thought he'd drawn the lucky straw, riding the footplate of the narrow-gauge armoured train that took his platoon back and forth to the dumps, until a German battery homed in on the furnace one night. A shell tore over the tender, as the driver raced for shelter in the next cutting, hitting the bank just feet away. But his luck held; it didn't explode.

During the day, despite his tiredness, he took every duty going, anything to distance him from Stafford and the unaffordable demands of the officers' mess. Then, one morning, Langham asked if he fancied going into Poperinghe. "I'm sure sergeant Houseman can manage things for an hour or two."

The invitation took Richard by surprise; Peverill was Langham's usual companion.

"Actually, I've never been into town," he confessed.

"Really? I'd've thought it's the first place you'd have gone, buying lace for mater and what-have-you. Famous for its lace; best there is."

"Are you sure it's all right?"

"Colonel's orders. He wants his new thunder box collected from the station. I'll get Bland to rustle up an extra horse."

Richard had straddled a horse only twice in his life, both times Crutchley's old nag, but he wasn't going to admit it.

An hour later the convoy assembled, two men on a G.S. wagon and two mounts. Aping Langham's every move, Richard managed to swing himself into the saddle. It was like sitting on polished steel.

"No spurs, old boy?"

"Left them behind."

Langham clicked his tongue; his horse walked on; to Richard's great relief, his own mount followed.

He'd always imagined a horse's gait to be a gentle sway, but this was like being perched on a drunken dromedary. He anchored himself in his stirrups, praying the animal wouldn't buck, bolt or otherwise make a fool of him, worst of all stop in its tracks. Yet, with each furlong negotiated, his anxiety ebbed. If this was a test, he was passing it.

It wasn't far into Poperinghe and 'Pop' wasn't much of a town, just a few narrow streets leading to the ubiquitous continental town square. Richard took in all that his horsemanship would allow, the old lace-makers in their upstairs windows, the Flemish architecture, the Pidgin English by the shop doors, 'Frish Fish', 'Washing Soup, Shaving Soup.'

A large black notice board hung over the Town Hall.

"The APM's taken it over," Langham told him. "The sign changes with the wind, 'safe' when it's westerly, 'dangerous' if there's a possibility of gas. By the way, if you're looking for anything from home, Ypriana is the place, books, gramophone records, stationary, you name it; a couple of sisters behind the counter; lost their parents to a Hun shell; quite pretty, really, though nothing tops Ginger; you'll find her over there in La Poupée, known to all and sundry as 'Ginger's'. Fifteen, if she's that and completely adorable, serves you dinner with one hand and steals your heart away with the other."

To the right of the town hall an ominous road sign pointed east; 'YPRES.'

"Macadam all the way; best road in the country, give or take the odd bomb crater. Pretty ironic, when you think about it. Look, the station's down there. It doesn't take two of us to complete the paperwork and, to tell the truth, I've rather made arrangements. Do you think you could manage on your own? There's nothing to it."

"Do I need any authorisation?"

"No, just tell them what you've come for and sign the appropriate chitty. I'll be up there, when you're done, at a place called Talbot House. You can't miss it, it's about halfway up, on the right. Pick me up there in, say, forty minutes? Tell you what, make it an hour and I'll introduce you to Ginger, when we're next in town."

Langham slid from the saddle and handed Richard the reins.

"Would you mind, old boy? Nowhere to hitch him. See you in an hour."

"Couldn't you...?"

But Langham had disappeared into the teeming khaki crowd.

"Move along, there," someone called from behind.

Richard's skin prickled; sweat broke out on his brow. He clicked his tongue, Langham fashion. His horse didn't budge.

His larynx filled his throat. He nudged the beast's flanks, then kicked harder.

"Try telling it to walk on, old chap, that usually does the trick;" a passing R.H.A. subaltern turned Richard's cheeks blood red.

Through gritted teeth he muttered the magic words.

"Abracadabra," the subaltern smiled, patting the rump of Langham's stallion in passing. "Nice horse. Looks like he's ready for his oats."

Too intent on staying in the saddle, Richard took no heed, until, halfway across the square, the animal began nosing his mare's withers. With a whinny of irritation, she broke into a trot. He pulled on the reins; she pulled harder, bouncing him high in the saddle. It was all going horribly wrong.

In desperation he tried to prise the pair apart, pushing harder and harder against Langham's stallion, until it veered away, leaving him suspended between the two like Tower Bridge.

'Oh, hell! Bloody hell!'

"Are you alright, Sir?" A voice called from the wagon.

"Take him, would you!"

A bobbing cap caught up; hands reached out and hauled the horses in.

Richard pushed himself upright, his face livid.

"Damned animal."

"Looked like she was about to bolt, Sir. Did well, Sir, if you don't mind me saying."

Richard scowled. He knew the man was being facetious, but he saw no smirk, no knowing wink to the driver behind. He looked around for crowers. None had gathered.

"Don't I know you, Private?"

"Short, Sir. Took you to the C.O. on your first day, Sir; well, to Captain Stafford, that is, who was C.O. at the time."

"Ah, yes; the talkative one," Richard remembered. "Well, Private Short, you'd better tie him to the wagon, out of harm's way."

"Begging your pardon, Sir, but that one you're on, she'll get all sorts coming at her once she rounds that bend. I've seen the best of 'em come a cropper there, 'specially when they've got the jitters. Might be best to tie her to the wagon, too, Sir, calm 'em both down. I'll sort the big fella out if he gets frisky."

Richard needed no persuading. Swallowing his pride, he slipped from the stirrups.

"Is it far?"

"Just down there aways; the second turning, Sir. You don't want to take the first; that's where they take the condemned. Deserters mostly; lock 'em up in the cells overnight then Bob's your uncle in the morning. Got a post in the yard."

"What, shoot them? Are you sure?"

"On me mother's grave, Sir. Put an end to one just the other day. Though, from what they say, he'd been a wrong 'un from the start. Murdered his sergeant."

"In that case, the second turning it is," Richard said, touching terra firma without mishap.

* * * * *

"Laura; what are you doing here?" Hettie Jameson's smile was framed in anxiety. She pulled the door to behind her. "Has something happened to Sarah?"

"Oh no, Sarah's fine."

"Then, shouldn't you be in school?"

"I sneaked out."

"So I see."

"I was hoping to talk to you."

"Ah, well, the thing is, I'm about to go out myself."

Having risked expulsion, Laura wasn't about to take the hint. Whatever Hettie was up to, she wanted to be part of it, even if Sarah didn't.

"It will only take a minute."

"Well... you'd better come in."

Laura could have sworn she heard a door close softly upstairs, as Hettie led her into the parlour.

"Now, what can I do for you?"

"Well, when we put that banner up in Tindal Square, I know nothing much came of it, but at least I felt I was doing something."

"I'd hardly call making the front page of every newspaper in the county nothing," Hettie retorted huffily. "However, do go on."

"I'm sorry, I didn't mean... Well, the thing is, I want to do more."

"And what exactly do you propose?"

Laura hadn't expected to be patronised.

"I don't know, but there must be something I can help with."

"Meaning what, exactly?"

"I don't know; that's why I'm here."

"Well, it's very kind of you, my dear, but there's really nothing at the moment. Now, without wishing to be rude, I have a hundred and one things to do; Sylvia Pankhurst's coming to town."

"There you are; I could help with that."

"Well, I suppose you could. The lodge is meeting in the George Street Methodist hall this afternoon; come along about five and I'll see what I can do."

Hettie may as well have said midnight.

"I'm afraid I have to be home by then; there's only one bus."

"Then, quite honestly, my dear, I can't see of what help you can be. And now I really must go."

Laura knew she'd been fobbed off. Whatever Hettie's secret was, it wasn't Sylvia Pankhurst, and she wasn't about to share it. Even so, she'd had no call to be so condescending. Laura sneaked back into school feeling considerably slighted.

* * * * *

The railhead had undergone a miraculous transformation since the battalion's arrival. The debris had been stacked to one side, the crater filled, the track re-laid. The buildings remained in ruins, but access had been restored. Richard went in search of the R.T.O. Within ten minutes, the colonel's dirt closet had been loaded onto the wagon.

"Wouldn't mind one of them myself," Private Short said, eyeing the commode. "No shovelling the shit with them; sort themselves out, they do. Bloody nifty."

"Oh yeh?" The driver raised an eyebrow.

"As good as. Once a week's no bother. Better than squatting over a bloody bucket getting your shirt tails all mucky."

"Amen to that."

"Thank you, Private Short, I'm sure we get the picture," Richard ended the imagery.

"Beg pardon, Sir; I wasn't meaning to be indelicate. It's just that, well..."

"Yes; thank you Private."

With the best part of an hour to waste, Short's mouth was clearly going to prove problematic. Tea at Ginger's or lace for his mother? With his few remaining sous, Richard couldn't afford both. He plumped for the latter.

"Do you know Talbot House, driver?"

"Toc H, Sir? Everyone knows Toc H, Sir."

"Toc H?"

"It's signals, Sir. That's what it means."

"Of course. Then I'll leave the horses with you. Meet myself and Lieutenant Langham there in forty minutes, would you? And for God's sake take care of that thunder box or the colonel will have all our guts for garters."

Toc H wasn't hard to find, a typical Flanders town house, three storeys high, the biggest in the street. A sign hung above the iron-grilled entrance; TALBOT HOUSE, 1915 - ? EVERY-MAN'S CLUB. Music and laughter gusted through the open door.

"What is it, some kind of Y.M.C.A.?" Richard asked a fellow subaltern on his way out.

"Something like that. Tubby's your man," the man nodded towards a bespectacled parson coming down the hall. "Sorry; must dash."

The padre barely reached Richard's shoulder.

"Come in, come in."

Bizarre notes were plastered everywhere; 'To pessimists, Way Out;' 'If you are in the habit of spitting on the carpet at home, please spit here;' 'The waste paper baskets are purely ornamental.' Most were by order of 'P.B.C.'

"Who's P.B.C?" Richard asked bemusedly.

"That's me. Clayton's my name, I'm the Chaplain here."

"Bowden; Second Lieutenant Bowden. I'm looking for Lieutenant Langham; he said to meet him here."

"Ah, yes, I believe he's in the garden. I'll take you through."

Rooms full of men opened, left and right, from the corridor, tea urns in one, a kitchen in another, the men laughing and joking, some quietly reading. Richard could have sworn he saw officers amongst the rank and file, but decided he had to be seeing things; fraternisation between the ranks simply wasn't allowed.

Caricatures, sketches, photographs and verses littered the walls.

"The men donate them, quite amusing, too, some of them. By the way, if you want to get in touch with anyone just post a note on the notice board over there giving all pertinent details, name, rank, regiment, and so on. It's astonishing how well it works; people who know the person or know of him pass the message on or leave a note as to his whereabouts."

The strains of a piano and a resounding chorus of 'If you were the only girl in the world' rattled the conservatory doors. Straight ahead more French windows led into a long, walled garden filled with tables and chairs, benches and hummocks. This time there could be no mistake; officers and men were mingling freely. Langham was close by, deep in conversation with a corporal.

"They're brothers," Clayton explained. "It happens quite often. Perhaps we could spare them a few minutes more. Let me show you round."

He led Richard back through the hall and up a steep staircase. On the first floor, another notice lay in ambush; 'No Amy Robsart stunts down these stairs. By request...'

"That's my room," Clayton pointed to a door across the landing. Above it a semi-circular sign set out his philosophy; 'All Rank Abandon Ye Who Enter Here'. "What do you think? I like to ask. A fellow from the trenches gave me the idea. He told me that in the heat of battle a man is judged not by his rank but by his character, much as God judges us. The Danté thing sprang immediately to mind."

"Doesn't the army object?"

"Not especially. At first it only applied to the Chaplain's room, but now we've

223

included the whole house; we've even had the odd general or two queuing for tea. Actually, what pleases me most about that quotation is the emphasis it places on the supplanted word, 'hope'; that's something we must never abandon. Over here is our library, such as it is," Clayton indicated a small room on the right, stacked with books and a pile of caps. "The men leave them as security. It works a treat. Rather than lose books, we seem to gain them by the day. Shall we continue up?"

Sleeping accommodation monopolised the second floor.

"This is the only part of the house confined to officers. We can sleep eleven in all, mostly on cots, but comfortable enough for those waiting for the leave train or vice versa. The only real bed is downstairs in the General's room, so called for no other reason than a general slept in it one night. It even has a proper bedsheet, though only one; the other is permanently in the wash. It's open to everyone, all donations gratefully received. There's a nominal charge of five francs for the cots, on the old Robin Hood principal, although you do get a bit of supper or breakfast thrown in, a cup of cocoa and Bath Oliver biscuits or a plate of cold meat, depending on whether you're coming or going. In the early days we used to hold services on this landing. Eventually it became too much of a crush and we moved to the loft. Mind how you go; the stairs are very steep."

At the top of 'Jacob's ladder' Richard found himself in the 'Upper Room', a hop-loft converted into a whitewashed chapel, where, according to yet another notice, all Christians, regardless of denomination, were invited to 'join us at the Lord's table.'

"Actually it's a carpenter's bench we found in the garden. Pretty appropriate, really; more so than the candle sticks; they came from a four poster bed."

"That's got to be the smallest font I've ever seen."

"Yes, well the smallest in active service, anyway; six inches square. It's modelled on the one in Winchester Cathedral. You'll find the detail quite astonishing. Believe it or not I was baptised in it myself, back in Queensland."

"Australia?"

"That's right."

"I would never have guessed."

"I was educated in England, at Saint Paul's."

"Hence the vocation."

"Hence the vocation. You'd be surprised how many we can cram in up here, well over a hundred, nearer two sometimes. Not bad for a floor that's been condemned. We form a circle and take it in turns to kneel, so as not to tempt providence. So far no one's fallen through. Would you care to pray?"

Richard had mumbled the Lord's Prayer in Church and in school assembly, but the only time he had truly prayed was for Laura. Perhaps he'd been too selfish; perhaps God hadn't heard, or perhaps He hadn't listened.

"Perhaps another time."

This man's faith deserved more than lip service.

"The door is always open."

CHAPTER THIRTY SEVEN

"Not a bad job, if I do say so myself." George Bowden swung the stable door on the new hinge he'd hammered from a bit of scrap metal.

The old man comprehended only his pride. "Kommen sie."

The Englishman stopped respectfully at the kitchen door, alert to the smooth pouring of beer over glazed clay. He licked his lips. A gnarled hand held out his reward.

"Prost."

George downed it in one, keeping an eye out for the corporal. Fraternisation was strictly forbidden.

"Dankershun," he gasped. It had been a long time since he'd tasted beer, and never a beer like this, not bitter, not sweet, almost metallic, like liquid steel.

While his fellow prisoners had been gleaning the fields, George had been detailed some much needed repair work on the farm. Despite his avowal of non-co-operation, he'd found himself attacking his task with as much energy as the pitiful prison rations would allow. The old man had appreciated his efforts. They'd struck up a nodding mutual respect.

George leaned too heavily on his gammy leg. The wound had gone septic a month earlier. The Camp doctor had lanced it, but it still troubled him.

The old man beckoned him over to a tree stump-cum-chopping block, scored with the blade marks of generations. He motioned George to sit. After a second bout of semaphore, George reluctantly dropped his trousers. The scar was livid, the flesh puffy, a build-up of poison obvious. The old man pressed. George stiffened.

With a shake of his head, the old man signalled for George to stay where he was and went into the house. He returned with his wife, a cut-throat razor, a bowl of evil smelling poultice, and some brown paper. George braced himself.

"Jesus Christ!" He clung on, as wizened thumbs dug under the inflammation. The woman wiped away the corruption; the old man dug again. George thought he was going to faint, and then he felt the cool, soothing poultice being applied.

"Was machst du gerade?!" The corporal's anger pierced the air.

George jumped to his feet. A rifle butt was jabbed into the pit of his stomach, then hammered into the small of his back. He fell to the ground, gasping like a landed perch.

By the time his faculties returned, his attacker was sitting where he had sat, guzzling beer, with enough bread and cheese on his lap to feed an entire section. Across the way the old couple cowered by the barn doors, their eyes overflowing with fear and the hunger that would be theirs for weeks to come.

"You bastard," George swore under his breath.

"Raus!" The guard snarled back, stuffing the uneaten food into his pockets.

George struggled to his feet.

"Schnell, Schnell!"

He was marched off at bayonet point. Behind the guard's back, the old man's hand raised no higher than a gambler's.

* * * * *

Friends and relations packed Ashleigh's ancient Parish Church for the wedding of Agatha, Maud Cooper, spinster, and Harold, Edward Scott, widower. The Baptist Coopers had bowed to pomp and circumstance and the Anglican Church to the bribe.

The house at Little Eastleigh had escaped serious damage. The plaster had been repaired and the broken windowpanes replaced; Scott's prayers had been answered; he'd had none left for the crew of the Zeppelin, said to have been shot down in flames over Hertfordshire.

Laura now knew Agatha's immediate family better than her own. She'd added a few lines to her father's letters once in a while, but she hadn't seen her grandparents since the outbreak of war. Her aunts, uncles and cousins were a more distant memory still; some she had never seen.

Scott had two sisters, one a social climber, the other a shrinking violet. The patrician had moved to Birmingham with her foundry-inheriting husband, the plebeian to Hackney Marshes with a market trader. The industrialist was still an industrialist, the market trader a patch of organic compost oozing from the earth somewhere near Thiepval. The letter of condolence was the first either sister had received from the other in years, while their mutual hatred of Marian had made Scott's neutrality all the easier.

However, on such an auspicious occasion and, in the socialite's case, in the light of her brother's improved circumstances, both attended, along with the surviving husband and samples of both's begetting, the surplus having stayed at home, the Birmingham brood to enjoy their recreation, the Hackney household to supplement the widow's pension. The London contingent was returning by train after the reception; the Birmingham Broadbents were spending the night at Elmsford's 'County Hotel', before being chauffeur driven home. They would be taking Laura with them.

There'd been a terrible scene. Laura had planned to stay with Sarah and delve into Hettie's secret during the happy couple's Norfolk coast honeymoon, but her father had been adamant; she was not going to associate with 'that Jameson woman' under any circumstances, however much she created, whatever oaths she took, and neither was she going to spoil Agatha's big day by sulking about it, he would never forgive her. Morosely, Laura had given in.

Scott's guests included members of Elmsford's commercial and civic hierarchy, along with ranking military men. The Bowdens felt uniquely out of place among the top hats, crinolines and full dress uniforms.

"Blimey, there's enough toffs here, ain't there?" Arthur whispered, standing at the back. "Wouldn't mind betting there's a title or two amongst this lot."

"I'm glad we're not going to the reception, Arthur," Beatrice told him, "what with all their forks for this and forks for that; wouldn't want to show myself up."

226

"Not you, mother; hold yer own against the Queen herself, you could."

Agatha followed family tradition by wearing her mother's wedding dress and her mother's before that. Minor alteration resulted in a faultless fit on the day. A bouquet of red carnations, matching Scott's buttonhole, set off the cream silk to perfection. Laura and Sarah and Agatha's two younger cousins competed in bridesmaid pink. Laura and Sarah won hands down.

"Dearly beloved....;" the betrothed took their vows, Agatha's hardly audible, Scott's stronger but tremulous. A lump rose in Laura's throat. It could, so easily, have been her and Richard kneeling before the altar. The tide swelled. She forced closed the lock gates. The 'Forbearance' resettled in emotion's dry dock.

The ring, the blessing, the lifted veil, the self-conscious kiss, the register; to the palsied wail of the wedding march, thanks to the bellows-boy – 'him what puts the wind up the Vicar's sister every Sunday' - bottoming out to bridesmaid ogling, the newlyweds traversed the aisle, the groom beaming proudly, the bride smiling humbly. Sarah dabbed her lashes, Laura blinked back sentiment's residue.

The photographer was waiting by the porch, the Bowdens by the lynch gate. Laura stole away.

"We'll be getting along now, dear," Beatrice told her.

"Oh, do you have to?" Suddenly, with her move to Little Eastleigh, Laura became aware of this farewell's finality, to the Bowdens, to her childhood, to her connection with the little house on the hill, to Richard.

"We promised Elizabeth we wouldn't be long. Well, don't suppose we'll be seeing much of you now, what with your move to Eastleigh. I shall miss you, my dear, I shall miss you very much."

The affection in the old lady's voice was touching, the honesty in her eyes heart rending. They were Richard's eyes.

"I shall miss you, too. Have you heard from Richard?" Laura couldn't help herself asking.

"He's alright, my dear, safe and well by all accounts."

A tear sprang to Mrs. Bowden's eye.

"Come on, mother," Mr. Bowden reminded her.

Clasped hands prolonged the bond for a few precious seconds more, then the Bowdens were gone, the tapestry of Laura's youth completed. She'd been distraught, she'd suffered abject misery, but she had never felt so sad.

A call went up for the bridesmaids. Laura hurried back, desperate to dilute the emotion distilling within her.

CHAPTER THIRTY EIGHT

The house was monolithically ugly, as were the Broadbents, especially Uncle Percy, a second generation ironmonger whose father had taken over a foundry and turned it into a gold mine too late for his progeny to enjoy a formal education. Laura found his broad, nasal Brummie nauseating. The bullion had grown to bank vault proportions on war profits and Uncle Percy was ashamed of neither its girth nor his gluttony.

"Muck and money, bloodshed and brass. Pass the gravy, Hilda. Our John's out there doing his bit, we're here doing ours, and long may it last."

'Our John' had gone to public school; 'Our John' was on Divisional Staff.

Hilda had come to the wedding. Frail, pale, Laura's age, she'd been car sick all the way home.

"Oh, Hilda, you're such a sissy," her brother had whined from the front seat every time she'd whimpered back into the Bentley. "I'm sorry, Laura, you can't take her anywhere. Well, apologise then, yet again."

"All right, Cyril," his mother had chided him dotingly. "Really, Hilda dear; we know you can't help it, but Harper can't keep stopping every few miles, we'll never get there."

"We should put her in the Flower Show under 'weed'; she'd win first prize," Schoolboy Cyril had scored a family of guffaws.

"Never you mind, Hilda," Broadbent had commiserated, considerably shrouding her in cigar smoke. "You're a late bloomer, that's all... blooming late!"

His wife had dutifully tittered, confirming Hilda as the butt of more than obnoxious Cyril's satire.

The gravy boat rattled as Hilda lifted it.

"Take it, Queenie, or she'll have it all over the cauliflower. Thank you, my peach."

At sixteen, Queenie was benefiting most from her mother's genes. Puppy plump with a rosy complexion, she was called 'my peach' and 'my dumpling' alternately by her adoring father.

Hilda stared resignedly at her plate.

"Eat up, girl. You won't get fat by looking at it."

All hope of beauty had long since been abandoned.

Drummond, second in line to the anticipated title, seemed more supportive, until he broke both his silence and voice with, "If you don't eat you'll get dog's breath."

"Cyril came up with a good one on the way home..." The Flower Show bloomed again. "A thorn among the bloody roses," Broadbent added the offshoot he'd been cultivating all afternoon.

"Perhaps we should call you 'Weed' from now on," Cyril sealed Hilda's fate.

Laura hated them all; Broadbent for his crudity, Cyril for his obnoxiousness, Dumpling for her dexterity in winding her father round her fat little finger,

Drummond because he was no bulldog, even if he slobbered like one, her aunt for her sycophancy and Hilda for her timidity.

"Why do you put up with it?" She asked Hilda in a private moment, to be answered with a hopeless bleat. The next ten days were going to be a nightmare.

Drummond was soon besotted, as was twelve-year-old Cyril, two years his junior, so besotted they came to blows over who was going to beat Laura at 'Battleships and Cruisers'. She reaped a certain satisfaction from their reciprocal pummelling, which ended in a bloody nose. Beanpole Drummond leaked off; the Butler summoned the maid to sponge up the blotches; fat boy Cyril scuttled himself in a sulk in the wake of Laura's broadside.

Rainy days followed, days of compendium games, tantrums, boredom and bull.

"What's that you're reading?" Laura asked, surprising Hilda in her father's study one afternoon.

Hilda fumbled the volume back into bookshelf obscurity.

"Oh, it's... er... nothing. A textbook, that's all; er... eighteenth century history."

"Really? May I look? I'll be studying exactly that for my exams."

"Oh, it's very boring. I don't know which one it was, now. Anyway, it's one of fathers."

Laura browsed. 'Harris's List' didn't sound overly inspiring.

"I don't think you should, Laura," Hilda fidgeted nervously. "Father's very particular about his books."

A plain dust cover presented itself. The pages were well thumbed.

"No! It wasn't that one! It was another; perhaps the one next to it." Hilda's fluster turned into a flap as Laura scanned the first few lines of Fanny Hill. "There's a much better selection in the library."

"Weed! What are you doing? You know you shouldn't be in here," Dumpling thigh-clapped through the door. Even through her heavy skirt, the friction was clearly audible. "Not father's books; he'll kill you. Oh, that one."

"I was...er...just telling Laura, it's very boring... history..."

"Never to be repeated in your case," Queenie smirked, her mouth paring into a pout at Laura's stoniness. "Anyway, we shouldn't be in here. If one of the tykes finds us, there'll be hell to pay."

"It's my fault," Laura shouldered the blame, slipping the book, unseen, into her skirt pocket. "I was being nosy."

"Yes, well Weed should've told you. Father doesn't allow anyone in here."

The Butler coughed politely in the doorway.

"What is it, Postlesthwaite?"

Laura had given up at her first attempted pronunciation and called him William.

"But that will never do, Miss," he'd protested.

"Nevertheless, I can't possibly call you Post..les..thw...thw...You see?"

He'd quite understood; he'd lost more employment for that very reason than he would care to say. However, heredity was sacrosanct. Postlesthwaite was his cross and the Broadbents his current Pharisees.

"Your mother would like to see you, Miss. She's in the drawing room."

"We weren't here, Postlesthwaite," Queenie reminded him.

"No, Miss."

They moved mother-wards.

"The rain has lifted. I thought we might go into Stratford, I'm sure Laura would like to see it," Mrs. Broadbent announced.

"Weed isn't coming, is she? She'll puke over everyone," Cyril complained.

"No she won't, dear, it's not far, and please don't use that word, it's vulgar."

"If it's all right with you, mother, I'd prefer to stay here. I'm feeling a little unwell," Hilda submitted, as she always did, to intimidation.

"As you wish, dear."

Stratford was as near to picturesque as the Midlands had to offer under its grey industrial skies. Drummond displayed his maturity by exacting belated revenge for his bloodied nose when no-one was looking, Cyril his lack of it with a vociferous public outcry and a retaliatory elbow on the threshold of Anna Hathaway's cottage, Dumpling her demureness by sprawling over that same hallowed step into the arms of the only eligible male for miles, and Laura's obvious admirer, and Mrs. Broadbent her sense of the Shakespearean by deprecating the tea-shop's famed French Fancies as 'much ado about nothing'. The patissier turned away, love's labours lost along with any chance of a tip. What the great man would have made of them, Laura couldn't hazard a guess.

It started to rain. The schoolroom would have to forego the honour of a Broadbent inspection. Besides, there wasn't much to see, Laura was assured, except Drummond's initials penknifed into a beam.

The chauffeur umbrellaed them into the car, Postlesthwaite out of it.

The knock fell as featherlight as the whisper.

"It's Hilda."

"Come in."

Hilda tiptoed to the dressing table where Laura was brushing out her hair.

"Laura, I... well... When we were in father's study, you... you didn't take that book, did you?"

"Book? What book?"

"You know...."

"Oh, that book," Laura finally remembered. "Actually I slipped it into my pocket when Dumpling wasn't looking. Why? Will he mind?"

"If father finds it missing, he'll go berserk."

"Oh, I see. Well, my dress is over there." Laura pointed to her discarded clothes. "Do you mind?"

"Not at all."

Hilda rummaged, clasping her find like the Holy Grail.

"What's so special about it?" Laura asked through her reflection.

"Nothing, nothing at all," Hilda blushed. "It's just father's, you know. Did... er... did you read any of it?"

"Haven't had a chance. Why, did Dumpling say something?"

Hilda gurgled at the use of 'Dumpling'. No-one dared call Queenie that except her father.

"No, no, but I'd better return it, then he'll be none the wiser. I'm sorry to have bothered you."

"That's alright. Goodnight."

"Goodnight."

'Strange family,' Laura thought.

* * * * *

The sandbagged hammerhead struck. The iron stanchion rang like a barely muffled Bow Bell. Someone had sent up angle irons instead of proper pickets; 'no screws; these will have to do.' The wiring party froze; Richard knelt instinctively, fraught with the fear of the trespasser in the divestment of no-man's land. No flare soared, no machine gun fired.

The hammerer swung again.

'Clung.'

Again Richard signalled suspension. He could sense his sergeant's impatience, but, on his first command, he was taking no chances. Silence reigned. "All right."

The hammer fell, and fell again, joined by the thud of mallet on stake, the rattle of wire.

"I'd best check on the covering party, Sir," his Sergeant whispered.

"It's all right, Sergeant, I'll do it. Keep the men at it."

Had he sounded like the schoolboy he felt? His self-effacement was short lived, squeezed from him by no-man's land's fearful grip. He crept forward, searching the darkness like a lost soul, adding extra strides for each skirted shell hole, crossing luck's palm with silver sweat. 'A straight line ahead,' the Sergeant had said. 'Seventy paces.' So where the hell were they?

The challenge came from his right, barely a whisper. He breathed the password and stole across. Three men lay prone in a shell hole, left, right and centre, boot against boot to nudge the alarm, cap-comforters covering all but their eyes. Richard crouched beside them. Sixty yards away, just a few seconds' sprint, even in army boots, the enemy wire lay cloaked in precipitous night, and, beyond that, the unknown, the demonic void.

Rain pitter-pattered onto his helmet and rubber cape. No one had told him helmets and capes were a no-no for this sort of thing. Still he could hear the iron's 'clink-clank', the stakes' wooden 'thud'.

The rain fell harder, gurgling in rivulets, plopping into streams in submerging alliance, or could it be treachery?

A sparking trail rent the night. The covering party clung to its crater, those encaged in the wire cowered in petrified, rain-patented display, as Richard did. One movement, one slip, and all would be lost. Ten feet away a skull grinned grotesquely; skeletal fingers stretched out from a sleeve where beady eyes sheltered.

The flare fell to earth in burnishing obituary. A final fizzle and glare-blinded blackness negated the nightmare.

'Damn your eyes,' Richard cursed himself; he should have looked away. For frustrating seconds red skull and green eye sockets were imprinted on his pupils, until finally they fused into grey and faded into the rainfall. Another lesson he hadn't been taught at training school.

He slid into the crater; the men shifted round, their thoughts easy to read; they needed no pipsqueak subaltern to poke his head up and land them in the shit.

The rain squalled away.

'Clink-clank, clink-clank.'

Richard shielded his watch; three thirty glowed green. Time was short; the carrying party had been late coming up.

A rifle cracked, but far away; from farther still, came the dull crump of guns.

'Clink-clank, clink-clank.'

'Fritz must be deaf.'

'Pitter patter'; the rain came again, then, through the sheen, 'clunk-clunk,' like an echo, 'clunk-clunk, clunk-clunk.'

So the Germans were at it, too; Langham had warned him they might, and they'd send out a covering party.

He'd felt that same anxiety an hour before, defecating in his dugout over an empty bully beef tin, eyes fixed to the entrance.

"Be on the alert," he needlessly warned, a boy telling men, and conscious of the fact.

A heel tapped his.

"Three of them, Sir, tucked into a shell hole, same as us."

He'd seen nothing. Now what did he do?

"No heroics, old chap, you're out there to wire. Live and let live and they'll do the same," Langham had told him. But would they follow the rules?

He pressed deeper into the earth, leaving only an inch between helmet's brim and crater's lip. He could feel the men's tension, hear it in their breathing. Was he a cub preparing to spring, or a buck about to bolt? Either way, they'd be for it; curse their bloody luck.

The faintest pinprick of light glimmered across the divide.

"Cheeky sod's got a fag on," someone whispered.

"They can't know we're here."

"Oh, they know alright, Sir. There'll be no fireworks tonight."

"Could do with a cigarette myself," Richard breathed lightly.

It seemed almost impossible that beside the hand that cupped the glow, another held a Mauser and could be aiming it at him at that very moment. They were thirty yards apart, no more, within easy bombing range.

'Clink-clank;' 'clunk-clunk.'

He should be getting back, the wiring party must be almost done; or would these three here think he'd got the wind up? 'Wish he'd crawl back to where he came from and leave us in bloody peace,' more like.

Along the line a flare shimmered, a solitary reminder of an awestruck young girl and a Guy Fawkes night of long ago. She'd be sleeping now, in rain lulled reassurance, if it was raining there too. He pictured her face on the pillow and floated back on her breathing's lullaby to an Ashleigh dawn and eternal belonging. God had given him the world and he'd thrown it away for the wilderness.

'She was the one,' his masochism reminded him, 'with Stafford, yes, Stafford, your Company Commander.'

His insides screwed into barbs as she gave herself on the rain's silver screen.

"Woodbines."

The password startled him from his torment.

"For Christ's sake," he scowled.

The messenger lowered his voice. "Sorry, Sir. We was afraid you'd got lost. Sergeant says they're all in; time to go."

"One at a time at ten second intervals," Richard hissed. "I'll be the last."

As each scuttled away, he kept rigid watch, his stomach compacting and then imploding with the realisation that he was all alone. His heartbeat drummed in his ears. Which way had they gone? Which way had he come? Oh sweet Jesus, why hadn't he checked, just a glance to be sure?

'For God's sake, get a grip. "Pole star to your left going out, to your right coming in," that's what Langham had said.' But there was no bloody Pole star. Was he laying left? Yes, he'd crawled in from the left, so back must be that way, it had to be.

No clinking, no clunking; Fritz had taken his cue. Now the truce was a race and God help the loser. He stared into the blackness, the wide-eyed fawn who'd lingered too long, and, on all sides, the predator waiting to strike.

His courage failed him.

'Just do it!'

He sprang up and fled, sweating terror with every stumble, fighting fear's paralysis, a child in reins, a runner on water, sobbing holy beseechment on every breath.

'The wire! Thank God!' He'd got it right.

His sergeant was there;

"This way, Sir."

He slalomed through the gap and leapt over the sandbags. A Very light soared. He basked in his salvation.

* * * * *

Hilda wasn't at breakfast.

"She's got a migraine," her mother said.

The boys sniggered.

"Be quiet or go to your rooms." The maternal nerves were frayed.

"I'll look in on her after breakfast," Laura volunteered.

"No," her aunt cried, adding with more restraint, "she's not to be disturbed."

Postlesthwaite's poker face had lengthened overnight; the maids were jittery.

233

Only Dumpling seemed her normal self, until she gave up after only the kippers. Broadbent had left early for the office. Something had happened and it had to do with Hilda, or the piglets wouldn't be snorting.

They ate on in silence, the tension building over each slice of toast: swordplay over the butter - "My knife was there first!" "No it wasn't!" - arm wrestling over the marmalade.

"Behave yourselves, for pity's sake, Drummond," Mrs. Broadbent snapped.

"Why is it always me?"

"Go to your room!"

The accused flung his napkin onto his plate. His chair screeched across the parquet.

"It's not fair!"

His mother's cheeks drew tighter, her eyes more restless; she followed.

"Stupid Weed," Cyril muttered.

"Be quiet, Cyril," Dumpling ordered.

"Well, she is."

"Cyril, you're not to say another word."

"Why, has something happened?"

"I'm sorry, Laura," Queenie apologised. "It's a family matter."

"Weed got caught in father's study," Cyril crowed.

"Cyril!"

Laura tiptoed along the landing, listening intently at each of the doors mirrored so evenly that they only furthered the monotony of the mustard walls and waist high wood panelling. By the staircase, a stained glass window cast its woefulness over a dingy display of dried flowers that reminded her of her mother.

"Hilda," she whispered by each of the doors, until footsteps on the stairs sent her scampering back to her room. A gentle rap was followed by a harder one.

"Miss Hilda?"

Laura peeked out. A maid was in the corridor with an armful of linen.

"Not today, Sally." Mrs. Broadbent hurried up. "Perhaps you could do Miss Laura's room."

Laura darted to the window; the same knock fell.

"Excuse me, Miss, is it convenient?"

"Please do," Laura told her, wondering why the servants' accents were so much more agreeable than her uncle's.

She looked out at the Broadbent's vast expanse. They were surrounded by more parkland than even the Staffords, but the acres were as bleak as the house itself, and over all hung the price of prosperity. Even ten miles from the belching chimney stacks the leaves were lustreless, the sills grimy.

"Have you been here long, Sally?"

"Oh, I don't know, 'bout eighteen months it must be, Miss," Sally replied, spreading a clean sheet.

"And do you like it here?"

"There's a lot to do, Miss. Mistress keeps us busy, and the Master can be generous when it comes to Christmas."

"And what about young Master Cyril?"

"Well, boys will be boys, Miss." Sally tucked in the folds.

"And Miss Hilda?"

"You'd best speak to Madam about Miss Hilda, Miss; I don't know nothing."

"About what happened, you mean?"

"As I says, Miss, you must speak to Madam."

The rain came at eleven and continued into the afternoon, giving Laura the perfect excuse for a nap. Having seen the maid knock with the linen, she knew which door to go to.

"Hilda? Hilda? It's me, Laura. Hilda?"

"Please go away."

"Don't be silly, open the door."

"I can't, it's locked. Look, please, you mustn't. If they catch you, there'll only be worse trouble and I couldn't bear it. You don't know what father's like. I'm not talking anymore. Please go away."

Laura returned to her rain spattered window. All this because she'd borrowed a book? It was utterly ludicrous to lock the girl up like that, monstrous, especially when she wasn't to blame. Damn Uncle Percy. She'd tell him herself as soon as he came home. It was pointless talking to her aunt. Oh, how stupid.

Broadbent returned at five. Undaunted, Laura disturbed him in his study.

"Hilda's no concern of yours, young lady. Now, if you'll excuse me, I've got things to do."

"But she is, you see. She was only returning a book I borrowed earlier."

"You borrowed? And from where, may I ask?"

"From over there. I didn't know we weren't allowed, until Queenie told me."

"Queenie?" He raised his eyebrows. "Postlesthwaite!"

The Butler came at his master's bellow.

"Get Miss Queenie for me."

"Yes, Sir."

"Now, which book would this be?"

"I'm not sure, I didn't have a chance to read it. It had a plain cover. Hilda seemed to think it was eighteenth century history..."

"Hilda?"

Laura felt her uncle's powers of intimidation.

"Yes, but she didn't seem too sure. Queenie seemed to know it better."

"Queenie? Queenie was in here?"

Laura balked. Broadbent thundered to the door.

"POSTLESTHWAITE. Get Miss Queenie for me, NOW! We'll soon get to the bottom of this."

"Look, I'm sorry if it's valuable or something. I wouldn't have borrowed it had I known. It's just that I'm studying..."

A flurry of footsteps brought Queenie's arrival.

"Laura says you were in here yesterday; is that true?"

"No, father, no, you know I wouldn't come in here, we're not allowed. Laura's got it mixed up with the library. We were in the library, weren't we, Laura; don't you remember?"

"Laura says you were and that you were discussing a certain book," Broadbent crushed the appeal.

Laura turned stool-pigeon crimson. Queenie blanched.

"Well?"

"It's a lie, father, I never did any such thing. I said she shouldn't be in here, that's all."

"So you were here."

"No! I was at the door, I was only at the door! Please, father, it's the truth. Tell him it's the truth, Laura, please!"

Queenie's fear was horrifying.

"The truth is it? We'll see about the truth," Broadbent snarled. "Thank you, Laura. You may go."

"But, really, Uncle Percy, it was all my fault...."

"Go." •

The rain still beat against her window. Laura flopped onto her bed. She felt like an informer; she was an informer, but she hadn't meant to be. Anyhow, at least, now, they'd let Hilda out. If Uncle Percy didn't want people to go into his study, he should bally well lock the stupid door. How was she to know?

The sound of sobbing escalated along the corridor. Her door flew open.

"I hope you're satisfied!" Queenie screamed in tears.

Queenie sat seething at the dinner table; Hilda remained in her room. As Laura despised them, they now hated her, all except Broadbent, in whose estimation her character seemed to have risen to the status of her looks.

"More spine than the rest of you put together," he scoffed at his squirming offspring over the soup, piling on the derision with each helping of roast beef, before pouring such plaudits on Laura over the plum-duff that Peach metamorphosed into jealous damson, then jaundiced prune.

However, any reciprocal regard Laura may have fostered was annulled in the dead of night, when she surprised Hilda coming out of the bathroom.

"Hilda!"

Hilda shielded her face from the lamplight. Laura caught a flash of ochre and puce.

"What on earth...? Let me look."

"Don't, Laura, please don't."

The left side of Hilda's face was one massive, swollen bruise.

"Dear God, did your father do this?"

Hilda's puckered brow nodded in admission.

"Because of that stupid book?"

Tearful confirmation.

"But that's insane!"

Taking Hilda's arm, Laura led her back to her room and closed the door.

At breakfast, Laura found her revulsion hard to contain. A semblance of normality had returned. Queenie, if sullen, was again Broadbent's peach. Laura wished them good morning. Broadbent grunted behind the Times, Queenie ignored her.

"Laura said good morning, dear," her mother reminded her.

"Oh, did she? Really, Laura, you should speak up more."

It wasn't too subtle for Cyril to smirk.

"Now, now, my Peach," Broadbent said gruffly, turning the page.

Laura took a piece of toast and buttered it distractedly. Had Hilda's courage deserted her?

The scrape of cutlery on plate, the rattle of cup on saucer, the pouring of tea, the rustle of broadsheets, all grated on her amplified hearing, until they were sucked into the vacuum of the maid's involuntary gasp.

Drummond's spoon suspended itself in front of his gaping mouth.

"Drummond, you're spilling your egg, dear. And please don't gawp, you look like a goldfish," his mother reproached him, following his boggle eyes towards the door. "Hilda!" She paled.

Broadbent's paper fell, his cheeks ballooned, his temples bulged.

"Go back to your room, AT ONCE!"

The chandelier rattled over Hilda's head, but she didn't falter.

Postlesthwaite hustled the maid out.

"DID YOU HEAR ME?"

'You can do it; you can do it,' Laura willed Hilda on.

"But, my dear, what happened to your face?"

Mrs. Broadbent's pretence stripped itself of all innocence.

"Ask father."

Broadbent boiled the colour of beetroot. Rising without a word, he flung his newspaper onto his chair and stormed out.

Laura saw nothing of him after that. It was a different house, a different family. No-one called Hilda 'Weed' any more.

"He can beat me black and blue, I don't care, I won't be their doormat, I just won't," she swore.

But would she be able to sustain her newly forged mettle? The boys had gone back to school; that would surely help. Nevertheless, as her luggage was loaded into the car, Laura could sense the impending cataclysm. For Hilda's sake, she was sorry to leave.

- CHAPTER THIRTY NINE -

On the night of September twenty third, twelve airships set out over the north sea to bomb targets from London to the Midlands, turning rapture into rupture as Harold Scott, back from his honeymoon, scrambled from his marital bed to watch Bocker's L33 float, ghost-like, over Ashleigh. It reached its vanishing point, somewhere south of Elmsford. Still Scott kept his vigil. The house had narrowly escaped just a few weeks before. It had been empty then; he would take no chances now. Then, far away to the South West, distant detonations alerted him to the silken thread of searchlights and the brighter specks of the Zeppelin's defensive flares.

"Come and look at this," he called incredulously. "It must be London. Good God."

But Agatha's eyes were set on his tousled hair, the crumpled outline of his pyjamas, the boy in the darkness, the silhouette of the son she craved.

While she enticed him back to bed, over London's East End, L33 emptied its bomb racks, setting an oil depot and a timber yard ablaze. However, it did not escape unscathed. Leaking gas like a sieve, the airship headed back to the Essex coast.

The shrill whistle of escaping hydrogen added eerie discord to the whirring rumble of aero engines, which, once more, propelled Harold from Agatha's arms. Why couldn't he see it? The night was crystal clear. It had to be close. He dashed from window to window, tearing back the curtains, until he found the gargantuan confronting him, its black underbelly barely clearing the tree tops.

"Dear God! The cellar, quickly!"

Barging through Laura's door, he dragged her bodily from her bed and down the stairs, deaf to her protests, trailing the bedclothes she clung to in bare-shouldered bewilderment. Agatha was waiting, lamp in hand, by the cellar door. Scott flung himself down the steps and urged them into his arms, instinctively wincing with embarrassment, as he realized Laura was naked.

Agatha offered her dressing gown. The air throbbed; the foundations shook; they crouched like primitives under the wrathful thunder of untold gods. Survival seemed impossible.

"Please, God, don't let it explode," Scott prayed.

Unbelievably, the noise began to fade.

"Stay put!" He ordered.

Unbolting the outside hatch, he scrambled up into the night, just in time to see the airship's tail fins disappear behind the oaks to the east.

"It's all right, you can come out now," he called. "Dear God!"

A flaming gauntlet lit up the Southern sky, clenching into a fireball as a second Zeppelin exploded in mid-air.

"What is it, Harold?" Agatha cried, clambering up behind him.

"Over there!"

"Poor devils."

"Poor devils be damned."

"It can't be the same one."

"It's not. Ours went that way. It's too low to see."

The crew of L33 also witnessed their compatriots' end, before their own craft staggered, stern up, and plummeted to earth. A young woman was among the twenty who dragged themselves from the wreckage. In perfect English, she warned some nearby cottagers to run for their lives, while a volunteer ran forward to destroy what remained of the ship, losing his legs and his life in the process. Turning their backs on his funeral pyre, his mourners set off for the sea, straight into the arms of a Special Constable and a posse of soldiers. However the man's martyrdom would be in vain, only the skin of the vessel would burn away, leaving the aluminium ribs and the engines intact.

The Scotts heard the explosion, but the topography denied them the flaming hull. As the distant glow subsided, they went back into the house. Laura dressed, before joining the others for a recuperative cup of tea. Scott's embarrassment still simmered.

"For God's sake, why weren't you wearing your nightclothes?"

"I was hot."

"Hot? You shed an eiderdown or a blanket, if you're too hot, not your damned nightdress."

"It's more comfortable that way. I really don't see what all the fuss is about; it's perfectly natural."

"To the beasts in the field, perhaps, or the pygmies in the jungle. I don't know what's got into you young lady, but, whatever it is, it's time you bucked your ideas up. In future, you will wear your nightdress at all times, is that clear? I've never been so embarrassed in all my life. I won't have this house turned into a den of iniquity."

"Oh, really!"

"And I won't be answered back! This is my house and you'll do as I say!"

* * * * *

As the Zeppelin raid interrupted Scott's passion, so it intervened in Elizabeth's adultery, catching her, quite literally, with her pants down. Despite the restrictions of living with her in-laws, her captivity was by no means complete. She'd seduced a sixteen-year-old during the harvest, making the most of her one opportunity on top of a haystack. It had been quite like old times. She'd met him again that day, out shopping in the village, and persuaded him into a midnight rendezvous at the Bowdens' back fence.

The plan had worked to perfection. The moon was full, her passions were high. She'd slipped off her draws and balanced herself precariously on the palings, peering through Arthur's bean canes for any signs of life from the house, while her fumbling paramour attempted to satisfy her with all the over-eagerness of youth.

It was during his still less than promising second wind that the airship's thunder woke little Doris, whose screams woke the whole household, sent Elizabeth squealing, rump punctured, from her perch and her panic stricken lover tottering backwards through Arthur's beans with an unstiflable "Aaahhhh!"

She saw the flicker of a lamp, a shadowy figure; she heard Mrs. Bowden comforting Doris, her own name called, then Arthur shout, "mind the blackout."

"Lord Almighty! Get up! Get up!"

Hauling the boy to his feet, she bundled him, bum high, over the back fence.

"Who's there? Is that you, Elizabeth?" Arthur was advancing, flashlight in hand.

"For God's sake, mind that light; it's them blooming Zeppelins again," Elizabeth cried, looking frantically around for her knickers.

Arthur was upon her, Beatrice close behind, little Doris in her arms.

"What's going on?" Beatrice demanded.

"Where's young George?" Elizabeth played for time.

"Sound asleep."

"That boy'll sleep through anything."

It was then that the second airship exploded, finally waking the budding Rip Van Winkle.

"Muuuummy!"

Never had an enemy brought such salvation.

"Sorry, dad, I bumped into them runner beans," Elizabeth apologised, cantering down the garden path.

With the danger passed, the children soothed and Elizabeth's young Casanova puff-full of pride and safe in his bed, the inquisition began over the kitchen table and the underwear exhibited thereon, found by Arthur over an up and coming cabbage.

"Must've blown off the line," Elizabeth told them. "Thought I'd lost a pair."

She found the extraction of the splinter harder to negotiate.

* * * * *

Autumn 1916 would see the last strategic Zeppelin campaign over southern England. With the advent of night fighters, losses became prohibitive. Lieutenant Leefe Robinson had been the first to shoot down a Zeppelin on September 2nd. Although a shellburst had riddled L33's hydrogen cells, a biplane piloted by Albert de Bath Brandon had also scored several hits, while L32, the Scott's flaming gauntlet, had been set alight by Second Lieutenant Sowrey's incendiary bullets. The visibility that night can be judged by the sighting of this disaster by L23, one hundred and fifty miles north over Lincoln.

By the beginning of October, the most feted Zeppelin commanders had gone down with their ships, Bocker, Peterson, in L32, and, the most famous of all,

240

Mathy. A further attempt would be made on the Midlands in December, but that, too, would end in flames over West Hartlepool and Lowestoft.

- CHAPTER FORTY -

Richard's battalion spent September in and out of the trenches in the Yser Canal sector, before leaving the battle zone to be brought up to strength by a draft of two hundred and nineteen fresh men. In early October, they were occupied in practice attacks for the final phase of the Somme offensive.

He was now a Platoon Commander, a veteran of some six weeks active service. Langham had, quite literally, gone West, sent thither by a 'Jack Johnson' as he'd stood on the parapet directing his men out of the line. Despite the care taken, the plod of too many hobnailed boots on duckboard or the chink of too many buckles must have alerted the enemy. Or perhaps it had been one of those fateful coincidences, a periodic salvo sent over to catch carrying parties in the darkness. Whatever the reason, for a few minutes, death had rained down. A shell splinter had ripped through Richard's sleeve, but, unlike Langham, he'd escaped without a scratch, further reinforcing his 'lucky' tag. However, he wouldn't fall into the trap of believing he was invincible.

"You never met Howlett, did you?" Langham had made the point after a previous narrow escape. "Extraordinary man; had no time for talismens. Believed in mind over matter, quite literally, wore it like some kind of body armour. Uncanny, really; he'd walk through the heaviest fire and come out unscathed, not even a nick. It was a shell that got him in the end, a ruddy dud of all things; hit him bang amidships. Strangest thing I ever saw. He didn't realise, you see; kept on going like a gradually sinking battleship and you could see right through him.

Then there was Smythe. His thing was cocaine; took it by the sack load; had it sent over from Harrods. Sniffed it like snuff. Gave it to his men once, just before an attack; had his sergeant slip it into the old rum jar. Fought like demons. Ne'r a one came back."

Richard missed Langham, he'd grown to like him in their few short weeks of fellowship. Langham had shown him a cutting from 'The New Church Times,' a trench newspaper published by some Sherwood Foresters from a dugout in Neuve Eglise. It was a cartoon entitled 'Questions a Platoon Commander should ask himself,' and portrayed a lanky, upper-crust subaltern, a typical 'Herbert', one hand in pocket, the other wielding a swagger stick. Underwritten was the immortal line, 'Am I as offensive as I might be?'

It had remained a running joke in the platoon for weeks. Langham had mimicked the character perfectly, amusing the men by swaggering up and down the trench lisping the legend, until he'd been caught in the act by the Colonel. It had been touch and go whether or not he'd be sent down. The episode had caused Stafford acute embarrassment, but still he'd won Langham a reprieve.

'Better for Langham had Stafford failed,' Richard reflected.

He'd soon realised that Langham's seeming indifference to death and mutilation had been both an instrument of mental self-preservation and a stabilising influence on those around him, and so it became with Richard. The numbness that had deadened the ravages of heartbreak came to his rescue once more, allowing the offal of human sacrifice to extract only momentary recognition of the horror and revulsion that would, in later years, haunt the sleep of thousands. Only the uncomprehending eyes of agonised, four-legged innocence, retained any immediate impact. However restricted his options, at least man offered himself by choice, Richard reasoned. What had horses done to deserve this, to deserve man? Such trust, such betrayal; surely Man was not the doyen of creation, but its greatest curse. He remembered his discussions with Langham about God and Darwin, man, beast and amoeba.

"It's now thought that each human body may harbour more life forms than there are people on the planet," Langham, a pre-war medical student, had told him. "Makes you think, doesn't it? Our own kind of universe within."

"Speak for yourself. We've got enough people playing God around here, if you ask me," Richard had groused.

"But that's the point, you see," Langham had continued. "What if the universe without is like the universe within, just another corpuscle in God's bloodstream, or worse still, a disease? Maybe all these ailments we try so hard to conquer are God's own prescription, purposely perpetrated to eradicate the blight of humanity."

Richard had smiled at the physicality of God scratching the itch as fruitlessly as he scratched his own lice ridden body.

"Hang on, Langham, we're not that bad."

"Well, I don't see much mercy and compassion coming from on high, do you? If there was ever a time, it's surely now. I tell you He hates us. Maybe He's given up on the old intravenous and taken to enemas."

"Maybe He's given up on our stupidity."

"Or, more likely still, He doesn't know we exist. After all, you didn't know there were millions of little whatnots floating around inside you, did you? Perhaps that's how it is with the Almighty and Man, only for Christ's sake don't tell the Padre, he'd do himself in if he thought all his communicative efforts were cried into a transcendental void. Although, on second thoughts, perhaps the hypocritical old bastard could do with a kick up the proverbial backside. I mean, for God's sake, 'thou shalt not kill' and there he is blessing the bloody maxim."

"Yes, he does seem a bit bloodthirsty for a Chaplain, all this 'eye for an eye' stuff."

"Actually, the one that gets my goat is the Eye of the Needle guff, when the Church itself is richer than Croesus. You should see the palace my uncle the Bishop lives in. No, as far as the old C of E is concerned it's horses for courses and always has been. 'Got a bit of a problem, Lord Moneybags? Worried about the old stash? Agonize not. Just slip us a few quid when the time comes and we'll give Saint Peter the nod, or, if you're really worried about it, dispense the old inheritance prior to lights out and ascend to the Pearly Gates with a clear conscience; knock, knock, I'm a pauper.'"

"Not a problem I'm likely to share," Richard had grinned ruefully.

"Nor me, old boy. The way things are going I'll be nought but dust long before

243

the old Pater kicks the bucket, God bless him. Unless, of course, I end up a cripple. 'I've had my legs blown off, father.' 'God moves in mysterious ways, my son.' 'Yes, so do I, now.' If all this really is God's Will, He has to be a complete sadist."

Bitter humour, Richard reflected, but had Langham been right? Had Man created God in his own image, rather than vice versa, forging faith into the greatest self-convincing con-trick of all? His capacity for expansive thought, his egotistic certainty of his primacy, his ability to create his own truth, perhaps these were the biggest hindrances, the impenetrable barriers to Man's understanding? Well, wherever Langham was, he was now privy to the secret, or not, as the case may be.

Richard closed the Langham book of philosophy and opened the hand-written pages Ralph had humbly bequeathed him, kept in his 'Oxford Book of English Verse.' Quite a poetry buff, Langham; they'd talked of a book, Richard's sketches, Ralph's poetry, an apt name for such an admirer of Morris. He'd also liked Hardy and the disgraced Oscar Wilde. 'If one loves, one loves, dear boy; the heart allows little option.' Langham's had been such an idealistic love.

Lie peaceful now and rest your fair brow on sorrow's breast.
Were that breast mine own, were mine hands the hands of God,
To heal your wounds and raise you up and carry you, full hearted,
From this dreadful place of filth, so envious of beauty, so pitiless of death.'

So he had written of Cope, Richard's predecessor, and of his seeming insensitivity;

The larks announce the dismal dawn,
And we stand-to with bayonets drawn,
Our hearts and minds to hardness honed,
Lest nature overwhelms us.

For standing we are fewer now,
Since death descended in our midst,
To steal the souls of those it kissed,
And leave to us the bloody mess.

Yet after sunset's ruddy glow,
Has tipped our steel with tint of blood,
In darkness, hearts will weep unseen,
And sorrow reign in silent scream.'

No, there'd been nothing sordid in Langham's love. He'd lusted only after life. Had he completed his studies, had he joined the Medical Corp, had Stafford not been so fond of him...

So soft the cheek that manhood deigned to spare from its insignia,
So full the sacred lips of youth that blessed each word's caress,
So innocent the eyes that stared in utter incredulity,

As death's disciple canonised his purity of breast.'

It could have been Langham's own epitaph; lost, like so many, in the perfidious well at World's End. Poor Langham; only his talisman had survived, a White Knight, grime infused by palm and pocket, yet still shining, a light in the darkness.

'Ah, well,' Richard sighed. 'Back to censoring letters.'

'Dear mum and dad,

I hope this finds you like how it leeves me in the pink and pass it onto Rosie likewise. Had a beer the other day, tell dad it was like nats you now what. Out at rest we was. That's a larf. Got more rest doing duble shift at Hoffmans. Now theres a name to cunger with. Mind you, wuodnt mind a pint rite now. We are back in the thick of it, but cant complain as the boys says we got it cushy compared to some. Thanks for the parsl. Fags always welcolm, not arf.

Keep smiling...

How many times had he read that? It was as if every letter was by the same hand, with the odd, pornographic exception. Like their bowels, the men couldn't open even their hearts without the Army knowing. He wondered if they realised he was the censor.

Which reminded him, it was time for a 'short arm' inspection. It was too ridiculous for words, he wouldn't recognise a dose of gonorrhoea or syphilis if it stared him in the face, let alone any of the lesser genital ailments. If he was an old sweat and some bloody schoolboy told him to 'raise the curtain' he'd tell him where to get off in no uncertain terms. But the men took it; the men took every degradation going and somehow turned it around.

'None more noble...'

Dear Langham.

- CHAPTER FORTY ONE -

On October 1st, Ashleigh's insomniacs watched Mathy's ill-fated Zeppelin float ghost-like over the village, headed for its fiery end at Potter's Bar, reset their clocks to 'normal hours' and went back to bed, leaving Arthur Bowden patrolling the lanes and Beatrice to read Richard's letter for the umpteenth time. He was safe and well and back in reserve. She thanked God. The previous week Elizabeth had heard from George, also 'in the pink'.

She was about to climb the stairs, when a frantic knocking startled her.

"Who's there?"

"It's Walter Taylor. Mrs. Gurny sent me."

The Taylor's were the Gurny's nearest neighbours. Beatrice opened the door.

"Sorry, Missus," the boy gasped. "Old Mister Gurny's been taken bad. Doctor says to come quick."

Elizabeth appeared, bleary eyed, on the landing.

"Granddad's been taken poorly," Beatrice called up, pulling on her coat and hat. "Soon as Arthur comes home, tell him that's where I'll be."

The old man was lying peacefully on his pillow, eyes closed, his breathing shallow. Mrs. Gurny, frail and gaunt, was at his bedside. There was clearly no hope, the shake of De'Ath's head merely confirmed it.

Beatrice sat gently on the bed. Her mother reached across.

"He just keeled over on the landing. Next door helped me get him into bed. Been like this ever since."

Gurny's eyelids flickered.

"It's Beattie, dear; Beattie's come."

"It's me, dad."

Beatrice squeezed her father's hand. A hint of a smile pursed the old man's lips. He sighed contentedly and was gone.

They buried him two days later, the Landlord of the Barley Mow arranging the unofficial loan of two black army horses to pull the gothicly sombre Victorian hearse, judged more fitting than a motor vehicle.

Jeremiah's was one of only two local deaths that year, both of men who had enjoyed long, fruitful and, in the main, happy lives; the Grim Reaper had far more bountiful fields to harvest. Mourning was hard to come by, even Elmsford's famed department store had failed to keep pace with demand.

The Bowdens suggested Gran Gurny move in with them for a while, but she preferred to stay in her home of sixty years, where every niche and knick-knack held its memories.

She took her loss stoically; her private tears were for a long life come to its natural end, rather than bitter tears for a young life cut short in its prime. Now she waited for God to reunite her with the only man she'd ever known, wishing only that they could have crossed the divide together. That there was a heaven, she had no doubt, to her the stars at night were the heavenly host, paradise was as real as that. It wouldn't be long before a rejuvenated Jeremiah would lead her through the Pearly Gates.

Before that happy event, she would like to see Richard safe and married. He'd done so well for himself, he'd made them all so proud. He deserved to be the father of children. She hoped Laura would be a better wife to him than Elizabeth, the harlot, had been to George. George was a good boy, but, by all accounts, no harm was likely to come to him now, she didn't worry about him so much. Maybe he would fall out with the strumpet when he got home, Lord knows, he had cause enough, but, where Richard and Laura were concerned, when things were right, they were right; they would have to be total fools not to see it and neither of them were that. She hoped she'd be around for the wedding, just so she could tell Jeremiah how happy they were.

* * * * *

The platform faithful and the ten or twelve members of the public who had bothered to turn out only emphasised the emptiness of a hall which could happily hold hundreds. For the heyday of Women's Suffrage had well and truly passed with the coming of war. Those who had so vehemently harassed Asquith's Liberal Government from the outset of office, had miraculously rallied to the flag. Even Emmeline Pankhurst, despite her years of imprisonment and hunger strikes, had forsaken the movement's green, white and purple for nationalistic red, white and blue, redirecting her oratory to the cause of military service.

'Patriotism had saved them,' Asquith would say in 1917. It had certainly spayed the Women's Movement. Of its hierarchy, only Emmeline's daughter Sylvia campaigned against the War. It was not a popular stand, as evidenced by the attendance. While the pike of European conflict gobbled up men in their millions, Women's suffrage was a minnow in the turbulent pool of political affairs. In many ways, the War had already delivered emancipation. Women were working the lathes, manning the busses, tilling the soil. The vote would come. It was enough for now.

Laura had been too young for the pre-war battles. She'd been fourteen when Emily Davidson had martyred herself under the King's Derby horse. Apart from the Tindal Square Banner, her support had been purely passive. Now, as Sylvia Pankhurst rose to speak, however unfavourable the climate, she was ready to be activated.

She'd been lucky, her father had gone to Wales on business. She'd simply telephoned Agatha from Elmsford Post Office saying she'd developed a migraine, felt too poorly to catch the bus and was staying with a friend overnight, leaving Agatha to remind the dialling tone about taxis.

However, her ruse was proving profitless; the eminent Pankhurst's rhetoric was as uninspiring as the attendance. She quoted Asquith's famous remark of 1913, 'Let

247

women work out their own salvation,' but her point was lost, like so many others, in the hall's reverberation. A veteran reporter from the local Chronicle fell asleep in his chair, blank notebook in hand.

It was more than disappointing, it was disillusioning. Laura had been ready to dedicate herself to the cause; now, despite Hettie Jameson's die-hard enthusiasm, the pulse of politics, like Pankhurst's oratory, was but yesterday's faint echo. Although there was nothing faint about the ensuing row between Hettie and Sarah, when the rally broke up, a row that ended with Sarah dragging Laura off, insisting that she *was* staying the night, and that was that, no matter what her mother said. "I promised her; she has nowhere else to go."

If Hettie was left fuming in front of her friends, Laura was left wondering what on earth she'd done to upset the woman so. Perhaps Sarah had been right about her mother's 'higher conscience' all along. Perhaps she should forget the whole thing, and university, too, and join the VADs like Sarah.

Why did everything seem so futile, she asked herself in her unfamiliar bed that night. Why did a future that had once seemed so bright, now seem so bleak? The answer was simple; without love, there was no future. But love was inadmissible. Laura had been ready for revolution, now she was a rebel without a cause and, more immediately, without motivation.

* * * * *

Spencer watched the raiders slip into no-man's land, faces blackened, hands clutching bayonets, bombs and homemade coshes. The covering party followed, Bowden leading. Spencer would have liked to have taken charge himself, but company commanders were barred from trench raiding.

The last man merged into the night. For twenty minutes nothing happened, then a sudden explosion shattered the stillness and German distress rockets turned night into day.

Spencer raised his binoculars. Through the clearing smoke he could see the raiders milling like cattle before the uncut wire. In its midst, their lieutenant was hopelessly entangled. The Bangelor torpedo had been a dud.

"Jesus Christ!"

Coal-scuttle helmets bobbed along the trench beyond; rifle barrels protruded over the parapet. His heart was gripped by the boy's terror, his ears rang with it, then the shells screamed down and the world exploded in mayhem, confining him to self-survival and the invocation of every deity of endurance.

Gradually the storm blew itself out; stillness returned, punctuated only by the spasmodic rattle of a machine gun. From the enemy wire, the cries of the wounded savaged his compassion, but he could do nothing for them, no one could.

Bowden brought his party in. He'd lost three men, two blown to bits and one badly wounded. Of the raiders, only four made it back, all, bar one, men of experience. The lucky novice had shown the good sense to stay close to his sergeant and do as he did, the rest had panicked, forsaking the earth they would now be buried in. A shrapnel burst over the trench had added another two wounded from Peverill's platoon.

Spencer retired to his dugout, telling Bowden to follow with his report. Half an hour later, the boy appeared.

"Come in, Bowden." The name was familiar to him now, but only militarily. Letters from Laura lined his top pocket, but she'd never revealed her ex-fiancé's identity; his memory banks remained time-locked.

He scanned the report, then put it to one side.

"Care for a whisky?"

"No, thank you, Sir."

"Relax, Bowden, we're not on parade here."

What was it with Bowden? There'd been a barrier from the start, verging on defiance. He'd never felt it with any of his other officers, but, with Bowden, even after two months or more, there was always an atmosphere. The boy had done well since Langham's demise, the men liked and respected him, his sergeant had nothing but praise for him and Sergeant Houseman was a man of sound judgement. So what did he, Stafford, represent that upset Bowden so much? Some kind of inferiority complex was the only plausible explanation. Bowden was clearly a 'temporary gentleman'.

"Have one anyway." He poured two fingers into a tumbler. "You shouldn't have helped that man in, you know, under any circumstances."

The reprimand was in no way malicious, but still Spencer sensed the boy's shackles rise.

"I felt it my duty, Sir."

Why did Bowden's every answer sound so bloody impertinent?

"Damn it, man, your duty is to obey orders. We've got few enough officers as is it, without you damned well throwing your life away."

Spencer hadn't meant to raise his voice, he'd had no intention of admonishing the boy, quite the contrary, but Bowden's attitude exasperated him.

"The man was wounded, Sir; I couldn't leave him to die."

"You know the rules, Bowden; it's every man for himself. If I can't rely on my officers to set an example, the discipline of this company will go to pot."

"It won't happen again, Sir."

"Make sure it doesn't."

It was another opportunity to clear the air, to get to the bottom of the problem, wasted. For God's sake, he actually liked the boy.

"All right, Lieutenant, that will be all."

Bowden placed his whisky, untouched, on the table, saluted and was gone.

Spencer sat wearily on his bunk.

"Damn it!"

Adding Bowden's whisky to his own, he slumped back.

* * * * *

Hettie Jameson hurried along Waterloo Road, cursing her daughter's obduracy. Sarah had known not to invite Laura to stay, that night of all nights. It had been beyond embarrassment; she'd been made to look a complete fool.

Turning into Dempster Street, she made her way to number eighty seven. Perhaps she could trust Laura, but the risks were too great, there were lives at stake, and a lengthy prison sentence for any aiders and abettors.

Mrs. Beckwith was waiting.

"Thank God you've come. I've never been so nervous."

"I'm sorry, Fanny," Hettie apologised shamefacedly. "Where is he?"

"Through there."

"What about your neighbour?"

A policeman had moved in next door to Mrs. Beckwith a month before.

"He left for work an hour ago, but his wife's in and she's got eyes like a hawk. I think we should wait 'til dark. What about your Sarah?"

"I'm so sorry, I don't know what got into her," Hettie apologised again.

"Is she all right now?"

"Oh, yes." If only for the simple reason that the girl had got her own way and was joining the VADs. "Well, I suppose I'd better say hello."

"I've made him up as best I can, but he doesn't have the smoothest complexion."

Hettie entered the room. The fugitive rose, slim enough to fit women's clothing, but far too manly to be wearing them. His eyebrows were thick, stubble shadowed his chin.

"My husband's been gone these past ten years," Fanny Beckwith apologised. "I'm afraid his razor's no longer up to the job."

"We'll have to wrap a scarf round his face. Hello; forgive me if I don't introduce myself, it's safer that way."

"Believe me, lady, there's nothing to forgive, not with what I owe you lot."

"You'll have to pretend you've got toothache. Would you mind walking about a bit?"

To cap it all, he was bow-legged. Hettie told him to take smaller steps, to straighten his knees, to hold his handbag 'like so'.

His gloves didn't fit.

"I've got a muff upstairs," Fanny volunteered.

"How you made it here on the train I'll never know," Hettie told him.

Fanny brought the muff.

"Now, let's try again."

He tottered about, trying his hardest; it would have to do.

"Do you mind if I sit? These shoes is killing me."

"I'm sorry; yes do," Hettie said. "I'm told you were in France when you deserted; how on earth did you get home?"

"On my mate's pass. He got leave, see, and I went down the trench aways to see him off; well, we'd been together since the start, him and me, you know how it is, though I don't suppose you do, really. Anyhow, I was on my way back, when this shell comes over. I knew he'd copped it as soon as I saw it land. I ran back, but he was a goner alright; not even his own mother would've recognised him. Bad luck for him, but a gift-horse for me. It's alright for the officers, they get leave regular, but I hadn't been home in over a year. Quick as a flash I nabs his pass, swaps discs and pay books and what-have-you, and hops it, not thinking of the consequences 'til it was too late. We was in the line, see; desertion in the face of the enemy. There's only one penalty for that, and we all knows what that is."

"But surely, if you swapped papers, they must think the dead man is you?"

"Exactly; I couldn't go back, even if I wanted to, and I can hardly go back as him, can I? I tell you, I've never been so scared as I was getting on that leave boat and then the train the other end. I thought they'd nab us for sure. Then it suddenly dawned on me that I couldn't go home neither. The whole street would've copped me. Hadn't seen my old lady for all that time and still haven't. Worst of all, she'll've got the telegram by now, saying I'm the one what's gone for a burton, and me old mate'll've been marked down as AWOL. He don't deserve that, not our Jack. If I'd knowed what I was getting myself into, I never would've done it, but I didn't think, see; spur of the moment. I'm only thankful that I came across you ladies when I did. Regent's Park, it was; pure luck. The rest I 'spect you know."

There was the basis of truth in it, though his eyes spoke of a deeper desperation.

Disguised as a woman, he'd been brought from London on the night of the rally to be left in Hettie's charge, until Sarah had thrown a spanner in the works and Mrs. Beckwith had stepped into the breach.

"You'd better try that walk again........"

- CHAPTER FORTY TWO -

Laura lay listlessly in her bed, watching the heavy October rain wash away the painful memories of the hot summer, leaving only one ineradicable reflection; Richard. Why, after six months apart, was he never far from her thoughts? She wondered where he was, picturing him in the arms of some mademoiselle before her jealousy gave way to reproof. He was more likely to be up to his neck in muck and bullets. He could even, at that very moment, be lying on the battlefield, mortally wounded. The thought was chastening, chilling. She saw Mrs. Bowden weeping over the grave, Mr. Bowden, head bowed to hide his distress.

She shuddered and changed the subject, wondering what on earth had got into Hettie Jameson. She'd called on her a day or so after the rally, sneaking out of school again to apologise for whatever she was supposed to have done. If anything, Hettie had been even more off hand; she hadn't even let her into the house.

Sarah had been posted to Rayntree hospital; she was living in a hostel.

'And who can blame her, with a mother like that,' Laura thought. If she didn't see Hettie again until hell froze over it would be too soon.

She'd told Agatha about the rally. Although angry, Agatha had said nothing to her father. The couple had driven into Elmsford to see 'The Man who Dined with the Kaiser' at the Empire.

The old house groaned in the wind, emphasising Laura's loneliness.

She'd heard of old Mr. Gurny's demise, Agatha had brought the news home from the village. Her heart had gone out to Mrs. Bowden. She felt so isolated from them, her second family, but, if the two or three miles which separated them seemed like two or three hundred, the gulf between her and Richard was even more unbridgeable.

Yet sometimes love seemed so close, almost close enough to touch through the transparency of parting, a clear dimension through which they had only to step. Then, at other times, it was a bottomless, fog filled chasm.

She side-stepped to Spencer. His letters were sometimes compassionate, sometimes anecdotal, although he never mentioned anyone by name. He'd made an exception in someone called Langham's case; he'd obviously liked him a lot. She did reply, relaying snippets of village gossip, but her letters were invariably short. She'd told him of the wedding and the near miss with the Zeppelin. She wouldn't tell him about Mr. Gurny; he probably hadn't known the man and, besides, she never mentioned anything pertaining to Richard.

The photographs were hidden behind her wardrobe. She brought them out occasionally. Now that the emotional dust had settled, she did find them mildly provocative, even arousing, when the mood took her. But the fomenter of that mood was always Richard.

She recalled the summer morning he'd arrived, drenched, on her doorstep after falling in the river, closing her eyes to savour the beauty of his boyish frame, the

252

catch in his voice when he'd lost control.

She remembered their furtive night of love, the light in his eyes. How she longed for his lips, his touch, that the hand stroking her breasts was his rather than her own.

Her fingers slipped down her torso. She moaned breathily at the delight of his caress. Her eyes flickered open to view the vase, which, months before, had held love's last white rose. It bloomed again to enfold her in its velvet seduction.

A ripple washed over her. She pictured herself and Richard making love in a summer meadow under a clear blue sky. The feel of his body, his masculine scent, the fiery passion of his possession, each fantasy heightening the tide, until she was swept away on ecstasy's yield.

The waves subsided; the rain had stopped; the night was still. A crescent moon broke through the clouds. She wondered whether, in Flanders, too, its silver beam had pierced the darkness. She would write to him, she had to write to him.

Her fingers delved into the tiny bedside draw; the dented locket melted into her palm. She held it to her heart.

* * * * *

Spencer stood in the trench, his collar turned up against the drizzle. Would it never stop raining?

"Looks like we'll have a nice day for it," Smylie, his adjutant, smiled sardonically.

The whole Battalion was to attack in the morning; 'B' Company would lead the second wave.

Petherill slipped through the gas curtain behind them to join the other platoon commanders in Spencer's dugout.

"He's the last."

"Then let's not keep them waiting."

"Attention!" Smylie called down the steps.

Spencer descended. The candle flared. He took in the gaunt faces. "At ease, gentlemen."

He spread the map and went through the plan of attack, making sure each officer knew his part. He'd placed himself in the centre with the newest arrival, posting Bowden to his right and Stevens to his left, along with the Company Sergeant Major, the sole survivor from the South African campaign. Stevens had been shaky of late; the CSM would be a steadying influence. Smylie had offered to take Steven's platoon across, but Spencer had said no, arranging his assignment to the nucleus left behind in all attacks. If the worst happened, Smylie would ensure that the battalion was rebuilt on good foundations. As for the fourth platoon, Petherill could be relied upon, the last of Langham's Mohicans.

"All right, Gentlemen, if there are no further questions? We all know what's expected of us. My advice is to catch an hour or two's sleep. It will be a long and arduous day tomorrow. You may dismiss, and good luck to you all."

The crowd cleared, Smylie folded the map, Spencer flopped onto his bunk. If the past two weeks were anything to go by, it was going to be a disaster.

The Battalion had joined the battle on the 9th, first as Divisional and then as Brigade reserve. It had taken them six hours to struggle four and a half miles through the mud to reach their positions, losing their Lewis Gun carts on the way.

The Warwicks, Duke of Wellingtons and Lancashire Fusiliers had attacked on the 13th, with the Essex supplying reinforcements and carrying parties. Only the Wellingtons had reached their objective, never to be seen again.

The Lancashires had been decimated. The Essex had taken over their trenches on the 14th, losing thirty men to their own artillery during six days of incessant bombardment, rain and glutinous mud. No sooner had they been relieved by the Scottish Rifles than they were told they were to attack on the 23rd.

"I think I'll take a turn, Sir, if that's all right?"

"Yes, all right, Smylie."

Spencer reached into his valise. Sensitive man, Smylie; Thank God, he, at least, would be spared. What was it the men said? Three to a loaf, tomorrow?

A small bundle moulded into his palm, Laura's letters. If only he had been whole, God, how he would have loved her, how he would have made her love him. But like this? If the War had taught him anything, it was to be a realist. Still her flowing hand reached out, inducing him into dreams of her dancing, nymph like, through lush Manor meadows, while he basked in her beauty.

* * * * *

Laura woke with a start. Richard! His aura filled the room. Something was wrong, something was happening to him. She sat bolt upright. Her hands were clammy; perspiration clung to her brow. She'd heard him call so clearly.

"Laura! You'll be late for school!"

She fell back onto her pillow, allowing the cosseting reality of the tangible to deprecate the credibility of the psychic. It must have been a nightmare.

It had happened before, one September night up in Warwickshire. She'd finally slipped back into sleep and woken in the morning knowing he was all right, but today there was no time.

"Laura?!"

"Yes! I'm up!"

* * * * *

The Batmen lined up with their officers' watches. Spencer liked to synchronise them personally. Smylie counted down; Spencer pressed on 'Zero', double checking each one before handing it back. The last looked vaguely familiar; this was no service watch; he knew this watch, but it wasn't Stevens', nor Petherill's, he knew Petherill's Batman. Whose on earth...

As he puzzled on one plane, his somnolent memory lurched through the jeweller's door on another, waking to Laura's sapphirine excitement. He turned the casing. There was the inscription. He remembered as if it was yesterday.

"Whose is this?"

254

"Second Lieutenant Bowden's, Sir," Rowe, Richard's Batman, told him.

Bowden? Of course! 'R.B.'; Richard Bowden. Bowden the plumber's son, the scholarship boy. This was that same Bowden. Good God! So that was it. Bowden knew. Of course he knew. She must have told him.

Smylie continued to count. Spencer clicked the winder on cue, but his mind ticked on.

In a funny way, the realisation came as a relief. At least he knew, now, Bowden's problem. The penny had dropped, the handle had been pulled; 'What the Butler Saw'; from their different perspectives, both he and Bowden were the butler. No wonder the boy was so surly. Did Bowden know about the photographs?

Rowe cleared his throat.

"Oh, yes." Spencer returned the watch. "That's the last," he told Smylie.

So, Bowden was the rival he'd envied to distraction. What he wouldn't have given, a few months ago, to be in Bowden's shoes. But now? As crushing as his impotence was, its surety blunted the emotional edge. He could only imagine the heartbreak Bowden must be suffering. Better the impossible than to have loved and lost.

How old was Bowden, eighteen, nineteen? He was only a boy. He would have it out with him, clear the air, Bowden had been a thorn in his side for far too long. But it would have to wait until after the attack. He reached for his helmet. 'Lucky Bowden', wasn't that what the men called him? Well, he hoped the boy's luck held.

* * * * *

The attack, scheduled for eleven thirty, was postponed until two thirty due to heavy mist. Through those three anguish-ridden hours Richard's men waited, crammed into their assembly trench, praying for reprieve, clinging to every straw, 'they won't send us now, half the day's gone,' willing the fog to last, and then cursing its callousness and the induration of those in command, when it suddenly lifted and the shells screamed over.

"We go."

The German counter barrage crashed down, setting earth and stomachs heaving. Somewhere ahead the first wave jumped off, advancing over the same ground, under the same conditions and to the same fate as the Duke of Wellingtons only ten days before; bullets and shrapnel ripped them apart.

The Essex moved up. The parapets were strewn with dead, the trenches choked with wounded. To continue the attack was futile, but the order had been given and orders were sacrosanct.

Richard gripped the ladder, his sinews taut, his heart pounding. A splayed hand stretched over the sandbags in death's benediction. A human remnant lay to his left, its intestines slopping over the boots of its retching replacement. Some were sobbing, others praying, some losing control of their bladder and bowels, but not even their mothers could hear them above the ear-rupturing din.

Whistle welded to his lips, Richard focused his entire being on keeping the ladder steady, on the onus of example, the injunction of command. Then, through the mayhem, came insanity's thunderbolt, the gut-wrenching rasp of Stafford's Acme.

Terror shuddered through him, blinding and paralysing, but it had to be done, duty demanded it, honour decreed. As if in slow motion, Richard rose to his destiny, blowing his whistle mutely into the maelstrom.

The mud sucked at his boots, the earth erupted around him, showering him with debris. A scream broke the sound barrier; the air around him was beating and fluttering, like a giant bird in the claws of a clowder of cats, all hissing and spitting, swearing and whining. He became conscious of a sporadic thudding, of men crying out and falling. Sergeant Houseman was beside him and then he was gone. Ragged khaki bundles littered his path, and numberless holes, multiplying through the smoke, some filled with ruddy water, others filling, marked by lingering wisps of cordite and scatterings of torn flesh and shattered bone.

"Keep going, men, keep going," Stafford's voice cut through the chaos, then the film slowed and its accompaniment slurred into sonorous suspension.

The whole landscape became shrouded in red, as if some crazed painter had daubed it with a giant brush. Richard wiped his temple; the rain was crimson and sticky, the back of his hand was smeared with it, like gooey water colour. Was it raining blood? Why wasn't he moving? Why was the world standing still? Why did everything echo so?

He could hardly see, it was getting dark, but it was only three. Laura? What was Laura doing there in the middle of a battle? She was calling him; he must go to her, he must go. He was swimming, the water was cool, it soothed his head, but he mustn't stay under too long. They said you couldn't breath under water, but you could. They were Waterbabies, he and Laura, but the water was murky, she was leaving him behind, he couldn't catch up, he had a broken arm, he was being sucked into a whirlpool, round and round, round and round...

Groggily, Richard opened one eye. The other was stuck, and he had an excruciating headache. The night was the blackest he had ever known and perishingly cold. A freezing tide lapped his chest; he was up to his neck in water.

Frantically he levered himself up. He seemed to be all right, except for this blasted eye that wouldn't open. Its counterpart began to ache with solo sight. Fearfully, he ran his fingers over the swollen lid. It was caked in something, completely clogged. He prayed to God that he wasn't blinded.

Pulling his sopping handkerchief from his pocket, he bathed it. Gradually the lashes freed, he could feel them fluttering. Gently he prised them apart. Could he see? It was too dark to tell. Yes, he was sure he could. Thank God.

His tongue felt like sandpaper. He searched for his water bottle. It wasn't there.

A Very light shot into the air. He shut his good eye to double check the bad, but as soon as he pressed his hand over it, pain caught him in its vice. He rode it through, then gingerly felt again, finally locating the congealed edges of a scalp wound.

He reached inside his right tunic flap for his Field Dressing. The waterproof cover had been ripped; the bandage and gauze were soaked through. Breaking open the phial of iodine, he emptied the contents over the gash, wiping the overflow away from his eyes in the nick of time. It stung like hell, but, bugger it, he was alive, he had all his faculties, what more could he ask?

A machine gun, close by, forced him back down into the water.

He wondered how Stevens had fared. The poor chap had been in such a funk, certain he was going to die. Had he plucked up the courage to go over? The Sergeant Major had been with him, he would have made sure Stevens did the right thing.

The firing ceased. Richard peered over the crater's lip to get his bearings. A German parachute flare went up; he ducked too soon to know from where, or even to care as vertigo span him on its axis.

Slowly it wound down. He looked at his watch; five fifteen. He'd been out for two hours? It seemed incredible, and even more incredible that it was so dark and so silent. Perhaps his watch had stopped. He looked again; five sixteen. So why no firing? It didn't make sense, unless... Christ! It couldn't be a.m.? He couldn't have been out all night?

Self-preservation centred him like a weather cock. Once dawn broke he wouldn't stand a chance; anything that moved would be shot on sight.

Another flare soared; again he raised his head. There was a blur of wire to his right, but whose? How far had he come before getting hit?

Then he suddenly realized that the ground in front was alive with giant salted slugs, writhing in their agony.

His head hammered. He covered his ears and screwed his eyes shut, but still their suffering seeped through his fingers, still they came on, trailing their slime, intoning their agony, until his temples pounded in crushing concussion.

Clammy hands clawed at his collar. Fearfully he fought them, but their grip was like iron, forcing Satan's stirrup cup to his lips. He opened his eyes in abject terror, to find the gargoyles of death were the bearers of life.

He gulped the water.

"Steady, Sir, steady."

* * * * *

As Richard regained consciousness, Laura slipped into sleep, her insomnia pacified by the surety of his survival.

A second telepathic shock had hit her in the afternoon, in the middle of English class, throwing her so completely that she'd asked to be excused. She'd gathered herself in the solitude of the locker room, but for the rest of the day her heart had palpitated, her hands trembled. She'd retired early, claiming a chill, forcing open telepathy's gate. When sleep finally came, it was the coma of a heart and mind stressed to exhaustion.

* * * * *

Of the entire battalion, only thirty two men had reached their first objective, a map

257

line drawn some five hundred yards beyond the German front trenches; of those only eighteen had made it back. Stafford had been badly hit, Richard was told at the aid post, he, Bowden, was the only surviving officer.

He was not a pretty sight. The left side of his face was bruised and swollen, the gash on his forehead was two inches long. His helmet had absorbed the brunt of the blow, but shell splinter or shrapnel had penetrated the metal. His skull hadn't been fractured, the injury looked worse than it was. An orderly bandaged him up and sent him down the line.

The Dressing Station more resembled a battered, blood-soaked Chinese Junk than a hospital, a Red Cross wreck floundering in a sea of misery. Where there was hope, the doctors did what they could, those beyond it were left to die, as were many others in the hours' long backlog. There was no time for consultation, no time for compromise; shattered bones meant amputation, abdominal wounds certain death. Richard was given an anti-tetanus injection and told to wait.

He trod carefully among the wounded, searching for familiar faces. He found five, waiting only for mortality to give up the ghost. The officers were slightly apart. He thought he recognised Stevens, but it was hard to tell. Padres were picking over the souls like dog-collared vultures.

"Bowden!"

The croak was barely audible. Richard turned to see Stafford's dawn grey face staring up at him. He looked so old. One glance told Richard the game was up; only death could ease his suffering now. He was shot through the lungs.

"Bloody shambles," Stafford wheezed. "Glad you made it."

Richard could only nod. Although he felt desperately sorry for the man, sorry for his pain, sorry he was going to die, he couldn't free himself from his hatred.

"It's up to you, now... I didn't know; not 'til... Miss Scott, Laura; there was nothing between us... Friends... that's all... just friends..."

Richard didn't want to hear, he didn't want to see, he didn't want to face his own crass stupidity.

"Orderly! Orderly! You'll make it, you'll see."

The blood bubbled from Stafford's mouth. Each breath was plainly torture. He gripped Richard's arm. "Friends, Bowden... You must believe me... Only friends..."

Richard's answer died on his lips. As with Laura, he discovered, too late, that it had all been a petty game he'd played right to the end. He didn't hate this man, he loved him.

Stafford's eyes stared from oblivion. Richard recoiled at their clamminess, then forced himself to close them, as guilt ridden as if he'd pulled the trigger. He'd seen men die, but he hadn't felt death's wax, he hadn't shuddered at its total impassivity.

He slipped the watch from Stafford's wrist, the crested ring from his finger. Such things were apt to go missing when left to the orderlies. He would give them to Smylie, he'd pass them on. The Colonel would write to the family, it had to be someone senior.

"The old buffer'd better do him justice, that's all," Richard sniffed, reaching into the bloodstained pockets.

Spencer's note book fell open at a battered photograph, but it wasn't of Laura, as

Richard had expected, it was of Langham. Poor Langham; he'd had no eyes to close and less to bury.

"Oh, God, dear God," Richard sobbed.

'The lines of age invest his brow...' Langham had written of his Captain. In the rejuvenating paradox of death Spencer looked almost boyish; but it was another of Langham's verses that surprised Richard's memory;

> '...........let not your spirit linger here in ghostly chains,
> Let we, the living, mourn thy loss, for other realms await thee.
> Realms where lush, abundant peace doth reign in love's eternal light,
> Realms where beauty such as thine shall bathe in Eden's Glory.'

There was no tattered battleflag with which to cover him. The sky had cleared a path for Spencer's spirit, let it also be his shroud.

Richard tucked the snapshot back into Spencer's pocket. Now Langham, too, would have a grave.

The rain resumed. Richard found the Battalion in the remains of Trones Wood. The Colonel had been hit, Smylie was acting C.O., Richard acting Company Commander. Even with no company left to command, he felt juvenilely inadequate. His Batman had been one of the lucky ones left behind; Rowe; thank God for Rowe. He'd scrounged some tarpaulin from somewhere and made a bivouac.

"Thought you might like a cup of tea, Sir."

Richard was deep in thought.

"Tea, Sir?"

"Oh, yes, thank you, Rowe." The luxury of meditation would have to wait. "Any news of the C.S.M.?"

"'Fraid he copped it, Sir."

"And Sergeant Houseman?"

"Him, too, Sir. No senior N.C.O.s left at all, just Corporal Walker from those left behind and one lance-jack, a bit the worst for wear."

Richard nodded and took a sip. The tea scolded his tongue. His hand shook. Quickly he put the mug down.

"Fetch Walker for me, would you?"

"Right you are, Sir."

"Oh, and Rowe, do you think you could find Captain Stafford's things?"

"Beg pardon, Sir, but there's no need to trouble yourself; Mr. Smylie'll see to all that."

"Even so, I'd like to ensure he gets them intact. We came from the same part of the world, Captain Stafford and I. We couldn't have been born more than a mile apart."

"Oh, I see, Sir. Well, the Captain's man copped it too, Sir, but I'll see what I can do."

259

That night, Richard wrote to Laura by the light of a solitary candle. Beside him were her folded letters, found in Spencer's kit along with several rolls of film and the camera that Richard had tried so desperately to avoid. Had Stafford caught him unawares? The concept of being captured by the same lens, which had once driven him to distraction, now raised only an ironic smile. There had been a photo of her, but only one, a portrait. Laura had sworn that Spencer had kept no others. He hadn't believed her then; he did now.

He hadn't read her letters. Yesterday he would have done, yesterday he would have been desperately jealous of them, but yesterday he'd been a boy, or perhaps an old soul waiting for his reborn consciousness to catch up.

> *'My dearest Laura,*
> *it is with the deepest regret that I must inform you of Spencer Stafford's death. No other Officer was so respected by his men.........'*

'No, no, no!' It sounded like an official bloody communiqué. He screwed up the page and flung it across the shelter.

> *'My dearest Laura,*
> *I wish this had been written under different circumstances, but it seems I am fated to bring you only pain. Spencer Stafford was killed today, leading an attack. I was with him when he died. As in the case of our love, it seems that only in destruction is the truth made apparent to me. I now know what an exceptional man he was and what he must have meant to you. We all miss him terribly. The men are desolate. His last words were of you. I know he must have loved you very much.'*

Should he add 'as I, too, will love you to my dying breath'? Even without it, he'd said too much. He'd come within a whisker of copping it himself more than once. If things went on as they were, 'lucky' or not, death could only be a matter of time. Why put her through it all again? Besides, would she even care?

Once again he put pencil to paper.

> *'My dearest Laura,*
> *It is with intense regret that I have to inform you that Spencer Stafford was killed today. Under the circumstances, I thought it best to return the enclosed to you, rather than to his family. His last words were of you. I am so desperately sorry.'*

It was very presumptuous of him. Perhaps the Staffords approved of the relationship, perhaps there was nothing untoward in the letters, without reading them he couldn't be sure. Still, returning them seemed the best option. He signed his name and placed the note in the envelope. Closing the flap, he called for Rowe.

- CHAPTER FORTY THREE -

Ashleigh's camp was dismantled at the end of October and the army moved into town billets for the winter, furthering Arthur Bowden's expectations of some lucrative repair work come spring. Even the village's shopkeepers were glad to see the back of the latest rowdy lot, but the melancholy that filled the void only emphasised the dearth of native men.

Elmsford, on the other hand, now overflowed with cocky, cockney conscripts, who saw, through the Priory gates, a vision of vestal heaven. The gauntlet they formed provided the perfect promenade and feminine rivalry did the rest. Compacts were concealed, powder and rouge, for outlawed application after the bell. Each coyly induced smile proclaimed a conquest, each wolf-whistle a femme fatale. Overt flirtation, jealous jibes, catty rejoinders, viper tongues, vixen claws: never had the Priory witnessed such behaviour.

Laura played the game as a matter of form, and why not? Richard's note, with so few lines to read between, far from nurturing her re-blossoming love, had all but torn it up by the roots. How her heart had leapt at his hand and how quickly it had crumpled.

How long had he and Spencer known each other? How much had they shared? How many of her letters had Richard read? All of them, she had no doubt. She'd written no lovelorn eulogies, they'd been mundane at best, in only one had she mentioned that day at the manor. It was enough.

She'd callously accused Spencer of betrayal, before her conscience had caught up with her. Poor Spencer; she wondered what those last words had been. One thing was certain, these were the last she'd ever hear from Richard. So why keep up this grass-widow pretence? Perhaps he'd been right all along; perhaps she was the whore he took her for. Perhaps, under the wrappings of revenge, her motive for seeing Spencer had been carnal, the art factor only a second layer of acceptability, pity not even its ribbon. In which case, why deny it; why deny herself?

Yet, for all her bluster, it was a license unendorsed by desire. She was finding that the very cynicism which unbarred the sexual gates, also retarded the animal within.

* * * * *

In the early months of the War, men had been able to enlist for 'Home Defence' service only. Now they, too, were being sent to France. Even the Roadmen, whether of conscription age or not, were asked to forsake the highways of Essex to mend the shell torn byways of Flanders for three shillings a day and an army allowance. Hardly an able bodied man was out of uniform.

However, the cut of his civilian suit was the last thing on Scott's mind, as he wandered down Elmsford High Street one lunchtime, until a girl pressed a white feather into his palm. He smiled kindly. It had been a while.

"My dear young lady, I only wish I were young enough."

"You look young enough to me," she sneered.

He'd expected an apology, not to be answered back. He swallowed his indignation.

"Well, it's very flattering of you to say so, my dear, but, I assure you, I'm old enough to be your father."

"In that case you're definitely a coward; my father was killed in France."

Her reproach was uncompromising; it caught him completely off guard. This girl was Laura's age, perhaps more.

"Was he a regular?"

"No, unlike you, he volunteered."

Scott was thrown completely. He'd been contemplating the evening ahead, totally unprepared for confrontation.

"And they took him?"

"Oh course they took him; he wouldn't be dead otherwise."

"Well, I'm sorry, my dear, but I really am too old; they wouldn't have me," he told her, wondering why on earth he was trying to justify himself to this slip of a girl.

"If you truly wanted to fight, you'd lie about your age as my father did. In France they need every man they can get, even cowards like you."

With that, she threw her head in the air and stalked off.

Scott was flabbergasted. In less than two minutes she had divested him of exemption's overcoat. She was right, he could lie about his age, everyone said he looked years younger than he was.

The realisation hit him like a thunderbolt. His sangfroid whirled into a tornado of moral confusion. Suddenly it was no longer her questioning his courage, but himself. He had no defence, he could hardly argue that lying was against his principals, he'd lied about Marian for four long years. He was in fair physical shape, he could claim no infirmity. He was constantly tired, but then who wasn't? Now that he thought of it, he knew men of his own age had joined up. How many others thought as she did? What were others saying behind his back?

He cursed the girl. Was it his fault he looked young for his years? He'd been slipped white feathers before; what made this one so different? He was too old, he had a family to support and a job of national importance, the commission simply wouldn't allow him to go; or did he have too much to live for? Didn't they all? Wasn't it his duty at least to try? Was his expertise really so critical? It was of profitable importance to his firm and to himself, but anyone with half a brain could tell one tree from another. For heaven's sake, if the truth be known, he was just as much a war profiteer as that brute of an in-law of his, Broadbent. He hadn't thought of it before, but, now that he had, would he really be able to hold his head high, when the war was over, and rest on the laurels of a fat bank balance?

Whatever arguments he put forward, they were no more than excuses. He'd debated the moral complexities with Richard enough times, the duty to oneself, to the nation. In his heart, he was no longer exempt; it was as if he'd cut his ego's artery and his self-respect was emptying into the gutter. Only the King's Shilling could stem the flow. The Recruiting Depot beckoned. Taking his hands from his pockets, he marched across the street.

* * * * *

While Richard's Battalion recuperated, the Battle of the Somme raged on into November. The weather worsened, the mud made movement impossible, but still High Command pushed on.

"Can't they see what they're sending us into?" a fellow subaltern complained.

Richard could only shrug.

Finally, with the last reserves floundering in the morass, the message seeped through; Kitchener's armies had been bled to death; the Generals would have to wait for conscription to replenish the coffers before embarking on another spending spree.

The retribution of failure began. Each Battalion was ordered to supply a Junior Officer as a Courts Marshal Prosecutor. 'Lucky' Bowden had been Duty Officer when the new C.O.'s gastroenteric vindaloo had emptied the mess. With the other candidates still in sick bay, he drew the short straw. His job was simple; to read out the charges, admissions and any written evidence, both damning and mitigating. He could have refused, but refusal would only have lumbered some other poor sod with the task of justifying the criminality of the High Command with the cowardice of its cannon fodder.

The accused said little, only their eyes spoke when the verdict was passed. As at Very lights, Richard learned not to look. Then, one night, he came across a familiar name in the prosecution notes for the next day's hearings, 'L/C. Crutchley, J.'

"Not Joe!"

He snatched up the file and hurried to the Provost Marshal's office. The Officer in Charge had gone, the Sergeant didn't know where, "out on the town, most like."

"But I can't prosecute this case. If this is who I think it is, I've known this man since childhood."

"Can't see how I can help you, Sir," the Sergeant told him. "You'll have to take it up with the Major."

"But he's not here, damn it," Richard remonstrated.

"Now, now, Sir, no need to raise your voice," the Sergeant objected respectfully. "'T'ain't my fault, is it, Sir?"

"But, don't you see, man, it's just impossible."

"I'm sorry if this man's a friend of yours, Sir, but it's the Major you've got to speak to, he's the only one what can help."

"When's he due back?" Richard tried to stay calm.

"Not 'til morning, I'm afraid, Sir."

"Not 'til morning? But that'll be too late."

"I'm sorry, Sir, truly I am, but, as I says, there's nothing I can do."

"Then can I see the man, Sergeant? I take it he is here?"

"Well, he is, Sir, but it's highly irregular."

"Yes, I know that, but the circumstances are rather unusual, wouldn't you say?

263

God dammit, if I'm supposed to try my best friend for cowardice, I must, at least, have the right to see him first."

The Sergeant reluctantly reached for the keys.

"Are you sure, Sir? May be best if you don't; only make it harder when the time comes."

"Yes, Sergeant, I'm very sure. Now take me to him. That's an order, Sergeant."

The cell was a stable, dark and dank with horse excrement and rotten oats. Richard requisitioned the Sergeant's lamp.

A figure stirred in the corner. The light fell on his face. It was Joe Crutchley.

"Joe? It's Richard, Richard Bowden."

"Bowdie? Is that you? Can't be!" Crutchley rose from his blanket, rubbing his eyes in disbelief. "Well fuck me sideways. Good to see you, old pal, good to see you. Cor, a bloody officer, no less; me dad said you was. Well, I'll be blowed."

"Not so good, I'm afraid, Joe. I'm the bastard that's got to prosecute you tomorrow."

"Oh, I see." Joe's face fell. "How the hell did you let yourself in for that?"

"Not much choice, I'm afraid. The adjutant volunteered me."

"Tomorrow is it?" Joe sank back on his bunk.

"Didn't they tell you?"

"Don't tell us nothing, my old mate."

"I'm going to speak to the Provost, Joe, there must be some mistake."

"Mistake?" Joe echoed wryly. "You could say that; biggest mistake I ever made, getting mixed up in this lot. My old man told me I was a fool to join up, but I wouldn't listen. Well, I'm in it now, right up to the neck. Ran didn't I; lost me nerve."

Richard sat beside his friend, horrified. He'd seen the name and 'Capital Charge', he hadn't stopped to read the rest.

"I don't believe it, Joe; not you. You've always had more guts than the rest of us put together. Remember Clayman's old bull? You took it on like a ruddy matador. There's got to be more to it than that."

"Guts?" Joe reflected. "Huh; I've seen more guts spilt these past six months than I've had hot dinners. You wouldn't remember old Smithy from out Belsham way; don't think you knew him. There was only him and me from our neck of the woods in our lot, so we got pally like. Awful it was. They had to scrape him off me, Bowdie, and there was this eye left there, stuck to my webbing. Next thing I knew I was back in the horse lines."

"Oh, hell, Joe," Richard grimaced.

"Yeh, I know." Joe's face crumpled. "Thing is, how's my old Dad gonna take it, me being shot for a coward?" A tear trickled down his cheek. "I've brought disgrace on the whole bloody lot of them."

"No you haven't, Joe, you haven't. Besides, it might not come to that."

"Oh, it surely will, Bowdie. If it wasn't for them at home, it wouldn't be so bad."

"They'll never know, I promise you. The telegrams don't say." But the telegrams did say, and Richard knew it. Only in the New Year, after much lobbying by Sylvia Pankhurst and constant questioning in parliament by Snowden, Hogge and the soon to be infamous Pemberton Billing, would 'Died of Wounds' replace the stark truth.

"Honest?"

"Honestly."

"Well that's something," Joe sniffed. "Anyway, what about you? You ain't had things so cushy yourself by the looks of you."

The scar on Richard's temple was still livid.

"Oh, that. Shell splinter; went straight through my battle bowler; wonder it didn't kill me."

"Not you, me old mate, got a charmed life, you, always have had." Crutchley forced a smile that quickly faded. "No, brought this lot on myself. Sooner they put an end to me the better."

"You can't mean that, Joe. You mustn't give up hope. Is anyone speaking on your behalf?"

"Not that I know. Make no odds if they did. I'm guilty as hell and they knows it, and you knows it too if you're honest."

"Look Joe, I'm going to tell them I can't do it, then they'll have to postpone the trial until they find someone else. At least it will buy you some time."

"No, don't do that, Bowdie. Better to be over and done with; I'd only have to sit here and rot another day or so, and I don't know as me nerves can stand it; don't want to make more of a bloody fool of myself than I already have. I know it's a lot to ask, but I'd rather it was you."

Richard wanted to be anywhere but in that courtroom, but Joe had left him no option. "All right, Joe, if that's what you want."

Crutchley leant forward and shook his friend's hand.

"Thanks, old chum."

As with the rest, Joe's verdict had been a foregone conclusion, though Richard wasn't there to hear sentence passed. His repeated interjections on the defendant's behalf had brought a string of officious reprimands and, finally, dismissal. When he'd reached his room, his bed had been stripped, his bags packed.

He caught up with his Company in a village untouched by war since the early days. One estaminet had been reserved for Officers. There, he found a table in an alcove and bitterly drowned his sorrows in vin blanc.

What gave those sanctimonious bastards the right to pass judgement on men like Joe, he raged. He'd like to see them endure fifteen months in the firing line. If they had, they might have found their courage failing them, too, probably after fifteen minutes, which was still a hell of a lot longer than he'd ever seen a geranium in a trench. The only one who'd ever honoured them with his presence had been a Major, and he'd hightailed it at the first 'whizz-bang'. It was them that needed shooting, the dirty bloody brass hats, not poor old Joe.

He'd often overheard the men muttering; 'be some bloody changes when this lot's over.' As with the War itself, it would only take one tiny spark to ignite a revolution. Men were dying in droves for what? If they had any sense they'd pack it all in and let the generals fight it out themselves.

So what was he doing there, if he felt that way? He could only repeat the 'auld lang syne' the Tommies sang on their way up the line. 'We're here because we're here, because we're here, because we're here!'

In the corner, an old upright piano broke his melodic train. A poignant tenor took up a different refrain;

> "Roses are shining in Picardy,
> In the hush of the silvery dew.
> Roses are flow'ring in Picardy,
> But there's never a rose like you.
> Roses will die in the summertime,
> And our roads may be far apart,
> But there's one rose that dies not in Picardy,
> 'Tis the rose that I keep in my heart."

For no-one else could the words have meant so much. Tears welled. The tree, his cardinal confessor, stretched out its boughs in absolution.

- CHAPTER FORTY FOUR -

On November 28th, London was raided by a single German aeroplane. Its bombs dropped on Knightsbridge, close to Lowndes Square. Buckingham Palace was thought to be the target, but the pilot had overshot. The nights of the Zeppelin were past, the days of the 'plane were just beginning. The following year, Gotha bombers would give Londoners a foretaste of what was to come a quarter of a century later.

Scott, in town for a Forestry Commission meeting, heard the blast from his Piccadilly rendezvous. He'd been turned down flat by the army medical examiner.

"Got a bit of a dickie ticker, old chap. I'd advise you to see your local quack," he'd been told.

De'Ath had confirmed the diagnosis and given him some pills. There was no need for further soul searching and, in the light of Agatha's news that morning, every reason to be thankful; she was expecting their first child. Scott was overjoyed.

Laura's happiness for the couple was bittersweet; it could so easily have been her baby, hers and Richard's. How badly she'd wanted his child.

The flirtations of school had been officially curtailed. Mother Abbess had complained to the authorities and the precincts of the Priory had been put out of bounds to the military. For a brief spell, the High Street had become the common stamping ground, until the Sisters had taken to patrolling the town centre. Now anyone caught in public with a serviceman, even an officer, was subject to a written enquiry to her parents regarding the claimed 'relative' or 'family friend', with expulsion hovering over the head of any unfortunate fibber.

With Elmsford reduced to the worst kind of garrison town, Scott preferred Laura to wait for him at school or to take a taxi, when he was away on business. Occasionally she would be invited to Rosalind Edwards's house for tea, and he would pick her up from there. The family's admiration had been boundless since Richard had saved Edwards junior's life at cadet camp. The boy, now a fifth former, was only too keen to dispense the latest reports on his hero, which, whether she cared to admit it or not, was Laura's main reason for going.

With so many Old Boys at the front, the Grammar's network offered considerably more insight into the reality of things than any amount of official bulletins. Edwards knew, for example, that Richard had been the only officer to survive the October attack and that he had been wounded, though not seriously.

Wounded? Laura had heard nothing from the village. If Richard had told his family, word would have got round. The news shook her. She raked over the fissure, denying the light to love's wintering tubers.

Now and again she would take tea with Annabelle Cousins in Sadler's Tea Rooms, usually when her father was away. Annabelle had fostered a chaste image at the Priory without being considered a Zealot. Never overly attractive, lately she'd been making more of an effort.

As Laura had confided in Sarah, Annabelle confided solely in her, confessing, over tea one day, to having an 'amour'. Laura's curiosity was aroused, if only mildly. Annabelle was so staid that a serious liaison was about as likely as an armistice.

"He's very handsome," Annabelle boasted. "He's going to be a flyer."

"And how did you meet this flyer of yours?" Laura asked out of politeness.

"We're neighbours, so to speak. He's billeted on Mrs. Marchmont, next door. She's a widow you see, she takes in lodgers. She and my parents go to whist drives together; that's when we see each other, while they're out."

"Really?"

"Yes; he comes round and we play cards."

"Oh."

Laura's interest lapsed in favour of a sporty looking lieutenant at a corner table. A pair of crutches were propped against the wall behind him. Instinct led her to the single brown boot. Just as instinctively, she shuddered at the thought of Richard losing a leg.

"Laura, do you think it's wrong to let a man, well, you know, take liberties?" Annabelle whispered, blushing profusely.

How could Laura answer without compromising herself?

"Well, I suppose it depends..."

"I mean, if two people really love each other?" Annabelle flushed an even darker purple.

Suddenly she had Laura's undivided attention. Was this a confession, a cry for absolution?

"You see, he says, if I don't, then I can't love him, and I do love him, I do. Oh, what shall I do, Laura, what shall I do?"

The solution was simple; tell the bounder to b..... off, in no uncertain terms.

"Do you really love him so much?" The question hardly needed asking.

"More than anything in the world. I'd do anything not to lose him, Laura, I couldn't bear it."

Laura thought of her own relationship. Were the truth to be told, it was always Richard who'd pulled back from the brink.

"And he feels the same?"

"He says he does."

They were words of infatuation rather than conviction. Annabelle's underlying insecurity was obvious.

"But if he really loves you, Annabelle, don't you think he'd wait?"

Annabelle had no answer.

"Well, don't you?"

"I don't know, Laura, I don't know. I mean, a man's needs are different to a woman's, and there's the War..."

Where love and war were concerned, Laura could reel off every rationale verbatim, her father's, Agatha's, Mrs. Bowden's, Richard's.

"Yes, but..."

In the end, sense seemed to sink in.

* * * * *

That same night, the Essex slogged, single file, through the Slough of Despond, outstretched hand to shoulder, like a battalion of the blind. The drizzle, incessant since October, dripped from their helmets and capes, turning the duckboard track into the highwire from hell. To step either side was to be lost to the slurry that levelled old shellholes and trenches, waiting to suck a man under. Even if the faller could be located in the dark, help usually came too late or proved suicidal. Many a line trudged on to suffocation's stifled screams. Drowning in mud had become as commonplace as death by enemy fire.

Richard remembered his first trip 'up the line' and the limber driver's warning about the mud at Wipers. The man had said the Somme didn't compare.

'How much worse can it be?' He wondered. 'So much for the absorbency of Picardy chalk.'

The shattered foundations of a street appeared through the gloom like a silt-swallowed Marie Celeste; the Gateway to Hell. The guide led on.

"All right, we're here," Richard whispered. "No smoking, no noise, pass it on."

As the communication trench deepened, so did the mire. The men cursed their way forward, levering themselves through the traverses, arms akimbo, like a giant, mud caked centipede, each hold-up at the front bringing a pile up at the back.

"Bit like my old woman's treacle pudding," some card said.

It took them four hours to cover the final half mile. Their reception from the men they were relieving was hardly amicable.

"Where the hell have you been?" Their officer demanded to know. "Blast your eyes, we'll be lucky to get back before daylight."

"Sorry, Sir; it's waist deep back there," Richard apologised.

"Well, let's get on with it. Mullery will show you where everything is. All right, Sergeant, lead off."

The Essex had taken over positions near Fregicourt and there they would remain until Christmas. Their new C.O. was a regular, but a novice nonetheless, a Curry-Wallah shipped back from India, where patrolling the Punjab had been no preparation for the Western Front. Richard was one of only two company officers with any experience of trench warfare. A handful of replacements had joined the ranks, but the Battalion was seriously under strength. It made no difference to G.H.Q.; a battalion was a battalion and would take over the corresponding yardage. The Essex would be thin on the ground.

'Please, God, they don't attack,' Richard prayed.

The outgoing Fusiliers had left the trenches in good order, there was little to do except get acclimatised and organise the sentry roster. Richard signed for the stores and supplies and got his men settled. When he returned to his dugout, Rowe had tea ready on the brazier. If ventilation was bad, sleeping men could easily succumb to its lethal coke fumes. There were worse ways to go.

By the glow of its embers, Richard read Elspeth's letter. The mail arrived in the top of the rations sack, often so rain-soaked that the ink ran into the bread below, as it must have done in this case; he could barely read it.

She hoped her 'Dickie Bow' wasn't having too bad a time of it and that he hadn't contracted any undesirable diseases from the love parlours she'd heard so much about from Jimmy. Jimmy, by the way, was dead, killed by some beastly bomb or other. Whenever he was in town, he must give her a call, her door would always be open to her most adorable paramour.

"Parasite, more like," Richard recollected her generosity, although barely Jimmy; he'd been too drunk at the time to recall much at all. He remembered Elspeth, though. How could he forget? She'd shagged his brains out. It was nice of her to write.

A 'Crump' triggered the inevitable shower of dirt. His hand automatically covered his tea. The cycle had started; death, destruction, fear and fatigue. It was all too familiar, like the irksome enteric he'd carried to the trenches. He would have to use the latrine soon, God forbid; better a bully tin. It would be just his luck to get caught in the act.

"What the hell are you doing, Boughden?!" The C.O. would ask.

"Crapping in a can, Sir."

The crusty old bugger had a lot to learn, not least how to pronounce his name.

CHAPTER FORTY FIVE

A day or so after their 'agony' session, Annabelle invited Laura to stay for the weekend. After satisfying her father that 'Cousins' was no pseudonym for 'Jameson', Laura accepted, if only to get away from Scott and Agatha's post-conception bliss. The Cousins were pleased; their daughter's solitude had been worrying them of late and Laura was obviously a girl of the right sort.

At last Mrs. Marchmont rang the doorbell. Friday night was whist drive night. After a brief introduction, parents and neighbour departed.

"They'll be here any minute. Do I look all right, Laura, do I? Oh, please say," Annabelle whined, frantically fussing with her hair.

"You look fine, honestly," Laura assured her a little shortly. Annabelle's nerves were having a knock-on effect. The pilot was bringing a friend, a shamefaced, last minute revelation on Annabelle's part. The situation amounted to a blind date. The mantle clock ticked temperamentally on, as if piqued by the chore, marking off the minutes of Annabelle's increasing trepidation.

"Aahh!" She nearly jumped out of her skin at the doorbell's sharp trill. "That's him!"

Laura stayed in the drawing room.

"Hello, darling. And how's my little girl tonight?"

The speaker's suave baritone oiled the hinges of the parlour door, as it carried through.

"This is Alex. You remember, sweetie, I told you about him; the game? You did promise."

"Yes, er, hello Alex," Laura heard Annabelle quake. "Er, actually, I have a friend with me, too."

"What?" The smoothness congealed into a truculent huff. The speaker applied a touch of solvent; "but, Annabelle, dearest, you knew about tonight. Alex has put off a very important engagement. Can't you get rid of whoever it is? Really, my sweet, you can't let me down like this, you really can't."

Laura peeked round the door. Annabelle was imploring the negative. The pilot's pressure gauge rose.

"It's just too bad. Perhaps we'd better call the whole thing off. If you can't keep a promise, well..."

"No, no! I just thought, with you bringing a friend..."

"You thought, you thought!" The gasket gave way. "And what about our agreement?"

"Our agreement?" Annabelle whimpered.

"The game. The sole reason Alex is here."

"Oh, Anthony, I cou... I..."

"God's teeth. When a person gives their word, they should damned well keep it. My apologies Alex," Anthony feigned to leave, "it seems I've brought you on a wild goose chase."

"No! We can still play, can't we?" Annabelle squirmed. "Just not....."

"I fail to see how; unless, of course, your friend....."

"No!" Annabelle cut him short. "No, she doesn't."

"I knew it. I should never have trusted you," Anthony seethed.

Laura's character assessment had been swiftly confirmed. "I'm sorry if I've spoilt your evening," she announced herself coldly.

"Anthony, this is Laura; Laura, this is Anthony... and.... er.... Alex, yes, Alex." Annabelle wrought her hands.

Anthony was nearer Spencer's age than Richard's, a lady-killer every bit as handsome as Annabelle had described him, the definitive conceited, cunning bastard, as self-centred and hard-hearted as Laura imagined herself to be. Beside him, Alex was consigned to sandy haired insignificance.

"It's of no consequence, a misunderstanding, that's all; Laura, is it?"

Anthony's smile was quickly frozen by Laura's glacial stare.

"Well, we'd better be off. I don't think we have anything more to say to each other, Annabelle, do you?" Calling Alex after him like a pet dog, Anthony plonked his cap on his head and stalked out.

"Please, Anthony, don't go! We can play another day... I promise... Please come back... Anthony!"

A breeze as spiteful as Anthony's parting words swept through the hall. Abjectly Annabelle closed the door.

"I'm sorry. I... well, I...."

"What on earth was he talking about, Annabelle? What game?"

Annabelle coloured. "It's nothing, just a card game. Oh, Laura, what am I to do?"

The tears fell. Laura led her friend into the sitting room. On the couch, the strip-poker truth was finally confided, and more.....

"Oh, Laura, if I tell you that..."

"Annabelle, you must."

"But you'll hate me, Laura; promise you won't hate me."

"Don't be silly, of course I won't hate you."

"Well... intimate things... you know...."

"Like?"

The extent of Anthony's hedonism shocked even Laura. Annabelle Cousins was telling her this? So much for her own sexual fable.

Now the words came rapidly, urgently.

"Only he wanted Alex to play, too, the three of us. I told him I couldn't possibly, it wouldn't be right, but he insisted. I didn't know what to do. I thought, with you here... Why did he want Alex to play, why?"

The reason for Laura's invitation was patently clear. Had the evening progressed, she may have been given the opportunity to prove just how much of a whore she was. She recoiled in repugnance.

"Oh, God." Annabelle crumpled.

"Don't, Annabelle, don't. He's not worth it. Listen to me. He was only using

272

you, don't you see?"

"Laura, you don't understand," Annabelle wailed. "I'm going to have his baby."

- CHAPTER FORTY SIX -

The Battalion's spell in the trenches had been the worst Richard had known, days of saturating rain and knee-deep mud, then deadly frost, then rain again to thaw the corpses, while, day after day, the line had been shelled incessantly. Hell itself could have offered no worse a purgatory.

The new C.O., desperate to prove himself, ordered a trench raid 'to lift the men's spirits'. That he could even consider it, given the conditions and the Battalion's weakness, was hard to believe; that it could possibly succeed was absurdity itself.

The subaltern chosen to lead came to Richard for advice.

"Only, with you out so long, I thought... I don't want to make a hash of it."

Richard had no advice to give. He'd only been on one trench raid, in charge of the covering party. The whole affair had been a disaster.

He voiced his misgivings to his Captain, who, despite his rank, was no more experienced. Had the captain relayed them with more tact the C.O. might even have listened; instead he exploded. No upstart bloody popinjay was going to tell him his business, particularly one whose recent Courts Marshal behaviour had disgraced the entire regiment. The conditions were to their advantage, the Hun would be caught off guard, and, as for fears of a counter strike, a raid of reasonable proportions would create an illusion of strength and deter retaliation.

Richard was given the assignment. If he succeeded, all well and good; if he failed, there would be one less argumentative little weasel to undermine authority.

Richard racked his brains trying to remember Spencer's strategy; no preliminary strafing, it gave the game away, and a small party, nine or ten at most; in and out before the enemy knew what had hit them. The Colonel agreed to limit the artillery to covering fire 'to aid your withdrawal,' but remained adamant it would be a full platoon affair. A platoon hardly constituted an attack in strength, fifty or sixty men struggling through the appalling mud would only increase the chances of annihilation, but Richard held his tongue; in its depleted state his black-hand gang only numbered eighteen.

As Zero hour approached, he blackened his face, checked his revolver and joined the men in the trench, anonymous in their matching minstrel masks. 'Bring on the Harlequin;' bitterly he pictured the C.O. leading the charge in 'Boy's Own' fashion. His Captain, the Judas witness to his death warrant, was there to wish him luck.

"I'm glad it's you, Bowden. The men have faith in you."

'The blind leading the blind,' Richard thought. "Thank you, Sir. Ready, Sergeant? England expects and all that."

Stealthily he climbed the ladder. A tape trailed out to the gaps cut in the British wire.

"Here we go."

He slipped over the bags. Immediately the mud sucked him to a standstill. A slurping 'ssshluck' proclaimed the extraction of each boot, a seething 'ssschlick' its replanting. Crawling was impossible; they would have to skate on their bellies, using their limbs like paddles.

At last he was through the wire, panting like a basset, his muscles aching, his head throbbing. Behind him, progress was despairingly slow. At this rate dawn would break before they got halfway. He damned the C.O. to hell.

"Sergeant; is Corporal Hatch up yet?"

"He's just coming now, Sir."

"Good. Tell him to spread the men out as they come up. They're to stay put, understand? And not a sound. When all hell breaks lose, he's to get them back, but not before, tell him. You and I will go on. Who else is there?"

"Mathison and the new man, Christie, Sir, over on your left."

"They'll have to do. Right, got that?"

"Yes, Sir, but what about the wire, Sir, the torpedo?"

"Sod the ruddy torpedo. We can't afford to wait. We'll make do with clippers, if we get that far."

"Right, Sir."

The sergeant scuttled off, leaving Richard in awe of the superhuman abilities sergeants' stripes seemed to bestowed. All he could discern over his shoulder was a line of slithering slugs. He shivered at the flashback. The Sergeant returned to his side.

"All right, Sergeant, I'll lead."

They paddled on, like mud bound newts, trying to avoid the fetid, waterlogged craters. The inevitable slip brought the inevitable gasp for help, the inevitable scramble to find the outstretched arm and pull its owner to sodden salvation.

A flare went up.

"Still!"

Night returned, silence, relief.

"On."

A putrefying corpse sat like a sentry before a death-trap cellar, brim full. Beyond it, rising ground offered better going; then another flare lit them up like a street lamp. Richard's watch ticked in front of his face, each second a minute, each minute an eternity.

The flare died. He struggled on, wallowing, swallowing mud, filth, yard after yard, minutes, quarters, time and mudtide. They had to be close; they had to be.

A stifled cough came from his right, but where was the wire? There had to be wire.

'tay here,' he signalled, snaking forward, breath on hold, nerves on hold, heart on hold.

A well fed rodent guarded a watery grave, its beady eyes watching; then a careless clink alerted him to a darker pit beyond.

A stinking, rancid, ragged heap offered cover. Its acridy filled his mouth. He thought he would choke, then something moved, he heard the cough again: a listening post.

Noiselessly he backed away, fear screaming in his ear to forget what he had seen, to just throw a few bombs and get the hell out of it. But he knew he couldn't; it had to be done.

He found his men where he'd left them.

"Knives and coshes; follow me."

Crabbing, crawling, skirting, stalking; a muffled cry, a gurgling slump;
A skull cracked open, wide-eyed terror, a brandished revolver; "Raus, raus!"
Soaring daylight, a belt of wire, starkly rusted, thirty feet;
"Hand grenades. Pull the pin; throw hard then run like hell!"
Flashes, explosions, erupting parapet, guttural agony; "Run, run!"
Firefly bullets, wildly angry, aching limbs, bursting lungs,
Sobbing men, stumbling, falling, sheet-white flarelight, "down, down!"
Praying, cursing, blinding blackness, sodding, sapping, trapping mud,
Screaming shells, descending, roaring, soaring filth, the fog of hell.
Slipping, sliding, clinging suction, death's seduction, "on, on!"
Webley pistol prodding, pushing, 'where's the wire, the bloody wire.'
A flying, crying, bloodstained bundle, breathing still, too weak to lift,
A stalwart Sergeant, bending, bearing, sagging shoulders, "this way, Sir!"
The wire, the gap; they stagger through, sandbagged sanctuary, helping hands.
Wounded, dying, death denying, still it takes them; there is no God.

The raid succeeded, if the loss of five men for one wounded prisoner, one dead sentry left at his post and the destruction of a few yards of enemy parapet could be called success. Mathison was missing, Christie had got hung up on the British wire and paid the penalty and three of Hatch's group had been blown to bits. The German losses to the grenades and covering fire couldn't be assessed and, therefore, couldn't be counted.

By contemporary standards, it had been a good show. The C.O. was magnanimous in victory, even offering Richard a whisky. Had he known that the bulk of his raiders had been left at the British wire, he may not have been so warmly receptive. The reports were ambiguous, the whisper went round; Bowden looked after his men; 'mum's the word.'

The Essex were pulled out of the line on Christmas Eve, marching to Maurepas. All festivities were postponed, although the Quartermaster did supply a free issue of beer. Still there was no rest; working details had to be found, supplies brought up, wiring parties organised. When the Battalion finally transferred to Camp 124 near Sailly-Laurette, it mustered little more than a hundred men and transport, a tenth of its nominal strength.

- CHAPTER FORTY SEVEN -

Despite his utter depression and the responsibility resting on his shoulders, Richard had managed to get a card off to his parents prior to the December stint, a silk embroidered nativity scene with the greeting 'Joyeux Noel', very colourful, very French. Its arrival brought tears to his mother's eyes.

It had been a traumatic year for the Bowdens, with Elizabeth's disgrace, the house-fire, Richard's conscription, his break-up with Laura and then his sudden departure for France. For five months Beatrice had lived in fear of the telegram boy, praying that she would see her son again.

Old Gurny's death in the autumn had added sorrow to the burden and now Young George had Scarlet Fever. He was a strong little boy and was showing signs of recovery, but the doctor said he wasn't out of the woods yet. There seemed no end to the family's misfortunes.

Through Christmas Eve and all of Christmas Day Beatrice kept one eye on the door, convinced that Richard would appear. It wasn't to be. Still, he'd sent a card and there'd been a letter from George; she knew her sons were safe. What more could a mother ask in such times? Even Young George seemed to have picked up during the day.

She said nothing to Arthur, but she would have liked to have seen Laura, Richard's Laura. Even if her intuition had failed her about him coming home, she was sure she was right about them. One day, when all this was over, they would be together again. Yes, she would have liked to have seen Laura.

* * * * *

Across the parish, Laura, too, was thinking of her second family. Despite their undoubted love for her, she was feeling increasingly isolated from her father and his new bride. Unlike the Scarlet Fever epidemic at the village school, reported by Agatha, their happiness demanded no quarantine, on the contrary, it was a beneficial infection, but, as much as their joy radiated to those around them, at its core there was only room for two.

She thought back to Christmas 1914 with its tree, goose, puddings and pies, even old Mr. Gurny's flatulence. It was the nearest thing to a 'proper' Christmas she'd ever had. This year's festivities, spent with her new grandparents, had only emphasised her demotion in the new order. The expected baby had monopolised the conversation. She'd had no Richard to brag about, she was no longer the centre of attention. Had she stayed home, she would barely have been missed.

But how she missed the Bowdens. How she wished she could put the clock back. How she wished that she, too, had someone to call her own, and that that someone was Richard. If only he was home, she would go to him, she would beg his forgiveness, she would make him love her again. How stupid they'd been, how

277

utterly, selfishly stupid.

She cursed herself for not sending him a card; after all, he'd tried to make things right. Why hadn't she listened? He couldn't know how she felt; how could he? But what chance was there now, after he'd read her letters to Spencer? It was hopeless, utterly hopeless, she'd been damned by her own testimony.

She thought back to her lunacy with Spencer. But for his incapacity, she, too, may have found herself pregnant like Annabelle. Poor Annabelle. Anthony, the bastard, had vanished without trace. Annabelle still hadn't told her parents. If only she would, even now, they would be sure to find him. The authorities would make him marry her, that is if he wasn't married already, ten times over.

She looked into the bedroom fire, snug and warm but lost all the same. She shouldn't be languishing at the Priory, she should be doing something positive, like Sarah. Even to think of University seemed so selfish when the world was tearing itself apart. If only there hadn't been a war, if only things could be as before.

Her overburdened eyelids demanded closure. Perhaps, in sleep, the years would fall away and Paradise be regained, if only for a few hours.

* * * * *

"Christmas comes but once a year and Santa Klaus forgot the beer! Still, who gives a fuck. Come on, Bowden, farts is trumps," Sarson let one rip. "Oow that's better. Put up or shut up."

"Paugh, do you have to," George grimaced at the stench, studying his cards. Ace, Queen, Jack and a couple of little ones, no Spades, the Ace of Clubs and nothing more to speak of; it was worth a fag. "Solo."

"You sod, I was gonna go that."

"Well, I've saved you the trouble."

Contentment oozed from every pore, cigarettes hung from every lip; the prisoners' bellies were full for the first time in months, courtesy of the Red Cross. Not everyone had received a parcel, but the Christmas spirit had prevailed. It would not prevail again. The following year men would fight like dogs over scraps of bread, some to the death.

The Boxing Day sun that had melted the frost on the window, now added its allure to the kitty of Capstans, Weights and Woodbines on the cardboard carton which served as a card table and would, when night fell, fuel the stove, if the Germans didn't confiscate it first.

Another resounding fart erupted from Sarson's rear.

"Do you mind," George complained for the umpteenth time.

"No," Sarson smirked, raising his leg, "and there's another. Make hay while the sun shines, that's my motto. First time I've been able to do that without shitting myself for fucking months."

"Pfahh! If you ask me, you bloody have!"

"Cor, savour that aroma; just like old times."

"My old man was a great one for the wind; he could blow a skiff clear across to the Isle of Wight," the Pagham man boasted.

"Dah, that's nuffink," Sarson told him. "Stick a nozzle up my old man's arse and he'd float a fucking Zeppelin. Snuff out a candle at forty fucking paces, just by bending over. Did it to a birthday cake full of candles once, the whole lot in one go, just so's he could have the whole fucking thing to himself, the selfish fucking sod. Who led Spades? You got a fucking death wish or something? He trumped the last fucking lot. I wouldn't've minded only it was my fucking cake. Backfired on him, though; went up like a gas fire; singed his arsehole good and proper. Served him bloody well right, the greedy bastard."

George took the hand with the four of trumps.

"Game over," Sarson groaned. "He's got the fucking Ace, Queen and Jack, and the King's already gone. I told you not to lead fucking Spades, Parsons, you bollock brain."

George added his winnings to his already considerable pile; his luck was in.

"You could open a fucking tobacconists with that lot, Bowden. Come on, deal the fucking cards; my luck's got to change some fucking time."

Sarson shifted uncomfortably. He, too, had a gammy leg, a hamstring peppered with shrapnel, which the camp doctor was leaving to work its way out. 'A proper case of pins and fucking needles,' as Sarson put it.

George's wound had pretty much healed, thanks to the old man's poultice. He still suffered the odd twinge and it still ached with the cold, but what part of him didn't? The fear of losing his leg no longer nagged at him and life was the sunnier for it. By way of gratitude, he'd curbed his swearing and mumbled 'amen' at church parade with more conviction. However, if his piety went unnoticed, his abstemiousness stuck out a mile.

"Call you fucking Quaker from now on," Sarson, whose 'dia-bloody-fucking-bolical' had made him exhalted among the heathens, had ribbed him.

"Do you reckon they'll give us some Charlie Chaplin tonight, seeing as it's Christmas?" Parsons asked hopefully.

"Will they fuck. Kaiser Bill handing out more Iron bloody Crosses, more like. Mind you, that Little Willie's always good for a laugh. Christ, with a son like that, who'd be a father? Should've drowned him at fucking birth. Can you imagine the poor old bleeding Kaiser's face when he popped out, fucking fish face? I'd hate to have been the one to tell him. 'Good news, Almighty One, it seems you've 'ad an 'addock!' I'd've thrown the bugger back."

"It's all that in-breeding," the Pagham man muttered, sorting his cards. "Pass."

"For Christ's sake, don't start on blue-bloods in front of bloody Bowden," Sarson warned. "He's a bloody expert on royalty; ain't that right, George? Jesus fuckin' Christ, did you shuffle these fuckers or what? Pass," Sarson moaned.

"Solo," George grinned.

"What, again?!"

- CHAPTER FORTY EIGHT -

On January 19th. a massive explosion ripped apart an ammunitions factory and nine hundred homes in London's Silvertown. In Ashleigh, thirty miles away; dinner plates rattled, dogs barked.

In the Barley Mow the suspension of Official Bulletins, barring a national emergency, was met with indifference, although the Government's proposal to conscript boys of fourteen and over into cadet corps led to some heated debates.

"Couldn't be plainer; they're just going to let it go on and on. Bloody glad I was born when I was; another couple of years and they'd be after me and all," Amos Harris said dolefully.

"I wouldn't count your chickens, Amos," Arthur Bowden told him. "They say the call-up's going to be sixteen to sixty soon. Reckon that Old Bill bloke's got it about right with that new cartoon of his."

"What one's that?"

"Bill and his mate Bert, is it, or Alf? One or t'other. Anyway, they're mulling over conscription, see. 'How long you up for,' Bill says. 'Seven Years,' the other tells him, all glum like. 'You're lucky,' Bill says, 'I'm duration.'"

"Well, I hope this new bread's not for the duration. It's full of bloody bits."

"Don't mind it, myself. At least it's got a bit of taste; better than that white ruddy stuff."

"It's all down to the government taking it over."

"And not before time. It was them demonstrations in London what did it and it's still not right," Arthur Treadwell joined the conversation. "There's us, all scrimp and scrape, while them with money hogs all the butter. Share and share alike, it should be. If things is short, all should go without. Have you tried to buy an egg recently? There ain't none; and them that's got 'em's charging an arm and a leg."

"Well, it don't make much odds, what with the miners on strike, we wouldn't have enough coal to cook it with even if we had one," Amos Harris sank deeper into dudgeon. "I don't know what the world's coming to, I'm damned if I do."

Over in Little Eastleigh, Laura physically retreated into the mental isolation that had stayed with her since Christmas, a bout of 'flu her justification. In reality it was no more than a bad cold, but with a baby on the way, De'Ath advised Scott and Agatha to keep their distance, thus ensuring the solitude in which despondency could incubate.

Laura had no reason to recover, no motivation to make the effort. Her evaluation of life was the sum of her summer assessment; she had no one, she needed no one. Even Scott and Agatha's good mornings and goodnights became intrusive. She kept her cold going, faking a temperature and a cough as necessary, longing only to hear the door close behind them each morning. Her father left at seven thirty after the pump boy had been, Agatha at eight, determined to enjoy one last term of teaching before pregnancy enforced her confinement. Mrs. Humphrey, the new 'daily', cleaned from nine 'til noon three days a week. Apart from that, Laura had the house to herself.

Defiantly, she continued to sleep nude; it had become a symbol of her insularity. The coal famine had minimal effect on the Scotts; they had plenty of trees to fell and wood from the yard. Laura's room was kept comfortably warm. She would slip into her nightdress when she woke in the morning to avert a tantrum when her father came in to make up the fire, but, other than that and slinging something on when Mrs. Humphrey's was about, she didn't bother. She even bared all behind the postman's back one morning, just for the hell of it.

A psychiatrist may have diagnosed a yearning for attention; Laura told herself it was contempt for bastards like Anthony and her Uncle Broadbent, for peeping-Tom pump boys and leering postmen. Then, one frosty morning, she heard Agnew arrive with the bread. She answered him from her father's window, wrapped in her dressing gown.

"Leave it inside the door, will you? It is open."

The old man gave her a quizzical look. Had he seen more than he should? She toyed with the idea of repeating her postal performance as he plodded back to his van. Instead she went downstairs to consume a slice while the bread was still digestible; by teatime it would be like solidified sawdust.

The loaf stood in a basket in the hall, Agnew's basket.

'That was nice of him,' she thought, careless of her dressing gown slipping from her shoulders as she stooped to pick it up, until the clump of boots on the step cast her in stone. Her heart thumped, primed for the knock, then beat into a frenzy as the door swung open.

"Miss Scott!" Agnew stood on the threshold, eyes bulging. "I'm sorry, Miss, really I am. I, er..." He span round. "I went to get some paper to stand the bread on. I need the basket, see. Not that the floor's dirty or nothing, I don't mean that. I do beg your pardon."

Laura remained rooted, unable even to blink.

Agnew arrested himself in mid-turn.

"Yes, well, I'd... er... I'd best be getting along. I'll fetch it another time."

Laura was only vaguely aware of the van pulling away. For long minutes she stared disbelievingly at the door, still half open, then at the bread in the basket, while the cold stole into her kidneys and finally shivered her back to her senses.

Dear God! Why hadn't she put her dressing gown on properly? If the pump boy had seen her at the window, or even the postman, she could have thought up some excuse, but here by the front door and by Agnew of all people? What on earth would she tell her father?

It was the Spencer nightmare all over again, only ten times worse. In Spencer's case, she'd been able to rely on his discretion, but Agnew was sure to blab.

"Please God, tie his tongue in knots, give him amnesia, laryngitis, anything, just please don't let him tell anyone."

By morning, Laura's 'flu would be back with a vengeance. Also by morning,

'Agnew's eyeful' would be all round the village.

* * * * *

Scott had been warned what to expect. It was the first film of its kind ever made, much of it shot as it happened, the rest re-enacted on Salisbury Plain.

"My wife wants to see it; her brother was there."

"I wouldn't advise it, Harold; it's a bit grizzly," Colonel Simpson had told him. "The Government thought it might boost morale, but I'm afraid it's rather backfired."

Scott had tried to talk Agatha out of it, using Laura's relapse as an excuse, but Laura had insisted they go. Even so, he'd been loath to leave her, she'd looked dreadful. He'd call De'Ath again in the morning.

The lights dimmed, the audience settled, the pianist played the overture, the title flickered onto the screen; 'The Battle of the Somme.' He took Agatha's hand.

How many eyes in how many theatres searched for a loved one, as Agatha's did, among the boys swinging along, thumbs-up and smiling, on their way up the line? How many hearts leapt, only to fall, deeper in sorrow, at mistaken identity? How many grasped the 'might-have-been' straw of celluloid immortality?

Scott took in the stockpile of shells marked, 'To Willie with compliments,' the galvanised gunners, stripped to the waist, loading and firing, and every one some mother's son and every gun some mother's nightmare; the earth erupting in spumes, yet, from farther away, looking barely like raindrops, sporadically bursting in the middle of nowhere; hardly the hurricane of newspaper proportions.

How many, like him, could scarcely equate these dirt piled ditches with the showpiece trenches in Kensington Gardens or Elmsford's own park, with their symmetry, sandbags and duckboarded sumps? How many noticed the biscuit tin patches? How many felt the weight of the packs? How many felt the fear in the faces, the cramping of muscles, the tautness of nerves?

How the skin prickled, how the blood chilled, as cold as the sweat in the palm, on the lip, as the piano strings hummed into sonic suspension and the caption came up; 'Zero Hour'.

Over they go, walking, not running, as if to a match, as if to the pub. Gasps as they fall, stunned realisation; this is no Chaplin, no Griffith production.

A soiled, crumpled Tommy, slumped in a traverse. "He's dead!" someone screams, while, up in the Midlands or some northern town, a horrified mother, or sister, or lover stares in disbelief at this face so familiar.

The wounded on stretchers are carried away past haggard survivors, and there, in the theatre, their families watch, dazed and bewildered, struck dumb beyond sorrow.

'The End;' yes it was, no more illusions, the end of the World.

* * * * *

Mrs. Bowden was hurt by 'Agnew's Eyeful'. She doubted whether Scott or even

Miss Cooper knew, those closest were always the last to hear. As Richard's school teacher, Agatha would always be 'Miss Cooper' to Beatrice, or 'Miss Cooper that was.'

Accosted with the gossip, Beatrice had immediately sprung to Laura's defence, even accusing Agnew of lying, although Laura being caught in her birthday suit, albeit midmorning and in the hallway, hardly ranked a spitting spark in the current firestorm of village scandal. Two girls had fallen pregnant to soldiers, one of them, Agnes Treadwell, married with a husband at the front.

Arthur was surprised that Beatrice took it so much to heart. "I don't know why you're taking on so. It weren't as if she was doing nothing. No one's accusing her; it's only by chance he saw her."

"Dirty old man. Shouldn't've gone in uninvited. I'm in two minds to report him to the authorities," was Beatrice's vitriolic reply.

"Don't be daft, woman. Anyway, he was invited."

The exchanges went on for days.

"How would you like it, if someone walked in on you like that, when you was in the tub?"

"Who said she was in the tub?"

"Well, she must have been, stands to reason. I don't know what all the fuss is about, really I don't. You'd think they'd have something better to do than gloat over a young girl's misfortune."

"You're the one who's making a fuss, mother. Sooner you let it pass, sooner there'll be an end to it." After more than a week, Arthur was fed up to the teeth with the subject. "Anyway, they've got a proper bathroom in that house and it's upstairs. Don't know what kind of bath she'd be taking in the hall, 'less she was planning on popping out for a birdbath." He couldn't resist it.

"Well you don't know everything, Arthur Bowden. Harold Scott might have had another bathroom put in; you're not the only plumber round here. Besides, she might have been taking a bath by the kitchen fire, the old fashioned way, specially in this weather. I won't have such things said about our Laura. That Agnew's to blame. He ought to be locked up, and so should you, the way you're talking. You should be ashamed of yourselves, the whole lot of you," she included the entire village.

"Facts is facts, mother."

"Well it's easy to see who's side you're on, Arthur Bowden. After all Harold Scott's done for you. There's plenty of others he could have asked, just as desperate for work. I'd've thought the least our Laura deserves is a bit of loyalty."

"Look, can we eat our dinner in peace?" Any allusion to work and money stuck in Arthur's gullet. Times were hard. He dug his fork into another potato. "Ain't right to talk of such things in front of the children. 'Sides, she ain't 'our Laura' no more, so let's just drop it, shall we? I've had enough, really I have."

Elizabeth had learned to sit silently through the daily argument. She'd poked her nose in when the news had first broken and had it bitten off. She was the last one to pass judgement, she'd been told in no uncertain terms. She'd only spoken in

Laura's defence, but, to Beatrice, support from Elizabeth was as tainting as tar and feathers. Nevertheless, an intervention was called for.

"Government coal wagon came round this morning; one and eight a hundredweight. Bit better than that thieving Brundle. And there was a letter from George."

"Oh, yes, how is he?" Arthur asked.

"Says he's fine. Got the latest parcel alright and glad of it he was, too. Things is very tight, apparently, and it's perishing cold, much colder than here, with nothing but a blanket to cover them at night. He says they do a bit of work and the Germans pay them for it, but then take it back off them for a film show. Says they have to go, all about how the Germans are winning the War. Says it's good for a laugh and they all gets into trouble. Huh, wish I could afford to go to the pictures."

"That's our George, chip off the old block," Bowden puffed proudly. "Perhaps I'll have a gander at it tonight, if I may. Good that he's alright. Nothing from Richard, I s'pose?"

"Not for three weeks or more. I do hope he's alright."

Arthur had given his wife something else to worry about.

* * * * *

Sarah had expected to scrub floors, clean lavatories and empty bedpans and bottles; what she'd never imagined was the filth and foulness, the lice and fleas, the writhing maggots, the ghastliness of gangrene and, worst of all, those riveting eyes. Watching stumps being dressed, wounds being drained, that was bad enough, but at least the patient was recognisably human. This man was no longer so. The remnants of flesh had been stretched and stitched over what remained of his facial structure, with apertures left for breathing and liquid diet. It was the most horrific injury she had ever seen.

"I'll be as gentle as I can," the Sister told him, telling Sarah more irately to hold the tray steady.

When the surgery had healed, a mask would be fitted, cold and expressionless, a sculptured coffin of a pre-war photograph, through which the eyes could stare, as they were staring now, from the grave.

He stretched out a hand. A crumpled photo lay on his locker, a portrait of a boy, perhaps nineteen or twenty, very handsome in his uniform.

He grunted like a hog.

Sarah broke down.

"Miss Jameson; leave the ward at once."

An arm reached out, but could not grasp her shadow.

* * * * *

Elizabeth had put the children to bed. Arthur seemed in a good mood, he'd smiled over George's film show, chuckled even; now was the time.

"I've got myself a job, Dad; munitions in Rayntree."

Arthur's eyes narrowed. "That's twelve-hour shifts, ain't it? And who's gonna look after the kiddies, as if I need to ask?"

"Mum said she wouldn't mind."

Beatrice knitted on, uncomfortably. Arthur returned to George's letter.

"Army allowance not good enough, then," he queried coldly.

"No, it ain't, Dad, not if the house is going to get fixed."

"I've already said I'll help with that."

It was an offer they both knew Arthur couldn't meet.

"It pays two pounds ten a week, and you can double that with overtime. I'd be daft not to take it."

It was more than Arthur was making, a lot more most weeks. Resentment added its payload to animosity, turning his chilliness to frost.

"And that's the reason, is it, the money?"

"Of course it's the reason. Why else would I be doing it?"

Arthur only looked at her. He'd long ago negated her threats of blackmail, the scandal over her Cameronian had seen to that. "Suppose you know you'll end up looking like a canary?"

"'T'ain't that bad, Dad. Besides, I'd be doing my bit and, as I says, we need the money. When George comes home, I want him to have a home to come to."

"Really," Arthur grunted caustically.

"And what's that supposed to mean?"

"I think you know."

Elizabeth had been expected this. She met it head on.

"Alright, I made a mistake, I admit it. But I ain't going to make no more, I swear. With George and the kids I got too much to lose."

"A mistake? Is that what you call it?" The ice cap erupted. "Didn't give a toss for them then, did you, long as you were getting your end away? Suppose that's what you're hoping for in this here factory of yours."

"Arthur!" Beatrice objected.

"Well, it's bloody right! And, as for you, I'm amazed you could fall for it. Fixing the house, my arse. I've never heard such codswallop. It's not George she's bothered about, or the kiddies, it's filling that gaping great hole between her legs, and if that ain't the truth, I don't know what is."

"Really, Arthur!"

"Jesus Christ!" Arthur stormed out, slamming the door behind him.

Elizabeth's face crumpled. "I ain't, mum, honest I ain't."

Beatrice spared herself from hypocrisy. "Look, leave it to me. He's got a lot on his mind at present. He could do with some help and there's none to have; he's losing more work than he's getting. Give him time; he'll come round."

- CHAPTER FORTY NINE -

The Essex were enjoying a hard-earned rest. Their billets were as atrocious as the weather, the worst in living memory, but, to men delivered from hell, the dilapidated barns and rat infested cellars were heaven indeed, the arctic conditions a minor discomfort. Even their urine froze, as did their wet hair when they boisterously bathed for the first time in weeks, in huge brewery vats, ten to a tub, while their clothes were stoved and fumigated. What did they care? For a few hours they would be clean and louse free.

Richard was happier still, so happy he was singing at the top of his voice in the driving sleet, on his way to a refresher course at Flexicourt, some thirty miles behind the lines. He'd thought Smylie had been pulling his leg, it had seemed impossible, yet here they were, he and Rowe, on the open-topped double-decker requisitioned from the National Bus Company, picking up others on the way. Spirits soared as each kilometre took them further from the firing line.

"Take me back to dear old Blighty,
Put me on a train to London town......"

Past supply columns, artillery horse lines, Red Cross Camps, ammunition dumps and, finally, within shooting distance of Army H.Q. itself, the bus trundled on into a landscape unravaged by war. Over huddled roofs, the spire of Amiens Cathedral threaded the clouds. Four whole weeks; like school summer holidays, they promised eternity.

Two officers had been chosen from each battalion, representing, it seemed, the entire army. To his great joy, Richard found Chapman, his old History Master, among them. However, where, for others, the course was by way of an unofficial reward, for Chapman it was the opposite. He'd been found too inclined to question the wisdom of glorious annihilation by his regimental adjutant, who'd dispensed with his services and, despite his age, assigned him front line duty, only to have him returned to H.Q. for the selfsame reason. If an example was to be made, Chapman would be it.

The bayonet Major gave him hell, sarcastically deriding his efforts at putting on the 'killing face' and howling like a Banshee. The demonstrating sergeant was a picture of well-rehearsed frightfulness; Chapman, by comparison, more resembled Charlie Chaplin at his most comically inept. However, thanks to a love of cricket, he was an adept thrower of Mills Bombs, the benefits of which, as a far more practical weapon of trench warfare, he took pains to point out, much to his instructors' annoyance. He became the bane of their lives in the classroom, they of his in the field. On face value, it seemed a fair exchange, but instructors were there to instruct, not to be lectured on the error of their ways.

He could have toed the line, as he freely admitted he'd done during his initial training, but now, having witnessed the futile slaughter for himself, the mentor of the school debating society could not let stupidity pass unchallenged.

For two weeks the class enjoyed the furore, until they assembled one morning to find their champion gone, returned to his unit. Richard missed him; Chapman had reminded him of home, the serenity of school, the tranquillity of the tree. He knew he should write to his family, he'd been neglecting them, they would be worried, but the truth was he'd run out of lies. Now he could tell them about Chapman.

Richard had looked forward to their nightly discussions. Despite being the man's pupil for five years, it had never occurred to him that Chapman was married with children. But there they'd all been, in the well-thumbed family portrait, staring seriously into the camera. Still there'd been something mischievous in the young girl's eyes. She was thirteen, Chapman had told him; his sons were eleven and six. His wife remained the apple of his eye.

"Constance takes after her," he'd boasted. "She'll be a real beauty when she's older."

Now the proud father had been hustled off in disgrace for daring to question the hallowed Army bible.

"The Infantry Training Manual, rather like the Old Testament, was drawn up before the coming of the new Messiah, in this case the machine gun," he'd told his instructor. "The Gattling gun and its successors have been demonstrating the weapon's potential for a quarter of a century, but, like the prophets, the message has been ignored. We are now paying the price for that ignorance."

It was a pity about Chapman.

Richard found the course re-humanising. In the trenches, he hadn't given much thought to his 'Officer and Gentleman' status; here class played its full part and Rowe was there to see to his every need.

If having a manservant remained a novelty to Richard, Rowe knew when he was well off. Being a batman definitely had its perks, like four weeks away from the firing line with nothing to do but ensure his officer looked spick and span and brew the odd pot of tea. Even in the line, he was excused all other duty, barring emergencies. No, the Army had snatched him from Bollingbroke's department store and made him a batman and 'lucky' Bowden's batman he was more than happy to be.

Wrapped in his greatcoat, Richard braved the thigh deep snowdrifts to roam the countryside in his free time, sometimes in company, sometimes alone. He imagined what a joy it must be in summertime with its tall poplars, lush elms and rippling streams, its barley and beet fields awash with poppies and cornflowers. Such thoughts led him, inexorably, to the woods and wheat fields of Ashleigh, and to Laura.

He had a small room to himself, slept in a proper bed, ate proper food, wore clean clothes, bathed every day and shaved in hot water. Most blissfully of all, he was able to defecate in private.

His new found freedoms lifted the repression of the trenches. Here he could fulfil his fantasies freely, fuelled by a nightly magic lantern show in the mess, where erotica was projected life-size onto a white bed sheet. In the light of Spencer's photographs, it was easy to picture Laura up there; in his more masochistic moments, he even found the idea perversely stimulating. Even Chapman, for all his sobriety, had enjoyed the titillation before his removal. One or two sophisticates aspired to lofty indifference, but few left before the end.

First among Richard's new confederates was 'Thomas of the Tank Corp', at twenty-one, older than Richard and a full lieutenant. He reminded Richard of Langham, a happy-go-lucky mask belying his true depth. Richard had never seen a tank. As Thomas had also arrived by 'bus, he was unable to satisfy his friend's curiosity, although, on Chapman's dismissal, he had threatened to fetch his contraption and flatten the camp and 'all the cretinous bastards in it'.

Thomas's flippancy was sometimes funny, often appalling, but his innate knack of delivery defused even the most slanderous jibe. When a subaltern, in the grip of patriotic fervour, trumpeted his English pride, Frank Thomas took up the goading rod.

"The best thing I can say about being English is that it makes me glad I'm Welsh."

"Well, someone has to be!" The retort brought the expected laughter.

"Now there's lovely for you," Frank gave them his best colloquial. "Jealously will get you nowhere, old boy. English, for heaven's sake? Jolly good, what-what, stiff upper lip and pass the kippers. And, as for the Scots, Och Aye th' noo! Could you image? And I don't think I'd wanna be Irish with all that shillelaghin', or Canadian, or South African or any of those other colonial types." Each nationality was delivered with the appropriate accent, ending with Australian. "Send 'em all to Sinai, that's what I say, let the old Hebrews sort 'em out with all their weeping and wailing, prostrations to Allah and what-have-you. None of that in a Welsh Chapel."

"They're Arabs, Thomas, for your information. The Hebrews haven't lived there for centuries," someone corrected him.

"Hebrews, Arabs, they're all the same to me. They cut off their willies, for Christ's sake. They say it's the sand, but it wouldn't surprise me if they weren't all Freemasons."

His expansion of the cutting edge whipped a protest from the billiard table.

"Sorry, old man, didn't recognise you without your apron. Must be a staff wallah, that's how they get the job, you know, a nod and a wink, funny handshakes in high places. Then there's those Haggis bashers," he turned his attention to some Highlanders at the bar. "All that whisky makes 'em fart so much they have to wear skirts to alleviate the pong. Put them in the line with a bellyful of Haggis, a bottle of Scotch and a strong wind behind 'em and they'd choke the jolly old Boche to death. Reckon that's why they started using Gas - retaliation. And loud! Heard the reports back in Blighty. Thought it was the guns, but it was only the old Jocks letting off!"

"More effective than your bloody tanks, Thomas," came the retort. "Might as well hit the Hun over the head with that leek of a prick of yours for all the discomfort you cause him."

"Ah, I would if I could, old man. Can't get close enough, that's the bloody trouble, keep breaking down. Oh, well, roll on duration. I believe it's my shout. Orderly! Drinks all round. He's paying," he pointed to the Scot.

* * * * *

Hettie Jameson was thirty yards down the road, hiding behind her umbrella, when the black Maria pulled up outside her house. Thanking God for the telegram stuffed in her pocket, she hurried on, slipping and sliding on the snow and ice, to warn Fanny Beckwith.

The police had beaten her to it.

"Damn him," she cursed the turncoat.

A string of deserters had been sheltered since the night of the rally. Stupidly, one had gone home. He'd been caught. With his life at stake, it was only a matter of time before the man turned King's Evidence, but there'd been other men in the system, other lives at risk; the cell had hung on. Now the members were being rounded up.

Hettie knew she'd been under surveillance. Luckily the man had stood out a mile with his walrus moustache, brown suit and bowler hat, like something grubby out of Sherlock Holmes. He'd skulked in the gateway across the street. He'd been easy to distract and lose when necessary, and to pick up again on the premise 'better the devil you know.' Now that particular game was over.

She swapped hands, carpetbag for umbrella, and walked on, intent on catching a bus to Rayntree, in the hope that Sarah could hide her. The train would have been quickest, but, with only up line or down line, far more vulnerable. Buses left in all directions and the police couldn't be everywhere at once, especially in this weather.

She was fully aware that her 'Inspector Lastrade' wasn't witless enough to have missed Sarah moving out and may have tracked her, but that was a risk Hettie would have to take, everyone else she knew would be either under suspicion or under arrest, except Sarah's friend Laura, and she could hardly call on her, by all accounts her father was Gladstone incarnate.

Nevertheless, as she ploughed on to the bus station, the very real possibility that Sarah may be under observation made her reconsider. Laura had been as keen as mustard, at one time. Obviously she couldn't hide her, but she might know someone who could. At the very least she'd be able to get a message to Sarah.

Hettie racked her brains for Laura's surname and then the name of her village. She knew it wasn't far; Sarah had been there the previous summer. Laura was bound to be home; the Priory was closed due to the weather. If only she could remember.

'Ashleigh' emboldened itself on the bus station's timetable.

"Can I be of any assistance, madam?"

The bus inspector's presence threw her completely.

"Buses to Ashleigh?"

"Stand two, madam, half past the hour, number fifty-two, although there's no way of telling whether it'll run or not; the snow's bad out that way. You'll need to get off at Ashtree corner; the Rayntree bus is the only one that goes through the actual village and that's definitely not running. The road's impassable. Belsham's completely cut off, drifts six foot high. The Army's doing their best to clear it, but I don't hold out much hope. Seems a bit daft to me, sending the roadmen to France to do the Army's job, and have the army over here doing theirs, but there you are."

For Hettie a twenty minute wait, even if the bus ran on time, was asking for trouble; the police might be slow but they weren't total imbeciles.

"How far is it, exactly, to Ashleigh I mean?" She cursed the clipped Afrikaans accent that surfaced under stress.

"Five miles, madam, straight down that road there," he pointed to a junction. "There's taxis at the railway station. You might get one of them to take you, though I wouldn't put money on it as things are."

She could tell he was suspicious. Women spies were popular fiction. She should have stayed away from the bus terminal; she should have kept her mouth shut.

"Thank you, I'll wait for the bus."

She could feel the inspector's eyes tracking her across the street and into the coffee shop. She took the window seat. Abruptly, he returned to his office. Did he have a telephone in there? Was he calling the police?

"Yes, Madam?" the waitress asked.

Hettie's mouth was parched, her extremities frozen, but she couldn't take the risk.

"Oh, dear, I'm so sorry, I seem to have forgotten my purse. So sorry."

She hurried out, scolding herself again for drawing attention to herself. How could she be so stupid?

Sense told her that Ashleigh was now out of the question, but, with the rest of the county cut off, she was left no alternative. At least she knew its general direction. She would just have to follow her nose and stay off the road wherever possible. If Stanley could find Livingston, Hettie could track down Laura. Deepest Essex was hardly darkest Africa, blizzard or no blizzard.

Four hours later, Hettie sat slumped on a stile, powerless to save herself from the man wading towards her through the snow. She'd taken the first lane she'd come to off the main road, and then the first footpath going in the right direction. Sheltered by hedgerow, it had escaped the main drifts and she'd made good progress, until the way had opened out into a sea of white. She'd kept going, stepping higher and higher as the snow deepened, her sodden clothing sapping her strength, until her knees had buckled under her.

The man drew near.

"My dear woman, you look all in."

He was tall and well muffled, and too young to be out of uniform.

"I'm looking for Ashleigh," she managed to ventriloquize through frozen lips.

"It's just beyond those trees. Are you looking for someone in particular?"

This time her tongue succumbed to the cold. She shivered intensely.

"Dear lady, are you all right?"

"Quite, thank you," she willed the words out. "Do excuse me."

She forced her limbs to respond, but they couldn't hold her. He caught her, taking her weight.

"We must get you to a fire immediately. Allow me."

She longed to give herself up to this man's well meaning.

"I c..couldn't possibly," she heard herself say.

"But you must, please. Have no fear; you will be quite safe. My name is Soames, I'm the vicar here. Now, let's get some warmth into you, otherwise I fear I'll be commending your spirit to the Almighty."

* * * * *

She was the first thing Richard saw through the swirling smoke, so much like Laura it was unnerving.

"I told you," Thomas smiled. "I don't know why you'd want to waste your last night in the damned mess staring at apparitions, when you can have the real thing. Let's grab that table, before someone else does."

They made it in the nick of time.

"If you think Janine's pretty, you should see her sister, an absolute corker. Reminds me of a girl I once had the pleasure of at Chepstow races, except she was Welsh, of course. Ma'moiselle," Thomas called over.

"Une minute, monsieur!" The waitress waved back.

"What are you having?"

Richard looked at the menu. "I'm not exactly fluent. How do you ask for a proper steak, as opposed to the horse variety?"

"Escargot."

"Very funny."

Janine arrived.

"Bonjour, monsieur. Qui voulez vous, s'il vous plait?"

Richard shrank into short trousers and a hand-me-down shirt, oversize enough to swallow him and his French. He blushed profusely.

"Eh bien. Et vous, monsieur?" She turned to Thomas.

He gave his order. "Red wine all right?"

"Fine," Richard mumbled.

"Et maintenant, monsieur?" The waitress returned to him.

"Le plat de jour," he managed to enunciate.

"Tres bon, monsieur," she teased him before pocketing her order book and heading for the kitchen.

"Did you see the smile she gave you? I'd say your luck was in, old boy."

"Frank, I made a complete arse of myself."

"Well it seems to have worked. Play your cards right and you could be sneaking back to camp just in time for reveille."

The food was brought. Richard's looked like a ladle of stew on a pile of ants' eggs.

"Q'est que ce?" His memory conjured from the depths, his confidence boosted.

"Cous-cous," Janine told him, "le plat de jour."

"Et q'est que ce cous-cous?"

Janine's explanation was pure, spellbinding, gobbledegook.

Someone called her name.

"Une moment, messieur!" She answered. "Eh bien. C'est tres bon, monsieur, le specialite de la maison. Bon appetite."

Richard kept track of her through the meal, jealous when she favoured others, joyous when she favoured him, until the estaminet filled and he lost sight of her. A group of Australians commandeered the piano. Richard knew the song, Jerome Kern's 'They didn't believe me,' but not the version he was about to hear.

"This is for all the staff officer's in the room," one of the Aussies announced.

> *"And when they ask us, how dangerous it was.*
> *Oh, we'll never tell them; no, we'll never tell them.*
> *We spent our pay in some café,*
> *And fucked wild women, night and day,*
> *'Twas the cushiest job, there ever was.*
> *And when they ask us, and they're certainly gonna ask us,*
> *The reason why we didn't win the Croix de Guerre,*
> *Oh, we'll never tell them; no, we'll never tell them,*
> *There was a front but damned if we knew where!"*

"Damned impertinence," Richard heard from behind. "Need shooting, the whole damned lot of 'em. They were just the same in South Africa. Why Haig ever agreed to waive the death penalty for them I'll never know. Worst day's work he ever did. Treat scum like scum and they'll respect you for it. Always have, always will. Bad show."

Richard had seen Australians in action; he knew their worth. He saw Joe Crutchley blindfolded and tied to a post.

"The telegrams do say, don't they Bowdie?"

Richard glared at the red collar flashes, at the Major's insignia.

"Are you all right, old man?" Thomas broke into his brainstorm. "Here, have another drink."

The Major lapsed into banality, demanding Janine's attention. Something went on, Richard didn't see what. Thomas warned him off with a puckered brow; Janine seemed to handle it, if not to the Major's satisfaction;

"Damned slut."

It was a while before she came by again. The Major's speech was slurred.

"Come here, my lovely..."

He grabbed her round the waist. Janine resisted. It became a wrestling match over the back of Richard's chair. His anger exploded.

"Get off her, you prick!" Seizing the major's arm, he twisted it until the man let go. Thomas hustled Janine away.

The Major was incensed. "What the hell do you think you're playing at? I could have you shot for that!"

"It was completely unintentional, Major," Thomas sprang to Richard's defence. "He was merely trying to mediate."

"He damned near had my arm off."

"I'm sure it wasn't meant."

"Yes it damned well was," Richard convicted himself.

"You see; he even has the gall to admit it. Arrest that man."

"Oh, surely not, Major. My uncle would have me sent down for insanity. You probably know him, his name is Gough, General Gough."

The name made an immediate impact.

"But this young pup assaulted me."

"Oh, I'd hardly call it that; after all, you were leaning all over the poor fellow. Heat of the moment, and all that."

"Oh, all right," the Major capitulated. "Just get him out of my sight. Stiles is my name, young man, Major J. D. Stiles. Cast it in stone; if our paths ever cross again, I won't be so lenient."

Thomas hustled Richard out. A voice whispered from the shadows, Janine's voice. With a warning to take care, Thomas kept going, making the decision for him.

It was no night of lust, but a night of love. It could have been Laura and there were times when, in the heat of passion, Janine and Laura were one and the same. Richard's only confusion was that he could love both at the same time, for, if not as deeply, he most definitely loved Janine, so the moment told him. It was the final confirmation that whatever had passed between Laura and Spencer would be of no consequence now.

He slipped from her bed in dawn's palest light, furthering the synthesis. He bribed the guard at the camp gates with his last shilling. He'd got back just in time. No sooner had he kicked the snow from his boots than Rowe was there with his shaving water.

The last roll was called, the course was ended, the men dispersed to their units, Richard with a bout of lovesickness, Thomas with a "dose of the clap, old man. Must've been that prossie in Amiens the other night. What the hell? Here today, gone tomorrow. Reckon it's a Blighty one?"

"You never know your luck, Frank, though more likely Rouen and a six inch needle in the bum, 'returned to duty, 'A. 1.' By the way, General Gough?"

"Pure inspiration, old chap."

"So you're not related?"

"Well, we could share the same ancestry somewhere down the line. Who's to say?"

"Well, let's hope our Major Stiles, or whatever his name is, never finds out or he'll have both our guts for garters."

CHAPTER FIFTY

'I'd drained the hot water to take a bath, added too much cold and nipped downstairs to top it up with the kettle, thinking Agnew had gone.'

Such was the story Laura had concocted overnight. It had sounded plausible enough and, by the time the scandal had reached Scott's ears, she'd been too ill to be seriously cross-examined, at one stage hospitalisation had been touch and go. But she'd been well cared for, Scott had hired a day-nurse and Sarah had come over on her days off, catching the bus to Ashleigh and walking the remaining two miles.

The police had tracked Sarah down, much to her embarrassment, looking for her mother. Two weeks later, a letter had arrived from London, saying Hettie was safe and well and that she wasn't to worry. Sarah had said her mother could rot in hell for all she cared, but her relief had been as evident as her overriding elation; she'd fallen in love with a doctor and found that love reciprocated.

The prolonged frost, so unwelcome to others through that bitter, coal-rationed winter, had sealed their courtship. Night after precious night, they'd gone skating in the moonlight on Gosling Lake, a local beauty spot. Now he'd been sent to France.

As for Laura and 'Agnew's eyeful,' Truelove's had lost a valued customer and Agnew his job, until, despite the allure of window cleaning, he'd offered Scott his shamefaced apologies.

"I'm sorry, Mr. Scott, I had one too many in the Barley Mow and it just came out. I never would've said anything otherwise."

The whole episode had blown over, with the exception of one annoying legacy, a Peeping Tom. Only once was he more than a shadow, a contorted face pressed against the window, glimpsed by the nurse. Scott bought a full-grown Mastiff called Max; the spying ceased.

Laura and Max became inseparable. At night he was confined to an eiderdown on the kitchen floor, during the day he sprawled across Laura's bed, squashing her into a corner. He was well trained, never made a mess and obeyed instantly. Laura adored him and the dog her. Once she'd been allowed up to feed him, his devotion was absolute.

He was Laura's salvation. He was more than her protector, he was her canine confidant, always there for a consoling cuddle, a playful romp, her reassurance that, despite everything, all was right with the world. After Max's recruitment, Laura's was a rapid recovery.

Scott was overjoyed; in Max he'd stumbled on the answer to his prayers. He'd lost his Laura months before; now Max, the faithful guide dog, was leading her back.

Agatha shared his relief. She'd expected a reactionary period, but she hadn't imagined that it would threaten permanency and be so radical. She, alone, knew the effect Laura's personality change had had on Scott, whose health also began to improve.

For them all, Max, the healer, was the catalyst of a deeper happiness.

* * * * *

Richard had received temporary promotion in the field after the October decimation. As the Battalion was brought up to strength, his lieutenancy remained temporary; the C.O. considered the refresher course was reward enough.

He hadn't tried to contact Janine; he didn't want to make a fool of himself. Major Stiles still nagged at the back of his mind, but, with an offensive in the offing, he had more pressing concerns, not least the hero worship of Appleton, the boy earmarked to lead the Colonel's trench raid before Richard had opened his big mouth.

The kid had led a charmed life since then, thanks to his asthma. How he'd got through the gas hut, Richard hadn't the faintest idea. The M.O. had been all for sending him down, but the brave little sod, more afraid of his father's detestation than death, had pleaded to stay. Now, with zero hour fast approaching, he was badly in need of another bout of asthma to save him from the fray.

"Are they really just going to let it go on and on?" Appleton asked dejectedly, one evening in billets.

Richard shrugged. Rumours of a German peace proposal had been doing the rounds since December.

"They can't know what it's like. I know my father doesn't; he seems to think it's some kind of rugger match. 'Boot the old Boche into touch,' he tells me. If the Jerries are willing to talk, surely it's worth a try. Anything's better than this."

"Na-pooh the peace proposals," Richard grunted, his pencil working overtime in the fading light. Chapman had written to him, giving him what details he knew. Betman-Holveg had approached the Americans back in December; President Wilson and the Pope had approached the Allies. The offer had been rejected out of hand. Now, with German 'U' Boats sinking any vessel bound for Allied ports, including neutral American ships, in a desperate bid to starve the allies into submission before the Germans, themselves, starved, there would be no more talk of peace.

He finished his sketch of a sundry hung corner, webbing and holster, helmet and gas cape. 'I'm useless at portraits,' he'd excused himself, when Appleton had hinted. Rowe was the only sitter left alive.

He looked over at his companion; Langham would have liked this fresh faced youth, probably have loved him. He was all of eighteen, going on seventeen. 'Look who's talking,' Richard reminded himself.

"Care for some Game Pie?" A hamper arrived for Appleton fortnightly, direct from Fortnum and Mason's, filled with jellied chicken and hams, tinned kippers, oysters and Fortnum's famed fruitcake. "Just time for a bite before the working party."

If he wondered why Richard received no such essentials, he never asked. Perhaps he knew of Richard's background; perhaps he never gave it a thought. Before the War, he would never have met a grammar school boy, let alone shared his hamper with one.

"Thanks, but I'm afraid your pheasants, or whatever they are, are a bit too gamey for me." Richard's previous partaking had left him with the raging runs. "I'll have a bit of that fruit cake, though, if there's any on offer."

"Do you think it'll be all right, going over I mean?" Appleton asked, slicing the Dundee.

"Piece of cake," Richard smiled, toasting his pun with the same. "We'll probably get reserve. We led last time."

"Only, well, you know."

"You'll be all right."

"I just hope my damned chest holds up, or people really will think I'm swerving."

"No one thinks that."

"Gower does. He told me, if I have one more attack, he'll appoint me 'Officer in Charge of Baths' on a permanent basis, and you know what that means."

Yes, Captain Gower was proving to be a right haemorrhoid and, if the 'Bombay boy buggering' rumours were true, was rather partial to curly haired Davids like innocent, blithely unaware and, thus, frustratingly unresponsive Appleton.

"I wouldn't worry too much about Gower, if I were you," Richard assured him, "at least, not as far as your asthma's concerned. Smylie thinks you deserve a medal simply for sticking it, I know that for a fact. If our illustrious Captain had what you've got, he'd be on the first boat home."

"Perhaps I should offer him some fruitcake," Appleton grinned impishly.

Richard smiled to himself. "Coals to Newcastle, old chap. I think you'll find he is one, or something of the sort. Come!" He answered the knock at the door.

"Sergeant says to tell you the carrying party's ready, Sir," Appleton's Batman reported.

"Oh well," Appleton sighed, reaching for his winter warmer, "duty calls."

* * * * *

Elizabeth straightened her mop cap in the grime-streaked mirror. A copper fringe haloed her face, halfway to an icon.

"Here, you're one of us, now," Edie said.

"Nah, it's them lights."

"Yeh, but you're catchin' up, soon be as chinkie as the rest of us."

"Oh well, all in a good cause." She'd saved ten pounds already and bought the kids new clothes. She'd never had money of her own; she'd never had money at all. It was a new experience and one well worth canary skin and matching bedsheets. "Not like you. You look like the Angel Gabriel."

"Do you mind, I'm a woman," Edie complained.

"Well, she can hardly call you the Virgin Mary, can she," Sandra wisecracked, paving the way for Ethel's "More like Mary Magdalene in her prime."

"Don't tell her that; she thinks she's God's gift already."

"Jealousy'll get you nowhere," Edie retorted to all and sundry, prising her mouth

296

open to poke an abscess embedded stump.

"You ought to get that seen to," Elizabeth told her.

"Yeh, maybe I will; it's really giving me jip. Talking of God's gift, have you heard them toffs talk? What the hell are they doing here, I'd like to know? I'd've thought they had money enough."

"Doing their bit, ain't they. I notice old Bloomers ain't put *them* on the monkey machines, the old arse licker, oh no; and they got new leggings," Ethel moaned. "Bloody stuck up you-know-whats; our canteen not good enough for 'em, have to have one of their own."

"Just as well, the way they smoke," Edie observed. "Bleeding hell, talk about chimneys. And they have the cheek to go on about our gin. Here, pass the flask."

"It's a wonder they don't ask for their own toilets," Ethel said.

"Use the guvnors, don't they," Sandra told her. "Leastways, her royal highness does. Got her own lav paper and everything, proper stuff, epigrammed."

"Go on!"

"Straight up. I've seen her going in."

"Probably the Times. You knows what they calls that, don't you? The Thunderer! Very apt," Ethel tittered.

"Well, I've never known any of them use ours, have you?" Sandra continued. "Nah, too afraid of catching the crabs, and if anyone's got them it's her, the dirty cow. Our Annie was in service at her place before the War. Says she was always at it; she even had the stable boy."

"Takes after her father, then," Edie cackled. "He'd have anything on two legs, whatever their accoutrements."

"Whatever their whats? That's disgusting."

"This was before the War, mind. I was walking out with the under butler in those days, well, he was a footman really. And have you seen Lady Muck? Bloody chauffeur comes to pick her up."

"He never does?"

"I've seen it. And where does the ruddy petrol come from, I ask? If they wants to work here, they should bloody well slum it like the rest of us."

A smart rap on the door led to a smarter concealment of flask and tumblers.

"Come on, ladies, let's be having you!"

"You ain't having me, Briggsy, and that's a fact."

"Sssshhh, Edie, he'll hear you," Sandra warned, coating her face with flour and starch, the girls' only protection against the ravages of TNT.

"Nah; daft old bugger's deaf as a post, ain't you, Briggsy?"

"Not as deaf as I can't hear you. Now jump to it!"

They filed onto the workfloor. In half an hour the coughing would start, only not tonight.

"Christ Almighty!"

They were blasted back. Shell and machinery shattered into shrapnel; billowing smoke choked the lungs; sheets of corrugated iron crashed from the roof; blacked-out windows rained sharded glass; then stillness.

"Is anyone hurt?"

The splutterings of survival;

"Ethel? Sandra? How about you, Lizzie?"

"Yeh, I'm alright, Edie."

Screams from the benches; crying. A white-faced foreman, Briggs, appeared through the dissipating cordite.

"Back to the restroom, please, ladies. There's nothing you can do here; leave it to them as can."

The shell shocked survivors shuffled off, all except Elizabeth.

"Mrs. Bowden? Lizzie?"

She was staring straight past him, at someone's kidney.

- CHAPTER FIFTY ONE -

In the event, neither Appleton's health nor Richard's luck were put to the test. The planned offensive was pre-empted by a German withdrawal to the Hindenburg Line, an impenetrable defence system secretly constructed during the winter, some thirty miles to the rear.

The British followed cautiously through the destruction of a scorched-earth policy executed to Prussian perfection. Whole villages had been levelled, cellars booby-trapped, wells poisoned, the most innocent looking objects fatally primed, any intact stretch of road mined and blocked. It was the Allies' greatest gain since trench warfare began and, even more ironically, bloodless.

Richard stood on the old German parapet, looking back over the pockmarked morass that had been no-man's land. Burial parties, handkerchiefs tied bandit fashion, gas masks on to combat the stench, were interring the season's dead. Limbs came away in their hands, carcasses disintegrated. There was little left of some but a rag-wrapped skeleton.

'So many men, and for what?' Richard asked hopelessly. Was that paltry patch of waterlogged wasteland worth dying for? Some of those pathetic bundles were men of his own platoon. Sergeant Houseman was out there somewhere, not that he'd recognise him now. He blinked back the tears. Apart from Langham, he missed Spencer most of all, the company just wasn't the same without him. If only they'd waited, if only the bloody fools had waited.

He shrugged hopelessly. Oh, well, there was no use crying over spilt milk. The problem was that blood was somewhat thicker, it congealed in the memory. Perhaps whatever whisky the High Command drank acted as some kind of anti-coagulant, at least where conscience was concerned. If so, that stupid bloody major who'd prattled on about the death penalty must have imbibed by the barrel load.

Once more Joe Crutchley rose from the dead. Richard turned from the spectre and trudged after his men, but he'd never be able to leave the past behind.

* * * * *

In Ashleigh, March brought little meteorological respite. There was another Zeppelin scare and, with it, more invasion rumours. Once again the village echoed to marching feet; even the specials were called out, causing Arthur Bowden to lose two precious days' work. More disastrously still, he lost the helping hands of Amos Harris, who put his back out manhandling a roadblock.

A Ministry of National Service had been set up under Neville Chamberlain to rationalise civilian employment by matching the skills of its workforce with the demands of agriculture and industry. So far it had failed dismally. Those who'd escaped conscription were far too wary of being drafted into the Army to co-operate.

After two weeks, Arthur's application for a casual labourer remained unanswered. He desperately needed an extra pair of hands and the only hands available were female, hardly suitable for the kind of work he had on hand, replacing the doctor's sewage system. Propriety apart, the pipes weighed a ton; she would need to be an Amazon. But help he had to have; the bad weather had kept the Army in winter billets; there would be no repair work until May. This job was all that stood between him and the begging bowl.

He was cycling back from Elmsford one day, saddlebags laden with miscellaneous plumbing parts, when Scott pulled alongside in his new Standard. Arthur looked at it enviously; it was a real beauty.

"I'd offer you a lift, but I can't fit a bike on the back of this one."

"That's alright, Mr. Scott. Actually, it's not a lift I need, it's a man to do some lifting," Arthur bemoaned his predicament.

"Why don't you apply for a Prisoner of War? We've got a detachment working for us, and quite skilled some of them are, too."

"Wouldn't let me have just one, surely? I can see the sense when there's a parcel of them, but they'd have to have a guard just for him; be a bit of a waste. Anyway, I know they got our George out there working like a Trojan, but it don't seem right somehow."

"No guards, Arthur; they drop 'em off in the morning and pick 'em up again at night."

"What, don't they try to escape or nothing?"

"We've never had any trouble. They're just happy to be out of the cage for a while. If the Authorities suspect a particular man can't be trusted, they keep him locked up. I'd give it a go if I were you. I'll help with the application; I know the people to contact."

"It's worth a thought."

"Well, don't leave it too long."

* * * * *

"One, two, heave!"

George put his back into it, happy to stagger on an empty stomach and to suffer the soreness of a day's hard labour. His leg was almost healed. Now, with a bit of decent grub inside him when the next batch of Red Cross Parcels arrived, if they ever did, he'd be quite his old self, fit as a fiddle, if as scrawny as catgut.

The lookout's horn interrupted his joie de vivre.

"Clear the tracks!"

The locomotive lumbered into view, trailing trucks as far as the eye could see. The working party moved back. George lingered.

"Schnell! Schnell!"

"Alright, keep your hair on."

"Schnell!"

George would never know what motivated him, whether it was the muzzle prodded into the small of his back, the raised rifle butt, or simply a sudden, insane rapacity for freedom. Whatever the impulse, the next thing he knew he was clinging to the side of a coal truck, his legs dragging in the shale, looking back at the guard he'd bundled over.

'What the hell are you doing?' George's common sense cried, as the man scrambled to his feet and raised the alarm. George saw the rifle being levelled, heard the 'clang' of the bullet ricocheting off the ironwork, then felt the sparks of another burn his hand.

'Jesus Christ, George, you're a sitting fucking duck. Let go, you numskull, let go!'

He followed his own advice, falling away from the wagon's lethal wheels to tumble into the trackside drainage ditch. Soles thundered on sleepers; heels crunched on shale. He turned on his back, ready to greet his arresters with a grin. The same contorted face confronted him, the same raised rifle butt.

"No! Not my leg! Aaaahhhh!"

* * * * *

After talking it over with Beatrice and a lot of soul searching, Arthur accepted Scott's offer and Gunther Redden arrived at the yard. Redden was a man in his early twenties, six feet tall with muscles to match. His blond hair was closely cropped, but still there was an air of amiability about him. As Scott had said, he was dropped off in the morning and picked up at dusk.

However, too many village lives had been lost to Redden's countrymen for his employment to pass without comment.

"How could you do it, Arthur?" Sirus Tate asked. "There's your boy out there fighting the bastards and you here making friends with them. Don't make no sense. It's doing you no good, Arthur, no good at all."

"They've got my George out there doing hard labour, I don't see why we shouldn't put them to work here the same," was Bowden's well rehearsed reply. "He don't find me none too friendly, I can assure you."

Most gave Arthur the benefit of the doubt. Yet, as the days passed, he found his surliness towards his captive labourer increasingly pretentious. Redden was a hard worker in every respect, he'd already picked up a little English in camp and tried hard to converse and learn new words, especially the plumbing vocabulary. In the very fact that George was also a prisoner, there was a certain bond.

In their anonymity Bowden had been able to hate the Germans, but, face to face, he couldn't equate Redden with the leering, Picklehaubed Hun of the newspaper cartoons. Gradually he untied his tongue; he took a bit extra in his lunch pack; he shared a joke with the man and Redden's emotions when he talked stiltedly of his Rhineland home. Finally, he took him home for a meal.

The children were wide-eyed, Elizabeth flirty-eyed, Beatrice ungiving. She, too, had suffered village animosity. Despite what George said in his letters, she didn't believe a German could be like them. It would take more than a religiously bowed head over a table unaccustomed to Grace, especially in a foreign tongue, or heartfelt thanks in faltering English, to allay her suspicions.

Elizabeth had no such reservations. A back-fence fumble with her sixteen-year-old was all she'd been able to manage for months. At the factory there was only Briggs, and he was hardly God's gift. The skilled men were in a separate building and the management toffs in another world. Now her father-in-law had delivered a towering trunk of virility to her very doorstep. He could not have initiated a more tormenting torture. While she drooled into her stew, she crossed her legs in frustration.

However, Elizabeth wasn't the only girl with eyes for Redden. Cissy Brewer's gaze also dwelt longer than curiosity excused on Gunther's handsome head, if not with the same degree of carnality.

Cissy worked at the surgery as receptionist cum cleaner cum dispenser. Despite being the prettiest girl in the village, she'd never married, due partly to her acute shyness, but mainly to her widowed father's belligerence towards any man who came near her.

The dispensary window offered Cissy the perfect vantage for admiring Redden, as he toiled in the garden trench, although contact only came when she carried out the twice-daily refreshments. They spoke not a word, but each furtive glance produced a reciprocal blush. Then, one day, Arthur returned from a conflab with De'Ath to find Cissy and Gunther in happy conversation. Had Bowden realised earlier he might have taken umbrage; had he fathered a daughter he may well have done so now, but he already liked Redden, in any other circumstances they would have made a well matched pair; he kept his peace.

However, while Bowden embraced Gunther, if not in fellowship, at least in humanity, Tom Brewer plotted revenge. He knew nothing of his daughter's fraternisation; if he'd thought she'd so much as given Redden a drink he would have chained her to her bed on a diet of bread and water for days, and even that would have been only a minor multiplication of his hatred.

He'd never got over the loss of his son early in the War and Redden's arrival had brought the festering canker to a head. An eye for an eye, the bible said. His boy's guts had been spilled by a bayonet, he'd got the truth from Billy White, the boy invalided home with half a skull and now too simple to tell a lie. Well, he didn't have a bayonet, but Billy did, and he knew how to use it, one-handed or not. Big as Redden was, he would be no match for the two of them, not if they took him by surprise.

* * * * *

Hettie watched Sarah get off the bus and walk up the lane towards Little Eastleigh. She longed to follow, to call out. Instead she remained motionless and whispered her farewells; she was returning to Africa.

Others in her circle had been gaoled for life; the minimum sentence had been ten years. Of those who had fled, she, alone, remained at large, thanks to the Reverend Soames and his sister Maud.

Soames had taken her back to the vicarage, where she'd discovered that her rescue was no accident. It transpired that Maud Soames had long been Hettie's admirer. She'd sat in the gallery when Hettie had been tried over the Tindal Square

302

banner, and had even found herself shouting 'shame,' much to her own amazement, when the judge had curtailed Hettie's oration from the dock.

However, the oakeness of dock and pulpit is where the commonality had ended. The Soames had followed a less conspicuous course of conscientious objection. Of all people, it was the village policeman who'd tipped them off about Hettie. Maud had bumped into him in the street and heard how he was on the lookout for Hettie, reported to be headed for Ashleigh. Maud had gone straight home and the Soames had put their heads together, deciding it was just possible that Hettie may have heard of them and was seeking sanctuary. Knowing that constable Johnson would stick to the main road and that Hettie would have the sense to avoid it, the pair split up, Maud taking the footpaths to the south, Soames those to the north. Hettie had been holed up at the vicarage ever since. Soames had posted a letter for her in London, telling Sarah she was safe. Maud had even paved the way for Hettie's public emergence with stories of a cousin coming from South Africa.

It had been a calculated gamble. With the hundred and one people who called at the vicarage each week, Hettie couldn't remain hidden indefinitely, and, for all her infamy, it was unlikely any local would recognise her, apart from Laura Scott, and she'd been confined to her sick bed.

Thus 'Felicity' Soames had arrived at the beginning of March. Even constable Johnson had tipped his helmet to her, and again, two weeks later, when he'd asked about her lost luggage and all-important paperwork. "Just a formality, you understand, but you ought to be registered. Could the Vicar let me know when it arrives?"

Then Laura had recovered. "A chill," Maud had excused Felicity's absence from Church that Sunday, followed by, "it's turned into a cold," the next. Then Agatha Scott had invited the Soames to tea, "as soon as your cousin is better." Whatever discretion Laura might possess, the risk was too great. It was time for Hettie to move on.

Soames found the means; a mission to Nyasaland. The boat would dock at Durban, a mere stone's throw from Hettie's home in African terms. It left Tilbury on the twenty-ninth; today was the twenty-seventh.

Hettie watched her daughter until the bend in the lane claimed her. The girl had gone her own way, the wrong way, perhaps, but one which deserved respect. Hettie had nursed wounded men herself, she knew its impact on a young girl. But she knew Sarah would cope, as, once, she had coped; there was hope for her yet.

Pride welled in Hettie's eyes. Even now she could catch Sarah up; but, no, it was better this way. She'd write from Natal; now that really would surprise her!

* * * * *

"How could you allow it, Beatrice, you of all people?" Mrs. Beasley's viper tongue forked outside the Post Office. "I mean, a blooming German. The whole village is up in arms. I heard it straight from Mrs. Truelove; if something ain't done about it, she'll refuse to serve you, and that goes for the other shopkeepers and all. If you take my advice, you'll leave that Hun-loving husband of yours before you get tarred

303

with the same brush. And as for Elizabeth, tell her there are certain stains that never wash out."

Beatrice told Arthur over supper. He stormed out, leaving her in tears.

"Never mind, mum, it'll blow over," Elizabeth attempted to console her.

"It won't unless he gets rid of that ruddy German," Beatrice sobbed. "I told him no good would come of it. I know times is hard, I know he can't manage on his own, but we'd get by, we always have."

"I expect she had a go at me and all, didn't she, bloody busybody?"

Beatrice couldn't hide the truth.

"Thought as much. Why people can't mind their own flaming business I'll never know. Anyway, I said it before and I'll say it again, he should knock it on the head and come and work at the factory with me; they're crying out for men."

And so Elizabeth had, to Arthur's face, and Beatrice wished to God she hadn't. She knitted on distractedly; the needles fell.

"Oh, I do hope he hasn't gone to the pub, there'll only be trouble."

Arthur sat in his yard, his collar turned up against the cold, frosted pipes sparkling in the shadows.

'Sod the War,' he groused. He'd been doing just fine, him and George, well respected in the village and work enough for the two of them, and the boy doing well at school. Now look at them. George a prisoner, Richard over yonder, his daughter-in-law a tart, half the village against him and barely two brass farthings to rub together. He couldn't even show his face in the Barley Mow without having shit flung in it. Fuck Brewer, it was all his doing, and that fucking old faggot Beasley. He wished he was younger; better the trenches than this.

'Hun-lover! How fucking dare they?'

He kicked a wood shard across the yard.

'Well, bollocks to 'em and bollocks to her, and all, the bloody whorebag," he heaped his aggression on Elizabeth's head. "Pity that bloody explosion didn't take her with it, save us all a parcel of trouble when our George gets home, if he ever does.'

"Arthur, boy, is that you?"

Joe the blacksmith's bandy legs bridged the gap in the gate.

"I was on my way back from the Mow, saw the gate open. Bit parky ain't it? Look, I got a jug with me. Come on home and have a jar."

CHAPTER FIFTY TWO

On April 6th, America joined the Allies; Scott read the news in the Times on his way to the Timber Commission.

"As soon as the Hun started sinking their ships it was only a matter of time," Colonel Simpson told him, asking his secretary to bring some coffee. "Mind you, bribing Mexico with half the southern states was hardly politic. Fancy Zimmerman admitting it, the damned fool. Makes you wonder what kind of people we're fighting. Still, all the better for us, given the situation in Russia."

"Any news on the Czar?"

"He wants to come here, but the King's having none of it, too afraid it might spark something similar. Well, we knew it was coming, Henry Wilson said as much when he came back from Petrograd."

"Yes, but you have to feel sorry for the man."

"Shouldn't have let his wife play around with that damned degenerate monk of hers. Bad enough that she was German. Undermined the whole chabanc. If a man can't keep his own house in order, how can he be trusted to run a country?"

"L. G. was all for the new order in the Commons the other day; said the revolution was the greatest service the Russian people have made to the war."

"Yes, and if the boot had been on the other foot he would have said exactly the opposite. I haven't forgotten him and the Boers. Just as long as they keep fighting, that's all. With over a million deserted already it's looking rather ominous. No one to stop them, you see, the officers have been stripped of all authority. It comes to something when the government of the day has to bow to the whim of a load of peasants ensconced down the corridor."

"Sounds a bit like the Commons and the Lords."

"Pah. Should never've given the hoi polloi the vote, never. And now they want to give it to women. I ask you."

"Actually I meant the Lords," Scott smiled.

"It's no joking matter, Harold. Damned anarchists are everywhere. The Welshman's even sending that fool Harrison over as adviser, and you can't get more radical than him. Wrong man; bad show. Need someone with a bit of go in him, keep this Prince whatever-his-name-is on the right track."

"Kerensky seems to be more the man."

"Pah, Kerensky's nothing but a weasely lawyer, no pedigree at all. Anyway, let's hope someone's got the wherewithal. Brusilov can't put up much of a fight when all his men are buggering off the other way. If something ain't done, they'll be fighting amongst themselves by autumn, you mark my words, and then where will we be? Damn the bloody lot of them, that's what I say."

* * * * *

Laura was home for the Easter break. She would be eighteen when School resumed. Some girls had already enlisted in the newly formed WAAC, or joined Chamberlain's scheme for non-military service. In London women were even driving taxicabs, but, despite everything, Laura's anti-war militancy prevailed. Every job she could think of aided the warmongers. There was nothing for it but to comply with her father's wishes and go to university; despite her long illness, Mother Abbess was sure she would pass the entrance exam.

Yet even that depository for her high ideals had been relegated to life's periphery, for Sarah's love affair and, above all, Max, had rearmed Laura's heart. She loved Richard, that was the simple truth; she owed it to them both to let him know. Whatever had passed between them, whatever had happened in the months of separation, her love had survived intact; perhaps so, too, had his.

She slipped the letter into the pillar-box.

"Thank you, Max, thank you," she said, burying her head in Max's ruff. "I love him so much. Pray for me, Max; if dogs can pray, pray for me."

* * * * *

Richard looked anxiously to the sky. The snow had eased; the clouds were clearing. They should have been off the road an hour ago. As much as the RFC was getting shot from the ether this bloody April, a column caught on the ground was a sitting duck.

"Into the ditch! Into the ditch!"

The black and yellow tri-plane howled down, guns blazing through its synchronised propeller, one bomb, another, up and away, while it's guardian circled menacingly.

A machine gun section frantically assembled its mounting. All was chaos, dead and wounded littered the road, a stricken mare screamed out her agony, mules bucked, drivers cursed, limbers overturned.

The black-crossed wings levelled, the engine's petulant whine grew into a roar and the second Fokker swooped.

Bullets clattered on pavé, a Lewis gun rattled in reply, rifle fire, two crashing explosions, the hiss of shrapnel, then tinitual silence.

Gradually, sound returned, whinnying horses, cracking wheels, groaning wounded. Richard hauled himself from the ditch.

"Are the men all right, Sergeant?"

"Smith caught a packet, Sir."

"How is he?"

The Sergeant shook his head.

"Anyone else?"

"No, Sir, they're all on their feet."

"And Lieutenant Appleton?"

"That was him on the machine gun, Sir."

Richard nodded wryly. "All right; get them organised."

Clouds closed the window on cue. A flurry of snow mocked their misery. The disembowelled mare was still kicking in her traces, her eyes wild and pleading. Her driver was kneeling over her. Richard couldn't stand it.

"Shoot the animal, man; for Christ's sake, shoot it!"

"I can't.... Sir....... I....." The driver sobbed.

"Can't you see she's in agony?"

The driver hugged his body despairingly. Tortured to fury, Richard cursed the man's weakness.

"Shoot it!"

The driver looked up distraughtly, all comprehension gone. Richard took out his revolver, held it to the horse's head and pulled the trigger. The animal jerked violently, then lay still.

The revolver shook in Richard's grasp. What else could he have done, let the poor beast suffer? Duty dragged him back from the brink. He rested a comforting hand on the driver's shoulder.

"It's all right; it's over."

There was no response, just the rocking of an overburdened heart.

"Pull yourself together, man!"

Blood-bathed fingers gripped Richard's sleeve. A dark stain seeped through the man's tunic.

"Stretcher-bearers!"

Leaving its debris by the roadside the column lumbered on into the mincing machine that was Arras. As far as the Essex were concerned, this had been merely an entrée for death's insatiable appetite.

"Uncanny, don't you think, how those things always seem to survive?" Appleton pointed to a roadside Calvary, trying desperately to disguise his breathlessness. "I mean, not even a scratch. There must be something in it."

Richard thought back to his conversations with Langham, racking his brains for a line Ralph had written. Ah, yes; 'Where was God when the gas cloud came?' Obviously looking after his own. It was an irony young Appleton didn't need to hear and, anyway, not a good analogy.

"There's a famous one up at Wipers, a wooden crucifix in the town cemetery, some say miraculous. The whole place gets smashed to bits on a regular basis, but that one always seems to survive. The only direct hit it took was from a dud; buried itself in the woodwork between Christ and the Cross. As far as I know, it's still there."

The light shone in Appleton's eyes. "I'll be damned."

'Aren't we all?' Richard thought.

* * * * *

While Richard was marching his men to the slaughter, Charlie Clayman, George Bowden's erstwhile brother in arms, was already up to his neck in the abattoir. He'd been made full corporal, a promotion he hadn't relished; he was a survivor, one of the few, and he hadn't survived by having responsibility thrust upon him. However, the allure of a bombing course behind the lines plus an N.C.O.'s wages, boosted further by the specialist pay of a bomber, had swayed him. Now the Army was calling in the debt.

"Corporal Clayman, take your section and see if you can get behind them," his lieutenant told him.

Over half the platoon had made it to the German line, a miracle in itself, but their objective was the support trench. A machine gun over on the right had them pinned down.

"Right you are, Sir."

It was a game of chance and reaction: the first sight, the first bomb, the only winner; two men leading, the rest a bay behind.

"You three, keep the bastards busy, you others follow me."

Charlie peered into the next bay. It's only occupants were two field grey stiffs. Stepping over them, he hurried on to the far end. Just feet away, behind the traverse, Fritz could be lurking, bombs in hand, bayonets at the ready, or maybe back in the dugout he'd just passed, waiting to take his men from behind. There was a simple answer to that, throw a couple of grenades down the shaft, but, with dugouts in every bay, they may as well carry a flag plotting their progress.

He waved his men on, zigzagging through the maze of smashed earthworks, nerves honed, senses razor sharp.

The machine-gun's rattle grew louder. They were getting close. Still he couldn't pinpoint it. He'd have to risk a squint over the top. Posting lookouts, he motioned for the nearest man to give him a leg up.

"Up, down, quick as you like; got it?"

Tensely he balanced in the interwoven fingers. A tap on the man's helmet and he was hoisted up.

Two seconds were all he needed to register direction and distance; one was all he got. His hobnailed boot slipped from its holders grasp and he tumbled into the bottom of the trench. The commotion distracted the lookout. A bullet whistled past the boy's face. He fired back blindly.

"Corporal! Grenade!"

"Shit........!"

Trapped beneath the man whose hands had been his stirrup and Evans, at whose feet the bomb had landed, Charlie had no choice but to play dead when the Germans charged through the bay, and again, when, fewer in number, they stampeded back. Through the tangle of arms and legs, he could see Evan's boot standing, almost comically, on the firestep, the flesh around the shattered tibia already alive with flies, the leather still smoking.

'His boots always were a bit whiffy,' Charlie thought caustically.

Blood dripped onto his face. He tried to shift round, but when he did a searing pain racked him from knee to groin. He could feel the weight of the dead on both calf and thigh, confirming his leg was intact. He also knew he had to free himself; as soon as darkness fell, the Germans would counter attack, if not before. However bad the pain, he had to get back to his own lines while the going was good.

Gritting his teeth, he pushed up, spitting and spluttering as an artery opened over him. The body tipped, then the thunder of footfalls sent him shrinking back into his burrow.

He sensed someone close.

"They're ours, Sergeant."

"Christ, what an observant little cunt you are, Williams."

Charlie grinned. He'd know that voice anywhere: Hollis, reported lost on the way over. 'Tucked himself safely in a shell hole, more like,' he muttered. 'I knew he hadn't copped it.'

"O.K., this'll do. Get that gooseberry up here; barricade that end," Hollis yelled. "And you, shift this mess."

"Mess? Is he calling me a mess?" Charlie protested, as Evan's corpse was pulled from him.

"Jesus Christ! Sergeant!"

"What now, Williams?" Hollis stormed over.

"Good afternoon, Sergeant. Any tea in the pot?"

"Clayman?" It took Hollis moments to recognise Charlie's blood caked features.

"Never thought I'd see the day," Charlie beamed.

"Hang on, son, we'll soon get you sorted," Hollis bent over him, breath like a distillery.

"So that's what happened to the rum."

"Do what?"

"Nothing, Sergeant."

"Stretcher bearers!"

"I'm alright, Sarge, its just my leg. It's them other poor buggers what copped it. All I need's an 'and up."

Hollis looked again at the blood-soaked tunic, the blood bathed face. "You just lie still. We'll have you out of here in no time. Stretcher bearers!" He bawled again.

"For Christ's sake, Sarge, keep it down," Charlie warned. 'Hollering bloody Hollis;' the nickname was well deserved.

Hostility flared in Hollis's pig-like pupils. He took it out on someone else. "Get them sandbags sorted! They'll be over soon as it's dark. And build up that fucking firestep!"

"Sergeant?"

"Fuck you, Williams, now what?"

"Stretcher's here, Sergeant."

"And about bloody time. Take good care of him lads, he's one of us."

'One of us? Who the hell does he think he is?' Charlie silently objected, before his legs were lifted and pain obliterated all thought.

"For fuck's sake, easy, I said," He heard Hollis complain. "You'll be alright, son, they'll sort you out."

The stretcher's support eased Charlie's agony. He propped himself up as they carried him away.

"Jesus, Sergeant, I never knew you cared!"

CHAPTER FIFTY THREE

The doctor's new sewage system was complete. Arthur couldn't have done it without the help of the big German who stood beside him mopping his brow with his patched prison sleeve. He had to admit he liked the man; they both deserved a beer and bugger the bloody-minded.

"Look, you hang on here; tidy up the yard," he ordered, fetching his beer can. "I won't be long."

Redden looked at him uncomprehendingly.

"You... stay... here; tidy up," Arthur indicated with his arms.

"Ah," Gunther grinned.

"How are you getting on with that German of yours?" The village's other Amos, Amos Crutchley, asked, as Arthur slavered at the bar, watching his ale being pulled.

"He's a good worker, I'll say that for him," Bowden admitted, his public disdain forgotten in the pleasure of a job well done and a lack of antagonists, with the exception of old man Brewer, sitting broodily in the corner. "Couldn't have done it without him. Suppose he's a decent enough bloke really. Didn't want to fight no more than our boys."

"No more than my Joe."

Crutchley's head sank into the secret he had shared only with Bowden. Even his own family had no knowledge of Joe's cowardice. Amos had burnt the telegram before anyone could read it. But the words remained etched in the headstone that was now his heart; 'Joseph, William, Crutchley was sentenced after trial by court-martial to be shot for cowardice in the face of the enemy and that sentence was carried out on November 24th. 1916...'

"Keep us company with a pint before you go back."

"Alright, but it'll have to be a quick one," Arthur agreed compassionately. "Don't think he'd run off, but better to be safe."

Brewer had been eavesdropping. He didn't talk to Bowden anymore; the man was a traitor. Draining his glass, he slipped out. Ten minutes later Arthur was just draining his, when Amos Harris burst into the bar.

"Arthur! Arthur! Come quick! I've just bumped into Brewer and Billy White. They're going after that German of yours with a bayonet!"

By the time the Barley Mow regulars reached the yard, Redden had Brewer in an armlock, twisting and turning him against Billy's thrusts.

Billy was disarmed, Brewer prised from Gunther's grip. It took four men to hold him, he was a man possessed, the fury of defeat compounding the dementia of hatred.

Blood dripped from the German's shoulder. One blow had found its mark.

"Get the doctor, someone," Arthur yelled, trying to stem the flow.

"I'd've got him proper, I would!" Billy proclaimed.

"He was trying to escape, I tell you, weren't he Billy? Let me go!" Brewer cried, lunging at Redden like a snared tiger. "I'll have you, you bloody swine, I'll have you!"

"Hold him, for Christ's sake!" Arthur warned.

Billy looked non-plussed. "But Mr. Bowden, he's a German!"

"That's right Billy, he's a German; and that one there's no better, the bloody traitor," Brewer glared.

"Get him out of here," Arthur ordered.

"You ain't heard the last of this, Bowden, not by a long chalk! 'T'ain't just me! You'll get what's coming to you, you mark my words," Brewer yelled as they dragged him away.

Bowden and Crutchley eased Redden over to Arthur's lean-to office. The doctor wasn't long in coming. Billy had missed the artery by a whisker. A cut on Redden's hand needed stitching, but the tendons were intact. They took him to the surgery, keeping an eye out for Brewer on the way, which is where Kipper Johnson caught up with them, twenty minutes later.

"You're not taking him in, Gordon, surely to God?" Arthur protested.

"From what I hear he was trying to escape."

"Trying to escape, my arse. The man was attacked! It's Brewer you should be locking up."

"Well I've got two men's sworn statements to the contrary. They say all the attacking was done by him," Johnson asserted.

"And that's how he got stabbed, is it?"

"Self-defence."

"Do me a bloody favour. With an army bayonet? It's obvious to a blind horse what happened. Look at the state of him," Bowden appealed animatedly.

"Well it ain't obvious to me, Arthur; I wasn't there and, from what I gather, neither was you," Kipper raised a censuring eyebrow.

"Ask Amos Harris, if you don't believe me. It was him what raised the alarm, ain't that right, Amos?"

Crutchley confirmed as much.

"Be that as it may."

"Dah; I thought better of you, Gordon, really I did," Bowden grumbled disgustedly. "Leave him with me 'til they pick him up; I'll vouch for him."

"It was you vouching for him in the first place what led to all this. Where were you when it happened?" Johnson made the point more bluntly a second time. "Call it protective custody, if you like, but he's coming with me, and that's an end to it. It's the safest place for him, Arthur, and if you can't see that you're blinder than that horse you keep on about."

* * * * *

'Ageless Peg' sat in swarthy concentration. In times past she would have been considered a witch with her herbal potions and palm reading. Before the War, few had professed a serious belief; now the path to her door was well trodden.

"Is he safe, Peg?" The offensive, as usual, was front-page news.

311

Peg opened her eyes. "He's well enough."

"Oh, that's a relief."

Peg handed back Richard's school cap, studying Beatrice across the table.

"How've you been of late?"

"Not so bad. Bit under the weather, but nothing I can put my finger on."

"Well don't you worry about him, nor that German neither; it'll blow over."

Peg left her seat and walked lithely over to her remedy cupboard. Stretching up, she plucked a navy blue bottle from the top shelf.

"Take a spoonful of this once a day 'til it's empty."

"Oh, no need, Peg, I'll be alright."

"'T'ain't poison!"

"Well, alright then. Thank you kindly."

"Make sure you do, mind," Peg ordered.

Beatrice crossed Peg's palm with the sixpence she'd been holding in her own, then reopened her purse. "How much for the medicine?"

"Dah," Peg grumped, gliding past. "You just take it, you hear?"

Beatrice turned at the door.

"Thanks, Peg, I was worried for him."

"Don't be. He's safe enough. I'll have the bottle back when you're done."

* * * * *

Across the valley, The Manor's drapes were tightly drawn. A solitary candle burned in the centre of the table; the ring of hope, scepticism, belief and charade was joined. Elmsford's most illustrious clairvoyant was also plying her trade. Not that Florence Corduroy's reputation was founded in fraud. She genuinely believed in her psychic powers. She only reverted to subterfuge to relieve distress when contact remained elusive. She settled into a trance.

"Is anyone there?"

Mary Stafford, young, impressionable, glanced nervously round the table. She'd pleaded to be excused; her mother had insisted. They'd toyed with the supernatural at school one night. The glass had spelt her name and come skidding towards her. She'd been scared stiff; that fear was returning.

Mrs. Stafford felt the tension in her daughter's hand. Mary had been closer to Spencer than anyone. Was she feeling his presence?

"Is there anyone there?"

'Stuff and nonsense,' thought Mrs. Avery. She'd nursed all the Stafford children, but Spencer had been her favourite. 'The boy's gone and that's all there is to it.' She'd accepted it now, not like her mistress, though it had taken a while. She'd mended his tunic. The Army had returned it, bullet-holed and bloodstained, with a picture of another young officer in the pocket. His mother had grasped at straws, but Mrs. Avery had known it was his alright, and known that he had gone.

"Grey Eagle, if you are there, give me a sign."

The candle flickered. Was it by indiscernible breath or freak draft? Mrs. Corduroy's companion smiled serenely. The flame resumed its perpendicular vigil.

"Who's Grey Eagle?" Mrs. Avery whispered a little too loudly.

"Mrs. Avery, please!" Mrs Stafford complained.

"That's Mrs. Corduroy's guide," the disciple told them.

'That's funny, didn't see him come in,' Mrs. Avery tittered to herself. 'Mind you, by the looks of her, she could do with a bit of guidance.' She studied the mystic's abundance, reflecting on her proud introductory boast, 'twenty years a Medium.' 'Then I changed to large!' The housekeeper added mischievously.

"I have a lady here, who wishes to contact her son, Captain Spencer Stafford, who passed over last October."

The maternal pulse quickened.

"If he is with you, can he communicate some sign to reassure his family who are here?"

The air vibrated with expectancy.

"Betsy; he says Betsy."

Mary stiffened, Mrs. Stafford blanched.

"Does the name Betsy mean anything to you?" The Companion asked.

Mrs. Stafford nodded tearfully. "It was his favourite pony, when he was a child."

Mrs. Avery flushed. 'How'd she know that?' It was uncanny, unsettling.

"Is there anything he wishes to tell them?" The Medium's brow furled. "He says you must not be... sad... He is very happy... You must not... fear..."

Suddenly she sat bolt upright. Sweat poured from her temples, her eyes bulged, the table trembled under her palms. The atmosphere became intense, threatening. The candle flickered violently, the crystal chandelier pealed out a warning of spiritual intrusion.

"What on earth is the matter?"

The ring was broken. Mary leapt back in terror; Mrs. Avery wriggled uncomfortably in her seat; Mrs. Stafford demanded an answer.

"I don't know!" The Companion panicked.

"Aaahhh!" The Psychic was struggling against suffocation. Her temples were throbbing, her veins protruded from her neck.

Her Companion grabbed her outstretched arm.

"For God's sake, help me, someone!"

They led Mrs. Corduroy to the settee. Her face was filled with dread. "No!" She screamed, forcing them back with demonic power. Then her eyes rolled, her body shuddered and she collapsed like an epileptic.

Mrs. Avery flung open the curtains; the room flooded with daylight; the convulsions subsided; the Medium lay still.

"Marian," she mumbled.

* * * * *

"I don't know what got into him, Mr. Bowden, really I don't. Gunther is going to be alright, isn't he?" Cissy asked when she called on the Bowdens after evening surgery. "He's not normally a violent man, Mr. Bowden, honest he ain't," she lied of her father. "It's just that, what with Raymond getting killed and all, well, I

313

suppose it's understandable, isn't it? He doesn't know Gunther like we do; it was too much for him."

"Gunther never harmed no one in his life, Cissy, at least not by choice," Bowden contended. "He ain't no different to our boys; just a normal bloke what got caught up in it the same as them. He had no say in the matter. He'd never have tried to escape in a month of Sundays, I'd stake my life on it. All he wants is for the whole thing to end so he can go home to his family, just like our George."

"Oh, I know, Mr. Bowden, I know. Are they going to charge him, do you think, my Dad, I mean? He never meant no real harm, I'm sure he didn't."

Bowden raised an eyebrow. "If stabbing someone's not real harm, Cissy, I don't know what is."

"But that was Billy, Mr. Bowden."

"Yes, and who put him up to it?"

Cissy sighed.

"Well, I don't rightly know," Arthur prolonged the suspense, knowing full well there was about as much chance of Brewer being charged as himself being elevated to the peerage. "By rights, he should be locked up and no mistake. Does he know you're here?"

"Please don't tell him, Mr. Bowden, he'd kill me."

Bowden frowned. "Someone's got to talk some sense into him, Cissy. If something ain't done, he'll end up like old Wilkinson, hanging on the end of a rope, German or no German."

"He won't do it again, Mr. Bowden; I'll see that he don't."

"Well I hope you're right," Bowden muttered, conscious of Brewer's parting threat.

CHAPTER FIFTY FOUR

Arras had been another cock up, another annihilation. There'd been rumours that the French poilus had baaed like sheep on their way to the Nivelle offensive, that there'd been mutinies, that the British offensive was being pushed to the limit to take the pressure off their allies. Richard's battalion had retched into Monchy le Preux over the cadavers of the county's yeomanry, massed in the village by some tactical genius, fully mounted and in full view of the enemy. A box barrage had done the rest. The stench had stripped the sinuses and turned the breakfast bacon to bile.

Appleton had wheezed across no-man's land unscathed, only to die in convulsions in a captured trench. They'd passed a battery of Livens' Projectors on the way up, cut down gas cylinders converted into electrically fired mortars.

"My worst enemy, gas," the boy had said, and so just a wisp of it had proved. Suffocating in his respirator, he'd taken it off too soon, at least for an asthmatic.

"Plucky little fellow," Langham might have said.

For all his resilience, Appleton's death had hit Richard hard, haunting him with his refusal to sketch the portrait the boy had so longed to send home, postscripted 'Front Line'. What harm would it have done? The curse had been exploded, as had been Rowe's chest that same day, ripped apart to expose the bellowing lungs, when the Bavarians had sprung their trap. Barely a quarter of the Battalion's nine hundred had made it back.

The Newfoundlanders, attacking in concert, had been equally decimated, but neither Battalion had been withdrawn; instead they'd been formed into carrying parties to support carbon copy attacks, pushed home ad nauseam. When they were finally relieved, barely two men in ten remained. Even so, getting leave had been a miracle. Scarcely able to believe his luck, Richard hadn't even packed in his haste to get away.

'Beechams Pills Worth a Guinea a Box,' 'Zam Buck for a Healthy Skin', 'Force is the Food that Raised Him': the trackside posters counted off the miles into London and out again.

Laura was waiting on the platform, as she'd waited before, but this time there was only joyful certainty, when he took her in his arms. He'd cleaned himself up as best he could en route, but he was no bed of roses. She said nothing, happy to simply glory in belonging.

He looked around. It was like stepping back to normality from the pits of hell. The protective shield he had striven to forge melted like porous ice. He quickly stemmed the flow before his pent up devastation made a fool of him.

The car was waiting, but not Scott.

"He's in London," Laura told him.

"So who drove you?"

"I did. Give it a swing."

Richard did as he was told, expecting her father to spring out of hiding.

"Well, get in, then," Laura smiled smugly, releasing the handbrake.

It was an emotional homecoming. The sight of Richard, alone, would have been enough, but to see them both in the joy of reunion was too much for Beatrice; in floods of tears she hugged the breath out of them. Arthur shook his son's hand as warmly as his inhibitions would allow, even patting him on the shoulder when doting eyes turned to the children and their awe of the French bonbons bought in Boulogne.

The scar on Richard's scalp was soon noticed.

'A training accident,' he told them. No one really believed him.

The housekeeping jar was emptied, the beanfeast prepared.

"Have I got time for a wash?"

"Of course, dear, I should've thought," his mother told him. "Dinner's on, but it'll be a while yet. I'll just shut the door."

Standing at the kitchen sink, Richard savoured the permanence of piecrust, the sanity of spring-greens, the harmonious bubbling of boiling potatoes, scarcely able to believe he was really there.

When dusk fell, he and Laura wandered along to the sad, silent house that had been her home. It remained empty, the garden overgrown, overlooked by the Land Girls who were putting every rood to the plough, every square foot to the fork, in England's efforts to feed herself. Across the valley the Manor paddock was already swaying with summer wheat.

The bower had been all but enveloped; the white roses had run riot. There they sat, as they had sat so often, sharing the fragrant sunset. England seemed so clean, so peaceful. England was Eden.

Laura reached for a rose. Gently, Richard stayed her hand.

"Too many," he said. "Too many..."

Astounded as he had been by Laura's driving, Richard was no less taken aback by the Grange; it reminded him of the tree, tranquil, old and wise. Little Eastleigh had been beyond his childhood horizon. The Manor's iron fence had been the terrible trio's picket line, with old man Wilkinson's 'Trespassers will be Shot' Kruger's warning.

Max greeted him like a long lost friend, Agatha in the final stages of pregnancy; "it could be any day, now. Why don't you show Richard the garden, Laura, while I make some tea?"

His deja vu was instant; his mother had said the self-same thing the first time Laura had come to the Bowden's.

Under an elm at the far end of the garden he restored the sapphire ring to her finger. It had lived by her bedside ever since the quarrel. The dented locket once more hung over her heart.

He said nothing about Elspeth or Janine; he wouldn't make that mistake again.

"I'm afraid we won't be able to use the car," Laura told him. "The new restrictions don't allow. I shouldn't have picked you up from the station, but it was the only way I could get there. Even Squire Stafford was fined the other day for driving his family to church. Father's exempt with the new Vauxhall, work of national importance and all that, but the Bentall's for emergency use only, and a bit of driving practice up and down the lane when no one's looking. Father told me there were only seven ever made, so it's a bit of a rarity. It'll be mine when the War's over, so it'd better be over soon."

The following day Sarah's arrival for a well-earned rest severely restricted the lovers'options. Half the week went by before they were able to grab some time to themselves.

Under a cloudless sky, they sauntered through the woods and out into the cornflowered wheat fields with Max at their heels. Laura said she wished he'd come earlier, when the copse had been carpeted with bluebells, and primroses and violets had scented the air. He wished he'd never left.

In a secluded corner, they kissed.

This time there were no recriminations. They made love more urgently than either had thought possible, oblivious of their surroundings, lost on the bed of wheat harvested by their need. She cried with fulfilment when he broke the final bastion. It was impossible that they had deprived themselves for so long, impossible. They rolled rapturously, locked in love's Elysium, laughing crazily, until, inevitably, he slipped from her and they bathed in ecstasy's afterglow.

Max lay dolefully beside them. Her harsh words had checked his participation; now her words were kind. Whatever he'd done wrong, he was forgiven. No explanation was necessary, he was a dog, he knew about human irrationality. Still, he was glad to be included again.

Laura rested her head on Richard's shoulder, tracing the stark collar line of the trenches. He became pensive.

"Laura; when we broke up... I'm sorry, I didn't mean what I said... I..."

She pressed a finger to his lips. "Ssshhh; it's all behind us now; a bad dream, nothing more. Anyway, it wasn't all you."

Even in Richard's deep contentment, betrayal rumbled like Flanders' unforgiving guns.

"I never dreamed it would be like this," he heard her say; but how much more would it have meant, how much more incredible might it have been, had they remained faithful? That was an experience forever denied them, the corrupting hand of another an irreversible fact, its eradication from the mind an enforced illusion. He should have taken her before the dream had been shattered.

"Mmmm," she moaned obliviously, offering her lips to be kissed.

A broken stalk registered its discomfort.

"Ouch!"

"That'll teach you to make love in a wheat field," he teased her. "We really should get dressed."

"But it's so wonderful," she sighed. "I could lie here forever."

"We pushed our luck last time, remember?"

She asked if he still had the sketch. He told her it was hidden behind his wardrobe. "You'd better have it, it'll be safer with you."

"No." She looked almost frightened. "I'd rather you kept it. Can't you take it with you?"

It was a superstition he shared. He forced the mayhem from his mind.

"We'd better be getting back."

He knew it was ludicrous to feel self-conscious about dressing, but he couldn't get his clothes on quickly enough.

"All clear," he said, then stood back in amazement as Laura leapt up to dance naked through the wheat like a white witch on the summer solstice, Max, her familiar, bounding along beside her. But would the seeds sown in such passion reap a harvest of their own? It was the first time, he told himself; she couldn't get pregnant the first time.

* * * * *

"Cor, bit of alright, this; just what the doctor ordered," Sarson beamed, wheeling himself along the veranda. "Talk about Southend on a sunny fucking day."

George manhandled his leg over his deckchair's support and sat back with a sigh, too weak to wipe the perspiration from his brow. Still he shivered. "Pah, I feel like death warmed up."

The rifle butt had split the old wound wide open and cracked the bone beneath. He'd been dragged back to camp and left tied to a post on tiptoe, hands above his head, until he'd been all but crucified.

He poked the puss corrupted bandage. "Augh."

"Bayonet, weren't it, the first time? Sarson asked. "Shrapnel, mine. You'd have thought it was gold fucking nuggets the way they keep poking about in there. If I charged them a pound for every bit they dug out, I'd be a bloody millionaire."

"Probably short of ammo," George mumbled drowsily.

"Bloody governments; all the fucking same; give it out with one hand and take it back with the other fucker."

"Where d'you get that from?" George belatedly puckered an eyebrow at Sarson's wheelchair.

"Let's just say I knew a man who wouldn't be needing it. Those fucking crutches was rubbing my armpits red fucking raw. Still, least we don't have to work for a living, hey? So what do you fancy for tonight, me lordship; 'party de fwar grah' or sandstorm soup? Soup man meself, which is just as bloody well, init? Americans eat grits; reckon it must be the same fucking thing. Wouldn't surprise me if they don't have us puking up over the fucking roads come winter, save them the trouble of sanding the fuckers."

George wasn't listening, he was over the hills and far away, until Sarson's elbow jogged the projector.

"Here, George? George! See him over there, that new bloke, the lanky fucker? Bloody conchy, weren't he."

George raised his head with an effort. "Obviously not conchy enough."

"Nah, neither would you be if they'd strung you up stark bollock naked in a prison cell in the middle of fuckin' winter, nothing but bars on the windows and a bloody gale whistling up your fucking arse'ole. Not that I blame them, mind; bastards like that deserve all they fucking get. Left his army clobber on the bed. Soon as the cold got too much for him, he puts it on and he's in."

"Well, he's out of it now," George sighed, easing his head back onto the canvas.

"Yeh, give himself up first fucking chance he got, lily-livered fucking swine. If I had my way, I'd string the fucker up by the balls and just let him hang there."

"Ah well, his mother loves him," George muttered, surfing back to a daytrip to Walton and Candy-Floss lips, the sun beating down on Elizabeth's tits as they rolled in the sand dunes, and sausage and chips, fried eggs on toast and jam Roly-poly, sunburn and camomile, just him and her in an empty compartment, all the way home; all the way home...

- CHAPTER FIFTY FIVE -

Near his leave's end, Richard called on Joscelyn, his old headmaster. In the early days, returning officers had been expected to extol the glories of patriotic sacrifice at assembly. Word had it that, since conscription, the practice had been dropped; however, fearing Joscelyn might make an exception in his case, Richard had delayed his visit until the last moment. The bell ringer was clanging away two-handed by the headmaster's door, ending the school day. He let him finish before he knocked.

"Come! Ah, yes, Bowden, or is it lieutenant Bowden now?"

After the preliminary pleasantries, Richard found himself with nothing to say, until he remembered his encounter with Chapman. Joscelyn was pleased to hear of his ex-history master; the Grammar's network didn't extend to North Country regiments.

"Funny old fish, Chapman. Good master, though, knew his subject. Debating Society's gone to pot without him."

Richard's mind flashed back to the fifth form.

"Today we shall debate the foreign policy of the Interregnum," Chapman had announced.

"All of us, Sir?" Cummin had piped up.

"Unless you've made other arrangements, Cummin," Chapman had engaged him.

"So it will be a mass debate, then, Sir?"

Out had rolled the old chestnut every generation of sniggering schoolboys believes to be its own.

"If you prefer, Cummin, you may relieve your evident frustrations elsewhere, although I'm sure the headmaster would be less than amused to find you doing so outside his study door. You, yourself, might find it a somewhat wilting experience," Chapman had turned the tables.

"And what of your own exploits, Bowden?" Joscelyn broke into the daydream. "I hear you were wounded?"

Oh, nothing, Sir, just a bump on the head."

"And something about a decoration?"

"A decoration? No, I don't believe so, Sir."

Obviously the old man had got himself mixed up with Richard's school medal.

"Oh, perhaps I'm wrong; one hears so many rumours."

The conversation drifted back to inanities until terminated by Joscelyn's timetable.

"I would invite you to tea, but I'm afraid I have a governors' meeting. Keep up the good work."

The tree beckoned. Richard stood in its shade, dwarfed by its magnificence. Yet none of it seemed real, none of it.

Richard bade goodbye at home; even his father shed tears. Grandma Gurny had wished him luck the night before and given him a bottle of rum old Gurny had been saving 'for a rainy day' - "Granddad liked a drop of rum" - and a pair of mittens her arthritic hands had been knitting since Christmas "for when the weather turns."

Elizabeth squeezed his hand and kissed him respectfully. Richard felt they'd grown closer, that she'd become more like a sister-in-law, although his mother told him Elizabeth said exactly the opposite, that she felt awkward in his presence, that he belonged more with the Scotts, or the Staffords up at the Big House. Whatever the truth, she was demonstrably proud of him. She and Mrs. Bowden had stuffed his pack with food and she'd self-consciously endowed his buttonhole with a sprig of lucky heather bought from a gypsy.

The farewells were prolonged; Scott had to drive hell for leather to get to the station in time. The train was already in.

"Good luck, my boy," he told Richard, leaving a five-pound note in his palm. "Now, you two, run like the wind."

The lovers bounded up the stairs. The guard was closing the doors; "Come on, Sir, come on."

They clung to each other, until the very last moment.

"Write soon!"

Richard hung precariously from the window, waving all the way across the viaduct until the station was lost to sight.

Securing the window strap, he squeezed along the corridor and found a seat, thanking God for his first class status. There were other occupants returning from leave, wishing to God time could stand still. A raised eyebrow, a resigned nod; 'You too, old chum; you too?'

What lay ahead didn't bear thinking about, yet neither did the love he'd left behind. He searched for distraction and found it in the irritant of Elizabeth's lucky heather. He freed it from his lapel and put it in his pocket.

A city slicker huffed over the collision of white spat and army boot. How incongruous he looked, this immaculate crow. 'Well, he'd better get used to it,' Richard thought, 'this collision of worlds, this us and them, this new world order, war without end.' Langham had written a poem about them. What was it now? 'As uniform as infantry in pinstripe grey conformity.' 'Whatever happens at the front, it's stocks and shares that bear the brunt', then something about 'Chu Chin Chow' and 'Aunt Matilda.' He couldn't remember it now; the vulture may be worth thousands but he wasn't worth the effort.

His father had been preoccupied with some bad feeling in the village, something to do with the Fritz he'd had working for him. Richard hadn't understood what all the fuss was about; by all accounts he'd been a decent enough bloke, a veritable Godsend, according to his father. Richard had offered to lend a hand, but he hadn't been needed; he'd been told to go off and enjoy himself, and enjoy himself he had.

A passing express thundered him back to the present, before the final acres of pastoral Essex returned him to Laura.

They'd made love once more, under the stars, taking an incredible risk. She'd sneaked out, ensuring Max's silence with a bone. He'd withdrawn in the nick of time; hopefully there'd be no repercussions. They'd marry on his next leave, whenever that would be.

Sarah had been ever present, he even suspected her of spying on them that night in the garden. He found the thought provocative. She was certainly attractive enough, blonde with light blue eyes and a fuller figure than Laura's. He'd felt like a veritable Douglas Fairbanks, when he'd walked the pair of them along Clacton prom.

"Need a hand, old boy?" A fellow lieutenant, too dapper to be on leave, had asked.

"I can manage," he'd assured the man smugly.

Sarah had been flirty, as if she knew his most intimate secrets, which, when he thought about it, she probably did, and more, if she had been watching from the shadows.

His loins stirred. He changed the subject; in another fifteen minutes the train would pull into Liverpool Street, little enough time to quell an impending uprising.

* * * * *

Laura, too, waved until the train was out of sight. In the three months since Easter, her transformation had been complete. Richard had replied to her letter, even sending her a belated birthday present, a paper knife Rowe had helped fashion from a shell casing, indented with a rose and 'Arras, April 1917'. Since then they'd written regularly. And then the phone call had come. How she'd panicked, unable even to decide what to wear, until she'd remembered his favourite dress. She hadn't worn it in over a year; it had needed pressing.

Through her hysteria, Agatha had exerted calm, until Laura had said she was taking the Bentall. She'd never driven solo; she'd stalled the engine, burnt the brakes, crunched the gears, nearly collided with an Army lorry, but she'd got there.

Waiting on the platform, she'd prayed it wouldn't be like last time. The train had been late, then, suddenly, he was there, a man, thinner than before, especially in the face, she hadn't even been sure; and then he'd smiled and she'd known he was her Richard.

She'd cursed her female cycle, she'd wanted to drive to the nearest lonely spot and seduce him there and then. When it finally happened, the gates of Paradise had opened. She glowed in the memory, thanking God that he hadn't found out about Agnew, it could have ruined everything. Though, perhaps not now.

Her father hugged her consolingly.

"Come on, old girl. He'll be all right, you'll see."

* * * * *

Richard had three hours to kill in London. He unfolded Elspeth's telephone

322

number. There was nothing between them, but he ought to tell her.

He found the restaurant easily enough. It was a scorching day, too hot to eat. Her breasts were evident through her light summer dress.

Her flat was cooler, as cool as the rivalry that teased him onto lips more practised and bewitching than any slip of a girl's. They'd been there before; she knew why he'd come, even if he didn't.

When it was over, he threw himself into his uniform and went like a bat-out-of-hell to Charing Cross. He'd lived with vermin, he'd messed himself in the trenches, but he'd never felt so filthy.

"Not this one, old boy."

Too confused to take umbrage, he ambled from the Staff's pristine Pullmans to the workhorse carriages for lesser mortals lining the adjacent platform.

He couldn't understand it. What on earth had possessed him? Why had he 'phoned Elspeth? Why the hell had he arranged to meet her? He'd known what would happen, he'd known. Was sex so irresistible; was his resolve so weak?

The demon of dented egos provided the answer, the curator of corrupting hands. Even though he'd taken Laura's virginity, the pedestal had already crumbled, the angel had already fallen. He didn't hate Spencer for it, he didn't hate her for it, or even blame her, his stupidity with Elizabeth had been the catalyst, but the bond had been broken and, even though the retied knot may have brought them even closer, in its two frayed ends lost fidelity would forever lay exposed to this retributive justification, which eased his conscience, as it had eased him into Elspeth's arms, reducing his guilt to a compact with perfidy to save Laura from hurt.

Had it remained intact, would he and Laura still have made love, or would they have waited, even now, until they were married? Would he have bedded Elspeth? He'd never have met Elspeth. And Janine? Not a chance.

Ah well, he was more than even now. Corruption had its compensations, but no more excuses, he would never cheat on her again.

A stiff breeze blew down the Grammar School playing field. The Copper Beech sighed.

- CHAPTER FIFTY SIX -

Agatha went into premature labour on July seventeenth, in the middle of an Air Raid. Two flights went over, looking, to one local observer, like 'a couple of flocks of starlings'. The previous month London's Liverpool Street had been the target, not long after Scott had left it. This time the General Post Office, St. Bart's, a Synagogue and some buildings along the Embankment took the brunt. Almost two hundred people were injured, thirty-seven fatally. It was all over by noon. Not so the birth; it took a red and angry-looking 'Harold, Henry, Stephen' another ten hours to end his mother's ordeal.

Laura hadn't conceived. Unmarried or not, seeing mother and child only increased her yearning. She consoled herself with knowing that everything had come right; perhaps next time - there would be a next time, she was sure, fate would not forsake her now.

On the last day of term, mother Abbess had read out a letter from Sister Rowena. It had taken six months to arrive from Russia and was as graphically descriptive as Priory vocabulary allowed.

'Without medicine of any kind, the wounded endure terrible suffering. There are no proper bandages, nor clean water. Operations are performed in the most primitive conditions with no anaesthetic other than Vodka, which is an abominable spirit rather like Gin, which the men are given to drink. During surgery, a piece of wood is inserted into the patient's mouth to bite on...'

Sister Rowena had said it was the most horrifying, yet rewarding experience of her life.

"And what are people doing here, hey Max?" Laura asked the dog sprawled across her bed. "Wearing purple ribbons to show they're eating less bread."

Each Sunday in May, a royal proclamation had been read out in church, asking people to eat less bread and avoid using flour in pastry. The campaign had been running ever since.

"What a complete waste of time and money," her father continually grumbled. "Why don't they simply ration the stuff and have done with it."

Laura wondered how they went about such things in Cambridge. She'd passed her University Entrance preliminaries, but was more confused than ever about taking up her place, caught between Hettie's 'greater conscience' and Sarah's support of the war, the quicker to end it. If Sarah was right, then she should forego Cambridge and volunteer as an ambulance driver in France. At least that way she might see Richard, as long as it wasn't with him on a stretcher.

From wounded to killed was a split-second progression. She blanked it from her mind and picked up the letter she was writing to him, filling the void with Max chasing the rabbits which had been invading the vegetable garden all summer long, getting into practice for the squirrels of autumn.

'He never catches them, they escape through the fence or over the stream and he hates water, he pulls up at the sight of it, sometimes too late, tottering on the brink before he falls in.'

She pulled the dog's ear. "You're such a baby."

'We often walk past 'our' field. The harvest is in full swing, but, so far, our love nest has escaped the scythe. We certainly made a mess of the wheat.'

Her thoughts returned to pregnancy and to Annabelle. The girl had been sent away in disgrace. The authorities had traced Anthony to France, where the Army needed all the pilots it could get, even bastards like him. He'd denied everything, claiming he couldn't possibly be the father. She hoped he was shot down in flames, it would be no more than the swine deserved, or got his thingummies shot off like poor old Spencer. Which reminded her, his mother had opened the Manor to convalescent officers; perhaps, she could help out up there.

She gazed out at a cloudy sky. Wherever Richard was, whatever he was doing, she knew he was safe.

The house was quiet; Agatha and baby Harold were taking their afternoon nap. Sliding her hand under the mattress, Laura pulled out the stiff, buff envelope she'd been too lazy to return to its proper hiding place.

"Look, Max, it's mummy."

She'd meant to destroy them; she'd told Richard she had.

"Your uncle Spencer took these. Naughty mummy."

Max's puckered eyes flicked enquiringly from the two-dimensional to the three, his tongue at rest over his white, untarnished teeth. Laura kissed his snout with a resounding smack. Joyously he keeled over.

"Oh, all right then."

Sighing deeply, he lay blissfully deep in dog heaven, while his mistress tickled his chest.

* * * * *

"Funny you never having been before, you living so close. Would've thought you'd've come here regular," Ethel said on Southend prom.

"It ain't that close really, not by train; well, you've seen for yourself," Elizabeth told her, licking the chip grease from her fingers. "Walton on Naze was always George's favourite; that and Clacton, been there once or twice. Real sea, he said; never fancied this place, said it'd be like swimming in a cess pool, what with all the muck that comes floating down the Thames, not that he can, mind, swim I mean; flaps about like a drowning spider, all arms and legs."

"I've never caught nothing," Ethel protested. "Apart from a cold. Anyway, that's not what you come for. It's the Pier, init; longest in the world, least it was before they blew a bloody hole in it."

"Sounds like my George," Elizabeth smirked.

"He didn't catch it there, did he?"

"Do what?"

"In the nether regions."

"Oh no. Least, I hope not," Elizabeth laughed. "No, we was going to come here once, but we caught the wrong train and ended up in London. You'd've thought we'd done it on purpose, the way the ticket inspector carried on. Wouldn't let us through. Said we'd have to catch the same train back and start again, and there was my George dying for the lav. Threatened to do it on the platform, he did, but they wouldn't have it. Called a policeman in the end and he took him. Well, that was it as far as George was concerned, it was Walton or nothing after that."

"Can't say I've ever been there."

"No? Nicer than here, more sand, though there's not much in the way of amusements."

"Come on you lot!" Ethel called to Edie, languishing behind.

"I'm waiting for Sandra," Edie shouted back.

"You should've seen it before the war; packed it was," Ethel continued. "Won a nice bit at housey-housey one time. You could catch a paddle steamer from the end of the pier there all the way to France. Came down from Tower Wharf. My Sid took me once, but I was that sick. Never again. And them French; dirty buggers. Your George would've been alright; do it in the street, they do, over there."

"Margate, too?" Edie said, catching up.

"Do they?"

"Do they what?"

"Pee in the street."

"Oh no; mind you my old granny used to straddled the gutter without so much as a by your leave. 'Needs must,' she used to say."

"Well, they had the skirts for it in them days."

"No, I meant the steamers, they go to Margate from here, too. Best fish 'n chips I ever tasted, in Margate."

"So where's Sandra?"

"Gone to get some toffee apples."

"What with all this sugar rationing? She'll be lucky," Ethel grumbled. "Wanted to make some jam. 'How many pounds are you making?' Her behind the counter wanted to know. 'What's it to you?' says I. 'Well I can only give you a third of what you ask for, according to how much you're making,' says she, 'regulations.' 'Regulations my arse!' I told her. 'It's jam I'm making, not a cup of ruddy tea!' Wouldn't let me have none. Got right uppity; told me I'd have to do without, the bitch."

"Same thing happened to my mum-in-law," Elizabeth commiserated.

"Don't know what the world's coming to, really I don't," Edie lamented. "Still, nice of 'em to give us the bank holiday. I never expected that."

"Nor me," Elizabeth said. "They're not supposed to; not supposed to have any holidays;" and she hadn't told the Bowdens about it. She deserved a day out, or the rest of the week, if she could get away with it. "Pity they blew it up," she returned to the pier. Would've liked to have gone on there."

"Had to, in case of invasion. Always was a bit rickety, mind; gaps in the boards you can see the sea through. Lost a tanner down one once," Edie reminisced. "Had to go without my supper. Well, sixpence was a small fortune in them days. Christ, did I get a thrashing. Wouldn't do to get your heel stuck in one on a dark night, I

326

can tell you that."

"I don't know; depends on who rescues you," Ethel grinned licentiously. "That young toff by the beach huts would do for starters, him in the bathchair. Wouldn't mind getting me hand under his blanket; I'd soon have him up and about."

"Yeh, hopping away on his crutches for all he was worth, poor sod!"

"Well he would if you came at him, that's for sure, Edith Brackley," Ethel huffed.

"Least I don't have a mouth like the black hole of Calcutta!"

"I hope you made a wish when you lost your sixpence," Elizabeth butted in before insult led to injury.

"Six of them, but never a one came true."

"Here you are, then," Sandra said triumphantly, arriving with some toffee apples. "Don't say I never give you nothing. There was only three, so two'll have to share."

"Well I ain't sharing with her," Edie protested. "Not with her teeth."

"Oh shut your gob," Ethel said, cocking an ear to the north. "Here, what's that noise?"

"Sounds like a load of farting seagulls," Edie said.

"Maybe old Briggsy's sent the Army out after us, decided to open up after all."

But it wasn't Sandra's army lorries, or Edie's seagulls.

"Look! Up there! It's planes! Must be thirty of them; big buggers, and all."

"I hope they're ours."

"Christ, they ain't!"

They watched in horror as the town centre erupted in smoke and flame.

"Watch out! He's coming straight for us!"

Bullets stuccoed the sea wall; the surf beyond spouted like a giant fountain, deluging the cowering works' girls in spume. Ethel was first on her feet, flinging her toffee apple after the Gotha as it lumbered over the waves; "Fucking bastard!"

"Get down, Ethel!" Elizabeth wrenched at her sleeve.

"Did you see that? He waved back! The bugger waved back!"

Ethel's expletives were lost in the din, as plane after plane roared over their heads.

"Jesus, Mary, mother of Christ," Sandra put her faith in Catholicism, clinging to Edie as though she were the Madonna.

The final Gotha winged away over the estuary. The women got to their feet.

"Christ, them ships was lucky; they're sitting ducks, stuck out there," Elizabeth observed.

"Fat chance of that," Ethel sneered. "Full of ruddy Germans, ain't they. Prison ships. Probably jumping for joy, the buggers."

"You're a human bloody encyclopaedia, you are. How d'you know that?"

"Just do, that's all. Here, Sandra, what's that on your blouse? Are you alright?"

Gingerly Edie dabbed the spot with her handkerchief.

"Dah, it's toffee!"

Their laughter was mandatory; the lunacy of Ethel throwing her toffee apple after the enemy like a stick-grenade would have to wait for another day. Gathering their belongings, they headed for the station.

The place was a shambles, the concourse strewn with masonry and mangled girders. Smatterings of blood dripped from the stanchions, forming pools along the platform. The wounded were being tended where they lay; those beyond help were simply covered.

"Christ; another half-hour and it could've been us," Edie stared.

"Just thank the Lord it weren't," Ethel told her. "Christ, can't even have a day out; nowhere's safe."

A train was standing at the platform, bomb-blasted but still on its rails. Inside a compartment, a woman sat sobbing among the shattered glass.

"It was awful," she howled into her handkerchief. "A little nipper, right in front of me, running for his mother. It took his head clean off, and his arm. And an old couple, they disappeared, just like that..." She couldn't go on.

"There, there, dear, it's over now," Ethel comforted her.

"We was all ready and waiting to go," the woman croaked. "Then over they came. We just left our bags and ran for shelter. And when I come back, they'd taken everything, all my money, everything. Who could do such a thing? I mean, how am I going to get home?" She wailed distraughtly.

"Here, will a shilling be enough?" Edie offered.

"Oh thank you, dear, thank you."

The woman looked up. From over Edie's shoulder, Elizabeth recognised a very familiar face.

"Mrs. Beasley!"

- CHAPTER FIFTY SEVEN -

Richard was lousy, lousier than he had ever been. Partridge, his new batman, seared the seams of his clothing night and day with a lighted candle. He even speared one or two of the translucent, lobster-like little monsters with a needle and frazzled them over the flame, but still the itching was incessant. All the ointments and preparations Richard's mother had donated did nothing. It was a standing joke in the trenches that lice waited for their treatment 'like sparrows for their morning bread.'

But Richard had contracted something worse; scabies. The microscopic itch mite laid her eggs under the skin. Constant scratching extended the hatching grounds. After three weeks and daily applications of Blue Unction, he was a walking, bright blue abrasion. Shin pains developed, and a temperature of a hundred and two; trench fever. He battled through it for three days, only for it to return with sweat-intense severity a week later. Some of the men had also gone down with it, but Richard's was a chronic case. They carried him from the front in a state of delirium.

By the summer of 1917 medical suspicions were being confirmed; the fever was the result of lice and scabies' excreta being scoured into broken skin. The scabies variety was the worst and extremely contagious. In the line or out, immediate isolation was compulsory. Even after the cause was discovered it remained a secret; if the men found out, they'd scratch themselves silly. An epidemic could empty the trenches, it could lose the War.

Of course, Richard knew none of this, he was barely aware of anything for the first few days. Finally, after interminable weeks of sulphur baths, he was sent to convalesce by the sea. He'd been hoping for home leave; nevertheless, the weather was fair, the food good and his presiding nurse pretty.

In bed he felt fit and well, but when he tried to take a little exercise, he soon discovered the fever's debilitating power. He wrote to Laura daily, but, for once, the remarkably efficient Army Postal Service failed him and he received few letters in reply, all dated weeks earlier and forwarded by Battalion H.Q.

His Military Cross came through, he got a letter from Smylie confirming the news, along with his promotion to full lieutenant. How Joscelyn had known about it, Richard hadn't a clue. Apparently the C.O. had recommended it after Arras, where Richard had brought in a wounded Subaltern under fire. Men had been carried in before, but this one had been no less a mortal than a Viscount's son. What's more, the boy had lived. It had taken Rowe ages to erase the bloodstain.

Richard smiled sardonically; here he was with a medal and the only German he'd confronted face to face was a terrified boy in a listening post. He'd seen helmets bobbing along a trench; he'd glimpsed a field grey back scampering round a traverse; he could have pulled the trigger, but he hadn't. He'd thrown a bomb or two, but, if he'd killed anyone, he hadn't seen them die.

Death in the trenches was so impersonal, so indiscriminate, shells, bombs and bullets directed at and by a predominantly unseen adversary. The old adage, 'if it's got your name on it', had never been truer. He'd been out longer than most with only a scratch on the head to show for it; others had copped it within days, some within hours. He supposed it was a survival medal more than anything.

He shared the news with his V.A.D., but no one else. Her name was Mildred; he called her Millie. She was tall for a girl, as tall as him, flaxen haired and came from Hampshire. She was blushingly smitten. He hadn't expected shyness from a nurse; it was very becoming; flirtation was good for the soul, good for the ego. After a week he was allowed out, after another he invited her to dinner.

They strolled through meadows, pine woods and sand hills to a small hotel at Hardelot. The ruddy brown sails of fishing smacks captured the sunset off Paris Plage, their timelessness, like life itself, compressed into a capsule by the guns' subliminal thunder.

He held her hand over the blue chequered tablecloth. Her candlelit lips shone as burgundy red as the wine, but he resisted the temptation. Only when they parted did he kiss her lightly on the mouth. His loins stirred, but he let his hand slip away. With Elspeth there had been no emotional repercussions, little remorse, but he felt something for Millie, to get involved with her would be an act of betrayal, and he didn't want to hurt her.

Their final goodbye was upliftingly poignant. She'd found some Military Cross ribbon from somewhere and sewn it on his tunic. Love, he decided, was circumstantial. Of all the women in the world, for how many could he fall? Probably thousands. One had to strip away lust to discover love's true meaning, the love he felt for Laura.

* * * * *

Despite Laura's maternal instincts, the novelty of a wailing baby and soiled nappies soon wore off. Her return to the patriotic fold had surprised her father as much as the relief of it had surprised her, but he remained adamant that she should go to university. Her dreams of ambulance driving were dashed. If she wanted to get to France, she would have to find another way, and find something to do in the meantime. The violet-sun-bonnet brigade were monopolising the fields, others the workplaces, and neither appealed.

"I had thought of helping out at the Manor."

Her father asked the reverend Soames. No help was needed. There were only four convalescents, more house guests than invalids, the Vicar reported. Then, two days later, he telephoned to say that Mrs. Stafford was looking for volunteers to man the new army camp's YMCA canteen. A number of local ladies had enlisted, including his own sister. Every girl was chaperoned, and the camp was within easy cycling distance.

Laura could hardly say no. However, she soon found that plying ha'penny and penny buns to a bunch of boisterous conscripts was little better than baby sitting, even if the odd vulgarity was a lexical education in itself.

She shared her shift with Mary, Spencer's youngest sister, each chaperoning the other. They became the darlings of the canteen. Laura was sure it was Mary she'd seen in Spencer's photographs. Then, one day, with every man out on parade, Mary spoke of him.

"He cared for you a great deal, you know. Often mentioned you in his letters. He and I were very close."

Laura told her the feeling had been mutual.

"The strangest thing," Mary confided, slicing a jam roll. "Between you and me, Mother tried to contact him, you know, seance and all that. She hired some trout from Elmsford, a mystic or medium or whatever one calls them. It was so scary. The woman threw a complete fit, writhing around on the floor, mumbling something about some 'Marian' or other. Not even Mrs. Avery knew of any Marians in the family."

If Mary noticed the blood drain from Laura's lips, she accredited it to the nature of the gossip.

"By the way, I've always meant to ask you, how did those pictures come out, you know, the ones he took when you came round that day?"

"What? Oh..." Laura mouthed distractedly. "They're splendid; he was such a good photographer."

"He took some of me, you know, with nothing on; well, next to nothing," Mary announced unabashedly. "Alice, too. I was just thinking..."

The seance was eclipsed; alarm bells rattled Laura's teacups. Had Mary stumbled upon her secret? Surely not; Spencer had sworn that he'd given her everything, even the negatives. Quickly she put the crockery down.

"No, no, nothing like that. Just some portraits." Her ears burned.

"Oh, Laura! Don't be such a prude! It's nothing to be ashamed of," Mary protested. "After all, he was my brother. Actually, it was quite fun, all Alice's doing. Poor Spencer didn't know where to look!"

Laura stabilised. But why was Mary telling her this?

"I was just wondering; you see I fou..."

The door banged open; the hut filled with drill-taxed soldiery.

"Oh well, back to the grindstone," Mary sighed.

It was almost an hour before the men returned to their training. Laura was just working back to the subject, when Mrs. Stafford arrived. She was organising a concert party and had been busy soliciting the services of Elmsford Operatic's Prima Donna. One of the officers from the Manor had already offered to recite some Kipling, while an enlisted man, a comedian by profession, had volunteered to supply the humour. All that was needed was a girl to sing a popular song or two and some kind of speciality act. Having heard Laura warbling away that morning over a particularly lovesick letter from Richard, Mrs. Stafford now thrust a selection of sheet music at her, forbidding any excuses.

That evening, Agatha and Laura cycled to the village school to rehearse, leaving baby Harold with his new nanny. The piano was more out of tune than ever, but eventually Laura got through 'On Sunday, I walk out with a Soldier,' as tonally as it was possible to tell. Left arm swung with left foot, and right with right, when she marched up and down, but Agatha said it only added to her appeal. Her second song would be the emotive 'Long, Long Trail,' if only she could memorise the words, for her mind remained preoccupied. Did Mary know about the photos? Worse still, had her own mother been watching her? Marian's supernatural existence and Laura's wantonness interlinked into the rattling chains of insomnia.

* * * * *

"Hold it down, boys, here comes Von Kluck. Had any postcards from the Kaiser lately, Bowden?" Brewer smirked over his beer. "Don't reckon you will, now, not with your boy getting the M.C. He won't like that. Put paid to your Iron Cross good and proper."

Arthur ignored the insult, or thought he had, until he forgot himself and offered to buy Kipper Johnson a drink. Round buying remained outlawed.

"Alright, Arthur?" Kipper frowned from the end of the bar. "Guns are loud today; must be the weather."

The area sergeant returned from the lavatory.

"Ah, there you are, Bill. Thought you'd got yourself lost for a minute."

"Should've come back sooner, Sergeant; you could've caught that bloody Hun lover red-handed. Offering a round, he was, and him a bloody Special. Doesn't say much for the force, does it? Needs putting behind bars, him, for more reasons than one," Brewer turned the screw.

"Asked the constable there how he was, that's all. Ain't that right, Arthur?" Bowden called on Arthur Treadwell's support.

"Do what?" Treadwell called from the dartboard. "Oh, it's you Arthur. Won't be a mo'. Double top and I'm done."

"See? You need your bloody ears syringed, Brewer. Wouldn't do your brain much harm, either."

"Alright you two, pack it in," Kipper warned.

A competitive groan issued from the ocky, as Treadwell's arrows flew straight and true. The atmosphere closed in behind them, hanging thickly over the sawdust.

More sniggering came from Brewer's corner; Bowden's eyes narrowed.

"If you got summat to say, Brewer, say it."

"Thought I had. Mind you, I always did wonder about that boy of yours, your youngest; never did stack up; you being his father."

The next thing Brewer knew he was flat on his back, clutching a broken nose.

* * * * *

The house seemed so small in its emptiness, as compact as the echo of Laura's footsteps on its bare boards. It hardly seemed possible that this was the parlour of dimensional memory. Had it only been a year? It seemed so long ago, the images a distant landscape of indiscernible shades, with no memorials on which to focus.

A creaking stair brought her first recollection of sneaking Richard out; the lamp on the landing, the bedroom window under which they had lain; but this was not the regression she sought.

Her mother's door was open, the room sunlit, as if to emphasise its exorcism. She could see where the bed had been, the chest of drawers with its crucifix, yet these re-papered walls were not those of their imprisonment. She closed her eyes, but could commune only with the present. Her mother was gone, at least from this place.

That left only the Manor, where her mother had been taken after her seizure, and where Laura had cavorted with Spencer, if cavorted was the right word. But she could hardly just turn up on the doorstep; she would have to be invited.

And why had they never visited her mother's grave? She didn't even know where it was, 'Hertfordshire' was all her father had ever said. Of course there was Agatha to consider, but, if she picked her moment, he would only need to tell her where, she could find her own way there, even drive there, when they lifted the ban. Suddenly it seemed strange that they had never been, Hertfordshire was not so prohibitively far in a motor car.

Downstairs a floorboard creaked. Fear gripped her.

"Is someone there?"

"Laura? Is that you? It's Mrs. Bowden..."

* * * * *

Kipper Johnson appeared in Arthur's yard.

"How is he? Dead, I hope," Arthur asked, unrepentantly.

"His nose is broke, right enough. Christ, Arthur, you do pick your moments, what with the sergeant there and all."

"Dah, he deserved that and more for what he said, the bastard."

"Well, that's as maybe, but he says he's pressing charges. I'll have another go at him once he's calmed down, but it ain't looking good."

333

"Duty calls." The last customer returned his cup to the counter and headed for the parade ground.

"Laura, about the photographs..."

Laura's stomach tightened. "Oh, I'm sorry, I meant to bring them with me." She'd decided to waylay Mary's suspicions with the portraits.

"No, I mean the ones I told you about, my ones!"

Laura's exploits were obviously of no interest. Still her heart pounded. "Oh yes."

"Well, do you think it shocking to do something like that?"

"I've never thought about it. I suppose it all depends on the circumstance."

"Only, I was thinking, perhaps we could do a tableau for the show, you know, behind a screen, Grecians bathing, that sort of thing. I found lots of props in Spencer's old studio, and there are even proper lights. It wouldn't be indecent or anything; one can buy stockings which cover the entire body and we could drape ourselves in silks and what-have-you. Anyway, they'd only see our silhouettes, they wouldn't even know it was us. We did it at school once and it was a real hoot."

Laura's relief was palpable. It was more than a reprieve, it was all erasing acquittal.

"I hardly think your mother would approve, do you?"

Even the mention of mothers no longer carried any soul-searching significance.

"No, but if I can't come up with an alternative, I've been ordered to ballet dance and I can't do that, it would be just too dreadful. I'm sure the men would like it."

"I'm sure they would," Laura laughed, piling sandwiches onto a plate. She'd just got Richard back, she wasn't going to jeopardise that for five minutes of tomfoolery.

"Only, if you were to do it too, I'm sure mother would agree," Mary pleaded. "She thinks very highly of you, and it is in a good cause."

"Mary, if we did something like that, it would be all round the village in an instant."

"Oh, the village. Who cares about the crummy village? Sometimes, Laura, you can be so.... middle class!"

* * * * *

The evening poured its contemplative light on 'Howard's End', begging the one, unrequited question;

"Daddy, I've been meaning to ask you; about Mother's grave...."

Scott read on behind the pages of the Telegraph. The Times had become too propagandist, even for a government contractor.

"Daddy?"

"What? Oh, yes, dear?"

"About Mother's grave..."

"Oh, yes..."

"Well, I was wondering...."

"I'm sorry, my darling, just let me finish this."

Laura returned to her book's great conundrum, 'only connect......' She was soon absorbed. Her father had reached the door before she realized.

"Oh, daddy, I wanted to ask you, while Agatha's upstairs..."

"Oh, yes, my dear; shan't be a tick; I'm just popping up to see how she is."

"It's about Mother's grave," she whispered urgently.

"Yes, all right; we'll talk later."

* * * * *

A despondent Arthur Bowden sat in his parlour, Beatrice beside him.

"Make us some tea, mother, there's a good girl."

"Sugar, Gordon?" Beatrice asked Kipper Johnson, sitting opposite.

"That's alright, Mrs. B., I've got used to it without."

"We've got some."

"Well, just the one, then."

Beatrice disappeared into the kitchen; Arthur gave Kipper the nod; Johnson lowered his voice.

"Why did you do it, Arthur?"

"You was there, you heard what he said. No one casts aspersions on my Beattie and gets away with it."

"Dah, he didn't mean nothing by it in her case; it was you he was having a go at."

"That's no excuse. He got what he deserved, the foul-mouthed bastard."

"Well, that's as maybe, but I'm going to have to suspend you, Arthur, got no choice."

"Come off it, Gordon."

"Sorry, old mate, Sergeant's orders. It's all down to the Beak now."

"But it'll be alright, won't it? I mean he's not going to lock me up or nothing, not for a piddling little thing like that? Christ, if anyone's been asking for it, it's him, after what he did to that Gunther. He could've killed him."

"Yes, and since you raise the subject, the least said about that the better."

"But it's bound to come up. I've got nothing to be ashamed of."

"You just mind what you say. Fraternising with the enemy won't stand you in good stead where old Rifkin's concerned, and ten to one that's who you'll get. He'd send you down for catching German measles. Lost his son, same time as Brewer."

"You don't think I was fraternising, surely to Christ, Gordon?"

"I might not, but I knows you; the old Beak don't, and Brewer's got a mouth on him the size of the crystal palace, as you've found out to your cost."

"Huh," Arthur humped. "And his!"

"Yes, well just you be careful, though I have to hand it to you, Arthur, you pack a mighty wallop. For a moment there I thought his head was going to fly off down the old alley and take the skittles with it. All swelled up, it is, eyes like coal holes.

Ain't you told your missus yet?" Kipper nodded towards the kitchen

"Not about what he said."

"Well, she's bound to hear. Anyway, as I said, he didn't mean anything on her account. Hey-up, here she comes. Mum's the word, then. Oh, thanks Mrs. B; nothing like a nice cuppa."

* * * * *

Captain 'Kipling's' monologue left his audience as stony-faced as his 'one-eyed yellow idol' and 'mad Karoo' heading hot foot for the Katmandu Law Courts, slander suit in hand. The comedian's jokes, purified in deference to the ladies, fell as flat as the army issue beer, while Mary's 'Swan Lake' drained what little patience the rank and file still retained, only the transparency of her silks, following her absolute refusal to wear a petticoat, securing a face-saving ripple. The men were getting restless; it was time to call up the heavy guns.

"Christ Almighty, Fred, it's Big bloody Bertha, herself!"

Elmsford's operatic diva let fly with an ear-piercing selection from Gilbert and Sullivan.

"Bloody hell, watch the glasses!"

"Glasses be blowed; that voice could shatter an effing tank!"

"Bring on the sodding policeman and arrest her, for Gawd's sake," some wag called.

She was hardly a nightingale, more a cantankerous crow. Her unappreciative flock gave her the bird.

"Fly South!"

She stalked from the stage. "Uncouth ruffians! I've never been so humiliated!"

Mutiny stared the Company in the face. The comedian was adamant, he wouldn't go back on unless he could 'spice it up a bit.'

Had there been a hook in the wings Mrs. Stafford would have hauled him off by the neck until dead, but the more ribald his jokes became, the better the Tommies liked it.

"Alright you lot, let's finish on a sing-song. Maestro, if you please."

The tune was notoriously familiar, even to a Priory girl.

"The mademoiselle from Armentieres..."

"Parley Vous!"

The girls were ordered to cover their ears; the Diva fainted in the wings; the Vicar half-nelsoned himself into submission trying to lift her.

"Inky-pinkie-parley-vous," Captain Kipling surreptitiously sang along.

"You're on, love," the comic grinned, striding triumphantly from the stage.

Laura's knees knocked, her face went into spasm. Only the tight lacing of her bodice offered any bolster. Mary had chosen her costume. Laura's father had disapproved. "It's barely decent, with bare being the operative word." Agatha had added a veil across the cleavage and sweet-talked him round. "You can't wear that," Mary had insisted in the dressing room, snatching the veil away. "It spoils the whole effect."

The pianist played the overture.

"Just march on, love, look, like this..." The comic marked time.

Laura forced her legs to respond.

"That's right, that's the way; nothing to it. Now, on we go!" Taking her arm, he marched her onto the stage. *"Da, da-da, da da..."*

"On Sunday, I walk out with a soldier..."

The men went wild. Primed by the comedian, any girl would have done, but one as physically uplifted as she, had got them, in their own parlance, 'by the short and curlies.' She couldn't have chosen a better song, the last stanza was the clincher;

"But on Saturday I'm willing,
If you'll only take the shilling,
To make a man of any one of you!"

The hut exploded. The men stood on their seats.

"More! More!"

Laura was elated, but lost. She looked frantically to the wings. Captain Kipling could only shrug.

"Bloody hell; not a fucking clue. God help us when we get to France, that's all I can say," the comedian muttered. "Get them to sing along!"

His prompt was drowned in the uproar, Laura floundered.

"Again," he yelled to the pianist, calling to the audience, "come on, you lot, let's hear what you're made of! Go on, love, sing it again!"

As Laura picked up the melody, the men raised the rafters with their own, rather different, version:

"I don't want to be a soldier,
I don't want to go to war,
I'd rather stay at home, around the streets to roam,
Living off the earnings of a high class whore!
I don't want a bayonet up my arsehole,
I don't want my bollocks shot away,
I'd rather stay in England,
In Merry, Merry England,
And fornicate my bloody life away!"

The song died on Laura's lips. She knew the impact those words would have on Mary and Mrs. Stafford. The comedian motioned to her to come off. The cheers turned to boos.

"It's alright, love, leave them to me."

Picking on the biggest hecklers, he restored order.

"Right, now this time I want to hear her sing, not you misbegotten bloody shower. I give you again, Miss Lily Scott!"

Her re-christening barely registered, her reception was tumultuous. The piano sounded the poignant overture; the hall hushed. Her nerves returned tenfold; her voice tremored like a child's.

"There's a long, long trail awinding,

337

Into the land of my dreams,
Where the nightingales are singing,
And the white moon beams.
There's a long, long trail of waiting,
Until my dreams all come true,
'Til the day when I'll be going,
Down that long, long trail with you."

In soft tones, the refrain was taken up, filling the hall with the men's longing for home, and with their love for her, for she was all women, their mothers, their daughters, their sisters, their lovers.

The last chord died into utter silence, then the place erupted.

After that no other act stood a chance. "You're a one," the comedian smiled as he took Laura hand and led the entire company in an extended finale of war tunes. The players sang along as best they could; it hardly mattered, the men knew the words by heart; all they'd really wanted was a good old singsong. As the pianist hammered out 'Good Save the King', they embellished the last bars with their own anthem:

"Glorious, glorious! One shell hole twixt four of us,
Soon there'll be no bleeding more of us,
Only the bloody old hole!"

Mrs. Stafford had long since departed, too upset to witness the final triumph and the final imperial blasphemy.

* * * * *

"Bloody hell, this egg's almost a chicken, mother," Arthur grimaced, lifting the stale shell.

"Well, either eat it or wait 'til it is, perhaps, then, we might all have a bit."

For what it cost, Beatrice was in no mood for Arthur's moaning, however deep her sympathy, of which the egg was a token. His expletives she would forgive, just this once.

"If you don't want it, pass it over here," Amos Crutchley eyed the oeuf enviously. "Well? How d'you get on, then?"

"Bound over to keep the peace," Beatrice told him. She'd insisted on attending the hearing; Cissy had sat opposite, a silent martyr to loyalty.

"Pah," Crutchley puffed. "Not even a fine? That put Brewer in his place, alright. So what are you so down in the mouth for, Arthur?"

"Bloody judge good as threw me out the Specials, didn't he. Said with a temper like mine I wasn't fit to serve."

"Christ, any man would've done the same under that kind of providication... provid.. oh, whatever they call it. Bloody beak must want his head tested."

"Sticks in my gullet, Amos, really it does. I'll say this for Gordon, though, he was on the right side of impartial, and old Arthur Treadwell put in a good word for me and all."

338

"Good old boy, Treadwell," Crutchley concurred. "'He's had his fair share, what with that Agnes of his. Oh well, Arthur, every cloud, as the saying goes; least you won't have to tramp the lanes of a night. Let Brewer do it, if he's a mind to, miserable old sod."

"Yeh, and I hope an owl poops on his head!"

"Arthur!" Beatrice objected. "Anyway, Gordon reckons, with things as they are, the worst you'll get is a reprimand," Beatrice put the record straight.

"That remains to be seen," Arthur moped.

- CHAPTER FIFTY NINE -

Richard was returned to duty at the end of September. The Essex were out of the line, rebuilding their strength. A bundle of post awaited him and the congratulations of his brother officers on his M.C.

"At least you deserve it," Smylie told him, resentful of the medals now being dished out to Base-Wallahs.

They went out and got roaring drunk. It wasn't until the following evening that Richard was able to settle down, still slightly the worst for wear, to read Laura's letters.

He seldom had bad moods; this was an exception. One of his men had gone awol, reviving the nightmare of Joe Crutchley. The Military Police were out looking for him. He'd been a good man, dependable, Richard had even recommended him for promotion. Another had shot himself in the hand, the second self-inflicted wound in Richard's platoon; three more had been blown to bits on a carrying party. He'd watched them go, lugging their loads like Christ and the condemned. Soon there'd be none of the old lags left. He tore open the first envelope, desperate for solace.

He was surprised to hear she was working at the camp. He smiled thinly when he read of her singing exploits. He lit a cigarette and inhaled deeply when she told him the show had gone so well she'd been asked to do more. There was nothing to worry about, everything was very proper and above board, she was escorted home after every show.

'I bet you are,' he scowled, picturing her on the arm of some suave Spencer look-alike. The old wound reopened.

'It's a real hoot. It's wonderful to be so appreciated. Photo to follow.'

The hardbacked envelope stood out from the pile. He opened it and took out the picture. It was verging on indecent. He flushed.

'Bitch. It's hardly surprising you get a standing ovation in that get-up.'

His latent jealously jostled past his inert common sense, as all the vindictive hurt came flooding back, Spencer, the photographs, everything. She was behaving like some Music Hall tart, openly exposing herself for the trollop she was and making a complete fool of him in the process. His imagination ran riot; the salted wound gaped.

A gulped Scotch raced to his belly, not to douse but to ignite his anger. The brazier flared as he fed his frustration with burning hatred, every page, every envelope. When nothing was left he took bottle and glass and skulked away to a nearby wood.

The following day, a missed open goal in a lost inter-battalion soccer match re-stoked the embers. Sporting a hangover, weak from lack of sleep and the aftermath of fever, he'd been a shadow of his former self, and she was to blame.

Boycotting the post-match commiserations, he retired to his billet to uncork his wrath, breaking lead twice as he poured out his presumptions in scorning sarcasm, turning the screw with each twisted comma. Officers were trusted, it would go through unvetted.

That night he slept like a log. When he awoke in the morning, his jealousy had evaporated. He leapt out of bed and pulled on his clothes. Partridge came in with his tea.

"Oh, Partridge, you'll be quicker than me. Nip down to the Adjutant's office, would you. I posted a letter last night; I don't want it to go."

"Right you are, Sir. Shall I see to your water first, Sir?"

"No, man, hurry!" His temper was back, but now it was anger at his own crass stupidity. "It's addressed to Miss L. Scott!"

* * * * *

The policeman walked across the lawn. The nurse left the pram and went to meet him. Something was said, but they were too far away for the fugitive to decipher what.

He sank further into his blackthorn hideaway. He'd spent the night in a ditch. Cold, covered with bracken, he'd slept little.

A voice called out, a female voice. He blinked back into focus. A big dog was bounding up to the policeman, the biggest he had ever seen.

"Down, Max!"

His heart thumped; this he understood, his own name! For mind-numbing seconds he thought he'd been discovered, until the dog obediently sank back on its haunches.

A very pretty girl kissed the policeman on the cheek. He looked embarrassed. The baby started to cry. The dog sniffed the breeze; the wind changed direction; the beast settled.

The nurse carried the baby into the house; the policeman sat; the girl relaxed on the grass, her arm draped over the dog's ruff.

The man cursed his nincompoop English tutor; if only he could understand what they were saying.

The nurse reappeared with a tray of what looked like lemonade. His breath escaped enviously over his parched tongue; all he'd had since daybreak was a swig of ditchwater and a gutful of raw cabbage.

The policeman emptied his glass and stood; the girl too. The dog followed them to the house and out of sight, its tail wagging.

Stealthily the fugitive skirted the grounds. There was an outbuilding at the front. It blocked his view. It smelled of oil. A garage?

He stole along its length and saw them again, the policeman astride his bike in the lane, the girl and her dog standing by the gate. He was downwind, yet still the brute seemed to sense him, until, once again, the girl's fawning distracted it.

The policeman cycled off; the dog took a last, lingering sniff, then ambled down the garden path at his mistress's heels.

Belly-crawling through the hedge, the fugitive crept to the garage door. It was

341

unlocked. He looked across anxiously at the house. Nothing stirred. Lifting the frame free from the gravel, he inched the door open.

In the dingy interior a miracle met his eyes, a car. With a car and a change of clothes he could get to the coast; there must be clothes in the house.

But the authorities would have set up road blocks. He would need papers, and better English than he had, to stand any chance of getting through; and, anyway, the car probably hadn't been driven for years.

Gently he rocked the chassis. Petrol lapped in the tank. It was an opportunity not to be missed; he might not get another.

The baby was the key. The girl must be the mother; she'd do anything to protect it. He could never bring himself to harm it, but she wasn't to know that. The threat would be sufficient. With hostages he would stand a much better chance.

The father had to be away at the War; that just left the dog. It was too big to tackle with his bare hands, it would be more likely to kill him than visa versa. Besides, he liked dogs, he had dogs of his own. The brute's behaviour would depend on its mistress. Even then it might not obey, not if it sensed her fear. Somehow he would have to lock it up, the nurse, too, preferably in the cellar, there had to be a cellar. Not now, though; he would wait until dark. The house had been checked, he should be safe enough.

* * * * *

"Nice to see you up and about again, George, even if it is on crutches," Sarson grinned.

George swung himself onto the bed. "Brought you a bit of baccy, though how you're going to smoke it, Gawd only knows. Had some myself; tasted like bloody cow dung."

"Bugger what it tastes like, a smoke's a smoke." Sarson thanked him, slipping the tiny wad under his pillow. "How's the old peg, then?"

"Bah; they won't do nothing; too afraid I'll do another runner. Not that they did anything before; it was that old boy what fixed it. 'Send me back to him,' I keep telling 'em; 'let that old man sort it out;' but do they listen? Do they fuck. If they don't do something soon, the bloody thing'll fall off."

Sarson's face fell. George could have kicked himself, even with his gammy leg.

"Sorry, mate, I wasn't thinking."

"Dah, that's alright," Sarson forgave him. "I'm better off without it; bloody thing was weighing me down like an anchor. Make the old woman happy, she was always having a go at me about getting through more shoes than her father's old nag."

"He's lucky to still have one. Bugger all left in our village; Army took every last one fit enough to pull a cart."

"Has to, don't he; Rag and Bone man, see; horse is his livelihood. This War's been the making of him. Talk about 'any old iron'; reckon he could buy the whole of fucking Lambeth with what he's got stashed away, fucking old miser. I keep telling her, get him to send some over here, let me buy my way out. I mean, what do they want to keep me here for, 'specially now?

342

A nice little boozer by the sea, that'd do me. A pint in one hand, the same of cockles in the other, and a barmaid with tits the size of footballs to rest my poor head upon when the old trouble and strife's at her mother's. Give me that, dear Lord, and I'll be happy as a fucking sandbag. Might even manage a game of skittles, once I've got me balance."

"Get back to my wife and kiddies, that's all I want," George sighed, "And get this leg seen to."

"Fat chance of that, good as a fucking ball and chain that, long as it stays the way it is. You shouldn't've tried it on, George. What the hell was you thinking?"

"Shouldn't've let go, you mean. Bloody wouldn't have, neither, if I'd known what bastards they'd be."

"Well, I've heard of some crazy fucking stunts in my time, but hitching a lift on one of the Kaiser's fucking coal wagons in broad fucking daylight just about takes the biscuit. Talk about asking for it. You must need your bleeding head examined."

"No need to rub it in. Anyway, my leg was better then."

"Yeh, and it'd be better now, if you'd used your noddle. Still, least you've still got the leverage; reckon my old woman'll have to learn a bit of jockeying if she wants her tinder to spark. Talking of which, I hear old Sparky gave the conchy a right fucking goin'-over."

"Half killed him," George confirmed. "Caught him with his hand in his food parcel, bloody warthog. How is it in here; feed you any better?"

"Do they fuck. Sandstorm soup and wood shavings. Only bit of meat we get's on a Sunday, if it ain't that evil smelling fish, and even that you could fit into a fucking matchbox. Christ, it's gone in one gollop and in the fucking bedpan the next. I know I used to moan on about it, but I'd give the other fucking leg for a bit of the old sausage and sauerkraut; even a dollop of that mangel-fucking-wurzel they have the cheek to call jam wouldn't go amiss."

"Same as us, then. Mind you, from what Hughesy says, they ain't faring much better themselves. He wangled kitchen detail to see what he could nick, but says there weren't nothing. Makes you wonder what it's like at home; the old food parcels ain't what they used to be."

"Still, a damned sight better than here, you can be sure of that."

"I hope so; wouldn't like to think of my kids going hungry."

"Nah, not there, George. Here, I think I spy our Little Willie on the prowl; better make yourself scarce. Thanks for the baccy."

* * * * *

Laura spent the afternoon singing along to gramophone records. She'd built a repertoire of ten songs. She loved winning over an audience, the euphoria of a standing ovation.

Of the original concert party, neither Mary nor the Operatic Diva had stayed the course, while the comedian had been packed off to France in disgrace. Nevertheless, the show had gone on and Laura with it, along with Captain 'Kipling', who'd persevered with his monologue, mostly for the sake of giving Laura a lift. He was hopelessly smitten; the others pulled her leg about it.

Her father remained as reconciled to her 'amateur theatricals' as his stage-struck daughter was to going to university. Quid pro quo was the bargain reached, Scott on the insistence that "that damned costume has to go," and Laura on the secret supposition that there had to be concert parties in Cambridge with the wherewithal to get her to France. The lace was sewn back into her stage bodice.

She'd been to the Manor at Mary's invitation. "It happened in here," Mary had said of the seance. Laura had recognised the room where her mother had lain, but she'd felt nothing from it, and nothing from Spencer's studio, now converted into the convalescents' tea room.

At half past three, she packed away her sheet music and headed for the garage. Constable Johnson's warning of a prisoner on the loose had given her a cast iron excuse for driving into the village to pick Agatha up from school. The new teacher was attending a funeral; Agatha was standing in.

"Mind out the way, Max."

She wrenched open the garage door.

Woken from his torpor, the fugitive vaulted groggily from the Bentall's back seat. The Mastiff was on him in an instant, clamping his incisors into his calf. The German cried out, punching the dog's muzzle, but Max had his man and he wasn't letting go.

"Get help! It's him! Phone the police!" Laura shrieked to baby Harold's nurse, who'd come running at commotion's call.

She wasn't the only one yelling for help. The man was rolling about by the car's back wheel, trying to prise Max's jaws apart. Summoning all her courage, Laura grabbed a garden fork, thrust the prongs determinedly before her and inched forward.

"Camerad! Camerad!"

"All right Max, here boy, here. Max! Heel!"

Reluctantly the dog relinquished its hold. The man sat up, his trouser leg in tatters, his face contorted.

"Hands up!" Laura ordered.

He complied with one hand, clasping his calf with the other. Blood flowed through his fingers. "Sheiser!"

Max growled menacingly. Laura gulped. What on earth did she do now? "Stay where you are, or I'll set the dog on you again!"

The German grasped the essentials.

"Nein, nein! I stay!"

He propped himself against a mudguard. A well-honed sickle hung on the wall, but out of reach.

"Don't you move!" Laura clung to Max's collar with one hand while waving the fork as menacingly as she could manage with the other, wishing to God she'd grabbed something lighter.

"I not move. Him Max? Me Max, also," the captive grimaced. "May I look, please?" Leaning forward, he carefully ripped open his trouser leg. "Mein Gott." He sank back in a daze.

The prongs of the fork clunked to the ground; Laura almost retched.

"Help's on its way." The nurse burst in, armed with Scott's knobkerrie.

"I don't think you'll be needing that," Laura told her.

"Oh, my Lord. Max?"

Laura nodded.

"Well we can't leave him in that state, he'll bleed to death."

"I no escape," the man assured them weakly. "Nice dog, nice... dog."

He slumped into the dust.

The nurse was tying the dressing when the Army arrived.

"Come on, let's be having you!"

Hobnailed boots clattered from the tailboard and up the shingle driveway.

"In here," Laura called.

"Sounds like our Lily!"

The captive was hauled to his feet.

"You'd better get him to a doctor," the nurse told them.

"You?" The Lieutenant asked Laura incredulously, looking at the garden fork.

"No, not me, Max."

The Mastiff raised its bloodstained jowls; Laura looked away.

"He's certainly a sizeable brute. Good boy, Max, good boy!" The lieutenant patted Max on the head with his left hand. His right was gloved and clearly prosthetic.

"Captured by a woman; the poor blighter'll never live it down. All right, Sergeant, take him out. I believe you can put that down now, Miss Scott."

The garden fork was still in Laura's grasp. Shakily she leant it against the door. It fell. The lieutenant righted it.

"I also believe you could do with a cup of tea."

"Yes, I believe I could."

She walked him to the lorry.

"Trust it to be you," a voice called from the back, followed by a general "Good on you, Lil!"

The men were from the local camp. She knew them all by sight, many by name.

"Max did all the work."

"Perhaps we should stuff a tin hat on his head and send him over yonder!"

"All right Smith, that'll do. Not a bad idea, though," the Lieutenant smiled. "Will you be singing for us soon, Miss Scott? I believe it's time you entertained the Officers, you know, can't let the men have all the fun."

"Oh, I'm not sure, Lieutenant. I'm off to university soon."

"Oh, we can't have that. How ever will we manage? No, I'll have to have a word with the C.O. and get you requisitioned for the duration. University? How could you even dream of such a thing?"

"My father's idea, I'm afraid," Laura explained.

"All secure, Sir," the Sergeant reported.

"Thank you, Sergeant. Well, at least I hope to see you again before you go. Dinner one night, perhaps?"

"Tough luck, Lieutenant, she's spoken for!"

"Quiet, that man!" The Sergeant snapped.

"Really?" The Lieutenant asked ruefully, climbing into the front seat. "Then all I can say is 'lucky beggar'. "Well, adieu for now. I don't know if they give decorations to dogs, but I'll see what I can do. Drive on!"

"Come on, Max," Laura smiled, as the lorry pulled away. "Let's get you cleaned up."

CHAPTER SIXTY

"*How* much, Mrs. Coombes?" Beatrice asked in disbelief.

"Two shillings a pound, I'm afraid, Mrs. Bowden," the shopkeeper confirmed, patting the butter into shape. "If you want some cheese, I've got Canadian at one and eight, and the New Zealand at one and four. It's a bit on the strong side, but it's alright for cooking."

'Rank, don't you mean,' Beatrice thought glumly. Even the cat had turned its nose up at the previous week's morsel. "You ain't paying good money for that," Arthur had told her. "Poison a rat, that would."

"No English though," Mrs. Coombes went on. "Can't get it for love nor money. I've been promised some eggs for Friday. I'll put some by for you, if you like. Won't be many, though."

"If you wouldn't mind," Beatrice saved face, wondering how on earth she was going to pay for them. Things were going from bad to worse for Arthur, and Elizabeth's purse strings were drawn tighter than a goat's bottom. Beatrice rued Arthur's prohibitive pride; she should have gone pea-picking, like the other women, and taken the children with her. Those who had were now enjoying the benefits of butter. "Just the margarine, then, Mrs. Coombes."

Doorbell and cash till jingled in unison.

"Morning Mrs. Beasley."

"Morning Mrs. Coombes; Beatrice."

Her subjection to the Southend air raid had elevated Mrs. Beasley to the front page of the Elmsford Chronicle, albeit it in the caption 'Eyewitness Account Inside.' No other villager had ever made it past the parish section. It was an exclusivity that, for once, had tied her tongue regarding Elizabeth's equal claim to fame.

"Any eggs, today?"

"Sorry, Mrs. Beasley, they just ain't laying. It's all on account of them guns, so they say. They can hear them even when we can't, Mrs. White was telling me. Apparently it puts them right off. I've been promised some for Friday."

"Friday it'll have to be, then. I just fancied a boiled egg," Mrs. Beasley sighed. "You and yours alright, Beatrice?"

"Can't complain," Beatrice said, pocketing her purse. "Good day."

"Good day. Give Elizabeth my regards."

For Mrs. Beasley to have a civil tongue in her head was unusual enough; for it to uncaustically include Elizabeth was stupefying. Beatrice walked home in a state of astonishment.

Arthur was poring over the coal card.

"Don't know what's got into that Mrs. Beasley," Beatrice told him, filling the kettle. "She's been right friendly since that air raid."

"Shell shock, I shouldn't wonder," he said, pondering the inclusion of every nook and cranny that sported a door in his room requirement for winter fuel.

"Even had a good word to say for Elizabeth."

"Huh."

The previous day Arthur had cycled to Rayntree, chasing work. A pint in a pub, a bit of eavesdropping, and the Works' outing had been Elizabeth's secret no longer. He hadn't told Beatrice.

"Pity she didn't get blown to buggery when that factory of hers went up, do us all a favour."

"Don't dig the girl's grave, Arthur. That's tempting fate."

"Fat chance of that; the Devil looks after his own, mother. Do you reckon the privy counts as a room?"

"Hardly, dear."

"I don't see why not," Arthur increased his tally to eight, including the stair cupboard. "I bet old Stafford puts his down. Don't see why we shouldn't."

"Because it's dishonest dear. Besides, since when did our privy have a fireplace?"

"Since they gave you extra coal for it, that's when," Arthur grumped, scrubbing it from his list.

* * * * *

Laura couldn't believe it. This was the Richard of her cruellest memories, the Richard he'd sworn he would never be again. Each paragraph was pure, punctuated poison. Why? What had she done? Surely all this couldn't be because of the YMCA; because of her singing; because someone gave her a lift home?

He had nothing to be jealous of, nothing. He knew she loved him; she wouldn't do anything to hurt him; she'd rather die than let another man touch her. How could he say such things?

She read on, her tears of pain turning to tears of anger at each vile innuendo, then came the teasing torment of the virtuous 'Millie'. His unembellished signature was the final spittle of contempt.

The spectre of his bitter hatred had risen from the dead like a vampire. Equally, as the fangs retracted, so the same old antidotes sealed the wounds. If that was what he thought, she'd give him something to be jealous about! It was ridiculous, totally ridiculous!

The letter had arrived by the afternoon post; she was performing that night. She couldn't cancel now, even if she wanted to, and, anyway, why the hell should she? She'd done nothing to deserve this, nothing. Why was he being so damn childish? No Elizabeth, she noticed; oh no! Spencer, Spencer, always Spencer, and each mention of his name another twist of the knife. And what about this Millie character he was obviously so fond of? Medication wasn't all she was giving him, by the sounds of it!

'Well, Captain Kipling does drive me home, as a matter of fact, Richard, and he is nice, very nice, and quite handsome, and his real name is Heywood, Thomas Heywood, and no, he's no relation to the famous playwright, whoever he was. If Millie's so wonderful, then damned well so be it!'

348

An afternoon's babysitting did nothing to improve Laura's temper. By curtain time, her innocent amateurism had hardened into the prostitution of the professional. She ripped out the lace Agatha had sewn into her bodice; the men stormed their approval. She felt like stripping off in front of them all and damning Richard and her father to hell.

The show ended. The charabanc was waiting. In Elmsford the troupe went their separate ways, Captain Heywood, as usual, drove Laura home in the Manor's Vauxhall.

There was a nip in the air; he offered her a snorter from his hip flask to keep out the cold. It tasted awful, it brought tears to her eyes, but the afterglow warmed her. She knew it was whisky; what the hell? Her second mouthful burned the back of her throat.

"Steady on," he warned, reaching over. "We don't want to deliver you drunk."

She whisked away the flask and took another long draught, wondering what all the fuss was about until the alcohol hit her stomach with the repercussion of a bomb blast.

"Miss Scott! Oh, God!" He stopped the car.

She'd had the equivalent of three double Haigs in as many minutes. Her eyes were wandering like an armadillo's.

"Actually, I don' know why you shay it's cold; I'm very, very hot, hic, as a madder of fact," she told him, flapping her open lapels. "What'sss so funny?"

His smile widened. "I think you'd better give that to me, don't you? If you have any more, I'll have to carry you over the threshold."

"Really?" She pouted. "Then I'll drink the whole lot."

He made a grab for the flask, she made a dive for the back. A rough and tumble ensued, until nausea overcame her.

"Miss Scott? Laura?"

She lolled sideways, grinning superciliously.

He took the flask and replaced the stopper, soaking up the spillage with his handkerchief.

She hiccupped, then yawned, so wide the moon caught her palate. Her dimples diffused; her face turned deathly white.

"I think I'm gonna be sick."

He got her out of the Vauxhall in the nick of time.

"Please God don't let anyone come, I'll be broken to the ranks," she heard him pray.

At last her heaving subsided; she began to shiver. He wrapped his trench coat around her and led her back to the car. She cocooned herself in her seat. He offered his handkerchief. It reeked of whisky. She shied away.

"I think we'd better get you home."

"I feel such a fool."

"'Twas the General himself what done it, guv'nor," he joked.

It didn't cheer her.

He shouldered the blame, she told him no, it was all her fault; and so it went on, until finally she broke down and poured out her heart.

His arms were reassuring, his voice consoling. It was hell out there, he told her, Richard probably didn't know what he was saying; he'd taken it out on the one he loved most, as people always do. He would write and explain.

"No. Thank you, but no." Her head was splitting. "I need to lie down."

"Yes, of course."

He slipped the car into gear.

She felt utterly defeated. "I don't know what you must think of me."

"Miss Scott, I've thought of little else but you from the moment I first clapped eyes on you."

His were such kind eyes.

"Even after tonight?"

"Even after tonight."

Heywood saw her to her door. Her father had waited up. She wished him goodnight from the hallway, not daring to go within sniffing distance.

"How did it go?" He called back.

"Very well; the best so far. I'm sorry, I'm so tired. See you in the morning."

* * * * *

George broke the surface, hauled up by the webbing from depths in which he could have happily drowned.

'Must've been sunk going across. Hope Charlie's alright. Must find Charlie....'

He rode the waves, choking for air through a tar-lined mouth, tar clogged nostrils. The swell settled. Groggily he opened his eyes. Ceiling planks emerged through the darkness.

"Ugh." His brain felt like a waterlogged greatcoat through which reality was slowly seeping. This wasn't his bunk; it was a bed, hard as nails, but a bed. They all had beds. This wasn't his hut. He must be dreaming.

"Jesus!" The pain in his leg was real enough, though, worse than bloody ever, right down to his bloody toes. He raised his head; his leg was caged; then his eyes gave out and his crown thumped back on the pillow.

'Young George could do with one of them for his train set, always wanted a tunnel.'

This had to be hospital, they must have taken him in. 'Bloody right, too. 'Bout time they did something. Old bollock bags must be in here somewhere.'

He leaned up, searching the speckled blackness for Sarson, until, once more, the world spiralled.

'Be alright now, though; be alright now,' he sighed back into sedation.

* * * * *

As it had with Richard, morning shed a new light on Laura's dilemma. If her hangover tunnelled her thoughts, Richard's second letter focused them. It was full

350

of apology. Nothing had happened with Millie, it was all lies. He loved her more than he ever thought possible. He'd tried to retrieve the first letter, now he pleaded to redress the hurt he knew it must have caused.

She knew he loved her; she knew she loved him, she would always love him, but equally she knew that, however much they tried, this phantom of lost faith would always be there to haunt their happiness, that forgiveness was as fictional as forgetfulness was temporary, it might overwrite the memory, but it could never erase it. Sooner or later, his jealousy would raise its ugly head again and she would react as she always reacted.

And this had been such a small thing; what would happen when she went away to university, if she followed a vocation? Wherever she went, he would always be suspicious. Where, once, she had revelled in their mutual possessiveness, now she felt trapped by it.

What they'd had had been so perfect, to accept less would be to defraud the past. Perfection couldn't be rebuilt on flawed foundations. She'd hoped they'd laid new foundations, but they'd simply relocated the old ones.

She was sad, unutterably sad, but not bitter. She would end it, however hard it would be for both of them, she had to end it. The ineradicability of memory worked both ways; by ending it now the good would always outweigh the bad.

Whoever Millie was, she hoped he would find solace in her arms.

* * * * *

"Charlie! What're you doing here?"

"Hullo Mrs. B. Just popped by to say hello."

"Come in, boy, come in. I'll put the kettle on."

"Well, if it ain't no trouble."

"'Course not; come through. Just keep the noise down, Elizabeth's on nights."

Charlie's hobnails clacked along the hall floor like tap shoes.

"You home on leave?"

"Spot of sick leave before they send me back."

"Didn't know you was wounded?"

"Well, I wasn't, really. Twisted me leg. Ligaments, they calls it."

"Sounds like rickets."

"No, not that," Charlie smiled. "Though there's many out there what must have been born and raised on them. I thought I was small, but you should see some of them; you could stand them on top of the parapet they still wouldn't see over."

"Small for your size, ain't that right, Charlie? Or big, depending on how you look at it," Elizabeth reveilled down the stairs.

Beatrice raised her eyebrows. What an alarm clock couldn't do in ten minutes, a man's voice could do in less than two.

"Morning, Liz," Charlie called back.

"I'll be down in a jiffy."

"Right you are."

"You was saying, Charlie, about your leg?"

351

"Oh yeh; never known such pain. Months it's been; plaster, walkin' stick, the works. You'd've thought I'd broke it. According to them I'd've been better off if I had. No use to man nor beast, but do you think they'd let me off? Not on your nelly! Had me sitting at a table filling out forms all day, and you can guess what kind of a muck I made of that, what with my spelling, elementary to say the least. Some other poor so-and-so had to do it all again. Total waste of time; I could just as well've been sitting at home."

"How is it now?"

"Still a bit iffy, but I got the feeling they thought I was putting it on. Can't tell, see; no swelling or nothing. Well, I wasn't having that, so I told them to sign me off and here I am. Anyway, have you heard from your George lately?"

"Not for a while."

"No; well; suppose it's difficult to get the stamps."

The joke raised half a smile.

"Least you know he's safe."

"Yes, there is that. We send over when we can, though it's not as often as we'd like. Elizabeth's saving for the house, and a bit extra's hard to come by, what with the restrictions and everything."

"Yes, didn't realise 'til I got home. They feed us alright in the Army. Me mum tells me it's that bad you can get had up for feeding crusts to the dog."

"Birds too, poor little beggars. Don't know what's going to happen to them when winter comes. They'll all starve, I reckon."

"I heard about the fire."

"Miracle no one was hurt. It's amazing what a spark can do," 'not to mention a gin bottle,' Beatrice mused maliciously, closing the subject before her temper got the better of her. "George always asks after you."

"Good old boy, George. Better off where he is 'til this little lot's over."

"Better off than that Billy White, poor soul. They say he'll never be right. Do you think it will ever end, Charlie?"

"Well, let's hope so, hey."

"Morning, Charlie."

"Afternoon, Liz." Clayman took in the copper fringe, the pitted, ochre complexion under the powder and rouge. "When did you get struck by lightening, then?"

"I'm on munitions, ain't I," Elizabeth objected, helping herself to tea. "Cheeky sod."

"Elizabeth!" Beatrice scolded her.

"Oh, Charlie don't mind. He's used to bad language in the Army, ain't you Charlie? If you think I'm bad, you should hear some of them others; effing and blinding all over, they are."

"It's a wonder they ain't mistaken you for one of them Geisha girls and packed you off to China," Charlie quipped.

'Ain't that the truth. No money for housekeeping but plenty for lip-gloss,' Beatrice scowled to herself, refilling the pot while Charlie repeated his ligaments saga.

352

"Talking about Coolies, we got thousands of them behind the lines, carting stores and what-have-you; darkies and all. French've got whole regiments of them, though ours is mostly the Indian type. Nearly got me throat cut by one. Great big fella he was, bigger than your George. Makes you wonder how we ever got one over on them in the first place. He's alright, then?"

"Seems to be. Says the grub's none too good, but apart from that it don't sound too bad. We send over when we can."

"So your mum was saying."

"They even gives them pocket money, but he don't send none home. Says they have to spend it on a film show. I wish I could afford to go to the pictures every week."

"Dah, if army pay's anything to go by, it wouldn't buy him a peppermint bullseye, let alone the tin to put it in. Clubbing together for a packet of fags, we was, on occasion; barely two brass farthings to rub together, and even they was French. Franks, they call them, franks and centimes. Here, did he ever tell you the one about the Colonel's cat?"

"No?"

"Well, me and him adopted this whippet, see, carried it in our rucksacks. The Sergeant knew, but he turned a blind eye, like. Marvel, he was, used to sit up on the old sandbags of a night on sentry go. Never barked nor nothing, just gave out this low growl if he thought something was up. And gas? He could sniff it out the day before."

"Had a nose for it, did he, Charlie?"

"Thank you, Liz," Clayman suffered the loss of his best line. "Who's telling this story?"

"Sorry."

"Now, where was I? Oh, yeh, the gas; the old mongrel had a different sound for that, more whimper-like. One whiff and....."

"I thought you said he was a whippet?"

"He was."

"Well whippets ain't mongrels."

"Take no notice, Charlie; the daylight must have gone to her head," Beatrice commiserated. 'Like my boot's gonna go to her backside, when I get hold of her,' she grumbled on silently. 'What was she doing in Southend, I'd like to know?' The Beasley tongue had finally loosened at the baker's that morning. "You was saying?"

"Well, I reckon Liz should tell it. That jaundice seems to have made her a mind reader."

"Oh, very droll."

"One whiff, Charlie," Beatrice prompted him from a memory long practised in a lifetime of listening and accusations of not.

"Right, Mrs. B. Well, that'd be enough for him, like; off he'd go and we wouldn't see hide nor hair of him for a week or more, until up he'd pop from out of the blue. Wouldn't matter where we was. Uncanny, how he found us."

"That's easy; head for the nearest pub."

"Oh, very witty. What do they feed you on in that blessed works canteen of yours, sarky sandwiches? Well, for your information, they don't have pubs over there, they have estaminets, 'estamints', we calls them, or 'just-a-minutes', take yer pick. Talk about omelettes; no shortage of eggs in France, Mrs. B., ten, twenty at a time, no bother. Well, the old cock's their national emblem, see, so I suppose it stands to reason."

Elizabeth choked on her tea; Beatrice tutted, shaking her head.

"What's mints got to do with it?" Elizabeth spluttered out her alibi.

"Mints?"

"Estamints."

"Look, do you want to hear this story or don't you?"

"I'm not stopping you."

"So where does the cat come in, Charlie?" Beatrice reminded him.

"Sorry Mrs. B, I was just coming to that, if I can get a word in edgeways."

"Don't look at me," Elizabeth protested. "You're the one what started on about whippets."

"Right; well, the Colonel had this cat, see, on account of the rats."

"Suppose he called him Fido," Elizabeth cackled.

"And our Captain borrowed it one night for the selfsame reason." Charlie ignored her. "Ruddy great ginger thing, it was; reminded me of your Jimmy, Mrs. B."

Elizabeth's cackling escalated.

"Will you give over, Liz!"

"Sorry, Charlie..... sorry...... I can't help it."

Beatrice's contempt lost its battle with contagion. She, too, began to chuckle. Charlie struggled on regardless.

"Well, it went missing, see. There was the old Adj. searching high and low. 'Has anyone seen the Captain's cat?'"

"You... you said.... it was the Colonel's," Elizabeth croaked.

"Ha.. ha, well it was the Captain's, when he borrowed it." Charlie also began to succumb. "Anyway, in the end, he figures it must've skidaddled over the top. Well, we had the old dog with us at the time... stop it Liz!"

"Go on, go on," she wheezed.

"'Send out the whippet,' the Sergeant cries. 'See if he can't chase the bugger back....'"

Elizabeth fell off her stool; Beatrice clung to the sink; "Oh, dear... Oh, dear!"

"... Sorry Mrs. B., but that's how he talks. Here.... ha, ha.... are you alright?"

"Yes... yes," Beatrice sobbed, waving Charlie on.

"Well, just then, the damned thing appears on the parapet. My Lord, you should've seen it. There they was, him and the whippet, haring round the trench like rabbit and greyhound, upsetting everything, and there was us diving about trying to catch the beggars."

Charlie had found his rhythm.

"Then off they goes, hurtling down the line. Could've ended up in Switzerland if they hadn't come across old Jonah Riley. Jumped over the top at the sight of him. Well, so would you, if you'd been them; ten foot tall and twice as wide. Talk about

Goliath. Built like a brick karsy, he was, so much so the birds used to crap on his head...."

Elizabeth grasped her sides; Beatrice gasped and gagged, too far-gone to complain. It would have made no difference, Charlie was flying.

"... No word of a lie! Dead now, though. Brass hats mistook him for a tank, stuffed a twelve pounder up his arse and told him to fire it! Talk about 'Hoo Flung-Dung', your Chinese compatriot, Liz!"

She flapped around the floor like a convulsed dolphin.

"Anyway, back to the old moggy. Off into no-man's land they fly and, would you believe it, he sends us out after them. Could've made a hand of the whole bloody platoon, pardon my French; flares and bullets flying all over, and all on account of the Colonel's ruddy cat! I ask you." Charlie took a gulp of tea. "Sid, we called him."

"What... the cat?" Elizabeth managed to splurt.

"No, the whippet!"

While the women laughed themselves sober, Charlie finished his tea, lost in the hell of Ypres. It was true enough, the Adjutant had sent them out after a cat and Jonah Riley had copped it, but George had been long gone by then and so had the whippet. His recovering audience waited in vain.

"Well, what happened, then?"

"What?"

"With the cat?" Elizabeth reminded him.

"Oh, he came back; wandered in along the line at morning stand-to, calm as yer like. Never did find the whippet, though; reckon the rats must've ate him. You wouldn't believe the size of them. Slimy great black beggars, big as badgers, they are, never seen the like...." But Charlie's humour had deserted him.

The laughter lapsed. The cups were replenished. They talked of the Brewer feud, and Richard's M.C.

"The whole village is that proud of him," Charlie told them.

"You wouldn't recognise him now, Charlie; proper gentleman. No side, though; same as ever he was," Elizabeth boasted.

"Met a bloke from his lot out there at Etaps. 'Lucky Bowden' they calls him. Bet you didn't know that. He's a real credit to you, Mrs. B."

"Yes, he's a good boy," Beatrice smiled modestly. "And our George."

"Yeh, good old George. Well, I suppose I'd better be off," Charlie roused himself. "Promised my mum I'd be back for dinner. Mr. Bowden down the yard is he?"

"Should be."

"I'll drop in on me way past. Thanks for the tea."

- CHAPTER SIXTY ONE -

Another shell buried itself in the sludge. Richard cowered on the shelf Partridge had hollowed out for him, the only elevation above water in his crumbling funk hole. The trench was waist-deep and floating with corruption, the dugouts flooded to their roofs.

"Platoon ready for inspection, Sir," his Sergeant summoned him through the rubber ground sheet that served as a gas curtain.

He forced himself from his womb, compelling his legs to respond.

The stench of fetid whale oil gusted from his waders, as they sank into the mire. His helmet shook in his grasp; it always did, no matter how tightly he held it. It was the same with his mug; he kept spilling his tea and fumbling his pencil; his writing was almost illegible. He blamed it on the fever, he hadn't been right since hospital, and Laura of course, she'd torn him apart, the same day Bohannon's brains had exploded into his face, filling his mouth, clogging his nostrils. It was his own fault; he shouldn't have had them open.

"H-have we g-got everything, Sergeant?" He cursed his stammer.

"All present and correct, Sir."

Sergeant Prentice was a guardsman; he lived by the book; all would be in Grenadier order. Richard stumbled out onto the firestep, itself ankle deep.

"G..give us a h..hand up, would you?"

The entire line was underwater; over the top was the only way forward.

"L-l-lead the m-men off, S-sergeant."

The mud was worse than at Arras, even worse than the Somme. Whatever tracks the Sappers laid, brick, ration-tin or duckboard, the sludge swallowed. Whole horses had been lost to its gluttony.

"Step into the foothold of the man in front..."

Still they stuck fast, while, on either side, the deep waited to claim them. The Sergeant was at the men incessantly, cursing and swearing.

There had been rumours of a mutiny at Etaples, of a sergeant being shot, of authority being defied, of thousands of men singing and cheering, telling the Base Wallahs it was their turn to do the fighting. Some Australians, sent down to restore order, had joined the mutineers. Finally, surrounded by H.Q. troops with machine guns, they'd been starved into submission. There'd been a string of executions. But it was all trench telegraph; nothing official, hush-hush it never happened; one hundred thousand men? Not a chance.

The Essex had been training for weeks, attacking dummy trenches through clouds of smoke, stifling in gas masks; bayonet practice, bombing practice, target practice, drill after drill. There'd been a procession of carrying parties, coils of wire, ammunition, duckboards. Richard had noted the gun pits, the shell dumps, the Aid Posts, the burial pits; he'd known what was coming. It wouldn't be long, now.

They'd moved up the day before. No attempt had been made to clear away the dead. Corpses had littered the rat-larder horizon, oozing puss, crawling with maggots, a liquorice all-sorts of body parts, horse, mule and human, scattered among the general debris of war, buckled helmets, redundant rifles, rubber capes, stakes, screw pickets, wire.

There'd been a shattered tank stuck fast, up to the cupolas in mud. Richard had wondered if it might have been Frank's, if the identity tag on the headless golliwog hanging from the hatch read 'Thomas'.

"Dr-drastic c-cure for the p-pox, Frank," he'd laughed hysterically.

The men must have thought he was mad. What fool sent tanks forward in this? What fool sent anything forward in this?

Now they were for it. There were no discernible trenches, not even craters, all had been blasted into the cesspits of hell. In daylight, the deeper, more dysentery-brown holes, with their bloated turds of humanity, betrayed themselves; at night one looked for the star-shells' reflection; the moon had given up in disgust. At sunset the battlefield might have looked like a gold-leafed ocean, but the sun never shone on Passchendaele, there was only the fathomless darkness of death, truly World's End.

At last they reached the jumping off point. Had it really taken four hours? It was only supposed to be a quarter of a mile. It wasn't a trench at all, just a barricade of rotting carcasses and sandbags slung up on slightly higher ground, an island in the fear infested swamp that was no-man's land. Here they would wait, waist deep in ooze, until dawn broke and the whistles blew.

Richard had lost three men coming up, undoubtedly sucked under. They would have to walk on water to reach the German lines. He wouldn't have been surprised to see a battleship cruising past, or the Margate paddle steamer, jam-packed with day-trippers come to see the sights. He blew it up with one blink.

'Let 'em taste what it's like, let 'em all drown in hell, the cretinous bastards.'

His entire body was knotted; his left arm felt curiously weak; there was a dead spot above the wrist. His heartbeat thumped irregularly in his ear, he felt lopsided.

'SPLOOOOOSH!'

A stray shell landed close by, showering him with muck. A black slug attached itself to his sleeve. Frantically he thrashed at it, until it fell off and plopped into the water; only then did he realize it was only a finger.

A sheet of lightening crazed the Western sky; thunder clapped along the line; the barrage. The shells clattered over, no longer reminding him of the Flying Scotsman, not in his wildest dreams.

Four hundred yards ahead, the greying dawn was pastelled by smoke and gas. He pressed himself deeper into the mud. Any moment now.....

'CRUMP, CRUMP, CRUMP, WHIZZZZZZ BANG! THUPP, THUPP.'

"Gas masks on!"

It was Sergeant Prentice doing his job for him.

The earth heaved; the parapet broke apart, deluging him in its hideous composite. Ribs ensnared his respirator; offal blinded its eyepieces.

"This is me, now, Bowdie, this is me," Joe Crutchley grinned from the corruption.

Kicking and screaming, Richard wrenched himself free. A giant insect was crawling towards him.

"Are you alright, Sir?"

He studied the apparition.

"Are you alright, Sir?"

The fly was shaking him; it sounded like an automaton.

He nodded. His left eye was twitching; he couldn't control it.

A whistle blew.

'Football? This was no place to play football.'

"Come on, Sir; on your feet."

Other wingless flies were being kicked from their pits. But he was a fly, too, just like the rest. He tried to follow the crowd, but he kept getting stuck.

"This is ridiculous; there isn't even a bloody ball."

Then something hit him on the arm, hard as a cricket ball driven full pelt. His sleeve had a hole in it, a perfectly round hole, it went in one side and out the other, and his side tingled. How odd; he would have to get Rowe to patch it up. The man to his left had holes in him, too, lots of holes; his uniform was torn and stained, his buttons weren't at all shiny. He would have to report him, the stupid arse should have polished his buttons.

'WHOOOSH.'

The man disintegrated.

'Silly Bugger! Oh, well, saved himself a rollicking.'

He'd better hurry or he would be left behind.

'Splosh!'

Head first into a pond; wouldn't you know it. Some evil sod had tied his bootlaces together. What was that, rising to the surface like a squishy marrow, someone's face?

"Ha-ha! Lost your head old chum, l-lost your h-head! Ha, ha! Ha, ha, ha!"

They found him twelve hours later, still talking to the facemask. Physically he'd been lucky, both bullets had gone clean through, missing bone and vital organ, there seemed little chance of gangrene despite the time taken to fetch him in. Mentally he was a mess, jabbering incoherently, laughing maniacally, seemingly impervious to pain, even when they swabbed through his wounds. The M.O. finally put him out.

He came round in a bed of white linen sheets.

"M-M-Millie? Is th-that you?"

The nurse came into focus.

"What h-h-happened to M-Millie?"

"You're in hospital. You've been wounded."

"Wounded? No, I've got the fever, I'm in hospital because I've g-got the fever. Where's Millie? Why have I been moved?"

He levered himself up.

"Ouch!"

His arm hurt like hell; his body was swathed in bandages. But how could he have been wounded in hospital? Had there been an air raid?

A doctor came.

"Ah, so you're awake at last."

The man spoke kindly enough. He noticed the blue and purple ribbon on the ragged tunic, hanging by the bedside.

"An MC, hey? Well, the wounds are clean enough. Let's see if we can't get you home for a week or two. Looks like a Blighty one to me, don't you think, Sister?"

Home? But he'd just come from there. And he didn't have an M.C.; it was obviously all a mistake. Oh well, if they wanted to send him home, who was he to argue.

The nurse plumped up his pillow. He settled back. Two days, had the doctor said? Home for two days? It hardly seemed worth it. He was tired, very tired. He'd just close his eyes for a minute or two.

* * * * *

"Aaahhhh!" Elizabeth's scream curdled the milk and rancidized the margarine. She flew into the kitchen. "There's something in there!"

"In where, dear?" Beatrice tingled with satisfaction.

"In the pantry," Elizabeth cried, cowering by the dresser.

"Oh; that'll be Arthur's rooks. He fetched them home last night."

"Ugh!" Elizabeth shuddered. "What'd he want to hang them in there for? Christ, they frightened the life out of me."

"It is the larder, dear," Beatrice chirruped.

"What's he going to do with them?"

"Eat them, of course. Thought you might like to dress them for me. They'll be nice in a pie. Had a lot of that when we was first married; anything we could lay our hands on in them days. I'm surprised George never asked you to make one; used to be his favourite, that and pigeon; brought them home regular when he was a boy; used to knock them down with his catapult. Dab hand at it he was; even nabbed a rabbit or two on occasion. Always reckoned it was better than shooting them, and he was right. Nothing worse than buckshot, ruins the flavour and plays havoc with the teeth, if you leave some in. George's granddad broke a tooth clean in half on a pellet. Pulled what was left out with a pair of pliers. That's how he came to have a gap."

"Should've gone to the dentist."

"Not him, never did. Had a good set of teeth, did Granddad."

"Actually, now you mention it, he did bring some home once. I buried them in the back garden; told him the cat had got them. Couldn't handle that."

"Then it's time you learned, young lady. There's a good bit of nourishment in a rook."

"Makes my skin crawl just thinking about it," Elizabeth shivered. "Evil ruddy things; worse than rats."

"The way things is going, we'll be eating them and all, before this War's over.

359

Now you just fetch them out and get the feathers off them, there's a good girl."

"I'd rather starve."

"Don't be silly. You've plucked chickens, haven't you? Rooks is no different. The kids've got to eat something, Elizabeth, and there'll be no proper meat 'til next Tuesday, and then only enough for a stew."

"Well they ain't having rook, not my kids." Elizabeth headed down the hall. "I'm going down the butchers. He must have something tucked away, restrictions or no restrictions."

"Suit yourself," Beatrice called after her, "but you're wasting your time."

"We'll see about that."

'About time she let the moths out of her purse,' Beatrice smirked. "Ooh, and get some butter while you're about it, there's a dear!"

* * * * *

His parents were at Richard's bedside in Rayntree hospital before the telegram arrived.

"H-how did you know?" He asked.

"Mr. Scott told us, he drove us over."

"It m-must have been Sarah." Sarah had been on duty when he'd been admitted. She'd seemed edgy, and even more so when he'd asked about Laura. He could have sworn she'd been avoiding him ever since.

Scott strode up the ward. "How are you, my boy?"

"Better for being here, I can tell you that."

"Where's this blooming medal of yours?" His father asked proudly.

"Oh, they h-haven't g-given it to me yet, dad, j-just the ribbon."

"I'd say there's a good chance your Richard will be going to the Palace for his investiture, now that he's here," Scott told them.

"Buckingham Palace? What the King himself? Well, would you credit it, Mother, our boy being decorated by the King. Well, I'll be."

Richard, too, was taken aback. He knew it happened, but surely not to him?

His mother straightened his bed. He could see she'd been crying, probably all the way over.

"Is L-Laura coming?" He asked.

The question seemed to embarrass them.

"I'm afraid she's away at university, Richard," Scott broke the silence.

"D-does she know I'm here?"

"No, not yet."

"W-wait 'til she hears. W-w-won't she be surprised!"

His mother started to cry again. Why on earth was she crying?

"There's n-nothing wrong, is there? L-Laura's all right?"

"Yes, my boy, she's fine; couldn't be better," Scott assured him.

"If you s-speak to her, please g-give her my love. I c-c-an't wait to see her. Is there any ch-chance of her c-coming down?"

There it was again, that embarrassment.

They asked how he was wounded. He told them he couldn't remember, he couldn't remember anything since his fever. Wasn't it silly? But he felt fine in himself, really he did; he just had this stupid stutter. He expected to be up and about in no time. He would go up to Cambridge, it wasn't far; that is where she was, Cambridge?

"I think you'd better stay with us for a while," his father told him. "Get some of your mother's home cooking inside you before you go gallivanting off."

"Quite so," they all agreed.

"G-God, won't she be p-proud, g-going to an investiture." Richard could see it now.

"Richard..." Scott began.

"Are they feeding you alright?" His mother cut in.

"Y-yes mother, f-fine, fine. You do f-fuss so."

"Well, a mother's got a right to fuss over her own son. These nurses don't seem to be too bothered; they've left a dirty mark on your forehead." She reached for her handkerchief.

"It w-won't wash off. They p-put it there when you're taken in to tell the n-next lot that you've had m-morphine. It w-wears off, in time."

"Talking of which, I must be making a move," Scott said apologetically. "I have a meeting at five back in Elmsford. May I offer you a lift?"

"If it's no trouble, Mr. Scott. Come on, Mother, we mustn't hold Mr. Scott up, he's got work to do. Let the boy rest. You can catch the bus over tomorrow."

"D-don't forget to t-tell Laura," Richard called after them. Laura would come, he was sure of it.

* * * * *

Scott left a message at the college; he would 'phone back at eight. Laura was waiting. He broke the news.

She thanked him for telling her. "I'm glad he's all right."

"I'm afraid it's a little more complicated than that," he said awkwardly. "It would seem he's lost his memory. Not totally, but he remembers nothing since his fever in August."

"You mean...?"

"I'm afraid so."

Laura was stunned. Fate could not be so cruel. It had taken all her resolve to sever the knot, to break her own heart as well as his. Had it all been in vain?

"Will it come back?"

"The doctors don't know; maybe tomorrow, maybe never. It's impossible to say. I'm so sorry, my dear, after all you've been through."

"He really doesn't remember anything?"

"Nothing at all. He still thinks... He talks of no one but you, I'm afraid."

"I see."

"I wasn't going to bother you with it, but there's always the chance he'll track you down. At least this way you've been forewarned. Sarah's on his ward. She's trying to get transferred."

"Poor Sarah. I'll speak to her." Laura felt drained.

"Look, don't worry, I'll tell him when the time comes. There's no point in putting yourself through it all again. It's just one of those unfortunate things, that's all."

"But he must still have my letters."

"Apparently not."

"I'd better come down."

"No, don't do that; just be out if he calls and leave it to me, it can't be rushed."

He asked about her studies, about Tom.

"Oh, he's fine. He's here, in fact, waiting to take me to dinner."

"Then I won't keep you. Don't worry, my sweet, I'll sort it out. Enjoy your meal."

She put the phone down.

"Is anything the matter, Miss Scott?"

"Pardon? Oh, no, thank you, Matron, everything's fine."

She'd believed she'd freed them from their entanglement, only to be caught on its last trailing barb.

Tom had driven up from Ashleigh with news of his own. Passchendaele had taken a fearful toll. Shocked and angered by the carnage, Lloyd George, now Prime Minister, had refused to release the replacements Haig had demanded. Boys and old men were all that were left. The Army would have to comb through its cripples to make up the numbers, badly gassed reciters of Kipling included.

Tom and Laura had become lovers during her traumatic severance from Richard. He'd been her point of no return. He'd also been caring, supportive and understanding. She didn't truly love him, he knew that, but she'd held nothing back.

They sat in the car; he held her hand. She relayed her news, he countered with his own, knowing full well that her distress had little to do with his own imminent endangerment. His heart sank. If she went to Richard, it would be over.

"Your father's right, there's nothing to be gained by your going. I'm sure he'll make it as painless as possible."

They drove to the restaurant. She ate little and spoke less; the white silk rose in the flower vase seemed to monopolise her attention. She said she was tired; did he mind terribly? She did love him, really she did, she hoped he understood.

Their parting was almost platonic. Not for the first time, he cursed Richard's unshakeable shadow.

* * * * *

When his mother returned the following day, Richard talked of nothing but Laura. She evaded the subject as best she could, until, her heart breaking for him, she could mislead him no longer. Richard refused to believe her. Why was she saying such things? It was lies, all lies! He wanted Sarah, she'd tell him the truth. There was a scene, he went berserk, screaming of exploding heads, of being buried in brains,

362

of being a fly, of floating faces. The doctor sedated him. When he came round, his mother was still there, both the gorgon of confirmation and the personification of the sorrow he couldn't face. He sat like Portland stone, staring into space, until she left.

Darkness hid his tears. He'd seen men beg for death at the loss of an arm or a leg. He'd lost his heart. To have it broken twice in so short a time was more than mind and body could bear. His suffered a complete breakdown.

They couldn't keep it from Laura, although they tried. She kept a constant vigil, sleeping in the private room Scott insisted upon, leaving only when the Bowdens came. Richard's eyes flickered open once, but only fleetingly.

She hadn't told anyone, not even Tom, but she was pregnant. He'd asked her to marry him. However bitter her regret, she would have to accept, and soon, he was to be posted after Christmas.

She cursed fate, and her own folly. Dear God, what a mess.

* * * * *

"Writing to the old missus, then, George?"

"Yeh, but I don't know how to put it."

"Let's see what you got."

Sarson took the frail, recycled paper.

"'Had a bit of trouble with me leg?' That's a bit of an understatement, ain't it?"

"Well, I can't tell her straight out, can I?"

"Why not? I did, mine. Here, look." He delved into his pocket. "'Dear, Hilda, won't be able to get me leg over no more, had it off. Love and kisses, Perce. P.S. Any chance of some fags?'"

"You've got to be joking."

"Nah, straight up. See for yourself."

The switch was easily sold.

"That's mine, you berk!"

"Oh, is it? Well there's a thing. Here, we're about the same size; what say we buy a pair of them Lotus all-weather numbers between us, always fancied a pair of them. Shouldn't think they sell them in ones, though, when this little lot's over, they might bow to demand. You can have the left one and me the right. Well, it wouldn't make much sense t'other way around, would it? Any preference to colour? Prefer black myself. 'Black goes with anything;' old Squiffy told me at the Café Royale one night, when him and me was having a spot of dinner, and if you believe that you'll believe anything. You can get all sorts down Petticoat Lane. Mind if I sit?" He leant his crutches on the bed. "Cor, that's better, needed to take the weight off. These crutches is rubbing my armpits red fucking raw. Talking of which, did I tell you the one about the old Jock?"

George raised an apathetic eyebrow.

"Well, there was this Jock, see; bomb landed at his feet and blew him all to bits, but he clung on, like; well, you know what them Haggis bashers is like, don't give nothing away gladly. Anyway, they gathers up what's left of him and chucks it down old Morris's well for a mend, and, would you believe it, not five minutes later he's shouting up that he's right as bloody ninepence. 'Gawd bless us,' they cry, 'it's a fucking miracle.' Well they start hauling him up, see, only every time they give the old rope a tug, another bit of him falls off again. Too soon, see; he hadn't had time to set; arms, legs, then the rest of him, 'til, by the time they get him to the top, all that's left is this eyeless head. 'What-ho,' says he, then his jaw drops off!"

"Don't know how you can be so bloody cheerful, really I don't," George moped.

"Well someone's got to show a bit of cheer, Christmas is coming and the goose was eaten at fucking Easter. I have to say, I'll miss the old panto; used to put on a good show at the Hackney Empire. My Hilda says they're doing Mother Goose this year, just so as they can eat the bloody thing afterwards. Be a scrawny old bugger if it came from here, hey?"

"If you say so."

"Ah, come on George, buck up. Least they can't make candles out of us, wouldn't be enough fat to make a flame."

"Huh," George wallowed morbidly.

"Down to boiling the old underpants soon," Sarson ignored him. "No nourishment left in the socks. Got more shit on me shirttail than mud at bleeding Wipers, might as well make the most of it. I mean, if flies can gorge themselves on it, why can't we? Ate enough of it in the Army."

"You're still in the bloody Army."

"Huh, for what it's worth. Wish the old Red Cross'd send over some proper bloody bogpaper; wiping the old arse 'ain't as easy as it used to be. Better for you, you've got more of a stump; mine pivots me round like a bleeding piston."

At last George cracked. "Pistons don't pivot."

"Gawd blimey, there he goes again. Too picky by half. Here, come on, let's hop over to nursey and see if we can't wheedle a pinch of baccy out of the old bugger. Tastes like bloody compost and probably is, but beggars can't be choosers. Roll on duration."

* * * * *

Laura slipped from the room. She'd fallen asleep in her chair; the whisper of Sarah's apron had woken her. Richard's eyes had been open; he'd been staring at her. "Laura's here," he'd said.

She ran down the corridor and out into the morning frost, crisp and sweet with his deliverance. Yet its aftertaste was more acidic than even the whisky of that drunken night. She'd thought it was over, she'd meant it to be over, but, as soon as she'd seen him, she'd known it would never be so. In truth, she'd known it when her father had first telephoned, she'd always known it. And when he'd spoken; 'Laura's here...'

Tears froze on her cheeks. 'God, dear God,' she railed. How could she marry Tom, when her heart bled for Richard? How could she bear Tom's child? Poor

Tom, he didn't deserve any of this. She was putting him through hell and it was all her fault, everything was her fault. She hadn't meant to hurt him, she hadn't meant to hurt anyone, but it seemed that was all she ever did.

She couldn't go back, she mustn't go back. She must never see Richard again, he must never know she'd been there; Sarah could convince him. There was no alternative, she had to marry Tom, but how could she?

Practicality and emotion swept her from impasse to impasse until her head pounded. She needed time to think.

She went back into the entrance hall and scribbled a note to Sarah. Her cuff was grubby. She couldn't remember when she'd last changed her clothes; she'd lost all track of time.

She shivered. Her coat was in Richard's room; she couldn't go back. She'd borrow Sarah's. Sarah wouldn't mind.

She headed for the nurses home and then to the taxi rank. It wasn't far to Little Eastleigh.

- CHAPTER SIXTY TWO -

In October Russia's Bolsheviks had swept to power. On the second of December, the country capitulated to the Germans, releasing trainload after trainload of German divisions for the Western Front.

In Britain, the King nominated the first Sunday of the New Year a day of intercession. On the Feast of Epiphany, the reverend Soames recited the royal address with its homilies to courage and sacrifice, dedication and steadfastness, and ultimate victory. Beatrice wondered why the nation didn't simply pray for peace.

While Richard languished in hospital, the army, bled dry by the extravagances of the previous years, waited in trepidation.

The first blow fell on March 21st., inflicting the greatest reverse on the Allies since 1914. The Somme battlefields were lost, Passchendaele relinquished, the sacrifice of millions ground into mud and mockery. 'With our backs to the wall...,' Haig exhorted those battle-deaf to eloquence to stem the tide. By May, Britain had suffered a further 350,000 casualties; fifty year-olds were being called to the colours. Paris was within the Kaiser's grasp.

Richard leant on the palisade of his childhood Sabbaths, looking across the fields towards the Manor. The apple trees were in blossom, the meadows and hedgerows filled with the tendrils of spring, little white 'Star of Bethlehems', Bluebells and red Deadnettles, but his sight, like his mind, was sepia. This wasn't the land he had looked on as a child. He felt nothing from it, no kinship, no warmth.

The sun was drifting down in the Western sky, but the world was cold. Was it really only man's imagination that made it smile? He had little imagination left, and no feeling. The horror was beyond imagining; and love?

He'd been diagnosed neurasthenic and moved to a London asylum, where his memory had returned, bringing the worst legacy of all, nightmares. He'd slept only when sleep had enforced itself. For an hour or two his subconscious had endured the agony before the barrier had been breached. But he'd learned to fool them; the boy in the next bed was always waking up screaming, as loudly as he would have done, when they'd cured his stammer, had his mouth not been stuffed full of electrodes.

He'd been caught out once since coming home, in the garden, frantically digging a hole with his bare hands and yelling at the dumbfounded children to take cover, when a battery, out on exercise nearby, had opened up. Some specialist or other had called, some acquaintance of Scott. His mother's pleading had climbed the stairs, his father's refusal; 'the boy's better off at home.' He'd had another board, his leave had been extended, his investiture postponed; the King couldn't be subjected to a man in his condition. He was better now, though; he only had the nightmares to contend with. He would be going out again soon.

He looked over at the Scott's old house. It was as if they'd never lived there, the garden as overgrown as it had been that last boyhood spring before Laura had come to turn his world upside down. It was as though time had stood still, as if it had all been an incredible daydream, except as a child he had seen colour where now there was none, and now he didn't have to jump the ditch, he could stride it.

His boots sank familiarly into the field's furrows. The tangled bower beckoned him on. Squinting into the sun, he swung a leg over the rotting paling.

"Who's there?"

Was that Laura's voice? No, he must be hearing things, he was always hearing things, shells exploding, whistles blowing, machine guns rat-tat-tatting, the screams of the dying. Like the nightmares, he hadn't told the board. Three months in a loony bin was long enough.

"Who is it?"

This time the call was more urgent. He decided he may as well answer; if there was no one there, only he would know.

"It's Richard."

"Richard?"

It *was* Laura's voice, it was coming from the bower.

"Laura?"

She sat like a forlorn sparrow in a wild floral wreath, come to glow in the memory of happier times.

Happier times? He thought they'd been a dream. "I'm afraid there's not much warmth left in the world, the War's seen to that." 'And you, of course,' he stopped himself from adding. "How's your father, and Miss Cooper - sorry, your step mother?"

"They're very well. And your own family?"

"Fine."

He searched in vain for something to say. At other sunsets in that same bower, their feelings had spoken for them. Without feelings, he had no voice. Still, he'd better say something.

"Are you..."

"They told me..."

They started in tandem.

"I'm sorry, please."

"No, you first."

"Are you better now?"

"Yes, all healed up apart from a dimple or two. They.. er.. they told me you'd married." The words almost choked him. Perhaps he did have feelings after all.

"Just after Christmas."

Her confirmation shattered his final fantasy that somehow the marriage had been fictional. He'd known all along, so why did hearing it from her hurt so much? And what of the twin of that last, lingering illusion?

"And a baby?"

"That too."

Now there were no dreams left, nothing to believe in but nightmares.

"When's it due?"

"July."

The arithmetic was simple. She hadn't wasted any time. He looked away. "How's the proud father?" He couldn't disguise his bitterness.

"He's dead."

The news threw him completely. He felt like a sulking child.

"I'm... I'm sorry, I didn't know."

"No, no one does yet, apart from me... and the War Office."

He hadn't noticed the crumpled telegram in her hand.

"Laura, I'm so sorry. Look, if you'd rather be alone..."

"No, it's all right." There were no tears. "I only married him because of the baby. I'm afraid I wasn't much of a wife. It was always you."

Her hypocrisy stung his heart. Then, for God's sake, why?

"Oh, Richard, I hurt him so much." Now the tears fell. "I didn't mean to. And you... I... I... It's all I seem to do."

"You and me both."

It was all he could say. Something was bursting inside him. He had to hold it back, he wouldn't survive. He searched for the anaesthetising drug of indifference and injected it into his soul. Now where was his compassion? Strange that he could stand here and feel nothing for this woman he had once loved so much.

"How's Max?"

"Oh, as adorable as ever," she sniffed. "He caught an escaped prisoner, you know."

"So I heard."

The serum was wearing off. So soon? He mustn't think. He must say something, anything.

"So no one's bought the house, yet?"

"No."

"Elizabeth's got her eye on it. She doesn't seem too keen on moving back to her old place. I think she quite likes the idea of having her own bathroom and a baby-sitter on the doorstep. She's made a small fortune at that factory, though they're beginning to lay them off now. No Russia, you see; the Americans can supply themselves. George is being repatriated. He lost a leg." He hardly knew what he was saying.

Laura shook her head abstractly. The irony of Elizabeth taking the house obviously hadn't registered with him. "Are you going back?"

"I must."

She flinched. Her hands clasped tighter. It gave him a cruel satisfaction.

"Why must you?"

"It's where I belong."

Her eyes locked into his, once more the glistening sapphires of memory. Now they spoke with the freedom of old, in the unity of silence.

Along the valley the old whitewashed watermill was dyed varying shades of sunset; the sky above was a wash of pastel pinks and blues. The tapestry of a love he thought long unwoven had unveiled his vision.

He mustn't make a fool of himself, he mustn't.

"They'll be wondering where I am. They've been keeping an eye on me, you know, since... since I came home." He forced a laugh. "They've probably sent out a search party by now."

"Yes, I should be going, too."

As she pushed herself up, her pregnancy became allergically evident. His diverted eyes found hers.

"Whoever comes here, this will always be our place."

"Always."

- CHAPTER SIXTY THREE -

It was a rough crossing; Richard staggered down the gangplank like a gas case. The train was better, however bad the fug, he was never sick on trains.

This time there was no two weeks' wait for a posting, he spent only one day at Rouen, next morning, his name was listed. At least he was going back to his old crowd.

Smylie had survived, he was a Major now.

"Bowden!" He was genuinely delighted. "Thought we'd lost you for the duration. You're just in time for the fun and games, we go back up tomorrow."

He took him along to the C.O. Richard was allotted his old platoon.

"The Sergeant Major will sort you out."

The face was familiar. Richard racked his brains. Baron, from cadet camp; that was it! He shouldn't be here, he was well past it.

"This way, Mr. Bowden, Sir."

Baron hadn't recognised him. Why should he? He must have trained thousands of boys. Besides, Richard had changed a lot since then. Should he remind him?

"I believe we've met before, Sergeant Major."

"At training camp it was, Sir. Correct me if I'm wrong, but you fancied yourself as a bit of a pit prop, as I recall."

He did remember.

"I see you got the MC, Sir. I'm sure it was well deserved. You showed a lot of pluck back then, a damned sight more than that other silly pillock, if you don't mind me saying."

Oh, yes, old 'Pee-brain'. Whatever happened to him, Richard wondered, and the others. Half of them dead, no doubt. As much as they'd hated Baron's guts, now it was like meeting an old friend.

They reached the shattered cottage that served as a Mess.

"Thank you, Sergeant Major, I can work things out for myself from here. Pleased to have you with us."

"Thank you very much, Sir. If I may say so, Sir, the feeling's mutual."

There were a couple of veterans, like himself, hauled from the scrap heap; the rest were schoolboys, some not even shaving. However, age was immaterial where whisky was concerned; they all got roaring drunk. Richard was sore-headed when the battalion assembled in the pre-dawn.

"Cor blimey, Lucky Bowden's back," he heard from the ranks. So there were one or two survivors. Not Partridge though; apparently he'd copped it soon after Richard. As far as anyone knew, he was still alive. He'd been packed off to Blighty.

Away they marched, towards the thunder of guns.

* * * * *

Amos Harris's milk cart trundled past the prisoners, sullenly sowing autumn cabbage.

"They're everywhere now, Arthur, look at the buggers, more of them than us and doing more damage than good with them rakes and whatnot, and well they knows it."

For all the aggravation Arthur had incurred over Gunther Redden, now every farm in the parish had its complement of captive labourers; they could even be seen ploughing up the Manor paddock and the Vicar's lawn.

"A bunch of them had the gall to jeer at one of our blokes the other day. How do you like that? Walking his girl, he was; invalided out, silver badge on his coat and everything and they jeered him. I'd've shot the bastards, if I'd been guarding them, which, of course, no-one was. Beats me how they can let them wander the lanes of their own accord, especially now; that's just asking for trouble."

"Just let them have a go at my George, when he gets back, that's all."

"Oh yeh, soon, init?"

"So we're hoping, though I'm not counting my chickens. I can see the sense in them swapping them over, when they can't fight no more, but I won't believe it 'til I see him with my own eyes."

"Well I'm pleased for you, Arthur, really I am. It'll be good to have him back. Here, look at her at the gate, flirting with them like there's no tomorrow," Harris scowled. "That's Truelove's girl init, her what married that bloke from Elmsford? You'd think they'd save it for their own boys. Mind you, you expect it from her. Poxed up to the eyebrows, so they say. It's a wonder she ain't been locked up like that woman from Hayfield what gave her husband a dose when he came home on leave, poor sod. Six months, she got, according to the paper. It's coming to something, when you can't trust your own missus."

Arthur kept his peace. As much as he longed to see his son, he was dreading George's homecoming.

"It's them bints from Rayntree what get me," Harris grumbled on. "Them at the works, there. Had a couple of them hanging over that same gate the other day, offering them Germans chocolate, bold as brass, and there's me getting had up for buying my own missus a drink. Dolled up to the nines, they was. They need tar and feathering, the whole lot of them."

"Suppose they've got nothing better to do, what with the factories laying them off left, right and centre. Got rid of a load from our Lizzie's place," Arthur grudgingly endowed his daughter-in-law with family status for solidarity's sake. "Though how they can do that when our boys are getting beaten to buggery, I don't know. I'd've thought we'd've needed all the ammunition we can get, but apparently not. According to her we've got huge stockpiles of the stuff. It's a rum world, Amos, and that's a fact. They'll be lining up down the old labour next, asking for a hand out."

"Already are, and they're paying them, twenty five bob a week. I ask you, slips of girls, not even married. Did you ever hear of such a thing? Wouldn't be able to look myself in the face if I was their fathers. And what about them others on the busses and what-have-you going on strike? Christ they've only been at it five minutes.

371

They say London's come to a complete standstill. By the by, did you put in for that extra meat ration?"

"Nah. Thought about it, give the kiddies a bit extra if nothing else, but I had precious little work on at the time and nothing you could call heavy labour. Haven't got much more now. Christ, before the War you could get a leg of lamb for tenpence; be lucky to get a ruddy chop for that nowadays. It's alright them saying we can have a bit extra, it's another thing paying for it. How about you?"

"No, didn't seem right somehow, though I'm beginning to wish I had, now, seeing them. You're working for that Mrs. Goodhall, ain't you, her of the exploding privy?"

"That's the one. She reckons one of them new fangle machines that flies so high you can't even see them, dropped a bomb on it. Though, if you ask me, more likely it blew up of its own accord. Probably that War Bread."

"Pity she weren't in it at the time," Harris scowled.

"Dah, she's not a bad old biddy. Makes a good cup of tea."

"I reckon that old bat Beasley getting her name in the paper's got more to do with it than anything. Put Ma Goodall's nose right out of joint. Probably put a bomb under it herself just to get some attention. Bad as each other, them two."

"Well, I'm not complaining; I got a week's work out of it. Never thought I'd see the day when I'd be beholden to a German bomb, if that's what it was, or War Bread if it weren't."

"Ruddy stuff," Harris grimaced. "I don't eat it no more. Old De'Ath gave me a note. Got the cramps something chronic. Weren't too bad at first, but this latest lot, well... Clayman lost half his pigs because of it; blew up like balloons, they did. Had to puncture their stomachs to let the air out. That's how come there's been so much pork about lately."

"Not in my house there ain't."

"Bad as that is it, Arthur?"

"Breaks my heart to admit it, Amos, but Elizabeth's the bread winner now, and even her money's been cut. Come August, I reckon I'll be out pea picking, and I ain't done that since I was a nipper. Got a permit for an extra parcel for our George a month back, but couldn't afford to fill it. Just as well as it turns out."

"You'd have been hard pushed even then, what with the food queues. Did you hear about that kafuffle in Rayntree the other day? And the other in Elmsford? Not far short of a riot, according to old Kipper."

"Yeh, and there'll be a riot here, too, if they don't soon get some beer in. Neither Mow nor Crown had a pint between them yesterday and precious few spirits. I don't know what the world's coming too, Amos. It can't go on like this. A man'll go without most things, but when it comes to his beer, that's the bloody limit. Reckon that's what's behind all these strikes."

"Send them over yonder, that's what I say, let the old Hun sort them out. Coal miners is different, I wouldn't want to go down one of them mines for love nor money, but, as for the rest of the bloody skivers, they should send them out to do their bit. Wouldn't be laying the women off then, neither."

"It's them Temperance people what's to blame, sure as eggs is eggs, and I haven't seen one of them in months. Did you see that notice in the paper, blaming the brewers for the sugar shortage? Bloody cheek. If they want to be tea-total, that's their affair, but I'm buggered if I'm going without my pint, war or no war. I pay enough for it."

"I can remember when mild and bitter was threeha'pence a pint, not even that. And what about those pies Mrs. Hancock used to make, Arthur, do you remember them?"

"Now you're talking."

The golden days were a pleasant place to linger, before a ripening cornfield brought them back to the coming harvest.

"Well you do could always go harvesting, Arthur. They reckon they'll be paying fifteen pounds this year. That's nigh on three quid a week, more if the weather stays fine and we don't catch this Spanish influenza they keep on about. You know Mr. Scott don't you? Course you do. Well, according to him, half the world's got it. Dying in droves, they are, and it's heading our way."

"Now you come to mention it, my Beattie's been a bit under the weather lately. I wonder if she's picked anything up. We went into town the other day to see the boy off. Broke her heart; mine too, I don't mind admitting. He's still not right. He reckons they'll give him a desk job, but I wouldn't like to bet on it, not with the ways things are."

"Well, fingers crossed, hey. That medal of his might just hold sway."

Arthur read the weathered milestone more by memory than sight, 'Elmsford 5 Miles.' The horse nodded into the village.

"Where do you want dropping?"

"I was going to say the yard, Amos, but maybe I'll call on the quack, ask him to take a look at my Beattie. Can't be too careful with this 'flu thing about."

* * * * *

After witnessing Agatha's agony, Laura knew what to expect, but the birth of her own child proved much easier than Harold Henry Stephen's. The Heywoods came to cradle the living link to their lost son. Laura was relieved when they left, insisting she stay with them as soon as she was strong enough to travel. They were already calling him Tom, after his father.

Depression set in. She'd made an utter hash of everything. How could she even think that Richard would come back to her now?

Still the future had to be faced. She had an income of sorts, her widow's pension, and a London flat, the marital home she'd never moved into.

Her father and Agatha wanted her to stay in Eastleigh where the children could grow up together, her son and infant brother. She could always follow in Agatha's footsteps at the village school. At least, if she stayed, she might see Richard. She could even move into the old house.

In late August an envelope arrived from France, bearing a sketch of a white rose. For a fleeting moment it was as if the meaning of life was in her grasp, as if within the petals' folds lay the ultimate understanding.

373

Perhaps there was hope still.

•

- CHAPTER SIXTY FOUR -

In the early hours of July 15th 1918, the Germans launched their final offensive, 'Friedensturm'. Since March the British had been battered into near collapse by successive onslaughts. Entire Divisions had been wiped out, every available man thrown in to plug the gaps. Now it was their ally's turn. However, this time, when the storm troopers advanced, they found the trenches opposite curiously empty. Isolated machine gun nests offered some resistance, but they were no more than an annoyance. What was going on?

They pressed forward. The annoyance became an irritant and then a hindrance, the counter barrage intensified, casualties grew, and still they saw no real sign of the enemy. The very edge of the battle zone was reached, the high-watermark of their own bombardment, and there, just beyond, they found the main French position awaiting them, fully manned and unscathed.

They crumbled before it. The French counterattacked; the pendulum swung. With more and more Americans arriving in the field, the Allies were in the ascendancy. In August, the counteroffensive began which would culminate in the Armistice.

* * * * *

Despite a few near misses, Lucky Bowden had survived. Smylie had appointed himself Richard's Guardian Angel, only calling on his experience when it had been absolutely necessary. He'd taken part in the assault on the Hindenburg Line and been as elated as anyone at its unexpected success.

Baron had died like an old soldier should, face to face with the enemy in a particularly bloody skirmish.

Now they were experiencing the novelty of open warfare, fighting in countryside previously unravaged by war, the 'boys of Bynge's Army', for boys they truly were. The bottom of the barrel had been reached, there were sixteen-year-olds amongst them.

Richard found it strange to be out of the trenches, to see the cavalry, redundant since the early months of conflict, in action. There'd even been sightings of Staff Officers in the danger zone.

The Germans staged a fighting retreat, sometimes grudgingly giving ground, at other times making a stand. Their boots and belts were made of cardboard, their bandages were paper, their uniforms threadbare, their rations non-existent, yet still they fought tooth and nail, inflicting losses as heavy as those of Loos and Arras, Passchendaele and the Somme.

The shallow valley looked quiet enough, with its meandering stream and dusty cart track winding away into the fields. For some reason Richard felt almost as if he'd come home.

A row of tall poplars shimmered in the pale October sun, betraying the presence of a sunken road. The field immediately in front was high in unharvested maize, blighted to buggery, useless to man or beast.

Richard refocused his battered binoculars, switching from the copse on the left to the dilapidated barn on the right. A Staff Officer rode up, complete with escorting Subaltern. Richard continued his surveillance.

"What's the problem, Lieutenant?"

"I don't like it, Sir. That copse on the left and the barn on the right there, it's just too convenient; and there looks to be a sunken road behind; perfect cover."

The Staff Officer raised his immaculate Zeiss lenses.

"Seems deserted enough to me, I don't understand why you're pussyfooting around. What say you, Markham?"

Richard turned at the affront, to find himself face to face with major Stiles, the man whose arm he'd done his best to disjoint in Janine's estaminet. Recognition was mutual and instant. They stared at each other in disbelief.

"Nothing at all, Sir," the Subaltern replied, leaning forward to pat his restless hunter. "Perhaps the odd field mouse."

'And a rat up here,' Richard fumed.

"Then you'd better proceed, Lieutenant." Stiles' bloodless lips pronounced.

"I'd be happier if the gunners gave it a quick once over... sir." The address was contemptuous.

"Oh, would you now?"

"Yes I would, especially that copse. You could hide half a battalion in there."

"Oh come now, Lieutenant, really." Stiles' condescension was sickening. "If we shelled the living daylights out of every clump of trees we encountered on the whim of some lily-livered lieutenant who'd got the wind up, we'd never catch up with the bloody Boche."

Richard stiffened. How dare the pompous bastard call him 'lily-livered', accuse him of wind up, especially that snivelling fart? This was probably the nearest he'd ever been to the enemy.

"It wouldn't take long... sir." Again the sneer. "A shell or two would soon flush 'em out."

"Damn your eyes, man, there's nothing down there. Now are you going to proceed or do I relieve you of your command?"

"I respectfully request artillery, sir," Richard said with total disrespect.

Stiles' face contorted. "Request denied! Now get down there, Lieutenant, that's an order."

Richard's eyes blazed.

"Did you hear me? I said advance!"

"Extended order, if you please, Sergeant Williams," Richard called, continuing the staring match. "If so much as one of my men gets hit going down there, I'll kill you, you filthy swine," he snarled with total conviction.

"What the hell do you mean?" Stiles blustered. "I'll have you court martialled for that!"

But he was raging at Richard's back.

"Bastard," the Sergeant spat under his breath.

The platoon advanced. Nothing stirred, except a bird or two, frightened out of the maize. Halfway down the slope Richard split his men into two groups, one heading for the copse, the other the barn. Silence reigned for another fifty yards, then all hell broke loose, as well-sited machine guns caught them in a deadly crossfire.

"Get back! Get back!" Someone screamed from his left.

The uninitiated were running like rabbits, and, like rabbits, they were being bowled over, spinning in the air and crashing to the ground.

"No! No!" Richard waded through the rotting grain. "Get down, GET DOWnnn....."

He could see nothing but whiskered walls and the blue autumn sky. High up a bird was circling, too high to identify, even for a country boy.

A burst of machine gun fire shucked the maize overhead. Someone came swishing by, a youngster, scared out of his wits, and then he was gone. He'd looked straight into Richard's eyes, he must have seen he was alive.

He tried to move. He couldn't. He couldn't even blink. His eyes should be stinging, but they weren't; he felt no pain at all. He tried to roll his pupils. They remained fixed.

The sky was getting brighter. Something was happening, he was drifting. Dear God! He had to shield his eyes, the sun would burn them to buggery, he would be blinded!

But no, there was the tree to shelter him, with his mother under its scarlet cloak. She looked younger somehow, and his father too. There was a young girl sitting on the playground steps. She was smiling. She *had* seen his goal after all. And there was Joe Crutchley, good old Joe, still in short trousers, carrying his coronation mug.

Miss Cooper was taking his hand; she was leading him to Laura in her blue dress. She had roses in her hair, white roses. They were stepping forward together, he and Laura, hand in hand. Scott and Joscelyn were looking proudly on, and his grandfather was there, on the Grammar school stage, with Chapman beside him, holding out a box of paints. And there was Sam, dear old Sam, to welcome him home.

But he had lost Laura! No, she was still there, different somehow, but still there. Laura would always be there.

* * * * *

The little boy followed his mother through the regimented rows of crosses, each as tall as himself. He had been before, he had been told, but he didn't remember. His mother stopped before a rose bush, conspicuously white against the blood red of those of the other graves. She'd brought it all the way from England, she said, the last time they'd come. He hoped it hadn't been seasick, like him.

The wooden crucifix gleamed in the drizzle. The earth beneath had been freshly turned.

"Is my daddy here?" He asked.

"No, dear, this is your Uncle Richard. Your daddy's in another place."

He'd never seen her look so sad. Letting go of her hand, he reached for the nearest rose and plucked it. His mother burst into tears. His joy faded, his brow creased. He offered it up in apology.

"It's for you." Why on earth was she crying? "He won't mind will he?"

She brushed his cheek with a tenderness that was almost scary, her eyes bluer than he had ever known, bluer than her dress, bluer even than the ring on her finger.

"No, my darling, I don't think he will."

THE POEMS

OF

R. J. LANGHAM

The Beginning:

Avenge Louvain!

Gird up thy loins,
Raise up the sword of righteousness!
Brave Belgium bleeds
And, in her hour of mortal need,
She calls to us to come, God speed,
To smite her desecrators.

The Kaiser's hordes,
That vilest race of all mankind,
Who blight the world
With sword and flame; foul murderers!
Avenge Louvain!
Incarcerate the Hun in shame's damnation!

Come Gallic host,
Courageous sons of French domain,
Whose hearts have bled
For lost Alsace-Lorraine too long!
For liberty, fraternity,
Onward march to victory!

For England

Please, God, give me the strength to face,
Unswervingly, the test to come,
Give me the courage to be worthy
Of the nomen 'Englishman.'
And if it be Thy will to take this life,
Then be it honourably,
On glory's field, in glory's name,
For England, sweet Jerusalem.

This land that ne'er I loved so well,
This land that swells my breast with pride,
This land of rolling hills and vales,
This land of fertile countryside.
This land that Thou have deigned to bless
With beauty in abundantness,
This land of Eden's purest bloom,
This England, this Jerusalem.

The reality:

All Creatures, Great and Small

The rodent raiders of the night,
In no-man's land will feast, 'til dawn's
Pale piper ends their gluttony
And calls them home to hidey hole,
Bloat-belly full of some poor soul.

When nought is left but blackened bone
To hone their teeth, then they will roam
The trenches, where, contemptuously,
They'll feed their face and scratch their fleas
While dragging clammy tail o'er ours.

In numbers greater than the Hun,
Though weaponless, they overcome.
Bullet, cudgel, bayonet sharp,
Nothing seems to find its mark
In the rat illusive dark.

Elephantine rats so gross
They'd feed a whole platoon, if roast,
That is, if they don't eat us first,
The rotten, rabid, rodent curse,
Of all our ills they are the worst.

Unless, of course, you count the louse,
Who clings and sucks and sets up house
In seams and socks and underwear
And anywhere you might have hair,
An irritation hard to bear.

Gnats and flies and beetle bugs,
Roaches, fleas and slimy slugs,
Bang the gas gong, ring the bell,
Chlorine's cloud of death will claim them
All, God's creatures, great and small.

In Silent Scream

The larks announce the dismal dawn
And we stand-to with bayonets drawn,
Our hearts and minds to hardness honed,
Lest nature overwhelms us.

For standing we are fewer now,
Since death descended in our midst,
To rent asunder those it kissed
And leave to us the bloody mess.

Yet after sunset's ruddy glow
Has tipped our steel with tint of blood,
In darkness hearts will weep, unseen,
And sorrow rage in silent scream.

Boys to Men:

The Captain

The lines of age invest his brow,
His eyes, worlds older than the sea,
Are fathom steeped in tragedy,
His wizened hands, perceptively,
Shake, as in senility,
Yet, he was young, but yesterday.

How perfidious is youth!
How swiftly doth its shadow flee
Before responsibility,
Prematurely memory,
While stress and strain exact, decree
The price of seniority.

Men and Boys

They march, boot clad, in naked rank
And comradely embarrassment,
As to the brewery baths they go,
Down river towpath, towel in hand.

Blue whiter than the virgin snow,
That fell less than an hour ago,
Yet still their carefree faces glow,
In flushed schoolboy exuberance.

Four by four they clamber in,
Ducking, splashing, in the swim,
Soaking in the grimy brine,
"Come on now, boys, you ain't got time!"

"Alright, my beauties, that's your lot!"
Moaning, groaning out they hop,
As sedimentary soup doth drain
And makeshift plumbing doth complain.

Now bloater pink from head to toe,
Back along the path they glow,

To stove and fumigation plant,
Scorched uniforms and underpants.

How simple things can bring such joy,
Make boys of men and men of boys.
How proud I am of these, my lads,
My khaki clad Sir Galahads.

The Humour:

The Legend of Jessop J.

Jessop, what a sorry lad,
Malodorous with breath so bad,
It curdles gas, or so they say,
As evidence they point to May's
Attack, when, with the men aghast,
He saw it through without a mask.

Though in trenches none can bathe
And personal cleanliness is gravely
Compromised, in Jessop's case,
No compromise can stand the pace.
E'en out at rest he has been seen,
To turn a bath a rancid green.

Few can stand to get too close
And even rats will flee the gross,
Disgusting stench. I ordered, once,
That he should take up residence
In my fair dugout for the day,
To shoo the blighters clear away.

It worked a treat, though never more,
Could I descend through dugout door.
But every dark cloud has its lining,
More to stop the men from whining,
O'er the door we hung his name
And Jessop's billet it became.

Thus the stink was localised,
With rubber capes we locked inside
Poor Jessop and his horrid pong,
And passed the spot with gas mask on,
Or held our breath for several paces,
Noses nipped and pulling faces.

Then, alas, the Colonel came,
Caught a whiff and went insane.
"For God's sake clean out that latrine!"
He choked and retched, "It's damned obscene!"
And so emerged young Jessop J.

And we set to with pallor grey.

Coughing, gagging, overcome,
The whole platoon did nigh succumb.
"A direct hit, that's what we need!"
As if on cue, at fateful speed,
A Johnson crashed on top of it
And blew the fetid place to bits.

O'er the lines the pall did drift
Towards the Hun, "Poor s..s, short shift
'T will make of them," the Sergeant said,
We heard the cries of guttural dread.
"My God, they're all surrendering!
Send Jessop J. to fetch them in."

The Sergeant raised an eyebrow grim,
"That's hardly cricket, Sir," he grinned,
For, as the lad approach-ed they,
Stampede they did, the other way.
That's how we captured Michelem
With Stinker Jessop, DCM.

The Sentiment:

To Bathe in Eden's Glory

So soft the cheek that manhood deigned to spare from its insignia,
So full the sacred lips of youth that blessed each word's caress,
So innocent the eyes that stared in utter incredulity,
As death's disciple cannonised his purity of breast.

A bearing of such godly grace could claim sweet Venus' motherhood;
A face so fair Olympian t'would melt e'en Daphne's heart.
Such beauty should immortal be, not savaged by atrocity,
But, here, fate rests, so blindly, in the lap of lesser gods.

Gods whose thunderous wrath doth roar and crash with hate's ferocity.
Gods whose sharded arrow tips rain down on fragile flesh.
The craven iron struck idols man doth worship with such blasphemy,
Exact the ritual sacrifice with gourmandistic zest.

Farewell, dear boy, let not your spirit linger here in ghostly chains,
Let we, the living, mourn thy loss for other realms await thee.
Realms where lush abundant peace doth reign in love's eternal light,
Realms where beauty such as thine shall bathe in Eden's Glory.

At Nightingale's Last Post

I stand, as the others stand,
As darkness claims the blood-soaked ground,
To shroud our comrades, where they fell.

When over all, so poignantly,
The nightingale's brave melody,
Sounds sad last post o'er open grave.

Ne'er Highland pipes played such lament,
Nor bugler's lips blew so intense
A requiem to tragedy.

In times far hence, when day is done,
At nightingale's sad evensong,
Please God, we will remember them.

Fair Youth

Lie peaceful now and rest your fair brow on sorrow's breast.
Were that breast mine own, were mine hands the hands of God,
To heal your wounds and raise you up and carry you, full hearted,
From this dreadful place of filth, so envious of beauty, so pitiless in death.

What Sport:

A Short Innings

"How goes the match?" "Alas, 'tis done,
An hour, less, the Hun had won.
Dispatched us all without reply,
On sticky wicket, though the sky
Set fair for batting endlessly,
He bowled with such ferocity,
Not even Grace would have survived,
All but the odd, occasional wide.

'T was plain upon the first to fall,
The self same fate awaited all.
A cunning trap in cover deep
Kept catching out our every sweep
From crease to boundary's sandbagged hump,
To leave us all completely stumped.
Yet, duty bound, in honour's name,
The first Battalion played the game.

The City Patriot

Rolled umbrellas, bowler hats,
And Topper's tall for fatter cats,
As uniform as infantry,
In pinstripe grey conformity,
With morning broadsheet under arm,
The City army marches on.

"Armaments and forestry,
Commodities for military
Consumption, money in the bank,
And have you heard about the tank?
There's fortunes to be made on them,
And aeroplanes have proved a gem.

Mill and textile, gold mines both,
Churning out the khaki cloth, and
Scrap, if you don't mind the certain
Stigma that is still attached.
So silly, when you estimate
The profit it can generate.

Bully beef, who would have thought?
And Maconachies! Should have bought
Up all the stock when War began,
By now I'd be a wealthy man.
Still, I suppose I can't complain,
I've got some Vickers to my name.

Whatever happens at the front,
It's stocks and shares that bear the brunt.
Poor Lloyds is near to bankruptcy
With all the losses on the sea.
Give credit now, where credit's due,
We do our bit for England, too.

Well, now, dear boy, I have to dash,
Your Aunt Matilda has this rash
Desire to sit through Choo Chin Chow,
I ask you! When I'm loaded down,
Not even time to stop for tea,

This War will be the death of me."

National Pride Supreme

'Sweet Victory - National Pride Supreme'

The sweeping headline smote its breast,
  Perhaps at General Haig's behest,
    'A trifle bold,' it seemed to me,
      With not a little irony,
    The testament of those that fell
    Would toll a rather different bell.

    But then I spied in column one,
     'Steady progress on the Somme.'
      How easily the eye deceives,
    How readily the mind perceives.
The 'National Pride' of headline mark,
Won 'Victory Sweet' at Haydock Park.

Home

Home; how strange. Familiar in fact alone,
For I feel only the shadow of lost emotions.
I am not the son that bade farewell,
Nor e'en the author of letters written,
Mine's not the face of filial smile,
But its mindful condescension.

For they are now the innocent
And I the worldly wise, as old as damnation.
I am lost in the land that bore me,
Lost in the hands that raised me.
For I am, now, eternally,
Of Flander's field fraternity.

No Illusions:

All Hope Abandon

'Abandon Hope....' So read the sign,
By hand of some sarcastic swine,
As entered we into the line.

Who, now, would change this destiny
For Workhouse gruel and poverty?
How sweet the taste of ignominy.

For we have passed this way before
And know what pleasures lay in store,
What charity for rich or poor.

A Blighty one through arm or leg,
For this small mercy all would beg,
A convalescent spring in Skeg'.

For others, hardened to the loss,
A missing limb is worth the cost,
A shell spun caber to be tossed.

An eye? Perhaps, but only one,
Maybe a gas corrupted lung,
A halfway house to Kingdom Come.

But, if the cup should overflow,
Please God keep sacred that below,
And face and brain from callous blow.

If death, then make it quick and clean,
Through head or heart or smithereen,
Not lingering through gut or spleen.

For faith we left at Church Parade,
And hope lies buried in the grave,
To charity we are enslaved.

God the Holy Ghost

He stands, hands clasped in solemn prayer
For those who are no longer there,
Commending them to Him above,
Our all embracing God of Love,
But, tell me Padre, please explain,
Where was God when the gas cloud came?

The Battlefields:

Ypres

The pride of Flanders, ruined now,
Where stood the Cloth Hall only shell remains
To tease posterity and glorify the memory,
Shattered by artillery.

Fair Ypres, once mediaeval jewel,
Now melted down to baseness, rat infested,
Gas ingested, streets congested with the
Putrefying flesh of horse and mule.

A house or two still has its walls,
The Square's still there beneath the fallen masonry,
And Cemetery, its contents strewn repulsively,
In foul display, Ypres ancestry.

One chimney stands redundantly,
While all around the fire doth rage and cackle
Like a gloating crone, whose brimstone breath doth
Fan the flames of agony, incessantly.

And, over all, there hangs a cloud,
So hellish dense it shrouds the living and the dead
In brick-dust red and particles, it's better said,
Defy imagination.

This, then, is Ypres, in whose defence
We fight and die in salient trench
Exposed, to honour history,
What other reason could there be?
That's all that's left but misery.

The Bitterness:

The Staff's Forbearance

While cower we at thunder's wrath,
Oblivious of the storm,
The Staff sit down to dine, immune,
In chateau safe and warm.

While lethal hale bites into flesh,
The succulent joint is carved.
While gas spills over firing step,
The gravy boat is charged.

While plum duff steams in pudding bowl,
Intestines steam in trench.
As port is passed and brandy glass,
We taste the sanguine stench.

As raise their glasses to the King,
In Flander's stinking mud,
We toast their precious ancestry
In misery and blood.

The General's Elevation

Nothing ventured, nothing gained,
But no-one killed and no-one maimed.
On balance, so it seemed to me,
A hundred yards of misery
Was hardly worth a spending spree.

The Captain's downcast eyes agreed,
But General's orders had decreed
That we must make a local thrust.
'For what? To satisfy his lust
For Glory?' I turned in disgust.

To boost morale and tactically,
Fair gift wrapped with 'strategically',
A necessary show of strength.
'To capture that quite useless length
Of trench?' I recoiled at the stench.

'In truth to spill Battalion blood,
To make our mark, once more, in putrid
Mud and sanguine slavery
To foolishness and knavery
To prove the General's bravery.'

But those were only thoughts, not words,
I stood as mute as all who heard,
In duty bound subordination,
One man's blind determination
To achieve his elevation.

Attrition, that's the Strategy!

Basil's gone quite mad, dear Jack,
Refused the order to attack!
'A futile waste of lives,' said he,
A spineless wimp if you ask me.
His figures for the month of May
Fair filled headquarters with dismay.

What earthly good's a General bent
On saving lives that should be spent?
I mean, we must be seen to try,
The men at least be seen to die
In numbers of sufficient sum
To match the Froggies at Verdun.

Who is there now that we can call?
Old Duncan's got the wherewithal.
He lost nigh a brigade last week
And damned near captured Zonnebeke.
Someone with unswerving drive,
No matter what the cost in lives.

July the first, now that's the way,
To show the Hun we'll make him pay.
There's plenty more where they came from,
Conscription's only just begun.
Attrition, that's the strategy,
Our Dougie's set for victory.

The Hell of It

'He's gone berserk, completely spliced!' The Devil did bemoan
Man's making such a Sheol on earth, it far surpassed his own.
'What fear lies there in Hades, now, what tortures of the soul?
Compared to this, Gehenna's bliss, an Easter Sunday stroll.

You'd better put the furnace out and save Satanic fuel.
Why waste the fires of purgatory on heating up the gruel?
We'll have to wait 'til things abate, too innocent are these,
He'll pack them into paradise, His conscience to appease.

But, never fear, our time will come and then the fun begins.
We'll get the Kaiser, that's for sure, that prince of mortal sins!
And all those generals, certain, too, will n'er get past the gate.
Discard my order of before, alert the stoker's mate!

I'll teach them to usurp my right to hell's monopoly,
They'll stew in boiling cauldrons of their own barbarity.
We'll make a no-man's land where they will, barbwired to a stake,
Suffer each and every evil they did perpetrate,

And every wound and agony by gassing, shot and shell,
While, all the time, will rain on them the molten fires of hell.
Then add to that, from brimstone vat, the tortures of the mind,
We will, for all eternity, fair pay them back in kind!'

Honour's Death

What binds us to this sadist's jest,
This masochistic hopelessness?
For honour's sake? For honour's shame,
For, after this degrading game,
Fair honour will be meaningless,
Killed within the very breast
That carried it so dutifully,
Along with sister chivalry.

The future generations may,
If curious, look up its definition
In a dictionary,
Where it will read 'stupidity';
Redefined by we, who blindly
Followed it, as though divinely,
Unto death. Pray let it rest
With us, its cursed, in Flanders field.

About the Author

Christopher Cass is the pen name of musician and producer Chris Baker. Educated at Chelmsford Grammar School, at 18 Chris chose the road over university and spent the next 30 years combining a playing career with production and the business side of music.

Once described by Melody Maker as a 'studio guru', he lectured on music business studies at MBS (London) during the late '80s and has written for a number of magazines and periodicals.

'To Bathe In Eden's Glory' is Chris's first novel and reflects a lifetime's obsession with the First World War.

Source material: The Flowers of the Field (Sarah Harrison)/Sergeant Michael Cassidy R.E. (Sapper)/The Lieutenant and Others (Sapper)/Haig's Command (Dennis Winter)/Death's Men (Dennis Winter)/The Old Front Line (John Masefield)/Up The Line To Death (War Poets 1914-1918)/The Great War and Modern Memory (Paul Fussell)/All Quiet on the Home Front (Richard Van Emden and Steve Humphries)/Fields of Death (Peter Stowe and Richard Woods)/In Search of the Better 'ole (Tonie and Valmai Holt)/Till the Boys Come Home (Tonie and Valmai Holt)/Tommy (Richard Holmes)/The Baby Killers (Thomas Feegan)/Myths and Legends of the First World War (James Hayward)/Tommy Goes to War (Malcolm Brown)/Men Who March Away (I. M. Parsons editor)/History of the First World War vol 1-8 (Purnell)/History of the First World War (Liddell Hart)/The World War 1 Data Book (John Ellis and Michael Cox)/Oh! It's a Lovely War (EMI Music)/Aces and Aircraft of World War 1 (Campbell)/First World War Tanks (E. Bartholomew)/The Roses of No Man's Land (Lyn Macdonald)/They Called it Passchendaele (Lyn Macdonald)/Somme (Lyn Macdonald)/People at War 1914-1918 (Michael Moynihan editor)/The Donkeys (Alan Clark)/August 1914 (Barbara W. Tuchman)/1918-The Last Act (Barrie Pit)/The Ghost Road (Pat Barker)/Regeneration (Pat Barker)/The Eye in the Door (Pat Barker)/Vimy (Pierre Berton)/Edmond Blunden (Pen&Sword)/Wilfred Owen (Pen& Sword)/Monchy Le Preux (Colin Fox)/In The Shadow of Hell (Paul Chapman)/A Haven in Hell (Paul Chapman)/Walking the Somme (Paul Rood)/Mud Blood and Poppycock (Gordon Corrigan)/Beaumont Hamel (Nigel Cave)/Poets and Pals of Picardy (Mary Ellen Freeman)/The History of the Great European War (Stanley Macbean Knight)/The Dardenelles (The Alfieri Picture Service)/Covenant with Death (John Harris)

Personal Accounts: With a Machine Gun to Cambrai (George Coppard)/Open House in Flanders (Baroness Ernest De La Grange)/Harry's War (Harry Stinton)/Toes Up (Paulo Monelli)/Storm of Steel (Ernst Junger)/The Patriot's Progress (Henry Williamson)/A Test to Destruction (Henry Williamson)/Drawing Fire (Len Smith)/My Bit (George Ashurst)/The Middle Parts of Fortune (Frederic Manning)/Nurse at the Russian Front (Florence Farmborough)/Armageddon Road (Billy Congreve)/Poor Bloody Infantry (Bernard Martin)/Echoes of the Great War (Rev. Andrew Clark)/The Bickersteth Diaries (Bickersteth)/Private 12768 Memoirs of a Tommy (John Jackson)/Have You Forgotten Yet? (C. P. Blacker)/The Road to St. Julien (William St. Clair)/From Vimy Ridge to the Rhine (Christopher Stone DSO MC)/Letters from the Trenches (Bill Lamin)/Memoirs of War (Marc Bloch)/The Bells of Hell go Ting-A Ling-A-Ling (Eric Hiscock)/All Quiet on the Western Front (Erich Maria Remarque)/ Verdun (Jules Romains)/Memoirs of an Infantry Officer (Siegfried Sassoon)/With the German Guns (Herbert Sulzbach)/A Farewell to Arms (Ernest Hemmingway)/Old Soldiers Never Die (Frank Richards)/Lice (Blaise Cendrars)/The Lousier War (W. A. Tucker)/No Man's Land (Reginald Hill)/To Hell and Back with the Guards (Norman D. Cliff)/Combat Report (Bill Lambert DFC)/A Sergeant Major's war (Ernest Shephard)/Testament of Youth (Vera Brittain)

Copyhouse Press

London

Lightning Source UK Ltd.
Milton Keynes UK
UKOW02f0807241115

263366UK00002B/19/P